Praise for No Freedom

"*No Freedom by Inge-Lise Goss is a suspense novel with a splash of something for everyone. It's fantasy, sci-fi-, dystopian, romance, and mystery all wrapped up into one imaginative, futuristic tale...grabs you from the first paragraph...This is a future movie!*"—Kristy Vee, Readers' Favorite Reviewer

"*No Freedom... is a unique science fiction story that is set in an age of intriguing technological advancement...The backdrop of the story was really fascinating, starting from laws put in place... to the ability of humans to purchase android companions...a must-read for science fiction fans.*"—Edith Wairimu, Readers' Favorite Reviewer

"No Freedom...is *a futuristic dystopian thriller...The plot is unique... The writing is tight with dialogue that sounds natural in a setting that is anything but...I am absolutely confident and comfortable in recommending it to others.*" —Asher Syed, Readers' Favorite Reviewer

No Freedom

Inge-Lise Goss

Olivebranch Press

To my husband, Peter, for all of his support, encouragement, and patience.

ACKNOWLEDGMENTS

My gratitude goes out to my exceptional editors, Jeff LaFerney and Nancy Buford. Their edits and comments always improve my stories and help me become a better writer. I wish to extend a thank you to Ernest Walwyn and Debbie Prince, members of the Las Vegas Writers' Group, for their professional critiques of my work. A special thanks goes out to all my readers for their continuous support. I also want to thank Margaret Daly for designing a fantastic book cover.

PROLOGUE

The conference room door flew open. As the board members filed out, the Founder of The Institute noted that some strode with a natural gait while others moved in a stiff-legged manner. He made a mental note to accelerate the elimination of that defect. His android and cyborg board members needed to exhibit the same confident walk as humans in executive positions.

The Founder, now eighty-years-old, walked alone to his office and took his chair behind the modern desk with a black slate top. The numbers revealed at the meeting gratified him. His efforts over the past decades showed measurable success. Many more androids and cyborgs had infiltrated society and gained positions of authority, far surpassing his initial projections.

A point of particular pride centered on the elimination of the rebel contingent in New York. The last member had received an implant a month ago. Since then, The Institute had tracked no new signs of rebel activity.

Communication, or more appropriately, the lack of certain types of communication, remained under control. It had been four years since The Institute had destroyed the Internet. The world's population believed The

Institute's propaganda that its destruction had been caused by a world-wide hack. The Institute's representatives instilled a pervasive fear that no network was safe—hackers were still at large.

The elderly man stared at the portrait of his father prominently displayed on the wall in front of him. Sixty years had passed since his father, a Nobel Peace Prize recipient, had been assassinated shortly after germ warfare and the retaliatory bombing had wiped out over two-thirds of the planet's inhabitants. His father had publically proposed a way to end the possibility of any future world wars and had gathered a growing number of followers on all continents. A group of organized dissenters, fueled by the Internet, feared his father's solution and wanted to stop him before his proposal made serious headway. As the Founder's father hovered near death, the dying man had never wavered in his belief that there was goodness in every person and had held no hostility toward his attackers. The Founder of The Institute vowed to carry on his father's work and achieve his goal. That vow between father and son allowed the older man the release he needed to pass on.

Unlike his father, however, the Founder wasn't as forgiving. Within a month of the funeral, every person behind his father's death had been killed.

Ironically, it was the shortage of manpower and the detritus of civilization after the war that offered the Founder the opportunity to begin to fulfill his promise more rapidly than he imagined possible. He knew his father would not have approved of the methods he was employing to reach that goal, but he doubted such a grand plan could ever come to fruition with a gentle hand.

Shortly after his father's funeral, the Founder established The Institute in New York and began mass producing androids programmed for the labor force. Had it not been for those androids, the world would still be rebuilding sixty years after the devastation. Demand for labor-force androids remained robust, and sales of newly designed domestic androids skyrocketed over the previous few years.

Even though the Founder had established a branch of The Institute in every major city across America and a few in Europe and Asia, more still needed to be established for his goal to be realized. After subjecting himself to a slew of "enhancements," he believed he would see his vision implemented during his artificially extended lifetime.

The buzzer on the Founder's desk sounded, jarring him out of his reflections.

He pushed the button. "Yes."

"The Los Angeles leadership team has arrived."

"Show them in."

The Founder pulled out his notepad and scanned over his notes. The active rebel group in L.A. was an obstacle to the fulfillment of his promise to his dying father.

When the team was seated, he gave the order. "Increase the number of androids infiltrating society. Place as many as you can in influential households. We might need those humans to help flush out the rebel leaders. No bars will stand in your way. Do whatever is necessary to accomplish this task, even if that means taking control of everyone in authority." A hint of a smile crossed his face. "Creating more cyborgs could benefit that city."

"It will be done." The man in charge of The Institute in L.A. never wavered from a commitment.

CHAPTER 1

The bubbling fountain contained the coins of my lost hopes and dreams. People in the crowd milled about. A few tossed coins into the fountain that dominated the open plaza. Affectionate couples and newspaper readers populated the surrounding benches. High-pitched children's voices screeched as they raced over the paving stones.

I stared at the coins in the fountain and wondered if the ones I had tossed in still remained from my desperate wish to be with the boy who had taught me to surf, stolen a kiss, and grown into a handsome man. But he was beneath my social stratum. No future existed for us.

After I forced myself to put aside all thoughts of my forbidden love, I met Emmett. He was attentive, charming, well-read, and enjoyable to be with. My parents liked him, and our friends thought we were the perfect couple. I actually believed he could fill the void left in my heart by the boy who would always be out of my reach. What went wrong? Emmett dumped me for a woman in his office, a woman who had just entered our stratum because her father had finally managed, after petitioning for over ten years and inheriting a partnership in a lucrative restaurant chain, to be accepted for advancement to a higher stratum. I didn't have a clue that Emmett was even attracted to her.

The end of that relationship drained me. I didn't want to attend social events alone in search for a replacement for Emmett, at least not for a while. At the same time, I couldn't allow Emmett the satisfaction of thinking I still pined for him. Mother suggested I visit The Institute and check out their offerings. Now, I stood at the meeting place arranged by them, waiting for Pellegrin Murr. It wasn't a name I would've picked, but that wasn't an option.

My eyes kept drifting toward the concrete stairs that led to The Institute. Finally, Pellegrin appeared. He had a very masculine bearing and looked exactly like his picture, immaculately groomed with every strand of hair in place. As his six-foot, well-built body came closer, his dark green eyes glowed while meeting mine.

"Miss Hobson, I presume." He spoke in a clear, baritone voice.

I took his extended hand and was a little surprised how warm it felt, about the same temperature as Emmett's. "Yes, Pellegrin, and please call me Paislee."

"Paislee. What a lovely name." He gave me a sensuous smile. I had expected a smile, but not one that held so much promise.

He nodded toward the fountain. "Did you make any wishes?"

"Not today."

"If you don't mind, I think I'll make a few."

"By all means."

Pellegrin pulled several coins out of his pocket. He gazed at the fountain for a few seconds, and then slowly tossed each one in, pausing slightly between throws. Was the android capable of making wishes?

"I've made reservations for us at Marco's." His hand brushed against my arm.

"My favorite restaurant. What time?"

He smiled again. "Seven. Of course, if you'd rather dine later, it won't be a problem moving the reservation."

"No. Seven is perfect."

Bangs, crashing sounds, yelling, and the pounding of feet erupted behind me. I looked over my shoulder and saw a man, carrying a box with a multi-colored emblem on it, plowing through people and knocking over any obstacle in his path. Two police officers, a distance from him, were in pursuit.

"I'll be right back." Pellegrin charged after the running man.

Within a few seconds, Pellegrin had tackled and pinned the man against the hard paving stones.

I hurried toward them as a crowd gathered. When the officers arrived, Pellegrin rose to his feet and brushed himself off.

While a policeman slapped cuffs on the man lying on the ground, the restrained man looked at the crowd and yelled, "Help me." One of the officers held a silver gadget against the man's neck while he continued shouting. "They'll never set me free. I have proof of…" His body went limp.

I figured he had been sedated, and then my eyes moved to the box next to the unconscious man. I recognized the logo for "The Institute" on it.

Pellegrin touched my shoulder. "Sorry about that. Part of my training is to assist law enforcement if I see any civil disobedience."

"Yes. I read it in the contract."

"Let me get you away from here." He led me out of the plaza. "Would you like to go for a drive along the coast before dinner?"

I glanced at my watch and saw we had an hour before our reservation. "I'd like that." I wondered what type of transport Pellegrin used since I had been told by The Institute to leave mine at home.

He took my arm, and we went up the stairs. As we strolled toward a TRL, a Transport Retaining Location, the doors to an HT-8, Hover Transport-8, began to rise.

My eyes fixed on it. I had an HT-6, but mine lacked the advanced features and technology of the transport in front of me. The HT-8 wasn't yet available for anyone to purchase. Pellegrin noticed me staring at it. "It belongs to The Institute. I've been given the opportunity to test drive it for a week."

"Well, then, let's go on a test drive. I've heard this model can float over waterways."

"Yes, and over the ocean. It can also hover above other HTs and land on their roofs, forcing them to power down. Transports like this will be a nice addition to law enforcement fleets."

As we drove toward the coast, a male voice came over the HT's intercom, giving directions. Each time I thought I had an opening to ask Pellegrin a question, the disembodied voice intervened. Unless I wasn't familiar with my destination, I turned off that system in my hover.

I couldn't tell how old Pellegrin was. Maybe he'd never been out of The Institute and didn't know how to reach the coast.

Then Pellegrin pushed a button, removed his hands from the steering wheel, and flipped off the intercom. "We don't need to listen to Wellington talk." The vehicle glided along without his assistance.

"The intercom voice in my hover belongs to Marcel."

"Marcel's voice is used in HT-5, 6, and 7. With the production of HT-8, Wellington's voice replaced Marcel's. Do you like it?"

"I prefer Marcel's."

"So do I. Wellington's voice has too much of a whiny tone."

The ocean came into view. "We're approaching the rocky cliffs. Oh, this is beautiful." I gazed at the aqua-colored water striking up foam when it hit the outcrop of rocks. "Can we go someplace to watch surfers?"

"Yes," he said. "Wellington, go to a beach with surfers."

The HT-8 zoomed away from the cliffs and headed down the shoreline.

"Do you surf?" Pellegrin asked.

"Yes." I looked at him. *Is it possible?* "Do you?"

The android nodded. "I've been trained in all sports, but I do need to wear earplugs in water due to an eardrum problem that started when I was a boy."

Interesting. He cited a human excuse for that condition. Something someone would believe if they didn't know the truth about him. I recalled that the contract warranty became null and void if Pellegrin's head ended up submerged in water without the earplugs securely in place. It also stated that he would be responsible for inserting his earplugs provided he was aware of potential situations that would require them and he was given adequate time to put them in place. So, unless I jumped on his back and forced his head under water, I didn't need to worry about that provision.

When we reached an area above the beach, Pellegrin said, "Wellington, stop here."

Through the window, I saw children playing in the sand and people lying on towels, soaking up the warmth of the sun. My eyes moved to the surfers in the water, and I wondered if one of them could be my forbidden love, the guy who had taught me to surf and now worked in the local market. Oh, how I wished he had been born to affluent parents like me.

"Do you see someone you know?" Pellegrin seemed to read my thoughts.

"From this distance, I can't make out anyone's features."

"I'd drive the transport closer, but that's against ordinance 36-10—'No hover crafts allowed within fifty feet of an occupied beach unless on official business.'

Would you like me to move our reservation so we can walk along the beach?"

"No. I'll just watch from here." I felt unable to relax around Pellegrin. Our conversation was stiff, unnatural. I seldom found myself lacking for words, but I had no idea what to talk to Pellegrin about. If I asked him about his childhood, where he went to school, anything like that, I figured he'd have answers, but no truth would be behind them. Maybe this type of a relationship wouldn't work out for me.

Pellegrin pushed a button and all the windows slid open. Then he chuckled and pointed out the window. "Look at that."

I followed the direction he was pointing in and saw the bare backside of an overweight man chasing two dogs. One dog had a towel in its mouth; the other held what I took to be clothing in his mouth. I laughed.

"That guy should think twice before he brings his dogs to the beach again."

"Maybe they're not his dogs," I said.

"Good point, but I hear him calling names."

I perked up my ears and strained to listen to him yelling, but I couldn't make out what he was saying. I guessed Pellegrin was equipped with supernatural hearing. As the dogs and man ran closer to the sunbathers, some rose and backed away while others laughed, which I managed to hear. A woman threw the man a towel. He quickly wrapped it around his middle.

"Ready to go?"

"Yes. We're probably not going to see any more nude adventures today."

His intense green eyes locked on me, and the corners of his mouth slightly curved up. "I wouldn't say that." Then suddenly, he pulled me into his arms and planted a hot, smoldering kiss on my lips.

His described attributes flashed into my head. Maybe this might work out after all. "You could be right." I gave him a warm smile.

"Wellington, directions to Marco's restaurant." Pellegrin's hands gripped the steering wheel. Before he took off, he looked at me. "I'd have Wellington take us, but I like the feel of driving the HT-8."

CHAPTER 2

When Pellegrin stopped near Marco's, my cell beeped. I pulled it out of a side compartment on my purse, looked at it, and saw the name of my best friend, Kara, appear on the screen. I had the urge to ignore her call but knew she would persist through dinner. "I better take this." Not wanting Pellegrin to hear my conversation and figuring she was calling to find out about my newly acquired asset, I climbed out of the HT-8 and softly answered, "Hey, Kara."

"What's he like? Is he as gorgeous as his picture? Have you enjoyed any intimate moments? How was it?"

"Kara, slow down. He looks just like his picture. And no, we haven't even gone to my house yet."

"Why not?"

"We drove along the beach, and now we're going to dinner."

"Where?"

"Marco's."

"Need to check him out."

"No. Stay away from here." I waited for her response. "Kara, are you still there?" The connection was silent. Irritated that she probably would show up, I slipped my

11

cell back into my purse.

Pellegrin came around the transport. "Is there a problem?"

"No. Not really."

After we entered the restaurant, the maitre d' said, "Hello, Mr. Murr. It's so nice to see you again. We have your table ready."

Based on that greeting, it appeared Pellegrin frequented the restaurant often, but The Institute had led me to believe he was a new model—their latest. Could he be a new model that had a prior owner? Or had his picture been circulated to the restaurant in order for their employees to give people the impression that Pellegrin was a longtime resident of the city?

Once we were seated and Pellegrin ordered a bottle of wine, my favorite Pinot Noir, I asked, "Have you been here before?"

"Yes. The unique, Italian flare of all their dishes keeps me coming back."

I knew he could eat food. I also knew it couldn't stay in his mechanical system long, but the time frame was not specified in the contract. "Have you lived with a woman before?"

He smiled. "Paislee, I'm surprised you would ask such a personal question. For various reasons, I'm not at liberty to say."

The waiter brought the wine and bowed slightly as he poured. Pellegrin ordered us both my favorite Italian entrée. *How does he know?*

During my last appointment at The Institute, I had been told that Pellegrin was busy working on a project that delayed our meeting for a couple of weeks. "What did you work on at The Institute?"

"I wasn't working at The Institute. I analyzed surveillance equipment and recordings at an undisclosed location in order to track down a couple from different strata who had become physically involved."

"Oh, you were working with law enforcement?"

"Yes. When they have difficulty locating individuals who are defying the law, they often request help from The Institute."

I wanted to ask him more questions but stopped when the waiter approached with our meals.

Between bites, I asked, "Did you find the couple?"

"Yes." He reached across the table and laid his hand on top of mine. "But that type of work is behind me now."

It seemed that Pellegrin was overqualified, or more accurately, over-programmed to be a companion, lover, and a domestic. Now I was beginning to understand why he cost so much more than other models. In his class, all of the models had a unique appearance, unlike the ones designed strictly for law enforcement. Maybe The Institute installed certain law-enforcement programs in all androids. Or maybe his model possessed more programs to accommodate the needs of different buyers. Pellegrin didn't hesitate discussing his latest job, so it must be standard work for his model.

"Couldn't they have…" I began and then stopped when I noticed Kara walking toward our table.

"Marten and I were waiting for a table when I saw you." Her eyes moved from me to Pellegrin. "And I thought I'd come and say hello."

There was no way she could have seen us from the restaurant's waiting area or from the bar, but I didn't want to point that out so I went along with her lie. "Oh, I'm glad you did. Kara, this is Pellegrin Murr. Pellegrin, this is my best friend, Kara Leeds."

Pellegrin rose to his feet. "I'm so happy to make your acquaintance, Ms. Leeds."

"Oh, please call me Kara."

Giving her a nice smile, Pellegrin nodded.

"Are you new in town?" she asked.

"No. I've lived here for almost five years. I'd ask you and your friend to join us, but as you can see, we're almost finished eating."

"Well, I better get back to Marten. I just wanted to stop by." Kara looked at me. "Are we still on for lunch tomorrow?"

"Yes. I'll meet you in the courthouse foyer at noon."

"See you then." Turning to Pellegrin, Kara added, "I've enjoyed meeting you."

"The pleasure is all mine."

Pellegrin sat down as Kara walked away. "Does Kara also work at the courthouse?"

Since Pellegrin hadn't asked me any questions, I assumed he had read over the documentation about me that I was required to provide The Institute. "No. She works for Dr. Morehouse in the medical building next to the courthouse."

"Have you known her long?" His tone sounded like an interrogation.

"Yes, since I was eleven."

The waiter came and cleared off the table. Then he asked if we wanted to see the dessert menu. We both declined.

After the bill was paid, we headed to the HT-8. While he drove toward my townhouse, a pang of uneasiness surged through my body. I had never lived with a man before. Emmett often spent the night and I spent nights at his place, but we never talked about living together. Also, we weren't intimate until Emmett and I had known each other for a while. Even if Pellegrin wasn't a human man, he certainly appeared to be. Could I share my bed with him?

He glanced at me and then placed his hand on my knee. "Don't worry, Paislee. We'll take it slow."

Since reading minds wasn't an android attribute, I figured a concerned expression must've appeared on my face. While I continued mulling it over, the garage door underneath my townhouse glided up, and the HT-8 entered, parking next to my HT-6.

As the door slid down behind us, we climbed out of the transport. After Pellegrin retrieved his suitcase from a compartment in the back of his transport, I led him through an interior door and up the stairs. On the way to my bedroom, I stopped at the guest bedroom. "This will be your room until we see how things go."

"Perfectly understandable. I hadn't anticipated putting my belongings in your bedroom."

He stepped into his room, and I continued down the hallway to my bedroom, feeling a little relieved that I'd have an opportunity to feel a little more comfortable around him before he shared my bed. I shook my head as I walked into my room. What was wrong with me? I was acting and thinking like he was a human, a person who I could form a relationship with. That wasn't a requirement of the contract, nor could it ever be. He was a machine. No emotions. He didn't need to like me, and I didn't need to care for him.

Suddenly, I felt masculine arms wrapping around my waist. As I turned, he smothered my lips with his, and he kissed me deeply while he began to unbutton my blouse. His lips moved down my neck as his hand tenderly stroked my breast. It had been over three months since I had enjoyed a man's touch. Even if the body pressed against me belongs to an android, I still felt blood surging into my cheeks, my heart pounding frantically in my chest and my desire for him growing.

He scooped me up in his arms and carried me to my bed. When he placed me on it, I gazed at his naked body. "Oh, my." Admiring him, I saw he was everything stipulated in the contract and a little more. Pellegrin's eyes glowed, and he looked like he was just as anxious to move forward as I was. He leaned down and slowly undressed me. I enjoyed his every touch.

An hour or so later, I snuggled in the arms of the android and felt blissfully sated. Neither one of us had spoken since the love making began, nor did we say a word before I drifted off.

When the alarm clock buzzed, I awoke and turned it off. Then the night before flashed into my head, and I realized Pellegrin wasn't lying next to me. As I sat up, I caught a whiff of bacon cooking and figured Pellegrin was busy making breakfast. Since I had to leave for work in an hour, I quickly showered and dressed.

Stepping into the kitchen, I saw Pellegrin wearing a pair of sweatpants and t-shirt. He sat at the eating bar with his eyes fixed on a monitor. I interrupted a news report to say, "Good morning."

His attention turned to me, and he stood up. "Good morning. I hope you slept well last night."

I smiled. "Perfect night."

He headed to the counter, opened a small compartment, and pulled out a plate filled with bacon, hash browns, scrambled eggs, and buttered toast. "Sit down and enjoy your breakfast," he said, placing the plate on the bar in a spot that had already been set with utensils and a napkin. He poured a cup of coffee and put it down next to my plate. He slightly caressed my arm, and then took the stool across from me. "You were wonderful last night."

"You were pretty special, too." I doubted my responses would make any difference to an android. As I dug into my breakfast, I thought how nice it was to have a domestic android that fulfilled other, more pleasant duties. At the same time, I thought it would probably take me twenty years to pay back my parents for the money they had loaned me to purchase Pellegrin, but he was Mother's idea. She probably didn't want me crying on her shoulder anymore after being dumped. Yet, she seemed overly insistent about me acquiring an android, which I couldn't understand.

"Is there anything special you'd like me to prepare for dinner?"

"No. Surprise me."

"While you're at work, I'd like to drive around to become familiar with the area. Would that be all right?"

"Sure. Once you've finished the domestic chores, feel free to do whatever you'd like, but I do insist that you be here when I get home from work, shortly before six. If I'm running late, I'll give you a call. Oh, I just remembered…you're scheduled to report every Thursday afternoon to The Institute. Let me know if that runs past six p.m."

Seeing it was almost time for me to leave, I hurried to the bathroom and brushed my teeth. I grabbed my briefcase and purse and headed toward the stairwell. Pellegrin stood near the newel post and placed his hand behind my head and softly kissed my lips. "Have a good day at work."

"Call if you can't find something that you need."

"Will do."

Five minutes later, I drove my HT-6 toward the courthouse while I thought about Pellegrin. He was an attentive lover and certainly fulfilled that prominent clause in the contract. He excelled Emmett in every way, but I couldn't shake the feeling that something was off. Maybe I was having a hard time picturing him as more than a machine. I wondered if my discomfort could be because he helped the police find two people who had broken the law, a law I wished didn't exist, that made me think something about him didn't add up. Maybe all I needed was just to get used to him. After all, I shouldn't expect him to only be programmed for domestic duties since I had requested an intelligent android, one that possessed the same knowledge as a college graduate. Lately, it seemed that law enforcement was always on high alert, so it made sense The Institute would program their androids to help out if needed. Otherwise, there'd be no need to include a provision in the contract stating that Pellegrin would step in if he observed anyone disobeying the law.

After parking my transport in a TRL, I headed to my

office near Judge Wilbur's chambers. As I headed toward my desk, my cell buzzed. I glanced at it and then answered, "Hi, Mom."

"How did it go?"

"He perfectly fit the description we had been given." I filled her in on my evening with Pellegrin, leaving out the intimate details.

"Does he have any traits that might lead someone to believe he's an android?"

"No. He even talked freely about his past—a human past. Of course, all made up, but unless you knew the truth, you'd never suspect. Now I know why The Institute referred to his model as their highest accomplishment. Each one has a unique appearance. There's no comparison between Pellegrin and the androids that work side-by-side with policemen. They all look alike and talk in a stiff monotone. No one would ever mistake them for humans. But I *am* feeling guilty about how much Pellegrin cost."

"Don't worry about it, dear. You can pay us back after you've established your own law practice."

"Pellegrin is supposed to have a good resale value, so who knows how long I'll keep him."

"Are you already thinking about getting rid of him?" Mother asked, sounding disappointed.

"No. No. But someday I might meet someone. Not now. I don't intend to even start looking for a while."

"Well, it would be nice to have grandchildren in my future."

"I'm not thinking that far ahead."

"I'd like to meet your young man."

"Mom, he's not *my young man*. He's an android."

"Our friends and acquaintances are going to be told otherwise. The Judge's schedule seems to be filling up more each day, but I have insisted that he keep Sundays open. Could you and Pellegrin join us for dinner this Sunday?"

Mom had called my father "the Judge" since he became

one twenty-four years ago, the same year I was born. "Sounds good," I said, though I wasn't anxious to start parading Pellegrin around. "It will just be dinner for the four of us, right?"

"Yes. Say five o'clock?"

"We'll be there."

After we disconnected, I looked at the stack of folders on my desk and wondered if we'd ever get back to having everything digitized, the way it used to be before the world-shattering hack. Having hard copies became the only way to keep court cases confidential. I began sorting through the folders to determine which case to work on first and ran across a folder marked "Judge Harlan" on it. Thinking one of Judge Wilbur's cases had been accidentally put in the wrong folder, I opened it and found myself staring at the pictures inside.

CHAPTER 3

I lifted up the first picture. A pregnant woman and a man clung to each other as an android policeman, with a pistol at the ready, stood over them. Strange. Policemen were never armed with simple weapons like that. They used zappers to temporarily paralyze and laser guns, weapons that when fired pierced a hole through the intended target. Those high-tech weapons were only allowed in the hands of law enforcement personnel. It was impossible for a civilian to acquire one. In the second picture, the man, covered in blood, was lying stretched out on the ground. The third and final picture showed the woman with a tear-streaked face, being pulled away from the man by a policeman. That policeman didn't appear to be an android.

Hearing footsteps outside my door, I quickly put the pictures back into the folder and slid it into the middle of the stack.

Britney, a law clerk for Judge Harlan, came rushing into my office. "One of Judge Harlan's folders is missing, and he's going nuts, like one of us snatched it. Did the receptionist by any chance give you one of his folders?"

I nodded toward the stack of folders. "All those were

20

on my desk when I came in. I haven't gone through them yet." Since Judge Harlan was temperamental, I didn't want him to think that I had the opportunity to look at the contents.

"Is it okay if I look through them? Oh, I'm not going to look inside any of the folders, but just to see if one has his name on it."

"Sure. I'll help." I moved the top half of the pile and started flipping through them.

Britney thumbed through the bottom half. "Oh…here it is." She held it up. "I better get this to him right away." She hurried out of my office.

I mulled over the pictures in that folder and figured the couple had committed a crime, probably cohabitating outside their respective strata, but that didn't rise to the level of the death penalty. Even if it did, the android policemen weren't allowed to carry out any sentences without a judge hearing the case first. Maybe the man had a weapon and put up a fight. Then the androids wouldn't need permission to shoot him. I might be jumping to conclusions; maybe the crime committed had nothing to do with cohabitation. My eyes drifted to the folders on my desk, and then I started working on the case files.

A couple of hours later, I needed a cup of coffee and headed to the break room. On the way, Britney stopped me in the hallway.

"Do you know anything about the case being heard in Courtroom 16?" she asked, scrunching her face in confusion.

"No. Why?"

"Judge Wilbur isn't presiding?"

"No. He's in his chambers."

"Something strange is going on. Judge Harlan is in there, and he has an appointment with the district attorney who has been waiting for him over a half an hour in Harlan's chambers. When I gave Judge Harlan that folder two hours ago, he rushed right into Courtroom 16. Two guards are standing by the door to make sure no one enters."

"It's not unusual to have guards stationed by the door. You know that."

"But Judge Harlan doesn't have any hearings on his calendar for this morning, and besides the appointment with the district attorney, he has another one scheduled in twenty minutes. Do you think he's testifying in a case?"

"How should I know that?"

"Phil has the day off and Janet is at a conference, and I don't know what to tell the district attorney or his next appointment. What should I do?"

Phil was Judge Harlan's administrative assistant, and Janet his chief law clerk. Britney had only been with him for a month. "Okay, tell the district attorney that Judge Harlan is involved with a case that requires his immediate attention and you don't know how long he'll be. At that point, the district attorney will probably say he'll reschedule the appointment. And then say something like that to Judge Harlan's upcoming appointment if he still isn't back in his chambers."

"Oh, thank you. You're the best." Britney turned around and hurried toward Harlan's chambers.

I strolled into the break room and filled my coffee mug. Savoring the caffeine boost, I noticed two android cops walk past the door. I peeked out into the hallway and saw them go around the corner in the direction of Harlan's chambers. Android policemen often came to the courthouse, but they were either bringing in a prisoner or stationed at a courtroom door.

A man yelled, "Let go of me!"

Then I caught a glimpse of the district attorney being physically escorted by the androids. I quickly backed into the break room and pressed myself against the wall, out of their view. I sensed it was better if they didn't see me.

The district attorney continued yelling, "You're both going to be neutralized for this outrageous behavior."

Britney was right when she mentioned something strange was going on. Over the past six months, all of the judges, including my father, seemed to be guarded in everything they said within the building. No joking or laughter went on anymore, not even in the break room or lunchroom.

Loud footsteps continued to pound on the hallway tile floor.

When I could no longer hear the footfalls, I peered into the hall and scanned both directions. Not seeing anyone, I walked at a brisk pace to my office. After entering, I closed the door and sank down on my chair, wondering what the district attorney had done and if Harlan had made an appointment with him just so he could be taken into custody.

A button flashed on my OC, the office communication device. It indicated an internal call, but not from Wilbur. I pushed the button. "Ms. Hobson. May I help you?"

"Paislee, you won't believe what happened," Britney said, sounding out of breath.

Figuring she intended to tell me about the arrest and knowing that everything said over the OC system was recorded, I blurted out, "Britney, sorry I can't talk now. I have to deliver a folder to Judge Wilbur."

"But this is…" she began, and I disconnected. Both of us could end up in trouble if we continued that conversation. People at the courthouse had been fired for much less. In case that call was scrutinized, I didn't want anyone to suspect I had lied. I picked up a folder, went to Wilbur's chambers and knocked on his door.

"Come in," he shouted. I was taken aback because that was unlike him to raise his voice.

I opened the door and stepped inside. "Judge Wilbur, this folder lacks the case files. Only a partially completed form is inside that gives the name of the defendant. It doesn't even state the charges. Would you like me to track down the documents?"

"Let me see it." He extended his hand for the file, and I gave it to him. He pulled out the sheet inside and briefly looked at it. "This case has been removed from my calendar. Give the folder back to central files."

"I'll do that." I left his office, wondering who had discussed the case with him since he never checked his calendar.

As I dropped the folder into the bin marked "Central Files," I noticed the time—12:05 p.m. I hurried back to my office, grabbed my purse, and headed to the foyer to meet Kara for lunch.

Kara was sitting on a bench and stood when I stepped out of the elevator.

"Sorry, I'm running late. Busy morning."

She smiled as we walked out of the building. "Yeah. I know."

"Huh?"

"I saw your dreamy looking android. Last night must've gone pretty good."

"What are you talking about?" I ambled with her across the street to a small café we patronized frequently.

"Paislee, I was at the window looking for Marten—he had left his sunglasses in my bathroom—when I saw that gorgeous Pellegrin walking into the courthouse. Did you summon him because you needed a little extra attention?"

I stopped on the sidewalk. "No! I didn't summon him. And I didn't need any *extra* attention." I smiled. "He more than took care of that last night."

"Oh, you've got to tell me everything. Was it strange doing it with an android?"

I held my index finger over my lips. "Shhh. No one is supposed to know he isn't human."

"Sorry, I forgot."

We found a table near the rear of the café, out of earshot from the other patrons, and placed our orders over the intercom attached to the wall.

"Pellegrin never came to see me this morning." I

adjusted myself in the chair.

Kara leaned forward. "Oh, come on. You can tell me."

"I *am* telling you. He never came to my office. I doubt he even knows where it is."

"Then why was he in the courthouse?"

I shrugged. "He mentioned he'd been helping the police on a case. Maybe it was something to do with that. I'll ask him this evening."

"You don't keep tabs on him? I thought he had to report to you if he left your place."

"Some people might handle androids that way," I said in a soft tone. "I've told Pellegrin he can do whatever he wants after he's finished his tasks, but he needs to be home before I get back. I want people to view him as a human. That image would be shattered if he was always kept locked up in my house while I worked."

A mechanical-moving android server brought our salads and placed them along with the utensils and bill on the table.

Out of habit, I said, "Thank you."

With a big grin on her face, Kara asked, "So how was it last night?"

"He's definitely worth every dollar I paid for him. Well, really, every dollar my parents paid for him."

"So…did he seem like a human?"

"Better than Emmett."

Her eyes popped wide open. "Really?"

I nodded while I ate. "He knew exactly what to do and when to do it. Awesome software."

"Can I rent him for a night?"

"What about Marten?"

Kara tilted her head and raised her eyebrows. "Marten is caring, fun to be with, and highly educated. Someday I'll probably marry him, but unfortunately, he isn't a great lover. I even rented some old triple-X rated DVD's."

"They're illegal. How did you get them?"

"Paislee, I can't blab about that. Strictly, hush hush.

The guy, who claims to be a handyman, probably lives off of all the money he receives from renting them out. They're in high demand. I can hook you up if you need them, but with Pellegrin around, that's not the case. And before him, you never complained about Emmett in that department."

"Did you and Marten watch them?"

"No. Well… I did. Marten only saw the first couple of minutes and thought they were disgusting. Hey, can we double date on Friday night?"

"Sure. Where should we go?"

"Bailey's. The band is supposed to be one of the best in the country." Kara cocked her head. "Pellegrin dances, doesn't he?"

"You know," Paislee mused, "I have no idea. He's skilled at all sports. Would dancing be considered a sport?"

"Maybe."

"I'll ask him. Even after the short time I had spent with him, I'd be surprised if he *didn't* know how to dance. Regardless, we can still go there. If he can't dance, we'll watch you and Marten. We'll pick you up. The Institute lent Pellegrin an HT-8 for a week. It's so cool."

"HT-8s aren't available yet. Marten's been wanting one. He'll love riding around in it. Can you pick us up early so we can float over water in it?"

"Sure. We'll pick you up at seven, drive around, and grab a bite to eat before going to Bailey's."

"Sounds good. I'll make dinner reservations for us at a place that has quick service."

We ate in silence for a few minutes.

Kara looked up. "Oh…what's wrong with Judge Harlan?"

"Nothing as far as I know. Why?"

"He's been in to Doc Morehouse almost every morning for the past week, but he doesn't look sick. He still has that same stiff walk and always looks gloomy. Never smiles. Can't figure out why your dad likes him."

"Dad invites all the judges whenever he and Mom have a party, whether he likes them or not."

"Your parents sure know how to throw great parties. Marten and I wouldn't miss one."

"Can't you just look up Judge Harlan's medical records when nobody's around to find out what's wrong with him?"

She shook her head. "I tried. Couldn't find it. Morehouse must have it in his office. I sure do miss the digital system. Having to always pull hard copies of everything is getting old. Do you think we'll ever be able to use network systems again?"

"I have no idea. According to the news, the three hackers that were caught tried to escape and were shot in the process. The hacking group keeps moving around without leaving any trace."

"We should probably be glad we still have television and radio. It must be tough on kids in school without the Internet. It sure made it easy to do research for school assignments."

"Yeah, we're lucky we made it through before the hackers took over." I glanced at my watch. "Time to get back to work."

* * *

During afternoon break, I decided to check on Britney since I had hung up on her. Walking down the hallway, I didn't pass anyone. Even the benches near the courtrooms were empty. The place seemed eerily quiet. The double doors leading to Judge Harlan's clerk's offices and his chambers were closed. I gripped the doorknob to open it. It was locked. Thinking they might be having a meeting and didn't want to be disturbed, I turned around and headed back to my office.

Sitting at my desk, I stared at the office communicator and contemplated calling Britney, then decided against it.

With the district attorney being arrested in Harlan's chambers, I didn't want to take a chance she might talk about it over the monitored OC system.

While I was doing some research on a case, I heard a loud voice outside my door. I couldn't make out the words, but it sounded too young to belong to 66-year-old Judge Wilbur.

A knock came on my door, and then it flew open.
Seeing an android policeman in the doorway, fear surged through my body.

CHAPTER 4

The android stepped aside, and I saw a familiar face.

"Thanks, A-4." Pellegrin walked into my office, and his attention turned to me. "I didn't know your location. A-4 was kind enough to show me the way."

Odd. With the stern, fixed expression on the faces of all android cops, I had a hard time envisioning any of them as being kind.

Pellegrin looked around the room. "Very nice." He gave me a sensuous smile. "But a couch against that wall..." He pointed to the one with two chairs. "...That would be a good addition for evenings when you're working late and you'd like company."

The image of spending time with Pellegrin on a couch flashed into my mind. My pulse quickened, and a tingling sensation spread through me. I took a steady breath to reel in the emerging desire. "Did you come here just to see me?" I was curious what he would say since I already knew he had entered the courthouse at least four hours before showing up in my office.

He moved closer to me and tucked an unruly strand of hair behind my ear. "Paislee, I always want to see you, but I had been called to testify in a case. The case I mentioned to you yesterday."

"Is it being heard now?"

"No. The hearing was this morning. Afterward, I was invited to go to lunch with Judge Harlan and the prosecuting attorney. Judge Harlan also invited his law clerk, Britney Sawyer. She mentioned you during lunch. You offered her some advice when she wasn't sure how to handle Judge Harlan's waiting appointment."

"It's unusual for a judge to take the prosecuting attorney, a witness, and a law clerk to lunch after a case has been heard. Was there something special about that case?"

Pellegrin shook his head. "Not that I know of. I've never been involved in any cases before, so I'm not familiar with the protocol. I am aware that Judge Harlan had another difficult situation that he had to deal with during the trial. From what I understand, that was settled admirably. That could've instigated his desire to have a break away from the courthouse, and I, along with others, benefited with a very enjoyable luncheon. Good food and stimulating conversation."

Pellegrin couldn't taste food, but I continued to be amazed at how well he was programmed to talk as if he were human. "I'll be off work in an hour. Should we have dinner somewhere around here?"

"That would be nice. Judge Harlan has a matter he'd like to discuss with me. Would it be all right if I talked to him while I'm waiting for you?"

"Sure." I wondered if Judge Harlan realized that Pellegrin was an android.

"I'll be back in an hour." He turned on his heel and headed out of my office.

My eyes dropped to the documents I had been summarizing, but I found it impossible to concentrate on them as my mind kept drifting to Pellegrin. He belonged to me. He was bought and paid for. Should I have refused to allow him to discuss any matter with Judge Harlan? Pellegrin must have done an excellent job testifying.

Harlan wanting to talk to him about something proved that. That *did* make him seem human. And whatever the discussion was about, would Pellegrin be able to provide him with appropriate input?

I could understand Pellegrin testifying in a case he had worked on before our meeting, but I didn't want him performing other tasks besides those I had delegated. Still, I had told him he was free to do whatever he wanted after he had finished his domestic tasks and before I came home. I dug into work and was surprised how quickly the completed documents stacked up.

"It doesn't look like you're ready to go." Pellegrin snapped me out of my concentration.

"Give me a minute." I gathered up the documents, put them back in the folder, and cleared off my desk.

After we stepped out of my office, I locked the door. "I thought we'd walk to the park and eat at the outdoor café."

"I'd like that." Pellegrin pushed the elevator button. "It'll give me a chance to see this part of town."

Pellegrin held my hand as we walked along the sidewalk. I wanted to ask him about the meeting with Judge Harlan but decided to wait until we were seated at the café. "Where did you go for lunch?"

"A & F Ristorante. Have you been there?"

"Yes. Many times. They serve some unique Italian dishes. What did you have?"

"I didn't go for one of their more exotic entrees. I ordered chicken parmesan. It was expertly prepared, probably the best I have ever had."

Then I noticed Pellegrin intensely eyeing a couple going the opposite direction on the sidewalk. His eyes stayed focused on them, even when the man returned his gaze as they moved past us. "Do you know them?"

"Who?"

I nodded behind me. "That couple."

"No. They're attired a little unusually. Don't you

agree?"

The woman wore cut-off jeans and a black halter with a shear black top draped over her outfit. The man had on a pair of light green baggy pants, a sleeveless t-shirt, and a cowboy hat. "They're casually dressed, but that's not unusual for this part of town." I doubted that was the reason Pellegrin had stared at them and wondered about Pellegrin's prior life—the life that started with his creation. Besides the investigation he'd told me about, had he worked on many before that? And, more importantly, was he *still* working on them?

After we placed our order at the counter, we sat at a table that overlooked the pond.

"It is pleasant here." Pellegrin turned his head back and forth. "All of these trees remind me of a forest."

"Have you visited many forests?"

"Yes. They seem to be a favorite place for people to hide."

"Hide? Pellegrin, have you worked on a lot of investigations?"

He nodded. "Yes."

The female food server brought us our hamburgers, fries, and drinks. So I said, "Thank you."

She smiled and went to another table.

I sipped my Coke. "Are you still working with the police on some?"

He shook his head. "No, not since I met the lovely Paislee with pale-blue eyes, flowing light brown hair, and the physique of a model." His eyes glowed. "I'm grateful that no one stole your heart before I came along."

How could I possibly be upset with him? After taking a few bites of my hamburger, I probed. "What did Judge Harlan want to discuss with you?"

"Other cases on his docket. According to him, there has been a surge in rebels either getting involved with people outside their stratum or trying to hack into secure systems."

"Hacking is a worldwide problem. Not just here. That's why all the documents at the courthouse are maintained as hard copy, no longer accessible through an electronic system. I didn't think there were any secure systems left."

"There are. The internal system at The Institute is secure, but it has become a full-time job for the communication department to keep it that way. No external transmissions are allowed. Also various internal law enforcement systems are secure. Unlike The Institute, they need to receive and send external transmissions, which go through another system. It ends up being a constant battle to prevent those transmissions from being intercepted. Sometimes they're not successful."

"You said Judge Harlan discussed cases with you. Besides mentioning the upsurge in rebel activity, did he want your advice or help with the cases?"

"Paislee, I'm afraid I'm not at liberty to discuss any specifics with you about the cases. As you know, that information is confidential."

"But he discussed them with you. You don't work for him. You work for me. You shouldn't be privy to that information."

He tilted his head. "Are you inferring that Judge Harlan was out of line when he talked to me about them?"

I wanted to say "Yes," but it appeared Pellegrin was somehow still connected to law enforcement, and I didn't fully trust him. He had only been with me for about twenty-four hours and it seemed like his past, whatever it was, kept him in some kind of loop. When I purchased him, I believed—and the contract reinforced—that he would only serve and be loyal to me. Maybe I needed to re-evaluate my purchase. Maybe see if I could get my money, actually my parents' money, back from The Institute since he wasn't living up to the contract. But he certainly was a good lover. I needed to carefully think that over.

"Paislee?"

"Oh. No, of course not. Judge Harlan would never break any rules. He's been highly commended for dispensing the law justly and equally to all defendants." To change the subject, I looked at the pond. "Isn't that cute to see the baby ducklings following their mothers around?"

"Are there any fish in the pond?"

"Yes. Last time I walked around it, I saw goldfish and Koi. Do you want to take a look?"

"You haven't finished your fries."

"I couldn't eat another bite." I stood.

Pellegrin grabbed our plates and dumped them in a trash container. He took my hand again, and we went to the pond. As we walked over the bridge, he pointed out other fish and gave me their names. He knew every species in the pond, and then he started naming all the various trees and bushes. I found the stroll around and over the pond to be educational, not exactly what I had hoped for.

It was almost 10:30 p.m. when I pulled my HT-6 into the garage and parked next to the HT-8. As I headed up the stairs, I heard Pellegrin talking. His back was to me, and I caught a few words—"tomorrow…won't work…gun."

Suddenly, he flipped around. "Talk later," he said into an odd-shaped gadget.

I had never seen a phone that looked like that.

Pellegrin must've noticed me staring at it, and then he held up the gadget. "This a CAD, a communication access device. It incorporates the latest technology. It's not available to the public yet, but The Institute was kind enough to give me one." He placed it on the counter. "I expected you to beat me home."

"I thought I would have too since you walked me to my transport. You must drive faster than I do."

"I let Wellington do the driving, so blame it on him." He moved closer to me, put his arms around me, and his lips curved against mine. "I've been looking forward to this all day." His warm breath, a nice feature that had been added to his model, brushed against my cheek.

Like the night before, he picked me up and carried me to my bed, and then began slowly removing my clothes. Each time he touched me, my skin tingled. My heartbeat spiked as I lay naked on the bed, sizzling with anticipation. I watched him strip. Within a few seconds, he was by my side, caressing and kissing every inch of my body. Concerns about his past and present loyalties vanished into thin air as a rush of excitement swirled through me.

* * *

The following morning, I sat down at the kitchen eating bar and drank coffee while Pellegrin dished me up a large waffle.

While pouring syrup over the waffle, I asked, "Do you have plans for the day?"

"Judge Harlan wanted me to take care of something for him this morning. If you'd rather I stay home, I can inform him that won't be possible."

I had the urge to pry but figured Pellegrin wouldn't reveal more. "Once you've finished your jobs here, you can help out Judge Harlan. And Pellegrin, I appreciate you asking me." Since I had already given him permission to do whatever he wanted to do before I got off work, I wasn't about ready to retract it this soon even though it didn't seem to be working out well for me.

"This afternoon I'll be going to The Institute."

"Yes. I remember. Tomorrow night we'll be going out with Kara and her boyfriend, Marten. Apparently, he wants an HT-8."

"I'd be happy to drive him around and explain all the features."

"Let's pick them up at seven. We can take a drive along the coast before we dine and head off to listen to a band. That'll give you plenty of time to tell him all about an HT-8."

"I'll be looking forward to meeting him and going out with your friends."

Before I left for work, Pellegrin held me in his arms and ran his tongue across my lips. "You taste so good."

CHAPTER 5

On the way to work, I listened to the radio and caught the end of the national news. The reporter was giving statistics about the lives lost and the damage the rebels were doing across the country. He went back and forth between calling them rebels and terrorists. Then it switched to local news. Nothing came on about the district attorney, and I assumed he had already been set free. Maybe the whole incident was just a mistake. The district attorney seemed too straight-laced to do anything so bad it would warrant his arrest.

While I unlocked my office door, Sophie, Judge Wilbur's administrative assistant, scooted her chair back and hurried to me. "Come with me to the restroom."

The restrooms were the only places in the building that didn't have cameras with listening equipment attached. Whenever female employees didn't want to take a chance of being overheard, or worse, recorded, they went to the women's restroom. I guessed the men used their restroom for the same purpose, but I couldn't verify that.

I dropped my purse on my desk and followed Sophie.

In the restroom, Sophie checked all the stalls to make sure we were alone. "Yesterday, Judge Harlan had the district attorney arrested."

"Really?" I feigned ignorance and tried to look worried.

"Yes. I overheard the assistant D.A. telling someone in the break room. He sounded mad. I didn't see who he was talking to."

"Where were you?"

"In the hall, ready to go into the break room. But then after I heard that, I hightailed it out of there. I didn't want anyone to know I overheard them, especially since Judge Harlan instigated the arrest. He's vindictive. He'd probably get me fired just for hearing about it. It's not on the news, and I doubt Judge Wilbur knows about it. He's pretty good friends with the D.A. and his wife. Can't tell him 'cause I don't want him to know I eavesdropped. I'm hoping the assistant D.A. stops by."

"Yeah, Judge Wilbur should know. Does he have the D.A. anywhere in his appointment calendar?"

"Tomorrow afternoon. Good idea. I could call to confirm. Someone there will tell me." Sophie touched my shoulder. "Thanks." She hurried out of the restroom.

I looked in the mirror and brushed my hair to the side and then noticed a mark near my hairline and leaned forward to get a better look. It was a small, round, blue circle. I grabbed some paper towels, lathered them up, and tried to scrub away the mark, but it remained firmly in place. Figuring I had accidently poked my forehead with the tip of a blue pen, it would have to wear off. I knew my hair would keep it well hidden, so I headed back to my office.

Mid-morning when I was busy working on a brief for one of Judge Wilbur's cases, he walked into my office.

"The district attorney has been shot. I'm heading to the hospital."

"How? Where?"

"I don't have any details. His wife called. She, of course, is extremely upset, and what she rattled off didn't make sense. I need to get there." He rushed out of my office before I could say anything else.

I'd talked to the D.A. and his wife at several social engagements. I knew them, but not well. My father always spoke highly of him. I wondered if Sophie had found a way to break the news about the D.A.'s arrest to Judge Wilbur before he received that phone call and went to her desk. She wasn't there, but Charles, Judge Wilbur's career law clerk, was putting some folders on her desk. "Do you know where Sophie went?" I asked him.

"No." He turned around and went back into his office. Charles was an average-sized man in his late thirties. He tended to keep to himself and seldom joined in any chit chat at the courthouse.

Then I heard shuffling of papers in Wilbur's chambers and looked in.

Sophie saw me as she gathered up documents and piled them neatly on Judge Wilbur's desk. "Did you hear?"

I nodded, moved closer to her, and whispered, "Were you able to mention the other matter to Judge Wilbur before the D.A.'s wife called?"

She shook her head. "I spoke with the receptionist at the D.A.'s office right after we talked, at least three hours before Judge Wilbur received the call from the D.A.'s wife. She had no idea where he was. She'd been trying to locate him. He missed an appointment, an attorney was waiting for him, and he had a scheduled meeting at 1:00 p.m. She sounded a little frantic."

"My father might not know about the shooting. I'm going to his office."

Going down the hallway, I passed six android policemen pacing back and forth and guessed their presence related to the shooting. Had the D.A. been shot by a family member of a sentenced person? Someone who strongly disagreed with the verdict?

"Hello, Paislee." Travis, my father's administrative assistant, leaned his lanky body against a file cabinet.

I nodded toward the closed door behind him. "Is my

father in?"

"No. Judge Hobson is in court."

"Do you know if he's heard anything about the district attorney this morning?"

"He's been in court since nine."

"Then he probably doesn't know."

Travis tilted his head with a puzzled expression on his face. "What about the D.A.?"

"He's been shot."

Travis's eyes popped wide open. "I knew something was going on. No wonder the android cops are swarming around here. Is the D.A. dead?"

"No. He's in the hospital. Judge Wilbur has gone there. I need to get back. Will you have my father call me when he returns to his chambers?"

Travis nodded. "Yes."

As I headed back down the hall, an android cop stepped in front of me, blocking my way. "What is your business in this building?" He spoke in a monotone.

"I work for Judge Wilbur. I'm a law clerk."

"Your hand."

I stretched out my left hand, knowing he intended to check my chip, located near the base of my thumb.

He placed a microchip reader over it and looked at the monitor. Then he tapped to the list of employees in the building. "You are free to go."

There had only been one other occasion when an android policeman stopped me. That time, it was right outside a courtroom and I had an emergency message for Judge Wilbur, who was presiding. Most people might not think it fell in the emergency message category, but his wife had insisted it did—their fourteen-year-old sick dog had passed.

As I worked through the case files, I kept expecting to hear from my father or news about the D.A. from Sophie. Finally, at 4:05 p.m., my OC buzzed. I grabbed it without even noticing if it was an internal or external call. "Ms.

Hobson. May I help you?"

"You sure can," Pellegrin said. "I miss those long, slender legs wrapped around my waist."

"Pellegrin. Everything said over this line is recorded."

"I'll have it erased."

I figured he might be able to pull that off, though I didn't have the foggiest idea how. "Is there a special reason for this call, or did you just want to hear my voice?"

"I'm at The Institute."

"Right. I remember your required Thursday afternoon visit."

"It's running late. The way things are going, I might not be home before 11:00 p.m. I've made chicken cacciatore for dinner. You'll only need to zap it a minute when you get home."

"Should I keep some warm for you?" I asked to find out how he'd respond.

"That won't be necessary. I'll grab something to eat at The Institute."

I had to hand it to him; he never gave even the slightest clue that he wasn't human.

After I disconnected, I strolled out of my office to see if Sophie had an update on the D.A.'s condition. "Have you heard from Judge Wilbur since he left?"

She shook her head. "No. I called Westland Hospital and the woman at the information desk wouldn't even tell me if the D.A. had been admitted. I even asked Charles. He doesn't know anything. I listened to the news. Nothing." She stood and whispered, "I started to wander the halls, looking for the assistant D.A., but an android cop stopped me. Since I didn't want to explain anything to him and there was only a slim chance the assistant D.A. was still in the building, I came back here. Why don't you talk to your dad and see if he knows the D.A.'s condition?"

"I've left a message for him to call me. I'd go and ask Britney, but I've already been stopped by an android cop once today. And since I have no business reason to see her, it's best that I don't even try with those policemen roaming the halls."

"The D.A. is such a nice guy. I hope he'll be okay."

"So do I."

Sophie stood up. "My bra strap in the back seems to be twisted. Can you come with me to the restroom and fix it?"

"Sure." I knew she wanted to tell me something in private as we walked down the hall without saying a word.

Like always, she checked the stalls. "Do you think the D.A. was shot while he was in police custody?"

"I have no idea. If he was, that will probably be kept quiet. Our police force wouldn't want it to get out that they couldn't protect their prisoner. Since you overheard about his arrest, pretend you don't know anything about it. Besides me, did you tell anyone else?"

Sophie shook her head. "No. And I agree, it's better not to let on I know anything about it. I still can't figure out what's going on around here. It's like no one trusts anyone, and everyone's worried they'll get kicked out of the courthouse if they say anything that isn't job-related. Has your father mentioned anything?"

"No. It seems his workload has doubled over the last few months. Mom's complained about it."

"Judge Wilbur's hasn't. Maybe it's because he doesn't handle the hard criminal cases like your father does."

"We better get back."

"Yeah. Don't want an android cop looking for us." Sophie opened the door to the hallway.

I returned to my office and decided to attempt to reach my father again to tell him about the shooting. I picked up the OC and punched in his extension.

"Travis Zaloom. May I help you?"

"Hi, Travis. My father still isn't in his chambers?"

"No. He came to pick up some folders. I mentioned you wanted him to give you a call. He asked if it was an emergency. When I told him 'No,' he hurried off to courtroom six. His calendar is packed today. He'll probably be working late. Paislee, do you want me to leave him another note to call you?"

"No. I just wanted him to know about the D.A."

"During lunch," Travis said, "I stood behind Janet in the cafeteria line. She was talking about the D.A. to a man I didn't recognize. I overheard her say the bullet struck the D.A. in his shoulder. He'll need some reconstructive surgery, but he'll be fine. If I don't see Judge Hobson before I take off, I'll leave him a note about the D.A."

Paislee sighed. "Oh, I'm so glad to hear that he'll be okay. From the way Judge Wilbur hurried out of here, I assumed the D.A. had been badly wounded. Maybe on his deathbed."

"With so many android cops still marching through the halls, I suspect the culprit who shot the D.A. hasn't been captured, yet."

"You're probably right, but the androids are good at their job. The perpetrator should be in custody soon." I hung up and went to tell Sophie the good news—the D.A. was going to be okay.

* * *

As I drove home, I decided to stop at the market to pick up some fruit. Or maybe it was just an excuse to catch a glimpse of Tate. I thought about him often, but we could never be together.

After entering the store, my eyes drifted around, looking for him, while I made my way to the produce section. Not spotting him anywhere, I moved up and down most of the aisles for a more thorough search. I gave up and began to fill a bag with oranges.

Suddenly, an arm wrapped around my waist and a hand covered my mouth as I was pulled into the storage room.

"Shhh. It's me." Tate released me.

"Tate, you could go to jail for doing that."

"Relax. You were standing in a blind spot and this side of the storage doors..." He pointed to one of the double doors. "…is also in the blind spot. We've been moving the cameras around to meet our needs."

"Who's we?"

"Friends." His eyes fixed on mine, and then he pulled me closer and kissed me.

I tried to refrain from kissing him back, but it was no use. My lips had a mind of their own. "This is dangerous. We could both go to prison just for standing this close."

He brushed my hair away from my face. "No, Paislee. Only I would go to prison. You'd be the innocent damsel in distress."

"Tate. I'd never let you take all the blame."

"It wouldn't matter what you said. That's how it would go down."

"Don't you care about your own safety?"

"I do. That's why we're in a blind spot."

A scraping sound echoed through the storage room.

I swung my head in the direction of the noise.

"Don't worry. It's a dolly being pushed along. Everyone who works here is on the same side."

"And what…" I turned my head and stopped when my hair caught on something. I reached up to free the strands.

"Hold still, Paislee. I'll get it." His hand clutched my hair.

I dropped my arm to my side, and then I saw Tate's teeth clenching.

"You didn't?" He stared at the top of my head, his eyes narrowed.

"What did I do?"

"This." He touched my forehead. "The blue mark."

"Tate, it's just ink. It'll wear off."

His eyes focused on it. "No. It's not ink. You've been marked."

"What are you talking about?"

He lowered his eyes to mine, and his handsome face darkened with rage. "I knew you were seeing a new guy, but an android?"

"Who I see is none of your business. You know as well as I do, that this…" I waved my hand between us. "…can never work."

"Paislee, you've been marked. Do you know what that means?"

"It's only a little dot….You really don't think it's ink?"

"It's not." He placed his hands on my shoulders. "Your android boyfriend has marked you. As far as all his android buddies are concerned, you belong to him."

I stroked his cheek. "No. He belongs to me. My parents loaned me money to buy him. I can resell him whenever I want to."

Tate shook his head. "That's not the way it works."

"That *is* the way it works."

"Why? Why did you do it?"

"Tate, you are not part of my life, and you never will be. After Emmett…"

"What a dipshit, dumping you for that blonde floozy."

"Actually, she's nice. After him, I didn't want to be with anyone. Mom thought having a human-like android could be a good companion until I was ready to date again. That's all there is to it…I don't know why I'm telling you this. I'm not your concern. What I do is none of your business."

Tate held me tight. "Yes, you are my concern, and you always will be." He kissed me again, and I loved the feel of his lips against mine. "Paislee, you're in danger." Then he pointed to the spot on my head again. "Watch this. See if it grows larger."

"What happens if it does?"

"Then you need to get away from that android any way you can," Tate responded without answering my question. "And come to me."

"How do you know about the android mark?"

"I've seen it before."

I wanted an explanation but guessed his vague answer was to keep me in the dark, probably for my own good. The less I knew, the easier it would be not to talk about it. With the strange atmosphere that had fallen over the courthouse, mentioning non-public information about androids could lead to trouble. Someone would demand to know who told me about it. If I refused to answer, I could find myself being interrogated by android policemen, and from what I had heard, their methods were persuasive and very unpleasant. I rubbed the spot on my forehead. "Can I put something on it to prevent it from getting bigger?"

"No. Don't allow the android in your bed. The more intimate you become with him, the larger the mark will become."

"How big?"

"Half an inch in diameter at the most. He's probably keeping tabs on you." Tate looked around. "Harvey, over here."

A heavyset, short, bald man walked to us.

"Have it show she went to the beach after she spent ten minutes in the market."

Harvey pulled an oblong, gray device out of his pocket, and tapped on it for a minute. "Ready."

Tate wrapped his hand around my wrist, and held my hand out. The man placed the gadget on top of my microchip, and a strange vibrating sensation ran through my thumb. Then Harvey lifted up the device. "All done." He began to walk away.

"Harvey, the sand box."

"Getting it."

"Sand? What for?" I asked Tate.

"To prove you were at the beach. Your new boyfriend will look for it."

I gritted my teeth. "He's not my boyfriend."

Harvey returned, pushing a dolly with a box of sand on it.

"Step into the box and wiggle your shoes."

"If I walked along the beach, I'd be carrying my shoes." I took off my heels, stepped over the rim of the box and stood in the sand, moving my bare feet around. Then I climbed out, brushed off some of the sand, and put my shoes back on. The grainy sand was pushed between my toes.

As Harvey pulled the dolly away, it dawned on me that more was going on there than adjusting cameras. I figured they had altered locations often on microchips to indicate someone was at the beach. This was more than a ruse to spend unobserved moments with me. *Could Tate be part of the rebel movement?*

"That will take care of you for another twenty minutes." Tate enveloped me in his arms, and I felt his heart beating, something I'd never feel being held in Pellegrin's arms. "You'd better head home."

I ducked out of the storage room and filled a bag with oranges. As I paid at the scanner, I noticed a short man with curly, blondish-red hair staring at me. He wore a shirt with the store logo on it. I had never seen him before and figured he must be a new employee. Then I wondered if he was staring at me because he found me attractive or, since Tate mentioned everyone who worked at the store was on the same side, could he be speculating if I was also on that side?

After climbing into my car, I mulled over everything Tate had said and wondered how he learned I had broken up with Emmett and there was another "man" in my life. It had been months since we had spoken. That conversation had taken place in a public spot in the store and only lasted a minute. I had no idea if Pellegrin was keeping tabs on me, but it appeared Tate was. Maybe he had known all along Pellegrin was an android.

It suddenly struck me....Could the whole mark thing be a wild, fabricated story Tate made up after seeing the ink spot? On a few occasions when Emmett and I were together, Tate told me Emmett was cheating on me. I never saw any sign from Emmett that was true, so I figured Tate was trying to break us up until Emmett broke it off with me. Other times, Tate had mentioned that androids were getting out of hand, given too much authority. The mark story might've just popped into Tate's head when he saw the spot, and he thought he could use it to keep me away from Pellegrin and all androids. But the look on his face didn't support that. I doubted he was that good of an actor. *Could it be true?*

My garage door glided up. The HT-8 was parked inside.

CHAPTER 6

How long had Pellegrin been home? I stopped my HT-6 next to the HT-8 and glanced at my watch—7:34 p.m. While I went up the stairs, the luscious smell of pastries baking permeated through the house.

Pellegrin rose from the couch when I reached the top step. "Did you run into any friends at the beach?"

"How did you know I went to the beach?" I placed the bag of oranges on the counter, knowing Tate had been right. Pellegrin was keeping tabs on me.

"I like looking at the ocean. Before coming home, I drove along the coast and saw you."

Now he was lying to me. "Why didn't you stop?"

"I wanted to make your favorite dessert, chocolate éclairs. You must be starving." He walked toward me.

My eyes drifted around the kitchen. A dozen éclairs were on a platter near the warming oven. "They look delicious, but how do you expect me to eat that many?"

Pellegrin smiled. "No. I thought your work colleagues might enjoy some tomorrow."

"It'll be a nice treat after today's problem." I sat down on a stool by the counter where a place setting had been laid out.

He took a plate out of the cabinet. "What problem?"

"I want to take off these shoes and wash my hands before I eat."

"Stay put. I'll take care of that." He picked up a bowl of soapy water, a wash cloth, and a towel from the counter by the sink and carried them to me. He certainly was prepared for my sandy feet. If I didn't have any sand on me, this might have turned into a difficult situation.

"Wouldn't it be easier if I just cleaned up in the bathroom?"

"I want to do this." He slung the towel over his shoulder and put the bowl on the floor.

He took each of my hands and meticulously wiped them with the warm, soaked wash cloth. Pellegrin had anticipated exactly when I'd arrive home; otherwise, the water would no longer have been warm. After he dried my hands, he slipped off my shoes.

"I'll clean the sand out of your shoes later tonight."

"I won't be wearing that pair of heels tomorrow, so no rush."

He proceeded to wash away the sand on my feet and dry them.

"Thanks." I watched Pellegrin put the bowl in the sink.

"I like taking care of you." Pellegrin poured a glass of wine and handed it to me. "What was the problem at the courthouse?" He dished up rice and chicken cacciatore. He placed the plate in front of me.

Since numerous people at the courthouse already knew about the D.A. getting shot, I briefed him about it.

When I finished, he looked perplexed. "You don't know if they caught the shooter?"

"I listened to the news earlier and nothing was even mentioned that the D.A. had been shot."

"I could make a call to find out the status of the pursuit."

"Could you? I'd feel better going to work tomorrow if I knew the culprit was behind bars."

While I continued eating, I watched Pellegrin pick up his CAD and tap on it. "Pellegrin here. How's the hunt for the D.A. shooter going?...When?...Why wasn't it on the news?...That's it...No...A-26." He put down the CAD. "The shooter has been taken care of. The D.A.'s wife requested that the shooting not be on the news, and they honored her request."

"Why would she request that? And when the potential killer was at large, the public should have been told about it. The press is supposed to keep us informed."

Pellegrin stroked my arm. "Sorry, Paislee, I don't have all the answers. I'll look more into the matter tomorrow."

After I enjoyed an éclair, Pellegrin handed me a letter. "What's this?"

"It's from The Institute."

It read:

> *Dear Ms. Hobson,*
>
> *Some unexpected matters have arisen that require the attention of our most knowledgeable and skilled androids. Pellegrin falls within that category. We would like to have him available for the next two weeks to help us resolve these matters. We do not anticipate this will consume all of his time, and we realize you may have social engagements on your calendar where you intend to have Pellegrin accompany you. Those engagements should go forward as planned. We do not want to disrupt any of your scheduled events.*
>
> *If you agree to allow Pellegrin to help us, we will refund you twenty-five percent of the price you paid to acquire him and provide a domestic android to clean your house and cook. We would appreciate your consideration of our proposal, and we look forward to hearing from you.*
>
> *Sincerely,*
> *The Institute*

I held up the letter. "Do you know what this says?"

"Yes. They discussed it with me. I do expect to be here during the evenings." He smiled. "I wouldn't want you to sleep alone."

"What do you want to do?"

"Paislee, that isn't my decision. It is yours."

"Well, it would be nice to give my parents back twenty-five percent of the money, and it would only be for two weeks. I guess I'll agree. When would you start?"

"I will check on a few things tomorrow while you are at work, but I'd like to spend as much time as possible with you over the weekend. Of course, I will make sure I am available to go with you and your friends tomorrow evening."

"My mother invited us to dinner at their house on Sunday, and I accepted."

"I would like to meet your parents. I won't miss that engagement."

"Outside that, no other social engagements are on the calendar. I'll try to keep it open so you can help The Institute."

"Thank you."

"I'm going to shower and wash away the rest of the sand." I headed to the bathroom and closed the door behind me. I sat on the counter, pulled my hair away from the blue dot and closely examined it in the mirror. To me, it still looked like an ink spot. Nothing about it struck me as unusual.

I slid off the counter, quickly stripped, and showered. Looking down, I saw granules of sand going down the drain. I hadn't realized that much sand had ended up on my legs. While I dried off, Pellegrin, wearing only briefs, opened the bathroom door and walked in. So much for privacy.

He took the towel and finished drying me off. He dropped the towel and pulled me close and traced my lips with his index finger. He lowered his mouth to mine and kissed me deeply, coaxing my mouth open with his tongue while he trailed his fingers down my body. My breathing accelerated and my heart pounded at a frantic tempo as I forgot Tate's warning and surrendered to Pellegrin's every move. He scooped me up in his arms and took me to the bed. His briefs fell to the floor, and he was mine for another night of overwhelming ecstasy.

* * *

When I arrived at work, I didn't see any android cops on the way to my office.

As I reached my door, Sophie said loudly from her desk, "They caught the shooter."

I walked over to her and set down the box of chocolate éclairs on the corner of her desk.

"What's this?"

"Treats to have with morning coffee."

She raised the lid. "Oh, yummy!"

"Don't worry; I won't leave the box on your desk. I'll put it on my credenza."

"You don't trust me with them?"

"Nope." I smiled. "Getting back to the shooting. Is it on the news today?"

"No. Not a word. Judge Wilbur told me when he got here. We talked in his chambers."

"Any idea why it isn't on the news?"

"Don't have a clue, and neither does Judge Wilbur. He stayed at the hospital yesterday with the D.A.'s wife. She had already been there for two days, sitting by her mother's side. The woman is dying, and Helen, the D.A.'s wife, is her only child. She saw her husband for a moment while he was being rushed into surgery and thought his face looked ashen white, as if he was dead. The two doctors, who were attending to him, wouldn't even tell her where he had been wounded. Had she not been at the hospital, she doubts she would've been able to see him at all. After the surgery, the D.A. was wheeled into the intensive care unit and visitors were prohibited. That's when Helen and Judge Wilbur were told the extent of his injury. They were both a little surprised and relieved that it wasn't worse. Helen pleaded with the doctors to let her see her husband, but they wouldn't relent. With that type of shoulder surgery, Judge Wilbur can't understand why the D.A. had to be kept isolated. He was worried that the doctors might be holding something back, but this morning Helen was allowed to see him. He's sleeping, doped up, but she seems to think his color is returning.

"The night before the shooting, she had received a message in the hospital that her husband had been arrested. Helen had called her house. No one answered, but, according to her, the D.A. is a heavy sleeper. Yesterday morning, she unsuccessfully tried to reach him at his office. Before she could do any more calling around, looking for him, he was brought into the hospital. When Judge Wilbur arrived at the hospital, he tried to track down the source of the message. It wasn't written on the form the hospital uses. He ended up turning the note over to the police.

"Can you imagine? The poor woman is in the hospital watching over her dying mother and someone gives her a phony message, and then her husband is shot." Sophie winked at me to let me know she was going along with the story about the arrest even though we both knew it wasn't a *phony message*. "No wonder she was hysterical when she called Judge Wilbur."

"I'm glad Judge Wilbur stayed with the D.A.'s wife all day."

"Judge Wilbur's wife went to the hospital last night. She kept Helen company so her husband could get some sleep. He has a full calendar today."

"How's Helen's mother doing?"

"The same. Helen's going back-and-forth between the two patients."

"That's rough. Let me know if you get any updates on the D.A.'s progress." I picked up the box. "Oh, do you want one now?"

Sophie nodded. "Mm hmm."

I raised the lid and she took one out. "I'll pass them around to our little group after I get settled. There's plenty, so you can have another one."

"I'm going to take you up on that."

I went into my office and sat down in the desk chair, thinking about the D.A. He had been carted off by two android policemen. Why was that arrest being covered up? And who had given Helen the message? A member of the rebel group? Was he shot in police custody? And worse, did an android policeman shoot him? Questions kept streaming through my head. I wanted answers.

Since Britney worked for Judge Harlan and witnessed the D.A. being taken away, she might know more. Judge Harlan didn't approve of his staff socializing during work hours. Not even for a few minutes. I needed an excuse to see her, and then the éclairs sprang into my mind.

Before going to her office, I walked into Judge Wilbur's chambers with the box of pastries. He looked drained. His eyes were droopy, and his shoulders sagged. The prior day had taken a toll on him, dealing with the D.A.'s wife and worrying about his friend. His first scheduled hearing was in less than thirty minutes, which was just the beginning of those on his calendar. I felt sorry for my 66-year-old boss as I offered him an éclair.

"I could use the sugar." He took one and held it up. "Your boyfriend made these?"

I nodded. Wanting Pellegrin's true identity to remain a secret, I didn't know another way to refer to the human-like android that lived at my place.

"I'm impressed. They appear professionally made."

"He's a gourmet cook."

"Wish my wife was."

I went into Charles's office. He wasn't shy. He took

two chocolate éclairs.

Stepping out of his office, I asked Sophie, "Do you want another one before I go and see if Britney wants any?"

"She'll want one all right." Sophie snagged another éclair. "Thanks."

Heading toward Britney's office, I didn't see one person or any android policemen in the hallway. "Want a morning treat?" I asked Phil, who sat at his desk outside Judge Harlan's chambers.

"Never turn down a treat," Phil, an overweight man, said.

I opened the box, and he looked inside.

"Did you buy éclairs on the way to work?"

"No. My boyfriend made them."

"Wow. They look awesome." Phil lifted one out and placed it on a napkin next to a stack of papers on his desk.

I noticed the napkin had crumbs on it, and figured the éclair wasn't his first morning treat. I swung around and walked toward Britney's closed door.

"Britney's not in." Phil's words were muffled from the éclair in his mouth.

"Sick?"

"Yeah, I guess. She missed work yesterday too."

"Maybe I'll call her at home and see how she's doing. Do you know her home phone number?"

The door to Judge Harlan's chambers opened, and he stepped out.

"Would you like an éclair, Judge Harlan?" I felt uncomfortable as his eyes swept over me.

"No. I don't indulge in sweets."

"Maybe Janet wants one." I moved toward her office.

"She doesn't indulge in sweets either." Judge Harlan turned to Phil and talked about some items on his calendar.

I decided it was time for me to take my leave and headed back to my office. As I opened my door, Sophie asked, "Do you have any left?"

"Yes. Are you ready for another one already?"

"Not right now. But maybe after lunch."

"I'll make sure to save you one."

I sank down in my chair and thought about Britney. She didn't seem like she had been coming down with anything on Wednesday, and Pellegrin said she went to lunch with them. Maybe she just ate something that didn't agree with her, but I sensed it was more than that. Phil didn't seem to know why she wasn't there. He just assumed she was sick. Could Britney have been fired because she saw too much that day? Guessing that Judge Harlan would be in court later, I made a mental note to call Phil in a few hours for her phone number.

A brief I had been working on needed to be finished before Monday morning along with the other documents in folders on my desk. Trying to put thoughts of the D.A. aside, I pulled out the brief and forced myself to concentrate on preparing the draft.

During afternoon break, I called Phil for Britney's phone number.

"Sorry, Paislee, Judge Harlan overheard you asking for her phone number this morning and told me it was inappropriate for me to give out phone numbers for any employees. If you want it, you're going to have to get it from human resources."

"I understand. Don't worry about it, Phil." I hung up, thinking hidden mics must be all over the courthouse. Otherwise, there was no way that Judge Harlan could have heard me requesting Britney's number. Or maybe Harlan just monitored his own employees. He was a control freak. That's why his previous law clerk left. She had to write down every time she walked away from her desk and the reason. Britney was still a new employee and probably didn't mind reporting her every move, yet. Phil and Janet had never complained about it, but Janet shared Harlan's work attitudes.

CHAPTER 7

Sitting on the couch, thumbing through a journal, I looked at my watch—6:28 p.m.—as I impatiently waited for Pellegrin. I tried to contact him on his CAD to make sure he would still be available to go out with Kara and Marten, but he never answered. If he didn't show up in the next fifteen minutes, I decided I'd call Kara and bow out of our planned get together.

I went into the bedroom to get another magazine when I heard a door opening. Hurrying back into the living room, I saw Pellegrin coming up the stairs, dressed perfectly for a night out on the town in his black, silk long-sleeved shirt, no tie, and gray slacks.

"Sorry, I'm running late. Everything took longer than anticipated." He stared at me, and it seemed like his eyes lingered on my bare legs. "Wow. You look great. I've never seen you in a short dress before."

I twirled around. "So you like my dancing outfit?"

"Yes. Very much. All the guys there will want a dance. If we're going to be on time, we need to be heading out. Do you need to get anything before we go?"

"No. I'm all set."

As he drove toward Kara's place, I wondered how he

knew where she lived. Nothing about Kara was included in any of the documents I completed for The Institute. Had he done research about her after they met at the restaurant? It was another sign that things about Pellegrin didn't add up, and The Institute wanting his services for two weeks amplified that. "Your éclairs were a big hit at the courthouse."

"I'm glad people enjoyed them."

"Britney hasn't been to work for a couple of days. Did she seem well when you went to lunch with her on Wednesday?"

"Yes. Completely. Has she seen a doctor?"

"I don't know. I tried to get her number to call her, but Judge Harlan doesn't want his assistant to give out employee numbers."

"I can understand that. Would you like me to get it for you?"

"Yes, if you could. I'd like to find out how she's doing."

Pellegrin stopped in front of Kara's apartment building. He leaned toward me, pulled me into his arms, and kissed me. "I've been wanting to do that ever since I saw you tonight but also wanted to get here on time. We're here three minutes early." He caressed my thigh and slowly moved his hand up. "Unfortunately, not enough time for more enjoyable activity." Pellegrin kissed me again and then looked out the passenger door window. "Here come your friends."

I straightened up my dress while I climbed out the HT-8. "Hi," I said to Kara and Marten, and then I briefly hugged her.

Pellegrin walked around the transport.

I introduced them. "Marten, this is Pellegrin."

"Glad to meet you, Marten." Pellegrin shook his hand.

"Nice to meet you, too, Pellegrin. I've heard so much about you."

I glared at Kara. She had promised not to tell anyone

that Pellegrin was an android.

Kara gave a slight shake of her head and mouthed, "He doesn't know."

"I hope it's all good." Pellegrin opened the back door for them.

"Yeah." Marten strolled around the HT-8, examining it. "That you have an inside track on getting one of these before they're available for the public. I've wanted an HT-8 since I read about the new features. How did you pull that off? Do you have a relative that runs the company or something?"

"As a matter of fact, my uncle is their head designer. He gave it to me to test drive for a week, and half of that time is gone. I intend to talk him into letting me keep it a little longer."

Marten ran his hand over the transport's roof. "This is so cool! Any idea when I can buy one?"

"No. The company's being pretty quiet about that. It'll probably be announced with great fanfare like the other HTs. Ready to take a spin in it?" Pellegrin held open the back door.

I stepped forward, touching Marten gently on his arm. "Hey, Marten, why don't you sit in the front passenger seat? I think you can get a better feel for the hover there."

Pellegrin smiled at me. "Good idea." He looked at Marten. "Then I can explain to you all the features as we go."

Excitement radiated from Marten's face as he moved toward the passenger door.

Kara and I climbed into the back seat. "Oh, this seat is so comfy," Kara said. "What's this material?"

"A specially treated leather." Pellegrin drove away from Kara's apartment as he pointed out the different functions to Marten.

While they chatted about the HT-8, Kara whispered, "Are you having fun evenings?"

I nodded. "Yep." With Pellegrin's super hearing, I

didn't want to elaborate and changed the subject to Kara's cousin's wedding. "How are Jessie's wedding plans coming?"

"Terrible. She keeps changing her mind about the color scheme, flowers, menu, you name it. Gene must really love her to put up with all of it." She smiled. "But you should see the bridesmaids' dresses she's picked out. Gorgeous. We are going to look great, even if there's still a question about the color."

Kara and I continued talking about the wedding until the HT-8 came to a stop and the front doors flew open.

I looked out the window and saw the ocean below the cliff. "Are we going to walk around here?"

"No." Pellegrin moved to the passenger door. "Marten's going to drive for a while."

Marten, beaming, turned toward us. "Over the ocean. Cool, huh?"

That got my attention. When Pellegrin drove me to the ocean after we met, he didn't hover over the water.

"Are you sure about this?" Kara sounded a little nervous.

Pellegrin looked over his shoulder at her. "Don't worry, Kara. Wellington won't let us plunge into the water."

A confused expression flashed on her face.

"Wellington is the operating system, like Marcel on my HT-6."

"Does he sound as sexy?" Kara leaned forward and looked at the dashboard.

"No." I shook my head. "Not even close."

Then Pellegrin gave some instructions to Marten. A few seconds later, the transport floated down to the water and hovered three to four feet above it. I peered out the windows as we glided along.

Pellegrin's tone changed. "You're getting too close to the surfers."

"I can barely see them."

"You have to pull up and go in another direction. Now."

The transport slowly turned around, and I found the ride exciting. I had been on numerous ships and boats, but this was my first time hovering over the waves and seeing the sun-bleached craggy rocks off in the distance. Looking in the other direction, the sky was ablaze with hues of oranges, yellows, and reds as the sun began to set. No matter in what direction I gazed, I saw spectacular views of the land and ocean. I thought about driving over lakes, rivers, and canals and hoped Pellegrin could sway The Institute into letting him keep the HT-8 but doubted they'd hand it over as a gift to him, and my budget was already stretched pretty thin.

"What time is the dinner reservation?" Pellegrin asked, bringing me back to the present.

Kara looked at her watch. "Oh, dear. It was for eight. We're late and the band starts at nine."

"There's a restaurant that overlooks the ocean not far from here. It's casual, but they serve their customers quickly," Pellegrin said. "Would you like me to call and see if they can seat us?"

Marten, sporting a huge grin, turned to Pellegrin. "Sure." He clearly relished driving the HT-8.

Pellegrin pulled out his CAD and placed the call. "Would you be able to seat a party of four in ten minutes…Pellegrin Murr…thank you." He disconnected. "We're set. Marten, do you want to drive there or should we turn that over to Wellington?"

"I want to drive. This is so much fun. I wanted one of these new transports, and now I'm going to be dreaming about getting an HT-8. Where to?"

Pellegrin rattled off the directions while Kara and I continued enjoying the views. My eyes opened wider when I saw we were approaching Ocean Hills, a casual eating establishment about ten feet above the ocean. There was a path from the beach that led to it. The place was often frequented by surfers, and I had gone there numerous times with Tate when I took lessons, lessons that lasted a whole wonderful summer. Did Pellegrin know about that? Or was it just a coincidence that we were going to that restaurant? Also, how did he manage to get reservations? Reservation never used to be available. It was a first-come-first-served establishment.

Marten parked by the entrance near the road. People were milling about outside. Some were seated on benches, waiting for tables to open up. It was something I had done often.

Pellegrin took my hand and guided me through the crowd with Kara and Marten right behind us. As soon as we stepped over the threshold, a middle-aged man, dressed in a colorful pair of plaid slacks and a short-sleeved white shirt, made his way around the hostess station.

"Mr. Murr, we have your table ready." He led us to one with an unobstructed view of the beach and ocean.

Within five minutes, we had placed our orders, and ten minutes later, our food was served. Marten and Pellegrin talked about the HT-8. Kara joined in. It sounded like she was just as excited for Marten to get one as he was.

The more time I spent with Pellegrin, the more something seemed amiss. He obviously had a wide depth of knowledge and connections that I hadn't expected him to possess. Being my companion and a domestic was appreciably below his intelligence and obvious qualifications. I still couldn't understand why The Institute sold him to me. Was he flawed in some way? Something that couldn't be corrected? But if so, then why did The Institute ask to borrow him back?

My eyes drifted around the packed tables until I saw a familiar face staring back at me—Harvey, a man who worked with Tate at the grocery store. He was the guy who adjusted my microchip. I scanned the faces of everyone sitting at his table and felt relieved that Tate wasn't among them.

Pellegrin touched my arm. "Are you ready for dessert?"

"No dessert for me. Thanks."

"I don't want any either." Kara looked at me. "But I need to touch up my lipstick before we leave for Bailey's."

"So do I." I went with Kara to the restroom.

"Pellegrin is dreamy, and he knows his way around." Kara pulled her makeup bag out of her purse. "You are so lucky, Paislee. I want…" She stopped when three women entered the restroom. "We need to go to lunch next week. How about Monday?"

"I'm swamped at work. How about Tuesday?" I leaned toward the mirror and applied lipstick.

"We're on." Kara fixed her makeup.

As we left the restaurant, Marten's face lit up when Pellegrin told him he could drive the HT-8 to Bailey's.

At 9:40 p.m., we arrived at Bailey's, and just like at the restaurant, a suit-clad host greeted Pellegrin and showed us to a table right next to the dance floor. "Would you care for your usual beverage, Mr. Murr?"

Pellegrin looked at us. "Do you all like champagne?"

"Yes," we answered in unison.

"I'll have a bottle delivered to your table." The host moved away to fulfill his promise.

"Wow, does everyone in town know you?" Kara said to Pellegrin, which was exactly my sentiment. "We've never scored a table this close to the dance floor before."

Pellegrin raised his brow. "Being a loyal customer for many years sometimes pays off."

Marten moved his chair closer to Kara's. "Does it ever."

Pellegrin extended his hand toward me. "Care to?"

He held me close as we danced to a slow tune. The next song was fast, and Pellegrin swung me all over the floor. I had a hard time keeping up. When that dance ended, we returned to the table, and Marten excused himself to go talk to a work colleague he saw at the bar.

As I sipped champagne, I spotted Harvey on the dance

floor and inhaled deeply, almost choking on the beverage. Did he follow us to Bailey's? Was he here to keep track of me?

Pellegrin gently rubbed my back. "Are you okay?"

"Just swallowed wrong. I'm fine."

Kara stood up. "Hey, Pellegrin. How about a dance?"

He looked at me. "Do you mind?"

"Of course not." I had anticipated that sometime during the evening we would exchange partners for a dance or two, and I wasn't surprised that Kara would make the first move.

I watched Kara and Pellegrin dance to a slow song. He didn't hold her as close as he had held me. I noticed instead of resting her hand on his shoulder, she rubbed the back of his neck. Didn't she realize that would do nothing for him? He was a machine. Had he been a human boyfriend, I would have gotten ticked off.

"Where are Kara and Pellegrin?" Marten took his seat.

"Dancing."

His eyes moved to the dance floor. The pleasant expression on his face faded as a tiny furrow of annoyance appeared between his eyes, and his lips were pressed together.

I looked at the couple on the dance floor and saw Kara was gazing at Pellegrin's face while her fingers combed through his hair. Was she completely oblivious that Marten could see the way she was behaving? And, I must admit, I was getting a little irritated that Pellegrin didn't try to stop her, maybe make an excuse to return to the table, anything. Finally, the music stopped. I expected that would end Kara's flirtation display, but instead, the music started up again and they began to dance again. Unfortunately, it was another slow tune.

My attention drifted to Marten. His mouth was set in a tense, grim line. He was fuming. Trying to defuse the anger boiling up inside him before smoke started coming out of his ears, I asked, "Care to dance?"

"Why not?"

As soon as we stepped on the dance floor, Marten pulled me tightly against his body and began to dance. "I've always really liked you, Paislee. How serious are you about Pellegrin?"

I feared where this conversation might be heading. "Pretty serious. We live together."

He loosened his grip on me and looked at my face. "Really? For how long?"

"He moved in on Tuesday."

"But Kara said you just met on Tuesday."

"I don't tell Kara everything. And until Tuesday, I wasn't sure how much he was committed to our relationship. I guess, unlike you and Kara, my relationship with Pellegrin is fairly new."

The music ended, and to my relief, Pellegrin escorted Kara back to our table.

We had just sat down when Marten said, "I must've eaten something that didn't agree with me. Pellegrin, would you mind taking Kara and me home, or should I call for a commercial transport?"

"Oh, I'm sorry you're not feeling well, Marten. Let me make arrangements for a transport to take you home."

"Pellegrin, why don't we take them home?"

"Is that what you would prefer, Paislee?"

"Yes."

Kara didn't say a word as we left Bailey's. Fearing that an argument between Marten and Kara could arise before we reached Kara's apartment, I insisted on letting Marten sit in the front passenger seat.

"We'll have to go there again," Pellegrin said as he drove them home. "Do they have live music every Friday?"

"Yes." Marten's voice was tense. "And Saturday nights."

By Pellegrin asking that question, it gave away that he hadn't patronized the establishment often as a loyal customer like he claimed when we first arrived. Neither Marten or Kara seemed to have noticed his mistake. Tonight might've been the first time he was there. But then how did the suit-clad man recognize him, and why was he given special treatment?

No one spoke until we stopped in front of Kara's place. We all climbed out of the car and said our goodbyes.

"Don't forget lunch on Tuesday." Kara turned toward the entrance.

"I won't." I slid into the passenger seat.

Pellegrin pulled away from the apartment building. "Have I done something to offend you?"

"No." I swung around to face Pellegrin. "But…"

He held up a hand. "Just a minute. Wellington, take us home." Pellegrin released the steering wheel.

"Kara and Marten are a couple. They've lived together for several years."

"Yes. She told me."

"Marten didn't appreciate her flirtatious gestures while you danced."

"Flirtatious gestures?"

"She rubbed your neck and ran her fingers through your hair."

"He was jealous?"

"Yes. That's why he no longer wanted to stay at Bailey's."

"Were you jealous?"

"No." I gave him a small smile. "Because it appeared she was the aggressor, not you."

"That's true. She said that she and Marten weren't getting along well. She hoped to make him jealous. It worked."

"That it did." Maybe that was all there was to it. Even if Kara would've liked a night with Pellegrin, that didn't mean she'd give up Marten for that isolated tryst.

As my garage door rose, I noticed a police HT parked close by my townhouse, and two android cops stood on my porch.

Pellegrin pulled the HT-8 into the garage and then climbed out and marched to the policemen. "What are you doing here?" His tone sounded angry.

Had The Institute developed a program for emotions so the latest android models would appear more human-like? Maybe it was just my imagination, but Pellegrin seemed to exhibit some emotions.

"You did not answer your CAD." The policeman addressed Pellegrin in a monotone.

"It was off. What's the problem?"

"You are wanted at The Institute."

"Go. Tell them you delivered the message." Pellegrin did not inform them if he intended to comply.

The two androids got into their transport and drove away.

Pellegrin headed back into the garage, and we went upstairs.

I dropped my purse on a chair. "Do you have to go?"

"Let me check." He picked up his CAD from the counter and placed a call. He turned his back to me.

Figuring he intended to have a private conversation, I went into the hallway and perked up my ears. I hoped I might hear something that would give me a clue about his job at The Institute.

"…no, not him. Shellman."

Harvey Shellman? Did he spot him at Ocean Hills, or was he talking about another person named Shellman? Then I heard a clanging sound. He had knocked something onto the floor. Guessing he might see me while he picked it up, I softly moved to my bedroom. Even though there was a possibility that Pellegrin had been talking about another Shellman, I still wanted to warn Tate, but I had no way to contact him except showing up at his store. The store closed hours ago. He'd probably be in bed, and I had no idea where he lived. Warning him would have to wait. Wondering if I'd have an opportunity to do it over the weekend, I got ready for bed. I had just hung up my dress when Pellegrin stepped through the doorway. "There's an issue I need to handle. I should not be gone more than a few hours."

"The Institute said it needed your help for a couple of weeks, so calling you in isn't unexpected."

He wrapped me in his arms. "I'll be home before you wake up." He kissed my forehead and then raised my chin and planted a long, deep kiss on my lips. Pellegrin's brilliant, green eyes gazed into mine. "We can finish this later."

CHAPTER 8

After he left, I decided to snoop through Pellegrin's
things to see if any of it would shed light on all the
questions streaming through my head. Since I knew he was
capable of quietly moving around the house, being caught
going through his stuff wasn't anything I wanted to deal
with. I went and locked the door leading to the garage.
Pellegrin had a key, but the clicking sound of the tumblers
if the door was unlocked, hopefully, would alert me to his
return, giving me time to move.

I walked into the guest bedroom. It looked exactly as
it had before Pellegrin moved in. No personal items were
on the bureau or nightstand. I opened the closet door. His
clothing was neatly hung up. Nothing was on the shelf. His
suitcase stood in the corner. I pulled it out and felt
surprised to find it locked. Years prior, besides teaching
me to surf, Tate had also taught me to pick a lock, a skill I
doubted I'd ever need. Staring at the suitcase, I wondered
if I could remember how to do it. I decided to give it a
shot after going through the drawers.

Underwear, socks, t-shirts, and sweaters were neatly
placed in three of the bureau's four drawers. The bottom
one held a plastic mechanical device. Upon closer

examination, I saw it had a mouth piece, a long tube, a cylinder container, and a metal box with a cord attached. I figured it was used to pump food out of his stomach—stomach was probably the wrong word—whatever inside his frame that held consumed food. I carefully put the device back into the drawer the same way I had found it.

I searched through the nightstand. In the top drawer were toiletries—combs, a toothbrush, and a blue tube that I took to be a special tooth polisher for an android.

The bottom drawer contained three folders. I lifted them out. In the first one were copies of all the forms and documents I had completed or provided to The Institute in order to purchase Pellegrin. Another file held copies of my medical records, documents I had not given to The Institute. Why did he have them? And how did he get them? Going through them, I noted that some items were highlighted—height, weight, and vaccines. I squinted when I saw a handwritten red star next to the birth control shot I had ten months prior, a shot I had when I was dating Emmett. A shot that prevented unwanted pregnancies for a year. Why was that marked? Androids didn't need to be concerned about that. Strange.

I continued flipping through the pages. Nothing else was highlighted, but on the last page was a handwritten note: "No physical problems, perfect fit." Did Pellegrin write this? Why did it matter? And "perfect fit" for what?

A loud knock echoed through the townhouse.

I jumped. Then I quickly put away the folder and closed the drawer.

Another loud knock.

I started out of the room and then remembered the suitcase. I rushed to it and put it back in the closet.

As I charged toward the front door, another knock reverberated through the air. I peered out the peephole and swallowed hard, seeing an android policeman on the other side of my door. Figuring he might force entry if I didn't answer, I slowly opened the door. "Yes?"

"Mr. Murr sent me."

"Why?"

"For your safety."

"Am I in danger?"

"Call Mr. Murr."

Leaving the door ajar, I took my cell phone out of my purse and ran my finger across the dark screen. When it lit up a small "4" flashed in the corner. Wondering why it didn't ring, I suddenly remembered muting it after we picked up Kara and Marten. I tapped on the "4" and listened to three messages from Pellegrin and one from Kara, wanting me to call them. Since an android cop stood within earshot, I returned Pellegrin's call.

"Why didn't you answer my calls?" He sounded urgent, but not mad.

"I put my cell on mute earlier and forgot to turn the sound back on when we got home."

"Is A-49 there?"

"I can't tell the android policemen apart, but there is one on the front porch."

"He'll be outside all night to watch for problems."

"What problems?"

"Some documents were stolen by an Institute employee. Before the employee was captured, she managed to pass on the documents to unknown parties."

"What does that have to do with me?"

"People and androids associated with The Institute have become targets for the rebels. Seven androids were terminated this evening."

"Can't they be repaired?"

"Vital components were removed from those androids before policemen arrived on the scene. A local factory that supplies those components has been destroyed, and the rebels have been successful in intersecting and confiscating shipments from a plant across the county."

"So because I had a transaction with The Institute, I've become a target?"

"No. I might be a target. It is unclear. Right now, only android policemen have been terminated."

"Is there anything I should do?"

"No. I did not want you to be concerned if you noticed any policemen patrolling around your house."

"Okay. Are you going to be home soon?"

"Not for a while." He disconnected without saying another word.

I opened the front door wider and looked at the android cop. "Mr. Murr has explained the situation to me. Thanks." I shut the door and thought about Pellegrin. Owning him hadn't turned out how I had expected. Probably just living by myself until I felt I wanted a man— a human man—in my life again would've been better. Since I agreed to let him help The Institute for two weeks, I had to wait until after that to make a decision whether or not to keep him. I also worried about Tate. Pellegrin was working against the rebels, and Tate might be one. Otherwise, why would Tate and his friends orchestrate blind spots and manipulate microchips? Was the rebels' goal to eliminate all androids?

As I continued mulling it over, I headed back into Pellegrin's bedroom to continue snooping. I opened the bottom nightstand drawer, took out the folders again, and looked in the third one. I sucked in a ragged breath when I saw the picture of a pregnant woman being pulled away from a man soaked in blood. It was the same picture I had seen in one of Harlan's folders, the folder Britney was anxious to retrieve. I flipped to the next picture and pressed my lips together at the sight of two men and a woman, with their heads covered in blood, lying on a pile of gravel. A few android policemen, pointing guns at the slain people, stood by the victims' feet. As I looked closer, it appeared the three people wore white lab coats. Were they medical professionals, or did they work for The Institute? Then I noticed they all wore badges. The names on them were too small for me to make them out. I went to the living room, got a magnifying glass out of an end table, and hurried back. Using it, I managed to read two of the names: Dr. Earl Jolson and Dr. Barbara McCarney. So I wouldn't forget the names, I got a pad and pen out of my bedroom and wrote them down. I returned the magnifying glass to the living room and stuck the sheet with the names on it in my purse.

Not wanting to see any more pictures, but trying to figure out everything Pellegrin was involved with, I forced myself to look at the third picture. Seeing a partially burnt and badly beaten body, I briefly closed my eyes. Looking at it again, I realized it was a woman. She was lying in a clearing surrounded by trees. Pellegrin had mentioned that people liked to hide in forests. Was that where she was found? Flipping it over to see the next picture, I saw a note on the back of the burnt woman's photo: "Spies cannot survive." Did she spy on The Institute? For the rebels?

Then I looked at the fourth picture, the last one in the stack, and sighed. No blood. No humans. Six android policemen were stretched out on the pavement, wires protruded from their heads and chests. Pellegrin mentioned that vital components had been removed from terminated android policemen. I wondered if those components had a useful purpose for the rebels or if they were just removed to permanently destroy the androids. Pellegrin had also mentioned that The Institute was having a hard time acquiring more of those components. The number of android policemen available to hunt down the rebels was slowly being depleted. Most likely that was part of the rebels' plan.

Suddenly, I caught the sound of a metal clicking noise, a key turning in a lock. As I heard a door opening, I quickly put away the folders, and rushed into my bedroom. I grabbed a book and curled up in the chair near the window.

"Why aren't you in bed?" Pellegrin said, entering the bedroom.

"I'm a little worried about Kara and Marten and want to clear my mind before going to bed." I held up the book. "Reading always helps."

"Why are you worried about them?"

"Marten seemed pretty upset. Kara called while my phone was on mute. That might not be a good sign. When I turned back on the ringer, it was after midnight. Figured she'd be asleep. I'll call her in the morning."

Pellegrin flashed me a mischievous smile. "There could be another way to get your mind off of your friends." He strode toward me, knelt by the chair, and pulled me into his arms. The pictures still occupied my mind as he trailed kisses down my neck. But Pellegrin seemed to know exactly what I liked, and it didn't take long before my body reacted to his every move. As heat spiraled through my system, I thought of nothing else but the handsome, desirable android making love to me.

* * *

I awoke to the smell of sizzling sausage and something baking, but I couldn't determine what it was from the aroma. Yet I knew Pellegrin was a great cook, so whatever he had prepared would be good. I hurried into the bathroom and then remembered it was Saturday. No work. I freshened up, slipped on a robe, and went to see what the gourmet cook had made.

Gazing at the filled platter, I said, "Croissants. Wow!"

"Are you hungry?"

I nodded. "You drained all my energy last night. I'm starving."

"Drained? No, I didn't drain your energy."

"Pellegrin, that was just a metaphor." I guess that was something he hadn't learned in android school. "I didn't literally mean you drained my energy. It was just another way to say you wore me out—not permanently, only temporarily."

"I understand." He smiled. "You drained my energy too." He dished up scrambled eggs and sausage and then put a croissant on the plate and placed it front of me.

To my surprise, he grabbed a croissant, sat on the stool next to me, and began eating it. Maybe he wanted to look like a human. He was an intelligent android. Did he harbor fantasies about being human?

"This is wonderful." I took another bite. "Where did you learn to cook?"

"I went to culinary school, and I used to be a chef at Marco's."

"So that's how the maitre d' knew you?" I couldn't believe I was going along with his story. Or was it possible?

He tilted his head and a confused expression crossed his face. "Yes…of course."

It appeared he wasn't being truthful, or had he been programmed not to disclose that information? I pried deeper. "Why did you leave Marco's?"

"I'm not at liberty to discuss that." Pellegrin finished his croissant. "What would you like to do today?"

"Go to the beach and swim in the ocean."

"I'd like that too."

I nodded toward the front door. "Is a policeman still out there?"

"Yes. One or two will be until the person or persons behind the theft of the documents have been apprehended and the materials are back at The Institute. At least one policeman will follow us wherever we go."

"Will a policeman follow me when you're not around?"

"No, but that could change."

Having an android cop hanging around my office wasn't anything I wanted. I already knew that the women's restroom was the only place I could talk freely in the courthouse, but away from that building, there were no mics I needed to worry about. If an android policeman was keeping track of me, would I be free to talk anywhere?

CHAPTER 9

While Pellegrin drove out of the garage, to my horror, I saw seven android cops standing by three police HTs. Were they expecting a battle in front of my townhouse? I watched two of them climb into one of the police transports, and then the HT-8 zoomed toward the ocean.

"I'm calling Kara." I tapped on her number.

"Hey. Why didn't you call me last night?" she asked with a trembling voice.

"Forgot to turn the sound back on my cell after I came home. Didn't know you had called until it was midnight. Sorry."

"Marten left me."

"What?"

"He was so mad, he wouldn't even let me explain." She sniffled. "All I wanted to do was make him a little jealous. Sometimes…he doesn't even notice me." She sounded helpless.

"Oh, Kara, I'm so sorry. Pellegrin and I are going to the beach. Why don't you join us?"

I looked at Pellegrin, knowing he could hear everything that was being said.

"But…but…you're a couple. I'd feel like a third wheel."

"That's not the way it is. We'd like you to come."

"I look a mess. My eyes are all swollen."

"Sunglasses will hide that. Do you want us to pick you up?"

Pellegrin shot me a quick glance.

"No. It'll take me a while to get ready. I'll meet you there. You'll be easy to find. No one else will have an HT-8 parked nearby."

"See you soon." I clicked off.

Pellegrin turned his head toward me. "We're not a couple?" His tone conveyed sadness.

I couldn't help but sense he had been given some feelings. "That's not what I meant. I just didn't want Kara to think she would be imposing on us."

A faint smile creased his lips. "I understand."

Pellegrin parked close to the spot where we had stopped the day I met him. He took beach chairs, an umbrella, blanket, and a small container that held various types of sunscreen out of the back of the transport.

I picked up towels and the picnic basket he had prepared. "Is there enough in here for Kara, too?"

"Yes. It's packed to feed six people."

"Did you expect others to join us?" I wondered if he had invited someone as we walked through the sand.

He glanced over his shoulder. "The policemen won't be eating with us."

My eyes drifted toward the HT-8. Two android cops stood at attention near it.

Pellegrin continued. "I thought you might run into friends here, and a colleague at The Institute mentioned he might be going to the beach. If I see him, is it okay if I invite him to have lunch with us?"

I assumed he was talking about a human, but it could be another android. "Yes. By all means. I'd like to meet your friends," I said, though I had never heard of an android having friends.

"Thank you. He has been looking forward to meeting you."

Did Pellegrin talk about me at The Institute? I helped him spread out the blanket and set up the chairs and the huge umbrella.

"Lie down," Pellegrin demanded.

"Huh?"

"You need to have sunscreen on. I don't want you to get sunburned."

I assumed he was programmed to look after his owner, though a provision like that wasn't in the contract.

"Okay." I took off my tunic top that covered my bikini and stretched out on the blanket.

Pellegrin squeezed sunscreen lotion on my stomach and began rubbing it in.

I jerked when his hand slipped into my bottoms. "Pellegrin, not there. Only put the sunscreen on the exposed skin."

He nodded.

Obviously, applying sunscreen was a new task for him. Prior to this outing, I thought Pellegrin had been programmed to the extent that no one would suspect he was an android. Now, I started to see he still needed to know a few things, but he was a quick learner.

He rolled me over on my stomach and began spreading the lotion on my back. I sighed as I enjoyed the massage he was giving me in the process.

His hands caressed my legs while he put the lotion on them. "All done. Ready to swim?"

"Are you?" I asked, checking to make sure he had his earplugs in place since they were designed not to be seen unless you peered deep into his ears.

He pulled off his t-shirt. "Yes."

I gazed up at his well-built physique. "Do you need sunscreen?"

"No. I never sunburn."

Pellegrin took my hand, and we ran into the waves. The water was a little cool but felt so good. I dove into the waves and swam farther away from the shore. Pellegrin followed. A second later, he was ahead of me and moving at such a quick speed, it was impossible for me to keep up. I treaded the water and watched him until he vanished from sight. I had never seen anyone swim that fast. Was it even possible for a human to go that fast? Probably not.

I swam around for a little while longer and then decided to head back to the beach and wait for Kara to show up. Pellegrin might have already reached Catalina Island.

Sitting under the umbrella on a beach chair and drinking a bottle of water, my eyes swept over the surfers. From the way they were all staring at the ocean and strolling around, I doubted they were happy with the size of the waves. The surfers I knew liked them at least double that size and more powerful, but they'd never pass up a chance to surf even if the waves weren't ideal.

A few surfers were riding their boards to shore. As they got closer, I recognized two of them. One was Tate. Was this my chance to warn him? I looked at the ocean, searching for Pellegrin. Not seeing him anywhere, I stood and moved toward Tate.

When I was halfway there, he spotted me and our eyes locked. I tilted my head in the direction of the women's restroom and walked at a brisk pace to it. I glanced over my shoulder and saw he was following me. I hurried behind the building and ducked down in the shadows on the other side of the commercial trash compressor.

"Over here," I said as Tate walked by.

He knelt next to me in the shadow. "You here with your android boyfriend?"

I held my index finger against my mouth. "Shhh. Not so loud. Yes, but I need to warn you. Yesterday, I saw Harvey at Ocean Hills and at Bailey's, and I think Pellegrin did too because he mentioned the name Shellman when he was talking on the phone."

Tate gently stroked my cheek, leaned closer, and kissed me. "There's something you need to know." His brow deeply creased, and his eyes fixed on me. "Your mechanical boyfriend is pretty high up at The Institute. He's not an android that would ever be sold. For some unknown reason, you were tricked into believing you've bought him."

"By my mother?" I asked since she was the one who suggested I buy an android.

"I doubt your mother's involved in the scheme. The Institute does sell companion androids. Your android just isn't one of them. He's dangerous and he's…"

Seeing an android cop wandering around, I interrupted. "I need to get back. I think I'm safe. Your friend might not be."

"But…" he took my hand and then immediately let go as his eyes moved to something behind me. "Go. They haven't seen us yet, or they'd be running this way."

I knew he was talking about the android cops. I hurried around the building and went into the women's restroom.

While I waited a few minutes to give Tate time to get back to his friends, I mulled over what he had said. Tate confirmed what I already figured—Pellegrin wasn't the type of android stated in the contract. Yet he did an exceptional job in fulfilling some of the provisions—a skilled lover and cook. I wondered if he did any of the other domestic chores outlined in the contract or if another android showed up after I went to work to free up his time. Given the power The Institute wielded, I needed to continue pretending Pellegrin was my property until I could determine why they wanted him in my life. Still thinking about it, I stepped out of the restroom and found myself face-to-face with Pellegrin.

"I've been searching for you." He put his arm around my shoulder. "Had A-32 not seen you getting out of the water, I would've first looked for you there."

"Sometimes…" I pointed to the restroom. "…I need the facilities, and I figured as fast as you were swimming, you'd be on the beach at Catalina."

He chuckled.

I was glad he caught the joke without me having to explain it to him.

We walked to our place on the beach. "Was I really going that fast?"

"Faster. No way could I keep up."

"I'll remember to slow down next time."

As we lounged on the beach chairs, an android cop approached Pellegrin. "Mr. Murr, you have a call." The android handed Pellegrin a CAD.

Pellegrin looked at me. "I gave A-32 my CAD before we left your townhouse."

I wondered why he said that. His CAD was lying on a compartment in the HT-8 while we drove here. Did he have two CADS? If so, why didn't he want me to know that?

He spoke into the phone. "Yes…No…Not today…Perhaps." He disconnected and placed the CAD on top of the picnic basket.

"Does The Institute want you to report to work?" I asked while I watched a four or five-year-old trying to build something in the sand. Each time he poured a little water on the sand, whatever he had started collapsed.

"Yes. I'll go there later."

I gazed at Pellegrin. It appeared he was also watching the youngster.

"Hi," Kara said, trudging through the sand with her arms full.

I rose. "Just put your stuff on the blanket."

Kara laid down her folded beach chair, towels, and a tote bag. Then she put on her wide-brimmed straw hat.

Pellegrin stood up. "Hello, Kara. Did you have any trouble finding us?"

"No." She pointed to the road. "Your HT-8 is parked

right there."

"It's not mine," Pellegrin clarified.

"Well. It is for a few more days," I said.

He gestured toward his seat. "Take my chair, Kara. I think I'll help that young man." Pellegrin gestured toward the boy. "Build a castle." He went over to the boy. "Would you like some help?"

"Yeah. You know how to make castles?"

"I've done it before." Pellegrin picked up the boy's bucket. "Can I fill this?"

The boy bobbed his head. Pellegrin ran into the ocean and scooped up water. He returned and sank down to the ground. He poured the water on the sand and chatted with the boy as they both worked on the project.

After resituating myself in my chair, I noticed how pale Kara's cheeks were. Her eyes still appeared a little swollen behind her sunglasses. "How are you doing?"

"Terrible. Marten won't return my calls."

"Do you know where he went?"

"No, but since it was late, he either went to his parents' or checked into a hotel someplace."

"Give him a few days. He's not going to permanently break up with you because you flirted with Pellegrin."

"Well...I'm sorry, Paislee, and you're being so nice, but I did a little more than flirt." Her lips quavered.

I went and hugged her. "Kara, it's okay. I already know how you danced with Pellegrin. I saw it." I whispered, "He isn't a real boyfriend. You know that."

"Yeah, but he sure seems real. Don't you think?"

"That he does." I took my seat again.

"Hey." She pointed to the surfers. "Is that..."

"Yes." I interrupted her before she could blurt out Tate's name. "And remember, it's best not to even say his name. He's not in our strata and never will be."

She leaned over and squeezed my arm. "I know."

I had often cried on Kara's shoulder about that problem since I couldn't even mention it to my parents.

She was my best friend and the only person I had ever talked to about Tate.

My eyes moved to Pellegrin's and the boy's creation that was developing in the sand and was beginning to look pretty impressive. Wondering where the boy's parents were, I looked around. A woman sat straight up in a chair about fifteen feet away, keeping a watchful eye on the construction of the castle. I guessed she was his mother.

"Pellegrin is so good with that boy." Kara gazed at me. "Someday he'll make a good dad." A cheesy grin crossed her face.

I raised my eyebrows. "He's a natural."

A blond-haired, good-looking man about the same size and build as Pellegrin tapped him on the shoulder. Pellegrin swung his head around. "Darren. Paislee's over there." He nodded toward me, and I smiled. "Go introduce yourself." He looked at the boy. "Charlie here and I want to finish this."

I stood as Darren approached. "Hello, Darren. I'm Paislee, and this is my friend, Kara." I shook his hand and then motioned toward my chair. "Take my seat."

"Oh, I couldn't."

Kara eyed him up and down. "Sure, you can."

I picked up her folded chair from the blanket, set it up, put it on the other side of Kara, and sat down. Based the way she looked at the guy, I figured she wouldn't have any problem talking to a good-looking man, and it might help cheer her up.

"Are you from around here?" Kara asked.

"I've only been in town a couple of weeks. I was living overseas when The Institute offered me a position."

"What do you do?"

"I'm a biomedical engineer."

"Oh, how interesting. I'm in medical school. Well, right now, I'm taking a little break from school and working for a doctor. I'll be back in school next year."

Then they began to compare medical practices. I tuned

them out, and my eyes drifted to the surfers. I couldn't see Tate anywhere. He was probably out riding the waves. Wishing I was with him, I closed my eyes and imaged being on a board with him again.

"Anyone hungry?" Pellegrin said, snapping me out of my reverie.

Darren nodded. "I'm starving."

I looked toward the creation in the sand and heard the boy talking to his mother about it. My attention turned to Pellegrin. "That castle looks magnificent. I had no idea you were talented in building castles."

Pellegrin smiled at me. "That is only one thing you do not know about me. As time goes on, you will discover more."

I already suspected that my knowledge about Pellegrin was limited, and the more I learned about him the more fearful I felt.

Pellegrin opened up the picnic basket and filled four plates, each with a ham and cheese croissant sandwich and some pasta salad.

I sat down on the blanket and ate next to Pellegrin, smiling as Darren and Kara praised Pellegrin for making such tasty sandwiches and salad.

After we finished eating, Pellegrin stood. "I hate to break this up, but I need to go to work."

Seeing a confused expression on Kara's face, I said, "Kara, I never mentioned that Pellegrin works at The Institute."

"Even on Saturdays?"

I was relieved that she seemed to have caught on and guessed she might've thought that he needed to go there for some kind of adjustment.

"The Institute is opened every day," Pellegrin said. "Workers come and go all the time."

Kara turned to Darren. "Do you also have to go to work?"

"Nope. I have the weekend off." His eyes moved to

Pellegrin. "Do you have to work this evening too?"

"I don't know yet."

"There's a bar close to where I live. One of the guys at The Institute told me they have a great country band. Would you all like to go?"

"Dancing?" Kara leaned forward.

"Yeah." Darren's eyes swept over us as we all looked at each other. "None of you like country music, or don't you like to dance?"

"I'd love to go," Kara said, which surprised me after last night's problem.

Pellegrin caressed my arm. "I'd like to dance with you again. If you're game, I won't work this evening."

"Sounds like fun," I said, hoping it would end up better than the night before. Pellegrin was a good dancer and, even if he had some kind of alternative motive why he was with me, I might as well take advantage of his skills.

"How about 9:00 p.m.?" Darren asked.

"Nine works for me," Kara said, and I nodded.

Pellegrin gathered up the dirty plates, put them in a bag, and looked at Darren. "You live close by, and I know where it is. We'll meet you there."

"Kara, we'll pick you up." I collapsed her beach chair.

Pellegrin glanced at me. "Let's go for a quick swim before we leave here. Work can wait a little longer."

All four of us headed to the water. As we swam, I looked back at the beach and saw seven android cops trudging around in the sand. It didn't appear they were going after anyone, but that could quickly change. I knew a couple of them were there because of Pellegrin and hoped, whatever the reason for the others being there, it had nothing to do with Tate.

CHAPTER 10

Pellegrin had just left for The Institute when Kara called.

"Hey," I answered. "Are you feeling better?"

"Am I ever. Darren is just as gorgeous as Pellegrin, and he's human. And we're going dancing. Can't believe how this day is turning out. Wonderful!"

It sure didn't take her long to get over Marten. Live with a guy for three years, and then it was over in a day? "Kara, maybe this is going a little fast. Did Marten return any of your calls when you were at the beach?"

"No, but he came here while I was gone and collected some of his things. Nothing might happen between Darren and me, but he's the first guy in a long time that's paid any attention to me. I told you earlier that Marten often ignores me."

"Other guys have paid attention to you. Just this last couple of months, three guys who work at the medical center have hit on you. Come on, you sound like you're a wallflower."

"Okay…okay…I get it. But I must admit, none of them look anything like Darren. Neither does Marten. I just want to have some fun. And I'm not sure if Marten will ever be back." Kara sounded a little down.

Her mood change was my fault for bringing up Marten, and it appeared he wasn't at all concerned about his relationship with my best friend. Still, I wasn't convinced that Darren was new in town like he had claimed. He might not even be human. In case he was an android, I didn't want Kara falling for him. But if Darren was telling the truth, I didn't want to spoil anything for her.

"We'll have fun tonight!" I tried to sound upbeat. "Pellegrin is a great dancer, and since Darren invited us, he's probably just as good."

"Hope so. Years ago, I bought this great outfit to wear to a cowboy bar, and I've never worn it. Marten hates country music. I'm going to wear it tonight. Do you think the cowboy hat would be too much?"

"You can't dance very close to a fella if you're wearing a hat."

"Good point. No hat."

The images of dead doctors suddenly flashed into my mind. "Oh, I have a couple of people I wanted to ask you about. I need to get my note." I dug into my purse to look for the sheet. Not finding it, I dumped out the contents and thumbed through them. It was gone. My heart beat faster and I swallowed hard, guessing Pellegrin had taken it. "I can't find it." I took a deep breath, trying to calm my nerves. "But one was Barbara McClare or something like that. She was a doctor."

"There's a Barbara McCarney who works at the medical center. She's still a doctor. She hasn't changed professions. That's the only Barbara I know whose last name comes close to a McClare."

So she's still a doctor, or was before she met an untimely death. I didn't want to alarm Kara. "What type of practice does Barbara McCarney have?"

"OBGYN. She delivers babies. Lots of them. She has a huge bulletin board that covers a whole wall in the hall with pictures pinned to it of all the babies she's delivered.

Thousands! Why do you want to know?"

"I saw her name, or a name similar to hers, on some documents at work, and I was just curious."

"Is she being sued or something? She's away on a vacation right now. Who knows? If she's being sued maybe she won't be back." Kara laughed.

I knew she wouldn't be back, but it had nothing to do with a lawsuit. "She's probably not the same person."

"Was the other person you wanted to know about also a doctor?"

"Yeah, but I can't remember his name." Changing the subject, I said, "Oh, I need to warn you. Some documents were stolen from The Institute, and it's caused quite a fuss. This evening some android policemen will be following us to and from the bar, so don't be concerned when you see them."

"Because of Pellegrin?"

"Yes. The project he's working on must be high priority."

"Yeah, you mentioned he worked at The Institute during lunch. I thought he was yours exclusively."

"The Institute asked if they could use him for a couple of weeks. They gave me quite an incentive, so I agreed."

"Well, I'm not crazy about android cops, but at least they'll protect us on the way there and back home again. Anyway, I'm going to head out. I want to get my nails done for tonight. See you later."

I disconnected and stared at the contents of my purse spread out on the counter. To verify the list was gone, I picked up each item and put it back in the purse. It definitely was gone. Then I wondered when Pellegrin had discovered it. Did he check my purse every day?

Since Pellegrin had found the names in my purse, I figured he had either moved the folders to his locked suitcase or he had taken them to The Institute. Still, I walked into his bedroom and looked in the bottom nightstand drawer. Empty.

I went to the closet and saw his suitcase in the corner. It stood in the same place as last time I searched Pellegrin's room. Before attempting to pick the lock, I headed to the garage door to lock it. On the way, I wondered if locking it, which was something I seldom did, would draw attention to my snooping. I sat down on a kitchen stool and tried to figure out another mechanism that could be used to alert me to Pellegrin entering the townhouse. My eyes drifted around the kitchen, and I briefly toyed with the idea of putting pans or newspapers on the floor. That would even be more obvious than locking the door. Since he found the sheet in my purse and the folders were gone, he already knew about my snooping. The evidence might be gone, but what I saw still lingered in my mind. That was something he couldn't take from me, but he could murder me or have an android cop do it like the other victims. Pellegrin had entered my life for some reason, and I doubted that reason was for some heroic purpose. Whatever it was, the purpose had not been satisfied yet. Until it was, I would be safe. With that thought, I marched down the stairs and locked the door.

I got two paperclips and straightened them. Inserting the paperclips into the lock, I went to work on the suitcase. It took over two minutes before the lock clicked open.

Inside were copies of newspaper clippings, a laser gun, and a pistol along with a box of bullets. The headline on the top clipping read: "An HT collision claims 3." Staring at it, I couldn't figure out how that could've happened. HTs had features that prevented colliding into each other. A crash would be impossible even if you were determined to do it, unless… the operating systems in both transports had been compromised. My eyes fixed on the name of the victims: Paxton Murr, his wife, Susanna, and their 4-year-old son, Reese. Mulling it over, I assumed that the family had a connection to Pellegrin Murr—maybe his designer, inventor, or software developer?

The next clipping was Paxton Murr's obituary. Paxton was only survived by one relative, his father, Maxwell Murr. It also stated Paxton had been a chef at Marco's. I thumbed through the other clippings looking for the wife's obituary. There wasn't one. The clipping below Paxton's obituary had the headline: "The Institute Names the Renowned Dr. Maxwell Murr as Head of Research and Development." At least I knew where Pellegrin received his last name. I wanted to read the whole article, but Pellegrin could show up at any time. I flipped through the other clippings and stopped when I recognized the D.A.'s name in the heading. I breezed through it. At that time, he was a practicing attorney, and he had defended the driver, a woman, of the other HT in the collision involving Paxton's family. The woman had been acquitted.

A soft beeping sound drifted from somewhere in the house. Quickly, I put the clippings back into the suitcase and pushed the lock, securing it again. I placed it in the closet and hurried into my bedroom.

The beeping continued. No other sounds could be heard. No creaking of doors opening or pounding feet.

I followed the beeps to the living room. On the floor by the front door sat a flashing, small, star-shaped gadget I'd never seen before. My survival instinct clicked in, and I ran down the stairs, unlocked the door, opened the garage door, and sprinted out of the townhouse. An android cop stood in my path, and I almost bumped right into him.

"There's a bomb in my house. It's beeping near the front door."

"What does it look like?" The android's monotone voice was oddly reassuring.

"Small, red, star-shaped."

"Is there anyone else in your house?"

"No."

"Do we have your permission to enter your house?"

"Yes." I had never heard of an android cop ever asking for permission, but my knowledge was a little limited in that area.

"A-41, come with me." Two androids went into the house through the garage while I backed farther away and worried it could explode any minute.

Within ten minutes, the androids returned. One held the gadget.

"There is no one in your house," one android said. "This malfunctioned. We will contact Mr. Murr."

"Thank goodness. I didn't want my house destroyed."

"This could not cause any damage."

"Then what's it for?"

"Ask Mr. Murr."

I dashed back inside, closed the garage door, and headed upstairs. Since it was after 7:00 p.m. and knowing food wasn't anything Pellegrin needed, I didn't want to go to the bar on an empty stomach. I devoured a leftover sandwich and a bowl of pasta salad he had made for lunch.

When I finished, I went into the bathroom to get cleaned up for the evening's activity. Before getting into the shower, I checked the blue dot on my forehead. It appeared a small fraction bigger, but I thought it might just be my imagination. After showering and blow-drying my hair, I searched through my wardrobe for a western-looking outfit. I pulled out the cowboy boots I wore once to a rodeo. Then I took out a jeans skirt that hit above my knees and a sleeveless dark blue blouse that had brass buttons. A cowboy belt could've added a nice touch, but I didn't own one.

While I was putting the finishing touches on my makeup, Pellegrin walked into the bathroom. I wished he'd knock sometimes.

"You look great." He placed his arms around my waist.

I gazed at him in the mirror. He had on a cowboy hat, plaid shirt, jeans, and a belt with a big cowboy-type buckle. I leaned sideways and looked at cowboy boots on his feet. "So do you, cowboy. Do you have a whole other wardrobe at The Institute?"

He released me and stepped toward the door. "Sort of. The Institute has a large stock of clothing. I can pick out whatever I want to wear."

"You're lucky."

"Lucky? No. You're the lucky one."

I had the urge to ask him why he thought that but sensed it would be better not to pry. If he had feelings, which he often acted like he did, he might not like the fact that he was an android.

"When you were gone, a star-shaped gadget in the front room started beeping."

"Yes. A-36 called me after A-41 checked your house. The gadget malfunctioned."

"When I saw the little star flashing and the beeping kept getting louder, I thought a bomb was about to go off and high-tailed out of here."

He smiled. "Sorry. I should have told you about the gadget before I went to work."

"What's the thing supposed to do?"

"The device was programmed to recognize you and me and should have only started beeping if anyone else entered your house, regardless of where they entered."

"So if someone climbed in through a bedroom window…"

"An alert would be sent to police HTs."

"Let me make sure I've got this right. The star-shaped gadget functions similar to other alarm systems. But unlike other systems, this one only needs to have a receiver in one room, and it's programmed not to beep when the people who live there come and go. And instead of sending the signal to just one place if an intruder enters, a signal is sent to all police HTs. Right?"

"Yes. The signal also goes out to the police before you'll hear beeping. A new device has been placed in the living room behind the couch."

"Where's the off switch? If I'm expecting a friend, I don't want our visit to be interrupted by that annoying beeping."

"You can't turn it off. A policeman will come within a few minutes, and you'll need to tell him that you have a friend visiting. He'll initiate the temporary deactivation mode."

Break-ins were almost non-existent in private homes due to the severe punishment associated with any crime. If a burglar's goal was not to steal, but to murder the occupants, that could be done within a minute. And I couldn't imagine anyone wanting an alarm system they couldn't control. This little beeping thing was just another method to keep track of my visitors. But complaining would probably be a wasted effort. At least with it in place, android policemen wouldn't be stationed outside my townhouse all the time.

* * *

Worried about Kara's infatuation with her new beau, I wanted more information about Darren. On the way to Kara's apartment, I probed Pellegrin. "Does Darren have a girlfriend where he used to live?"

"He did. She didn't want to move here. They broke up."

Was there any truth to his answer? Most likely, he would've given that same answer if Darren was an android. "How long have you known him?"

"Two weeks. We did a project together right after he started working for The Institute." He reached over and squeezed my knee. "You're looking out for your friend. If you want to know more about Darren, I could probably get you a copy of his résumé."

I smiled at him. "Oh, could you? That would be great."

"You'll have a copy by Monday. I intend to work tomorrow, but I'll be available to go with you to dinner at your parents' house. What time?"

I smacked my forehead. "Glad you said something. I

had completely forgotten. But Mother will be calling sometime tomorrow to remind me. She always does when I'm expected at their place. I think she said 5:00 p.m. That doesn't mean we'll eat at five. They like to socialize before dinner."

Kara stood outside her apartment building when we pulled up. She looked very western in a black blouse that hung off her shoulders, a cream-colored, mid-calf skirt that flared at the bottom, a belt with a big buckle, similar to Pellegrin's, and cowboy boots. She darted to the HT-8 before I had a chance to open her door. "Why the rush?"

"It's 8:45. I don't want to be late." Kara climbed into the backseat.

"I like your outfit. You look great in it."

"Thanks. Do you think Darren will like it?"

I thought she was acting like a school girl on her first date, as if Kara had never gone out with anyone else before. And since Darren invited all of us, I didn't think tonight fell in the date category. "Kara, I don't know Darren well enough to make a judgment call." I tapped Pellegrin's arm. "He's your buddy. What do you think?"

Pellegrin looked over his shoulder at Kara and smiled. "He'll like what he sees."

His answer sounded charming. Pellegrin had been well programmed.

Kara blushed. "Thanks."

CHAPTER 11

The HT-8 stopped in front of a western-looking structure that reminded me of a rugged cabin I had seen in books. People chatted and milled about near the building's entrance.

"I'll have one of the policeman find a place for the HT-8 in a TRL," Pellegrin said. "We'll get out here."

We all climbed out of the HT-8 and Pellegrin went and talked to the android cop in the police HT behind us. Then he returned and escorted Kara and me into the establishment. The place was packed. Darren made his way through the crowd to us. His cowboy outfit looked so similar to Pellegrin's that I wondered if he also got it at The Institute.

"I've secured a table for us by the dance floor." Darren eyed Kara up and down. "You look fantastic."

She grinned. "So do you."

He took her hand and led her to the table. Pellegrin and I followed. A pitcher of beer and four glasses stood in the center of the table. On the platform at one end of the dance floor, the band members were busy setting up their equipment.

"Hope everyone likes beer." Darren's eyes moved from Kara to me. "If you ladies would prefer something else, I'll flag down the bar server." He pulled out a chair for Kara.

She sat down. "No, no. Beer goes perfect with country music."

"Paislee?"

"I like beer."

Darren poured a glass for everyone.

As I sipped the beverage, I glanced around and speculated about how Darren managed to score a table right by the dance floor. Was he here extra early? Or did all employees, whether human or android, of The Institute receive special treatment from all establishments?

"The band was supposed to start at nine," Darren said. "They're running a little late."

A squealing static sound came through the speakers.

"Good evening, folks!" The band leader, holding a mic, strutted with a bounce in his step as he moved back and forth on the platform. "Ready to whip up your heels and have a good time?"

Cheers and hollering "Yep" came from the crowd.

"Okay. Let's get started." The leader signaled the other band members and the music began with "Seein' Red."

Pellegrin touched my arm. "May I have this dance, Miss Hobson?"

In a similar mode of faux formality, I answered, "Yes, Mr. Murr." I took his hand, and we stepped onto the dance floor. Like I expected, he was just as good at dancing to country music as he was to the tunes played by the contemporary band the night before. I noticed Kara and Darren dancing not far from us. They danced well together.

A slow and romantic song started. Pellegrin held me close to him. I inhaled his pleasant, sexy smelling cologne, a scent he always wore. Strange, there weren't any cologne bottles in his room. His body felt good next to mine. How could I feel that way when I knew he was using me? *Who knows what devious plan might be underway?*

When that song ended, we returned to our empty table. Kara and Darren were still on the dance floor. I gazed at them. They were smiling and chatting while waiting for the next tune to begin.

Pellegrin picked up his beer glass and took a big swig.

Knowing he had to pump it out, I wondered why he didn't just sip it, but that probably wouldn't look macho enough.

He rubbed my hand. "I'm glad I can spend all night with you."

I gave him my best fake smile. "So am I." But there was no denying that he was a great lover and part of me was definitely looking forward to having him in my bed.

After that tune, Kara and Darren came back to the table. Darren looked at Pellegrin and me. "How about changing partners for the next dance?"

Pellegrin glanced at me.

"Okay," I replied and then looked at Kara. She sipped her beer and didn't seem fazed that we were exchanging partners for a dance.

To my relief, the band played a fast song. Darren took my hand and Pellegrin took Kara's, and we all went out on the dance floor.

As I danced with Darren, I caught a whiff of his cologne. It smelled just like Pellegrin's. Did that signify he was an android? Did all androids in Pellegrin's class smell the same? Then I felt a scab on Darren's hand and sighed—androids didn't have scabs.

Darren continued swinging me around the dance floor. He was a good dancer but not quite in Pellegrin's league.

We switched partners, and I danced with Pellegrin to another slow tune. As we headed back to the table, he dug his CAD out of his pocket and glanced at it. I didn't hear it ring. Pellegrin could have turned the volume way down where only he could hear it or set it on vibrate, assuming his CAD had that feature.

I sat down while Pellegrin talked into his CAD. All I picked up of his conversation was "Yes…No…That will work."

When he was seated, I frowned. "Do you have to leave to go to The Institute?"

"I don't intend to go there until tomorrow morning." He put his arm around my shoulders and pulled me close to him. "I'm looking forward to enjoying this night, all night, with you."

"Hey," Kara said as she returned to the table with Darren. "Do you want to go to the restroom with me?"

I guessed she wanted to tell me something in private. "Yes."

As we zigzagged through people on the way to the women's restroom, I spotted Harvey leaning against the bar. Again? Was he keeping track of me for Tate? Or was he here for another reason? My eyes swept around him, looking for familiar faces. No one stood out.

In the restroom, a few women were waiting for stalls to open up and others were lined up in front of the mirror, applying makeup.

Kara leaned toward me and whispered, "I wish we were alone so we could talk freely."

"Do you want to go outside?"

"No." She took my arm and pulled me to the other side of the room. "Tell me, will it be okay if I bring Darren with me to your parents' house tomorrow for dinner? Your mom invited me and Marten. She expects that I'll have someone with me, and it sure won't be Marten."

Mom told me, in fact she almost promised, she wasn't inviting anyone else besides Pellegrin and me. I squinted. "Mom invited you for dinner?"

Kara's forehead creased. "You don't want me to come?"

I patted her arm. "No. that's not it. Mom said it was just going to be her, Dad, Pellegrin, and me. She wants to meet Pellegrin. I should've figured she'd make it into a party." I chuckled. "Mom calls Pellegrin my 'young man.'"

Kara laughed. "Oh, I love it, especially since she knows the truth. So, what do you think? Is it okay if I bring Darren?"

"Sure. She'll want to meet your new *young man*." I sighed. "I'm glad yours has blood running through his veins and not man-made components. But Darren might think you're rushing things a bit—bringing him to a social engagement this soon in your relationship."

"He had already asked me out for tomorrow, so that won't be a problem. He'd probably like to make new friends in town. Right now, it sounds like the only ones he knows work at The Institute."

I briefly hugged her. "I'm glad you'll be there tomorrow. I wonder if there will be anyone else even close to our age there. The guest lists Mom and Dad tend to put together mainly include older folks."

"So true." Kara grabbed the door to a stall that just became vacant. "I'm going to quickly use the facilities, and then we better get back. Don't want any of the single ladies out there hitting on our fellas."

The band was taking a break when Kara and I sat down at the table. Another pitcher of beer had been delivered while we were gone. Darren topped off our glasses.

Yelling and screaming suddenly came from the direction of the entrance. Pellegrin and Darren jumped to their feet.

I didn't bother standing up since I knew I wouldn't be able to see over everyone's head. "Can you see what's going on?" I asked Pellegrin as the shouting continued.

"No. I'd go and check it out, but I don't want to leave you here alone in case it's a serious problem."

"If it's serious, won't the policemen that followed us here handle it?"

"Yes, unless…"

A gunshot echoed through the building. People screamed. Clanging, banging, and crashing sounds followed. Men and women near us leapt out of their chairs, tipping them over, and ran toward the building's back door.

"Let's get out of here," I yelled in order to be heard over the chaos.

Pellegrin dashed to the other side of the table. "No. I can handle this situation."

Darren wrapped his arm around Kara and pulled her with him underneath the table. I just sat there frozen, not knowing what to do. Then I covered my head as if the ceiling were falling in.

A second later, a burst of gunfire reverberated from the front of the structure, sending a horde of people charging toward the back door. They trampled everything in their path. Pellegrin spread his arms to divert the crowd from crashing into our table. A couple of the men attempted to dislodge Pellegrin. Big mistake. Pellegrin swung his hand, hitting both men in their throats. The injured men tumbled to the floor and end up being stomped by the people behind them as the flock continued rushing to the back door. Using a chopping motion Pellegrin struck everyone that came within his reach. Those hit landed hard on the hard-surfaced floor.

The shooting went on. I heard zapping sounds and assumed the android cops were returning fire. My eyes drifted to the carnage left in the path of those that fled to the back exit. I looked over my shoulder and saw a crush of people climbing over each other, fearing for their lives, as they tried to get through the doorway and escape the mayhem in the building.

Another onslaught of patrons leapt over the broken chairs and bodies as they charged toward us on their way to the door. In that group, two men held guns. One shot an armed man by the bar. Then the shooter swung his weapon around and aimed at Pellegrin.

"Watch out, Pellegrin," I yelled and dropped to the floor.

A nearby shot rang out, followed by a fusillade of high-pitched zapping sounds. The table wobbled and a woman's screams pierced the air. My eyes moved to Kara and Darren huddled together. Tears ran down Kara's cheeks as she trembled in Darren's arms.

The gunfire and zapping noise ended, but the sound of feet thumping on the floor continued. I stretched my neck and peeked over the top of the table. Seeing Pellegrin flopped in a chair, holding his arm, I jumped up and looped around the table. Small wires protruded around his hand that grasped his injured arm. I guessed it covered a gunshot wound. I stroked his face. "Oh, you've been shot. What can I do?"

"Nothing. I'll be fine."

Three men dressed in blue scrubs came jogging toward us. Two carried medical cases.

The third man, who was taller and leaner than the other two, sprinted out in front of them, carrying a white towel. The sprinter reached Pellegrin first and wrapped the towel around his damaged arm. "This man's been shot!"

My eyes opened wider when I saw what looked like blood soaking through the towel wrapped around a non-bleeding, mechanical arm. The special towel was probably just another tool to give the illusion Pellegrin was human.

The scrub-clad, tall man opened one of the medical cases and pulled out a sling. Securing Pellegrin's shot arm in it, he left the red liquid-stained section of the towel clearly visible. "Can you walk, sir, or should I have a gurney brought it? The ambulance is right outside the entrance."

Pellegrin stood. "I can manage to get there on my own."

"You can lean on me, Pellegrin," Darren said, walking toward him with Kara by his side.

I hadn't even noticed them getting out from under the table.

Pellegrin put his good arm over Darren's shoulder, and

he sluggishly ambled toward the entrance. The bullet hadn't affected his android legs, but I figured that Pellegrin was putting on a show to make him appear human. My attention moved to Kara. She looked scared and pale. I grabbed our purses from the floor, took her arm, and followed the injured android while sirens whined.

As we hedged toward the door, I gazed around the destroyed bar. Blood, bodies, and wounded people seemed to be everywhere. Some of the casualties were being attended to, but most were reeling in pain while someone near them shouted at the medical workers for help. Too few medics had been dispatched to handle what had gone down at the western-themed venue.

My eyes drifted over the crowd gathered around the HT ambulances and noticed Tate among the spectators. He had his arm around an attractive blonde. When our eyes met, he slightly shook his head. I had no idea what he meant by that, but I quickly turned away in order not to draw attention to him. I hated seeing him with another woman, but I couldn't expect him to remain celibate and spend his life pining over me. Even though he still lingered in my heart, I had tried to move on, and it appeared he had also. But I couldn't deny how I enjoyed our chance encounters and feeling his lips against mine.

Pellegrin was directed to lie down on the gurney near the ambulance's back door. He complied without putting up any resistance. Once he was strapped in, he reached over and took my hand. "Don't worry. I'll be home tomorrow afternoon. We won't miss your parents' dinner engagement. All day, I looked forward to spending the night with you. The rebels spoiled our plans."

I stroked his arm and gave him a sympathetic smile. "There will be other nights. Should I drive your HT-8 to the townhouse?"

"No. A policeman will take it to The Institute so it'll be available for me tomorrow."

Darren came closer to us. "I'll make sure Paislee gets

home safely."

"Thank you, Darren."

Darren held Kara's hand. We watched the medical staff move Pellegrin into the ambulance. A few seconds later, the HT ambulance glided into the air and zoomed away at the high altitude permitted to emergency HTs.

I turned toward Kara. "How are you doing?"

She briefly shut her eyes. "I don't know."

Darren hugged her. "I'll take care of you. Tomorrow will be a brighter day." He led us to his place, an apartment building, a couple of blocks away. He stopped by a light gray HT-8 that stood in front of it.

"You have an HT-8 too?" I stared at it.

"Yes. It was a nice perk that came with the job. Seems like wherever I go, I keep hearing it's not available to the public yet. The Institute must have been on the top of the list to get a supply of HT-8s." He tilted his head. "Pellegrin has one too."

"His is a loaner. He wants to keep it, but that seems unlikely."

"Well, I'd be surprised if they made him give it back." Darren opened the passenger door for Kara, who hadn't said a word since leaving the bar.

"We'll have to see." I climbed into the back seat.

Darren gripped the steering wheel. "Where to?"

I rattled off my address and then also gave him Kara's, thinking she wasn't up to the task.

Within fifteen minutes, Darren's HT-8 reached my townhouse. To my disgust, two android policemen were stationed in front of it. Would I ever have my privacy back? Would I ever feel safe again?

CHAPTER 12

A harsh buzzing sound shattered my dream about being with Tate. I raised my hand and pushed off the alarm clock. Through foggy vision, I glanced at the time—7:00 a.m.—and couldn't remember setting the alarm. Then the havoc of the night before flashed into my head. I wondered how many people had been killed and wounded in the fight. But what preyed on my mind the most was *why*. Pellegrin had said that he was in danger, but it didn't appear that he was the main target. Maybe he wasn't a target at all. He could've been shot because he was at the wrong place at the wrong time. Nothing more. Had the shooter intended to put him out of commission permanently, he would have plugged a bullet into Pellegrin's head. Even if the rebels had a target inside the bar, storming in and shooting up the place made no sense to me. Had the two android policemen that were there to keep Pellegrin safe been terminated before the shooting began?

I wanted to sleep and clear my mind of the whole ordeal, but it had taken over two hours to fall asleep the prior night after the melee. With the sunlight streaming through the drapes, I was wide awake. Dragging myself into the bathroom, I freshened up. After checking the blue mark on my forehead, I noticed something sticking out below the window and went to it. I pulled out a folded note. How did this get here?

The note read:

> Last night's mayhem was planned and executed by The Institute. It controls the police department. Eight police HTs arrived shortly after you entered the bar. We're still trying to determine what role they intend to have you play in their scheme. Whatever you hear today about the carnage won't be true. Be careful. It is not safe to talk any place within the walls of the courthouse, not even the restrooms. If you have an opportunity tomorrow, go outside for lunch and enjoy the good weather.
> Love Always
> Destroy this note.

No signature appeared, but I knew it was from Tate. The note was printed, not handwritten. Not traceable. I guessed his last sentence meant he would show up if I went outside. Staring at the note, I couldn't figure out how he managed to squeeze it in under the window without being caught by an android cop. Then I opened the frosted glass window to see if any cops were in the back yard. One stood about ten feet away. I closed the window, read over the note again, tore it into tiny pieces, and flushed them down the toilet.

I sat down on the chair in the bedroom and thought about how simple life seemed to be when I was dating Emmett. After that relationship ended, buying an android never would've occurred to me if Mom hadn't suggested it and offered a loan. The more I mulled over the purchase, the more I couldn't imagine Mom coming up with that idea on her own. Had someone approached her about how wonderful a companion android would be for me? Mom was pretty easy to talk into things and had lied for me numerous times in the past. When I was in high school and wanted to stay out beyond Dad's 11:00 p.m. curfew, Mom told him I was at a sleepover. Assuming I was on the right track, who was the guilty party, the persuader? I decided to try to get Mom alone during my visit, but it would be tricky with so many other guests.

I went into the kitchen and brewed coffee. While I drank it, I listened to the news to find out how the devastation at the bar would be reported. A reporter kept talking about some policemen who had been ambushed on the other side of town. Three android policemen had been terminated, one human policeman had died at the scene, and two had been hospitalized. Patiently, I continued listening, waiting for the reporter to talk about the incident at the bar, but he moved on to the weather. Irritated it hadn't been mentioned, I leaned over to change the channel to another news source. Before I pushed the button, the reporter blurted out, "Rebels terrorized The Corral, a western bar in the suburbs last night. Details are sketchy, but what we've learned so far is that over a dozen rebels charged in and started shooting while patrons were dancing and enjoying a Saturday night. People fled out the back door. At least sixteen went to the hospital and seven are known to have perished. The final count might be higher. The names of the victims have not been released. No motive for the shooting has been given. One surviving victim, who was shot in the leg, told a reporter earlier that he saw two of the gunmen handcuffed and hauled away in a police HT. That has not been confirmed. The police department's spokesman will be holding a press conference this afternoon to update the public on this horrific act of violence. Attacks on innocent people are occurring almost on a daily basis in the city. The police can't be everywhere all the time. We all need to pitch in and do our part to help them handle this explosive problem by reporting anything we see that appears suspicious."

I switched off the device and thought about what the reporter had said and what Tate had written in his note. If the police were responsible for last night's attack, maybe they were responsible for all of them. Why would they do it? To bring public outcry against the rebels?

As I looked in the fridge for something to have for breakfast, my cell rang. I picked it up from the counter and saw "Kara" displayed. "Hi. Are you doing okay today?"

"Oh, you won't believe what a wonderful, beyond words night I had after you were dropped off." Her excitement was effusive. "I'm completely worn out, but I wanted to tell you before I fell asleep."

"You haven't slept yet?"

"No. Well, occasionally I drifted off a little. Poor Darren had to go to work. He's really going to be beat when we go to your parents' house."

"I take it that Darren stayed over?"

"Yep. Talk about an awesome lover. He went way beyond the videos I had watched. I never felt such ecstasy. Now I couldn't care less if Marten ever returns my calls. He's in my past, and that's where he's going to stay."

"Kara, you were with Marten for three years and Darren for only one night."

"But what a night." She sighed.

"Just make sure if Marten calls you that you really don't want him in your life before you tell him to get lost."

"Don't worry about me. I think Darren feels the same way about me as I do about him. The things he said! And he told me he was in our stratum." Her tone suddenly changed. "Oh, I feel bad about last night."

"Huh? You just said it was wonderful."

"It was. But at the bar, I should've helped the injured, like the paramedics. They were so understaffed. Even if I'm not a doctor yet, I still plan on being one someday.

I've learned a lot working for Dr. Morehouse. I could've taken care of a lot of those people in such terrible pain. Moans and groans echoed through the place, but I felt numb, like I wasn't really there. Bodies, people bleeding, and paramedics running around, and I never moved into action."

"Kara, you were there when the fighting was going on. Your life was in danger. The medics never experienced that. No one would have expected you to leap to your feet and dig in helping others."

"Darren said something just like that. So you don't think anyone will think I'm an awful person for not helping out?"

"No. Everyone who knows you will be happy that you made it through the attack without being injured, just like I am."

Kara sighed, relief clear in her voice. "That makes me feel so much better. You're the best friend in the whole world."

"Get some sleep."

"That's exactly what I intend to do. See you at your parents' house."

After hanging up, I thought about Darren while I fried an egg and toasted a slice of bread. I could understand Kara wanting attention from a man since her self-esteem was probably in the toilet from Marten up and leaving her. But Darren had just met her that day at the beach. Why was he rushing their relationship? He immediately evoked in me the same feeling Pellegrin gave me shortly after I met him. Something about both of them was off. Now I knew my suspicions were right about Pellegrin—he was much more than a companion android. Could Darren be an android too? I recalled touching the scab on his hand. Not possible for an android. Was that a planted imperfection so people would believe he was human? How could I find out?

My cell rang again and "Mother" appeared on the small

screen.

"Hi, Mom."

"Hello, dear. I'm calling to make sure you haven't forgotten about dinner today."

"I remember."

"Well, that's a first. How is your *young man* doing?"

I rolled my eyes. "Fine." Then since I wasn't sure about the time, I asked, "You want us there at five, right?"

"Yes. And *do* try not to be late again."

I had the urge to complain about her inviting other people, but knew it wouldn't change anything. "Will do."

* * *

I examined the blue mark on my forehead. It hadn't changed. It remained slightly bigger than a dot, but still not very noticeable. I put on a dark blue, sleeveless dress and heels for the dinner engagement. I dreaded parading Pellegrin around and introducing him to Mom and Dad's friends, but it was unavoidable.

On my way to the living room, out of the corner of my eye, I caught a glimpse of something sticking out on the other side of the Pellegrin's bed. I stepped into his room to check it out and saw a file-sized box. I had gone by Pellegrin's room several times during the day and once looked in. If the box had been there earlier, I would have noticed it. Could he be home? I moved back into the hallway. "Pellegrin, are you in the house?"

Not receiving an answer, I quickly looked into all the rooms to make sure he was nowhere in my townhouse. Satisfied, I went back to his room to snoop in the box, but hesitated, knowing he could show up any minute. Curiosity got the best of me, and I was just ready to raise the lid on the box when a thought sprang into my head. Could this be a trap? I stared at the box. Had it just been pushed a little farther on the other side of the bed, it would have been completely concealed from the hallway. I wasn't sure who had put it there, but guessed it was one of the android cops. Would bells or whistles go off if I raised the lid?

I glanced at my watch—4:30 p.m. It took me about twenty minutes to drive to my parents' house. Since Pellegrin drove faster than I did, he might not pick me up for another fifteen minutes. With that thought, I boldly lifted off the lid. Nothing happened. So far, so good. Just as I anticipated, it contained file folders. I thumbed through them and stopped at the folder labeled "Barbara McCarney," a name I recognized from a photo in Pellegrin's nightstand drawer. She was one of the victims. Keeping my ears on high alert for Pellegrin, I took out the folder and opened it. The top sheet was a press release. There was a line at the top for a date. It was blank. I quickly read it over. It stated that she had become another rebel victim during a shootout the rebels had instigated with the police. Two officers had also been slain. The press release listed her accomplishments. I skimmed through the following documents and a different story emerged.

Barbara was eliminated due to her refusal to perform some medical services for The Institute. During her time there, she had acquired information that would discredit The Institute. As I flipped to the next page, I heard a door opening and quickly put back the folder and closed the lid. I pushed the box slightly so it couldn't be seen from the hallway and then walked at a brisk pace to the living room.

"I was starting the think you weren't going to make it." I eyed the well-attired Pellegrin in dark slacks, a blue dress shirt, and a blazer. "It must be nice working in a place that provides an endless wardrobe."

"It is. Are you ready to go?"

"Yes." I turned and picked up my purse. "How's your arm?"

He moved it up and down. "As good as new."

When his HT-8 began to move, a police HT followed closely behind us.

Since the news reporter said there might be more than seven dead and I had seen more bodies than that on the floor, I asked, "Do you know how many casualties there were last night?"

"Thirty-four."

I knew seven was too low, but thirty-four seemed way too high. A dreadful grief rolled over me. Thirty-four lives lost, for what? And why didn't the android cops call for back-up at the first sign of trouble? With the speed of law enforcement hovers, reinforcement could have arrived within five minutes. Lives could've been saved, but maybe protecting humans was no longer their top priority.

"The rebels seem to be getting more dangerous every day." Pellegrin spoke with authority. "The police are working 24/7 trying to restore order, but their numbers keep declining with every rebel confrontation."

"I heard on the news that two gunmen had been captured. Have the police been able to find out the reason behind the attack?"

Pellegrin, with a perplexed expression on his face, glanced at me. "No one was captured. The news reporter must have received incorrect information. A few rebels were terminated. The rest took off. Their faces were partially covered, like always. There's nothing concrete to go on."

CHAPTER 13

HTs were parked in a neat row in front of my parents' house. Pellegrin parked at the end of the row, and we climbed out of his transport.

Mom stood by the open door, probably watching for us to arrive. "Come in; come in." She extended her hand to Pellegrin. "Oh, you must be Pellegrin. You're even more handsome than your picture."

"Thank you, Mrs. Hobson." He took her hand, raised it as he bent down, and kissed it.

Mom beamed. "Please call me Lillian."

"I'm pleased to make your acquaintance, Lillian."

Taking Pellegrin's arm, Mom guided him inside. "Let me introduce you to our friends. They've all been so anxious to meet you."

What a relief. One job I didn't have to do. I took a glass of wine from a server and watched Mom parading Pellegrin around and proudly introducing him to her friends as my boyfriend.

Dad walked over to me and gave me a big hug. "I'm sorry I never had a chance to call you at work. Things have been crazy. My workload grows by the day. Travis said you were calling about the D.A. Your mom and I went and

113

saw him last night in the hospital. He's regaining his strength. Eating well. It won't be long before he's back at work." He stroked my arm. "Is everything okay with you, sweetie?"

"No complaints." I doubted he knew I was at the bar that was attacked the prior night, but I figured he'd start worrying about me if I mentioned it. "Just so you won't be surprised when Kara shows up, she has a new boyfriend."

His eyes narrowed. "What happened to Marten?"

"They had an argument that ended very badly."

"We ran into him last night in the TRL by the new dessert lounge downtown. Your mom wanted to try it out after we left the D.A. She told Martin we'd see him tomorrow. He never mentioned that he wouldn't be here. Their fight was probably over his fancy new HT-8. That must have set him back quite a bit."

"Marten has an HT-8?"

Dad nodded. "He showed us the interior and talked about everything it could do. It's a pretty nice transport. Do you think I can talk your mom into letting me get one?"

Dad was joking. If he wanted one, he'd just go out and buy it. "She's going to be a hard sell. You're going to have to turn on all your charms."

Kara and Darren strolled toward them. "Sorry we're late."

"It's my fault," Darren said. "I got absorbed in my work and didn't notice the time."

"I understand how that can happen," Dad said.

As soon as I finished introducing them, Mom moved to the other side of me. I introduced them.

Darren extended his hand. Mom reached out, and just like Pellegrin, he kissed it. "It is so refreshing to meet young men who have such nice manners." Mom smiled at him.

While they talked and were served wine, I scanned the room. Pellegrin was conversing with Judge Wilbur. I felt relieved when I didn't spot Judge Harlan anywhere.

Mom stepped away, and I followed her into the dining room. "Mom, can I talk to you privately after dinner?"

She touched my cheek. "Well, of course, dear." A concerned expression flashed on her face. "You and your young man aren't having problems are you?"

She acted and talked like he was a real human. "No. That's not what it's about."

"Thank goodness. I'm having a hard time understanding Kara and Marten breaking up. The Judge and I saw him last night. Didn't say a word about it, even after I told him we'd see him tomorrow. But I will say, Kara certainly has found a nice young man." Mom picked up a place card from the table with the name Marten on it. She always put out place cards whenever they had more than a few guests for dinner. "Have they been dating long?"

"Several weeks," I lied. Saying one day would not have set well with Mom.

She opened the top drawer of the buffet and took out another place card. "We certainly don't want Darren to see Marten's name on the table." Mom wrote Darren on the card and placed it where Marten's card had been.

"Well, we'd better get our guests seated." She whispered, "Some of our older friends have a hard time staying awake past nine."

I found myself sitting between my Uncle Edward and Louise Quest, a frail, 98-year-old woman. Pellegrin fared slightly better. He sat between Mom and Judge Wilbur. Kara was on the other side of Wilbur and next to Dad. Darren was sandwiched between two middle-aged friends of the family.

Conversations sprouted up all over. Everyone seemed to be talking. No one appeared bored.

Louise was more concerned about her food than talking to anyone, so I chatted with my Uncle Edward, whom I'd always felt sorry for. Fifteen years younger than my dad, his brother, he was a bit of a non-conformist. Like me, Uncle Edward had fallen in love with someone that wasn't in our strata. He'd bought her a business and petitioned unsuccessfully several times to get her moved up to a higher stratum. After the last petition, a warrant for their arrest was issued for the crime of fraternizing with a person in another stratum. The authorities couldn't find her. Uncle Edward was hauled off to jail and claimed he had no idea where she was. Dad worked with my uncle's lawyer to help put together the legal arguments in his favor, which for that crime weren't many. A trial date had been set, but before that date arrived, the woman along with two other people drowned when their boat capsized. Since his lover was dead, the judge set to hear the case dismissed it. That was nine years ago. Uncle Edward still mourned her death. He didn't date and rarely socialized. He used to constantly complain about the government but seldom did that anymore.

When I was young, he always played with me and called me his favorite niece. It wasn't until I was around six or seven that I realized I was his only niece. He still referred to me as his favorite.

Uncle Edward owned a chain of grocery stores that he inherited from my grandmother on Dad's side. Tate worked in one of his stores. I doubted Uncle Edward had a clue that the surveillance cameras inside are sometimes moved around, but I also doubted that he would care. Before he inherited the stores, he was a programmer and set up computerized systems for all the government buildings, including the courthouse. When the worldwide computer hack occurred, he was asked to work with a team of experts to try to fix the problem. He refused.

"How's the grocery business going?" I asked between bites.

"Good. Steady. As long as people *need* to eat, I'll stay in business."

I wondered why he emphasized the word "need." *Does*

he think androids might impact his business? Not wanting to dwell on it during dinner, I decided to talk to him about sports. He had medals for all the races and swimming events he won years ago.

When we had almost finished dessert, Louise, who couldn't hear fireworks if they exploded in the living room, asked me in as loud a voice as she could muster, "Have you set a date for the wedding yet?"

Everyone's attention at the table snapped to me. I patted Louise's arm. "I'm not engaged."

She looked confused. "Oh, you're not?"

I shook my head. "No." My eyes drifted to Kara. Her mouth was tightly shut, suppressing a laugh.

A few of the guests left right after dinner. The rest of us went into the living room, and various dessert wines were served along with an assortment of chocolates. Some of the men enjoyed a brandy.

I stood by the fireplace and chatted with Kara and Darren until Mom came over and rubbed my arm. "Excuse me," I said and stepped away.

"Dear, everyone seems engaged in conversation. I think we can sneak away for a few minutes and have that private talk you mentioned."

I went with Mom into the den, and she closed the door. We sat down on the couch.

"Mom, did anyone suggest a companion android would be good for me before you talked to me about it?"

"So this is about Pellegrin. Is it not working out well for you?"

"Mom." Then I began my lie. "I just wanted to know if any of your friends might realize he was an android. If someone had suggested I buy an android, that person might surmise he is my property and not human."

She leaned over and patted my leg. "No one here, except the Judge and me, well…and Kara, knows he's an android. My goodness, Louise even thought you'd be marrying Pellegrin soon. He is so charming. All our friends here like him."

Maybe Mom came up with the idea on her own. "The Institute's advertising that they sell domestic androids but not companion androids. How did you find that out?"

"One day when I was having lunch with Helen, the D.A.'s wife, she mentioned it." Mom smiled. "But don't worry. I never told her that I discussed it with you. If Helen should see you with Pellegrin, I doubt she'll think he's an android. It probably won't even enter her mind. Was there anything else you wanted to talk about before we rejoin the others?"

Helen? I wondered how she knew about companion androids. "No, that was it."

"Rest assured, dear, we'll keep that little detail about Pellegrin secret. You have nothing to be concerned about."

Little detail isn't exactly how I would phrase Pellegrin being an android. "Thanks, Mom."

An hour later, Pellegrin and I were back in my townhouse.

"It was so nice meeting your parents and their friends. Besides your Uncle Edward, do you have any other uncles or aunts?"

"No. He's it." That information was on the documents I completed in order to buy Pellegrin. Why had he asked— to verify I had given The Institute accurate information? "Darren and Kara certainly have hit it off," I said, hoping he might reveal something.

"Yes. Darren was smiling and joking with everyone at work today. First time I ever saw him like that. After last night's problem, I didn't expect that type of behavior. During lunch, he told me how crazy he already was about Kara."

"That seems a little early in their relationship."

Pellegrin put his arms around me. "Paislee, that was exactly how I felt about you after we spent that first night together." He bent down and kissed me. "Let's take a shower together. We haven't done that before."

I had the urge to say no, but I sensed that could be dangerous. I needed to continue playing the role of a woman wanting and needing a companion android in her life. I smiled at him. "I'd like that."

* * *

Climbing out of bed, I felt tired and worn out. Pellegrin gave me quite a workout as he made up for not being able to spend Saturday night with me. As much as I wished I hadn't, I'd enjoyed every minute of it. The intimate things he did to me, I had never read about. In college, I heard whispers that erotic books had once existed, but they had been banned and burned before I was born. Maybe they weren't all destroyed like the videos Kara had seen. *Could The Institute have acquired some erotic videos as training tools?*

I trudged into the bathroom and got ready for work. Slipping on my shoes, the smell of something frying floated through the air. My stomach growled and I headed to the kitchen. "Oh, you made eggs Benedict." Gazing at the platter on the counter, I said, "That looks good."

"I hope you like it. That's what I had intended to make you yesterday morning. Unfortunately, I was in no condition to cook."

After a taste, I said, "I'm glad you're okay now. And this is as delicious as it looks. Eggs Benedict is one of my favorite breakfasts. I'll have to go on a diet if I keep eating these big breakfasts."

"You look wonderful, Paislee. You shouldn't lose any weight."

"I don't need to diet right now, but I will if I continue devouring this much food for breakfast. For the remainder of the week, I just want to have cereal in the mornings. And then, big breakfasts for the weekends."

"Cereal? I'll make some special kind for you."

My thought was that cereal in a box would be fine but

didn't voice my opinion as I took the last bite of the eggs.

Pellegrin refilled my coffee cup. "I might not be home this evening. I'll call you at work after my schedule has been established."

I nodded with my mouth full.

CHAPTER 14

Even though I kept busy at work all morning, time dragged on. Finally, it was noon—my chance to walk outside and hopefully see Tate.

I sat on a bench on the courthouse plaza while my eyes searched around. I didn't see Tate or any of his friends. Maybe he didn't want to meet me this close to the courthouse. I stood and strolled along the sidewalk. Several stiff-looking androids moved by me on the pavement, and I wondered if Pellegrin had enlisted them to watch me if I left the work.

One female android going the opposite direction, her hands loaded with boxes, stared at me. When she was a few feet away, she stumbled on the uneven pavement and all the boxes flew out of her hands and landed at my feet. When the android quickly bent over to gather them up, I knelt down to help her.

"Miss Hobson, go and buy a hot dog at the stand in front of you." Her voice was the standard android monotone.

I glanced around, expecting to see Pellegrin close by. Wondering why he wanted me to buy a hot dog, I proceeded to the stand and waited in the line. Within a few minutes, I had placed my order.

The man behind the counter gave me my order in a cardboard tray like all the other orders he had distributed. He pointed to the sign attached to the cart which read: "Keep the sidewalks clean. Deposit trash here." Under it was an arrow to a trash bin. Then he said, "Don't forget to put *all* your garbage and other things you need to discard in that trash bin."

Something struck me as unusual about the way he had said that after pointing to the sign. I walked away and looked down at my wrapped hot dog. Underneath it was the corner of a brown object. That was when I figured that the female android had been sent by Tate, not Pellegrin. I headed to the park across the street and found an empty bench partially shielded by the trees.

I lifted up the hot dog and saw a mini-recorder with an ear bud attached. I pushed the ear bud into my ear and hid as much of the cord as I could with my hair. I unwrapped the hot dog and pushed the play button on the recorder.

As I ate the hot dog, I listened: "Paislee, something has been scheduled by The Institute that involves you, and it will occur on Wednesday." It was Tate's voice. "We haven't been able to obtain any more details, but we are still working on it. Don't go anywhere with your boyfriend after work or Kara and her new boyfriend on Wednesday. Make excuses. Kara's boyfriend is an android. We have not picked up any chatter that she may be in danger, but with an android boyfriend, that could change quickly. I'm close by. It's better that we don't meet in public, and with your boyfriend keeping close tabs on you, even a private place would be difficult. I will communicate with you in this same manner on Wednesday. Maybe I'll have more to report then. Paislee, you are the woman of my dreams. Please be careful."

I pushed the erase button and looked around, hoping to get a glimpse of Tate. No such luck. I crunched-up the napkin and placed it over the recorder in the cardboard tray, and then went back to the hot dog stand and dropped the container in the trash bin.

Returning to the courthouse, I ran into Britney in the hallway. "Glad you're back to work. I tried to get your phone number from Phil to see how you were doing, but Judge Harlan wouldn't let him give it to me."

"Employees aren't allowed to give out that type of information, and the Human Resource Department has strict rules regarding when they can divulge employees' personal information."

I stared at her, wondering why she was talking in such a businesslike manner. Then, recalling there was no place safe to talk inside the courthouse, my eyes swept over the walls and ceiling. A surveillance camera was over twenty feet away. Within five feet of us, I spotted a small brown box covered with pin holes tucked underneath the brown chair rail, an object I wouldn't have noticed if I hadn't been searching for listening devices. My eyes followed the chair rail. There was a row of boxes, about five feet apart.

Britney was aware that hallways contained surveillance equipment, but I doubted she knew the magnitude. Still, I figured she must be putting forth a public effort to defend her boss about enforcing the strict personnel policy—no phone numbers given out. "We should go to lunch sometime this week."

"I don't believe that will be possible. I need to catch up on a lot of work." Her face looked stern. Not even a hint of a smile.

Maybe she felt she needed to show she was a devoted to her job. "Let me know when you're free to have lunch with me."

"I will, Paislee." She continued down the hall toward Harlan's offices.

Thinking Harlan had really chewed her out over talking about the D.A.'s arrest and probably threatened to fire her, I decided to give her a few days to get caught up and then ask her to go lunch someplace away from the courthouse.

All employees were entitled to an hour lunch. Harlan couldn't prevent her from going.

I strolled into my office.

Pellegrin sat in my desk chair. "You're late." His tone held a trace of anger.

"Yeah. I had a hot dog and went to the park. I'll stay late to make up the time. What are you doing here?"

"I couldn't reach you on the phone, and Judge Harlan wanted to see me. I decided to stop by your office on the way to his."

There was no point in asking Pellegrin why Harlan wanted to see him since a straight answer wouldn't be forthcoming. "Earlier you said you might not be home tonight. Is that because of something you're working on with Judge Harlan?"

"No. That's another matter."

I looked at the papers on my desk in front of him. "Since you're settled into my chair, are you planning to help me get my work done?"

"No." Pellegrin rose and walked to me. "Just wanted to find out if your chair was comfortable."

"And what's the verdict?"

"Not bad." He wrapped me in his arms. "This is what I really came here for." Pellegrin smothered my lips with his. "I can never get enough of you."

Smiling, I wondered why he was really here. Did he have someone watching me when I was at the park? If he did, I doubted any of my moves would have seemed suspicious. "Will you be late tonight?"

"I'm not sure. If the meeting with Judge Harlan is over before five, would you like to return to the park and have a bite to eat before I report to The Institute?"

"That would be nice. I always like going there."

After he left for his meeting, I sat down at my desk. The brief I had been working on was no longer in plain sight. It appeared everything on my desk had been rearranged. Pellegrin must have gone through all the documents. Looking for the brief, I thumbed through the papers and found it among the stack on the corner of my desk. Then I checked my drawers. All the pens, pencils, paperclips, notepads, and miscellaneous items were nicely placed in an orderly fashion, not the way I had left them. Nothing seemed to be missing. With the added surveillance and atmosphere at the courthouse, I never left any personal items in my office. Was Pellegrin searching for something?

I tried to work on the brief, but I had a hard time concentrating. What Tate had said on the recording kept replaying in my mind. Something was going to happen on Wednesday that involved me. What? Another gunfight? Would I be the target this time? I couldn't imagine anything I had done or said would put me in that type of danger.

Judge Wilbur walked into my office. "How are you doing on drafting that brief?"

"It's coming right along. You'll have it first thing in the morning."

"Good. It was nice meeting your boyfriend yesterday. He's such a pleasant person."

I smiled. "I think so." That wasn't what I thought, but I couldn't stop pretending.

"I need to get back to court."

Knowing I was running out of time to finish the brief, I forced myself to focus on it and put all thoughts about Wednesday aside. It was shortly after 5:30 p.m. when I finished.

I stood and looked out my door. Everyone had left for the day. Should I go home or wait a little longer for Pellegrin? Leaving my office door open, I went to the restroom to freshen up. Ten minutes later, I was back in my office. Still no sign of Pellegrin. I grabbed my purse, stepped out of the room, and locked the door. Then I decided to check if any of Harlan's employees were working late so I could leave a message to let Pellegrin know I'd gone home.

Silence had descended over the courthouse. I didn't hear a sound while walking along the hallway, not even the cleaning crew. That changed the minute I turned the corner to another hallway.

"That is exactly what you will do," I heard Pellegrin say in an authoritative tone.

The double doors leading to Harlan's offices were slightly ajar. Pellegrin couldn't see me, and I wanted to keep it that way. I swung around to head to the elevator when Britney's voice drifted through the opening. "But, what if I…"

"You will do that on Wednesday. This discussion is over," Pellegrin said.

I hurried away, trying not to make any noise. Reaching the elevator, I pushed the button and waited anxiously for it. I sighed when the doors slid open and quickly stepped in and pushed the button. As the doors glided together, a hand appeared between them and forced the doors apart.

Pellegrin smiled. "I was headed to your office when I saw you getting on the elevator. I'm glad I caught you."

I returned his smile. "Since it was almost six, I figured you weren't going to have time to eat with me."

He moved closer and took my hand as the elevator descended. "That meeting lasted longer than I anticipated. I won't be able to spend as much time with you as I would have liked, but I don't want you to go home hungry."

"With all the leftovers in the fridge, I wouldn't go hungry long."

As we walked out of the courthouse, I saw two police HTs parked near the entrance. No android cops were in sight. The glare of the sun hit the windows so I couldn't see if any cops were sitting inside the transports. I squinted when we went by them and looked in. No cops. Scanning the area again, I couldn't spot one policeman.

"Are you looking for someone?"

"Yes. The android policemen. I thought they were

supposed to be close by to protect you. You've already been shot once this week. I don't want a repeat performance."

He caressed my cheek. "Paislee, don't worry. They don't always stay out in the open, but they're nearby. They'll swing into action if any problems arise. And worst case scenario, if we get caught up in another unfortunate situation and I'm struck with a flying bullet, I'll heal in no time. You're the one I worry about. You won't heal as quickly from a bullet. That's why I have android policemen watching over you all the time."

Did he say that to let me know his android buddies had me in their sights during lunch? No wonder Tate kept hidden.

At the outdoor café, I ordered a seafood salad and Pellegrin ordered a hamburger like he did last time. It didn't take long before our food was served.

While we ate, Pellegrin's eyes fixed on something or someone by the pond. "I like the way the bridge support beams curve over the pond."

I looked at the bridge. "It is picturesque. I enjoy walking over it and seeing the water and fish on both sides. Do you have time for a little stroll after we finish eating?"

"Yes. I can be a little late to The Institute."

Fifteen minutes later, we were headed to the bridge. Unlike the last time when Pellegrin was giving me a lesson on the various types of fish that occupied the pond, this time he put his arm over my shoulders and held me close to him as we walked at a slow pace across the bridge. Near the middle of it, he stopped, leaned down, and pressed his perfect lips against mine. He gently caressed my shoulders, and then he trailed his fingertips slowly down my bare arms, sending a pleasant warmth through me. Pellegrin might be a devious android, but he did know how to please a woman.

"Do you have any idea yet how late you'll be working tonight?" I couldn't help myself; I wanted him.

A sensuous smile crossed his face. "I'll try to be home before eleven, but I can't make any promises. It depends on how a project is moving along." He embraced me. "I need to get to work."

While we headed to the TRL, I heard commotion between two buildings and looked that direction. Two android cops handcuffed a man and then slapped tape over his mouth. After that, since Pellegrin was moving at a fast pace, they were out of my line of sight. He hadn't even glanced between the buildings. With his supernatural hearing, he couldn't have missed the noise. Maybe his attention was all directed at getting to The Institute. His android brain might have been focused on the project waiting for him there.

Driving home, I went by the store where Tate works and gazed at its large windows covering the front façade. Like always, the place was packed with customers. Then I thought about what Uncle Edward had said. "I'll be in business as long as people *need* to eat." I wondered if more human-like androids had blended into society than I could possibly imagine. Pellegrin and Darren were prime examples of androids that easily passed as humans. Kara suddenly flashed into my mind. I had to tell her that Darren was an android. I didn't want her to fall in love with a machine. From the way she talked on the phone Sunday morning, that might already be too late. Still, she needed to know. Would she believe me? And she'd want to know how I found that out. What could I say? Mentioning Tate was not an option. I had to come up with some kind of a believable lie before we went to lunch on Tuesday.

I pulled my HT-6 into the garage while the android cops patrolling my townhouse stood watching me. Closing the garage door and seeing them vanish from my sight brought a smile.

Shortly after I changed into a pair of jeans and t-shirt, my cell rang. "Hi, Kara."

"Just calling to make sure we're still on for tomorrow. I have so much to tell you, but I'm going to save it until I see you."

I thought the same thing. I didn't want to spring it on her over the phone that Darren was an android.

She went on. "Oh, you won't believe this."

"What?"

"Marten has an HT-8. A friend at the medical center saw him near a restaurant showing it off to some of his buddies. I checked to see if HT-8s had become available to the public. They haven't yet. How did he get one?"

"I have no idea."

"I left Marten another message—not to get him back—but I was curious about it. He'd been talking about how much he wanted an HT-8 for almost a year. And then right after he drives Pellegrin's, he manages to get one. The timing seems too coincidental. Anyway, Marten hasn't returned any of my calls. Could you ask Pellegrin if he pulled any stings to help Marten?"

"Why does it matter to you, Kara?"

"Well, I know this sounds silly, but I thought Pellegrin liked me more than Marten. And when people break up, their friends sometimes chose sides. I wondered if Pellegrin had chosen Marten's side. Making him feel better by helping him get an HT-8. Pellegrin even seemed a little put out that I showed up at the beach. He acted nice to me at the bar, but that might've been because of Darren. I'm probably being pretty petty about the whole thing."

"Kara, Pellegrin is an android. He doesn't have emotions like you and I, but I'll ask him about the HT-8."

"Thanks. I better go. Darren will be here soon, and I'm baking cookies."

"See you tomorrow." I hung up thinking it hadn't sunk into Kara that Pellegrin wasn't human. But I couldn't understand why she seemed so insecure. That wasn't like her. Maybe it had to do with Marten. She might not want him back, but Marten never returning her calls probably struck her like he had never cared for her. Before the breakup, Kara said that Marten sometimes ignored her. I worried that she wouldn't take it well hearing Darren was an android. Would it be a terrible blow to her self esteem?

I wandered into Pellegrin's bedroom to look for the file box that had been there the prior day. It wasn't on the floor or in the closet. I checked his bureau to see if he had piled the folders in a drawer. Nothing.

Feeling disappointed, I sank down on his bed and heard a soft crunching sound. I stood up and raised the corner of the blanket. Nice and evenly laid out on the sheet were documents. I picked up the closest one. My eyes sprang wide open when I saw the first word.

CHAPTER 15

Wednesday was written in bold letters along the top. Under it were splashed colorful symbols. I had never seen such odd-looking signs. Below them was a list:

- 4 policemen
- 7 witnesses
- 2 paramedics
- 1 ambulance
- 2 police HTs with more to be dispatched.
- The guilty party will be immediately taken into custody.

Then more symbols. In the margin near the 7 witnesses were scribbled initials—PH. Since Tate had said in the recording that I'd be involved in something scheduled for Wednesday, I guessed that stood for me—Paislee Hobson. I figured that meant I'd be one of the witnesses. At the bottom of the page was a brief handwritten note. "Pellegrin, there is no other way."

Staring at the note, I wondered what that meant. Was there something about the planned event that Pellegrin didn't like? As I continued mulling it over, I picked up the next document. It detailed medical information for

Pellegrin and indicated he had some heart issues. Everything on that page referred to medical conditions applicable to a human, not an android. Without spotting a drop of blood, I had seen wires sticking out of his injured arm. It had been completely limp. Nothing on that arm twitched or moved. Pellegrin was definitely an android. Then an unpleasant thought bounced into my head. Was Pellegrin going to be terminated, and someone would be framed for murdering a human? If that wasn't the case, why did Pellegrin have medical records—human records— and why would those records be among the documents summarizing what was needed for Wednesday's event? The note at the bottom of the first page suddenly made sense to me. The Institute was sorry that Pellegrin had to be terminated, but "there is no other way." Had I figured it out right? Was that The Institute's plan for Wednesday, or was my imagination working overtime?

As I lifted up the adjacent page, my cell buzzed. In case it was Pellegrin, I ran to the kitchen counter where I had left my phone. Seeing his name, I tapped on it. "Hey. Are you on your way home?"

"No. Not yet. The police have picked up some viable threats against me."

"From whom?" I asked, wondering if that was just part of the set up for Wednesday.

"They're working to identify the source. That person or persons might think I am at home with you. I want you well guarded. With the recent losses of android cops, would you be amenable to allowing a couple of them into your living room? They can't protect you if they're terminated. Leaving them exposed outside or sitting in their HTs might make them easy targets."

The idea of android cops occupying my living room turned me off, but I couldn't think of a way to refuse his request. "That will be fine. Will they still be staying in the living room after you get home?"

"Yes, but they won't be allowed to wander freely

through your house, and we'll keep your bedroom door closed."

"Should I go and invite them in, or are you going to tell them?"

"I'll handle it. All you need to do is unlock the front door."

"Got it."

"I'll be home in a couple of hours."

I laid down my cell, unlocked the door, and charged into Pellegrin's bedroom to put the papers back where I had found them and straighten up the blanket. As I was running my hand over the bed to smooth out the last ridge, the front door opened. I peeked into the hallway. Not seeing the cops, I hurried into my bedroom and closed the door. Since the android cops weren't guests in my place, I didn't intend to exchange any words with them.

Noticing it was almost 10:30 p.m., I changed into my nightgown and crawled into bed and then mulled over the events of the day: the warning from Tate, the angry words Pellegrin spouted at Britney, the documents in Pellegrin's room, Kara's phone call, and Pellegrin's hubris to sit at my desk. From what I had gathered from the documents, it appeared I'd been slated to be a witness on Wednesday. I guessed whatever was going to happen would be pinned on a rebel. Would it be Tate or one of his friends? Thinking about how to contact Tate to tell him to stay far away from me on Wednesday, the hot dog stand bounced into my head. I decided to pass the owner a note when I inserted my credit card into his machine. As I closed my eyes the image of Tate appeared. I drifted off wishing stratum rules would fade away.

Feeling my nightgown lifted over my head, I awoke with a start.

"Relax, it's me." Pellegrin dropped my nightgown on the floor. He leaned toward me and covered my mouth with his. The tip of his tongue against my lips sent a surge of excitement swirling through my body. He pulled me closer so our bodies touched more intimately. He deepened his kiss, and every stroke of his tongue intensified my desire. Then his lips moved down my neck and lingered on my chest. My breathing became ragged. All my concerns about Pellegrin vanished as his hands began exploring every inch of my body.

* * *

The next day, I delivered the brief to Wilbur. "How is the D.A. doing?"

Wilbur's brow furrowed. "Something seems off. Besides being shot in the arm, I think he sustained a head injury in the ordeal. When I've tried to broach the subject with Helen, she says he'll be back to normal once his arm heals. I doubt she believes that. She's pale and has red, puffy eyes. Not the way a woman would look if she truly believed her husband would be well soon. Helen barely leaves his side. She only goes home to shower and change clothes. I've talked to one of the D.A.'s doctors. He's sticking with the original prognosis—he only sustained a bullet wound in his arm."

"Helen's mother being sick isn't helping anything I'm sure."

"Her mother, who was supposedly on her death bed, went home from the hospital yesterday morning. She even did some grocery shopping in the afternoon. According to Helen, her mother hasn't gone to a store for ten years— ever since the elderly woman acquired a domestic android. Helen thinks her mother's personality changed in the hospital, but the woman might've just needed the rest." Wilbur lifted the brief. "I need to read this over."

"Let me know if there are any changes you'd like me to make to it." I turned and left his office.

Sitting at my desk, I still wondered if the D.A. had been shot by an android policeman. Helen and Wilbur weren't aware that the D.A. had been arrested in the courthouse the day before the shooting. There had to be some kind of connection. Maybe the police wanted information from him that he wasn't willing to give. They knocked him around, thinking that would loosen his tongue before he was shot. Something like that could account for the D.A. behaving in an unusual manner, but if he sustained a head wound, why would the doctors cover it up?

I set the alarm on my cell so Kara wouldn't have to wait for me again. Then I dug into the stack of documents that had kept growing since I had spent more time worrying about rebels and androids than getting my work done.

Soft beeps came from my cell. I tapped off the alarm, stood, and stretched. Then I picked up my purse and headed to the foyer to meet Kara.

She walked through the entrance the same time I stepped out of the elevator. Perfect timing.

"Hey. You look great." I really meant it. Her cheeks were rosy. Her light brown eyes shined. Her short, print-patterned dress showed off her curvy legs.

"Oh, I feel great." She eyed my pink silk blouse and dark blue silk pants. "You always look good. I'm still amazed that Emmett left you for that bleached-blonde."

"Don't want to talk about him. He's history. Any place special you want to go?"

"The usual. Juan's Southwest Grill. It's a good place to talk."

The restaurant was only a block away, and its booths had high back rests, providing a nice degree of privacy.

Ten minutes later, we were seated and the waitress had taken our orders.

"Darren is so gorgeous. He could have any woman he wanted. I'm having a hard time believing he wants to spend all his free time with me." Her voice slightly quavered, and her glowing eyes dimmed.

"Kara, you're cute. A lot of guys would want to spend

time with you." I reached across the table and squeezed her hand. "You and Marten were a couple. You weren't available. Some guys at the medical center still asked you out. Do they even know that you and Marten have broken up?"

"Well…no." A big smile flashed across her face. "But now…Darren calls me his girlfriend. Isn't that awesome! I wouldn't think about going out with anyone else."

Seeing her face light up, I couldn't bring myself to tell her that Darren wasn't human. That conversation could wait for another day.

Kara, still beaming, opened her mouth to speak, and then immediately closed it when the server brought our orders.

"This looks good." I picked up my fork and had a taste.

Kara sipped her water. "You won't believe this, and I know it seems a little early, but Darren wants me to move in with him." Excitement radiated in her voice. "His place is nicer than mine. And I think it bugs him that Marten used to live at my apartment. What do you think?"

"What did you tell him?"

"Well…"

I guessed she might've already said yes. "Kara, you've only known him for three days. Are you sure that's what you want to do?"

"Uh-uh." A goofy grin was plastered on her face.

"How will your parents take it? They weren't very happy when Marten moved in with you, and you'd known him for over a year."

"Well…that might be a problem. They don't even know that Marten and I have broken up. Anyway, I did tell Darren I wanted him to meet my parents before I moved into his place and I needed to give the apartment manager a thirty-day notice—that's in my lease—so it's not going to happen right away.

"Your parents really seemed to like Darren and so did their friends. I think my parents will too. But I'm a little worried about my dad. He went fishing often with Marten, and he'll probably be disappointed that we broke up." She hesitated and then a determined expression appeared on her face. "But I am twenty-four. I really don't need their permission to move in with anyone."

"Before you make arrangements for your parents to meet Darren, why don't you call your mom and tell her Marten broke up with you? Sound sad. My mom went overboard to try to make me feel better. Since then, Emmett's name is never mentioned in their household." I had no idea why I was giving her advice on how she could make Darren more acceptable to her parents when I wanted the android out of her life.

Her cheeks became rosier, and her face glowed. "You are the best friend in the whole world. No matter what I do—like the way I danced with Pellegrin—you are always there for me. I can always count on you. I'm going to call Mom as soon as I get back to work."

We smiled at each other and then continued eating.

As I chewed, I felt a little bad that I wanted to rip Darren away from her when she so desperately wanted him in her life, but she didn't have a clue he was an android. Then I had a fleeting thought that it might not make any difference to her. She acts like Pellegrin was a human, and she knew the truth.

When we were heading back to work, Kara stopped me. "Oh, I forgot to ask. Did Pellegrin pull any strings to help Marten get an HT-8?"

"Pellegrin came home pretty late last night and left before I got up. I didn't get a chance to ask him. I intend to do that when I see him today."

"Thanks."

Before I entered the courthouse, we briefly hugged each other.

"I'll let you know how it goes with Mom." Kara smiled and walked with a bounce in her step toward the medical building.

* * *

Around 3:00 p.m., Pellegrin called. "I have to work again tonight, but I don't plan to show up until nine. How would you like to go out to dinner at a casual place?"

"The outdoor café in the park?"

"No. We've already patronized that place twice in the past week. I was thinking of the amusement park across town. Then we can also go on some rides."

That was a good choice since Pellegrin didn't need to eat. "I haven't been there for a long time. Maybe three or four years. Sounds like fun. After work, I'll go home and change my clothes, and then we can take off."

"No. I'll bring you an appropriate outfit. Then we can leave from there to go to the amusement park."

The amusement park was significantly closer to the courthouse than it was to my place. Given the fact that Pellegrin had a limited amount of time, that option made sense. "Okay. See you at five."

As I hung up, I wondered about Pellegrin. Did he want to go out today because it was going to be his last? The image of the handwritten note at the bottom of a hidden document came into my mind: "Pellegrin, there is no other way." I didn't understand everything on that page—especially all the symbols—but I felt confident that a crime would be committed and someone would be arrested. Based on the falsified medical records relating to Pellegrin, he was probably the victim. Despite my distrust of him, that thought made me feel sad.

I had just finished a couple of the jobs Wilbur had given me when Pellegrin strode into my office, carrying a duffle bag. He eyed all the stuff on my desk. "You don't look like you're ready to leave work yet."

Glancing at my watch and seeing it was quitting time, I stacked the papers in front of me. "No. The rest of this work can wait another day." I stood and walked to

Pellegrin. "I take it that the outfit you selected for me is in the duffle bag."

"Yes, and a pair of shoes." He handed it to me. "I'll wait here for you."

I headed to the restroom and set the duffle bag on the counter to see what he had brought for me. I pulled out a pair of shorts, a sleeveless blouse and a pair of sandals. None of the items belonged to me, which was not what I had expected. All the clothing appeared to be new. He probably got it out of The Institute's vast wardrobe. I stepped into a stall and changed into the outfit. Then I checked myself in the mirror. It fit me well, but the neckline of the blouse plunged more than I would have liked. I gathered up my clothing and put it along with my heels in the duffle bag and went back to my office.

I twirled around in front of Pellegrin. "So what do you think?"

"It looks good on you, but you're gorgeous no matter what you're wearing."

We smiled at each other. It still amazed me how human-like Pellegrin was. His facial expressions, gestures, and words. Nothing would have given him away, but when he was shot in the bar, he didn't bleed. Being shot would expose him for the android he was. Unless, like at the bar, if he was the intended victim, a paramedic would be close by to wrap the wound in a towel that provided the illusion of blood seeping from it.

On our way to Pellegrin's HT-8, an android cop approached him. "Mr. Murr, the suspect has been taken into custody. Where would you like us to take him?"

"The Institute."

CHAPTER 16

I watched the android cop walk away. "Was he talking about the person who made threats against you?"

"We suspect the man arrested is the culprit, but we lack evidence."

"Why's he going to The Institute and not to jail?"

"The Institute has at their disposal more sophisticated interrogators. They'll help the police determine if the man is guilty and if he has any accomplices." He turned and his eyes fixed on me. "Paislee, I'm not the only one in danger. Everyone who works for The Institute has received threats."

"Maybe I made a mistake by letting you work for them for two weeks. You'd be safer not going there at all."

"No. You made the right decision." He stood next to me while I slid into the HT-8. Then Pellegrin climbed into the driver's seat and told Wellington to take us to the amusement park. "Tomorrow night there's a party at The Institute to celebrate the successful testing of their latest product that will soon be offered to the public. I'd like you to attend with me."

Tate's warning sprang into my head—don't go anywhere with Pellegrin on Wednesday. And I wasn't positive I had correctly interpreted the document I found.

"Oh, I don't know. I promised Mom I'd go shopping with her after work," I lied and made a mental note to call Mom to set up a shopping spree. "But maybe I can get out of it. I'll call her later."

Pellegrin reached over and took my hand. "I'd really like you to go with me so you can meet everyone I've been working with."

"Tell me about this new product."

"I don't know what it is. It'll be unveiled tomorrow night at the celebration. The celebration is private. Only employees, consultants and a few guests are invited."

I assumed whatever was going to happen on Wednesday, it was going to take place during the party. But then the witness count mentioned on that page didn't make sense. The Institute had hundreds of employees. There'd be more than seven present; unless, during the celebration, small groups were taken on a tour of the facility or something like that.

The Wild Wheel, Deadly Drop, Roller Spin, and the other towering amusement park rides came into view.

"We have reached your destination." Wellington's voice came through the speaker.

Pellegrin and I left the HT-8 and strolled toward the park entrance.

"Hello, Mr. Murr. It's been a while since you've been here," said a stiff-moving female android. She motioned other people through the gate.

"Yes, it has, C-18."

When we were out of her earshot, I said, "I didn't realize you'd been here before."

"Many times. I used to…" He lowered his head, and a weird expression appeared on his face.

I had the impression he was trying to grasp something he had forgotten. I rubbed his arm. "Pellegrin, are you okay?"

He raised his head. "Yes. Of course. Do you want to eat now or after we've gone on some rides?"

"After."

He led me to the Wild Wheel. The attendant, who was either a human or looked like one, strapped us in, and then clicked the switch. The speed of the turning wheel kept increasing. My stomach churned, and I began to feel nauseous. I closed my eyes, hoping the ride would end soon. Then I heard laughter. *Pellegrin?* I turned my head toward him and opened my eyes. He was laughing. He could laugh?

The ride slowed down and stopped.

Holding onto my stomach, I trudged off of the platform.

"Paislee, are you sick?"

"I didn't remember how fast that ride went, but you liked it."

"Yes, I did. We'll go on the Ferris Wheel next."

When we were seated on it, Pellegrin put his arm around my shoulders. The wheel moved at a nice, slow speed, and my stomach started to settle down.

As we neared the top, Pellegrin raised my chin and gently kissed my lips. His green, glowing eyes focused on me. "I like the way your hair shimmers in the light." He brushed his hand over it. "Are you feeling better?"

"Yes. Much."

"You must need something to eat."

"I am getting a little hungry, but let's walk around first. Like I told you earlier, it's been a long time since I've been here."

After that ride, we ambled through the amusement park. Pellegrin wanted to play all the arcade games. It didn't take long before my arms were full of stuffed animals. We competed against each other in the game of Shooting Water to fill up a balloon until it popped. Pellegrin's balloon popped first, so he won another stuffed bear. That attendant noticed me gathering up all the prizes Pellegrin had won and gave me a bag to put them in.

As we sat at a round table eating tacos, I decided to

bring up Kara's question. "Do you know that Marten has an HT-8?"

"Yes. I saw him parking an HT-8 in a transport retaining location."

"Did you help him get it?"

"Why do you want to know that?" he asked with an edge in his voice.

"I don't care if you helped him or not, but Kara wanted me to ask you."

"Does she want one too?"

"No. That wasn't the reason she wanted to know." I rubbed my head, trying to figure out how to explain. Then I decided to just blurt it out. "Kara thinks if you helped Marten get an HT-8 that means you like him more than you like her." I pressed my lips together, thinking how childish that sounded.

"No. I like Kara more. She's going to move in with Darren soon."

It surprised me that Pellegrin already knew about that. "So you didn't help Marten get an HT-8?" I put the last piece of the Taco in my mouth.

"Are you through eating?"

I nodded, assuming Pellegrin did not intend to answer my question about Marten's HT-8. That probably meant he *did* play a role in Marten acquiring it.

"I want to go on another ride before we leave."

Pellegrin threw away our garbage and then took my hand and headed to the Roller Spin. We stood and watched it violently twirl. When it stopped, the riders climbed out and wobbled and swayed as they went to the ride's exit gate.

"I don't think I'm up for this ride. Why don't you go on it? I'll stay here and watch."

"You don't mind?"

"Nope. Since I just ate a taco, it's better if my feet stay firmly planted on solid ground." I swung my hand toward the ride. "Go. Have fun."

Pellegrin didn't hesitate getting into the line and moving with the other people into the eight-foot roller. He took a seat. The bar lowered, securing him in place. The ride only lasted five minutes. That would've been five minutes too long for me.

Like the other people I had watched go to the exit gate, they all swayed and waddled, but not Pellegrin.

"I wish we could stay longer, but I have to get to work." He took the bag of prizes from me, and we headed to his transport.

A police HT was parked next to the HT-8.

"Is there a problem?" Pellegrin asked an android cop.

"Yes." The android cop looked at me. "This is a private matter."

That obviously was my cue to walk away. I strolled toward the amusement park entrance.

"Paislee, stay where I can see you."

When I was about forty feet from them, I swung around and saw Pellegrin and two android cops looking my direction. They probably figured I was out of earshot since they turned toward each other and talked.

After a short conversation, the android cops got into their transport, and Pellegrin gestured for me to join him. Walking back to him, I thought how right Tate was— Pellegrin didn't belong to me. I belonged to him regardless of what the contract said.

In the HT-8, I asked, "Pellegrin, are you ever going to share any of your work with me?"

"Share?" A confused expression flashed on his face. "You don't have the ability to do what I do."

"I didn't mean literally share. I meant tell me about it."

He put his hand on top of mine. "No."

Well, at least he answered my question, but I had expected an explanation even if it held no truth.

Pellegrin pulled into the courthouse's TRL and parked next to my HT-6. We both got out of his transport, and he wrapped me in his arms. "Paislee, I might not make it home tonight, and I will miss you." His lips touched mine and he kissed me passionately. When he released me from his embrace, he gazed at my face, and his glowing green eyes seemed to dim a little.

I sensed Pellegrin felt sad. How could I think that?

He remained outside his HT-8 while I got into the HT-6 and left him.

"Marcel, take me home," I said to my transport's operating system. Then I clicked Mom's number on my cell.

"Hello, Paislee. I was just thinking about you."

"Good thoughts?"

"Always, dear. The Judge and I are planning a garden party. It'll give Pellegrin a chance to meet more of our friends. Would two weeks from Sunday work for you?"

"Yes," I said, doubting that Pellegrin would be available. "My social calendar is pretty empty right now. Mom, I want to buy Pellegrin a present. I want it to be a surprise, but I have no idea what to get him."

"Oh, I'm so glad that things are going that well between you two. How can I help with the present?"

"I thought we could go shopping together, and you could help me find the perfect gift."

"I'd love to go shopping with you, dear. I've already got a few ideas. When would you like to go?"

"How about tomorrow night, or is that too early for you?"

"Well, I had intended to go to an art show, but this is more important."

"Great! I'll pick you up right after work. Oh, pretend we've had this shopping excursion planned for a long time. I don't want Pellegrin to suspect it has anything to do with him."

"I will, dear."

"Thanks, Mom. See you tomorrow."

I hated lying to Mom, but she wouldn't handle the truth well. I wasn't even sure what the truth was. I lacked any concrete facts about what was going to happen on Wednesday. Even though one of the documents convinced me that someone would be arrested probably for a crime they didn't commit, it was still circumstantial. No hard proof. Tate warned me something would happen, but he never provided any evidence. Maybe his recorded message that I'd get at the hot dog stand during lunch on Wednesday might give me more details. I needed something concrete that I could count on.

My townhouse came into view. An ambulance with its lights flickering, three police HTs, and a mixture of android and human cops were in front of it. A man was being dragged from the side of my house. When I saw his face, a flash of utter disbelief ripped through me.

CHAPTER 17

I charged out of my transport and ran toward the action. "Travis, what happened?"

"Paislee, tell them you know me." He sounded meek and scared as an android cop slapped handcuffs on him.

I grabbed his shoulder. "This is Travis Zaloom. He works for my dad, Judge Hobson, and he's my friend. Let go of him!"

"He was caught trying to break into your house," an android cop said.

"Paislee, that's not true. I came here to meet your dad."

"This is my home, and he always has my permission to be here. Release him now." My voice rose with each word.

A human policeman, or an android that looked like a human, stepped toward me. "Miss Hobson, after Travis Zaloom mentioned he knew you, we contacted Mr. Murr. We are following his instructions."

"Pellegrin? Like I said, this is my home. I say who can come and go here, not Mr. Murr."

"You will have to discuss that with Mr. Murr."

"I don't have to discuss that with anyone. This is *my* home!" I snapped, anger churning inside me.

Two android cops ignored me and placed Travis on a gurney.

Still fuming over Pellegrin, I eyed Travis up and down, and couldn't see any visible injuries. I leaned over him. "Did they hurt you, Travis?"

"I tripped over your patio furniture when the police charged into your backyard. My ankle is sore. It might be sprained." He glanced at the paramedic strapping him in. "It's better that I'm going to the hospital than jail."

"Why did my dad want to meet you here?"

A human policeman and an android cop moved closer to us, probably to make sure they didn't miss anything that was said.

"I don't know. The message just said to meet him here. When no one answered your door bell, I went to see if he was on your patio. The cops appeared as I was about to call him."

"Message? A phone call?"

"No. It was stuck to my door when I got home. I didn't go straight home from work. It could've been there for a while. Your dad probably got tired of waiting for me and left."

"He never called you?"

"No. And I've never gotten a message from him like that before. I had gone to a movie so my cell had been off."

"Have you still got the message?"

"Yeah. It's in my pants pocket."

Since Travis's hands were handcuffed, pulling it out of his pocket would be a difficult move. "Is it okay if I get it out?"

"Sure. Right front pocket."

As I lifted it out, the human policeman grabbed my wrist. "We'll take that."

"I'll give it to you after I read it."

His gripped tightened around my wrist, forcing me to open my hand. He took the note.

"Judge Hobson is going to hear about your brutal behavior." It appeared the policeman wasn't fazed by my threat, so I added, "And so will Mr. Murr. He won't approve of you manhandling me." That *did* cause him to flinch.

"Miss Hobson, I am sorry that you view it that way. I am only doing my job."

"And your job is to manhandle innocent civilians?"

The corner of his mouth twitched. Then he turned on his heel and joined his cop buddies.

The paramedics picked up the gurney.

"I patted Travis's arm. "Don't worry. I'll call my father. He'll take care of this."

Travis's lips quivered as he was pushed into the ambulance.

I noticed the name "Southern Community Hospital" plastered on the side of the emergency HT when the human cop climbed into the ambulance behind the gurney.

When it was out of sight, I slid into my transport, pushed the button to open my garage door, and drove it in, honking at the policemen in my way. Had they not immediately stepped aside, I wouldn't have hesitating knocking them down, but Marcel would have prevented that.

I quickly closed the garage door, headed up the stairs, and called Dad.

Mom answered after four rings. "Paislee, are you okay?" She sounded anxious, probably because it was past 11:00 p.m. I never called my parents at that late hour.

"Yes, but I'm not sure Travis is."

"Travis? What's wrong with him?"

"It's a legal matter. Can I talk to Dad?"

"Of course, dear."

Dad came on the phone, and I spouted out everything that happened from when I arrived home to Travis being taken away in an ambulance.

"Sit down, sweetie, and breathe deeply."

I figured I must have sounded overly agitated, which I was. I followed his instructions. "Okay, Dad. I'm calming down."

"Good. I never sent or gave any message to Travis to meet me at your house. I'll call the hospital to find out how he is doing and then call the police chief, but I doubt I will be able to reach him until tomorrow morning. I suspect this is a misunderstanding, and when the facts are laid out, Travis will be released. I will ask the chief to compare the note taken from Travis to the note given them by Judge Wilbur. He mentioned that Helen received a prank note in the hospital from an undetermined source, which he turned over to the police department. It dealt with a different matter, but there could be similarities."

"I didn't even think about that." Then I wondered if I should tell him Helen's note wasn't a prank but decided against it since the airwaves might not be secure.

"Go to bed, sweetie. I'll handle it from here."

"Give Travis my best if you get a chance to talk to him."

"I will. Sleep tight."

As soon as I disconnected, I tapped on Pellegrin's number.

"Hello, Paislee. I expected your call."

"Then you know what went on here. Was it all according to your instructions?" I didn't attempt to hide my anger and assumed it was evident in my tone.

"Not everything, Paislee. I did not tell Travis Zaloom to break into your townhouse."

"Then you must also be aware of how a policeman forced me to give him a note by squeezing and twisting my wrist until I couldn't stand the pain anymore. I've been keeping a cold pack on it to bring down the swelling." I realized that was laying it on a little heavy, but I wanted to know Pellegrin's reaction.

"That isn't exactly how Eugene described the situation."

"So, you're calling me a liar, and believing a policeman named Eugene? Of course, he's not going to tell the truth that he was involved with police brutality."

"Paislee, please calm down. We can talk about this when I see you tomorrow. I'll bring an ointment home that will soothe your wrist."

I held up my hand and checked my wrist. There wasn't even a black-and-blue mark on it. "Pellegrin, Travis never broke into my house. He was given a note to meet my dad here. Did your android cop buddies tell you that?"

"Paislee, you sound upset. But even before this evening's incident, Travis Zaloom was under surveillance. Now I want you to go to bed."

Grinding and scraping sounds came through the airwaves.

"Pellegrin, you can't…"

"I need to get back to work."

The line went silent. "Pellegrin?" I said to verify he had hung up on me. Any lingering question that I might have some control over Pellegrin completely vanished. Pellegrin called all the shots, and I had no say in anything. It also appeared he had significant influence over the actions of the police. Tate had said that Pellegrin was high up in The Institute. The more I thought about it, the less it made sense that Pellegrin would be the intended victim in whatever was planned for Wednesday. The whole thing didn't add up to me.

Hoping the android cops were no longer stationed outside my home, I lifted up the corner of the drape and looked out the window. No such luck. Two cops stood prominently by their HT, watching my townhouse.

On the way to my bedroom, I made a detour into Pellegrin's room to get another look at the documents. I raised up the corner of the blanket. The documents were gone. I wasn't ready to give up and searched through his drawers and the closet. No documents. His suitcase was also gone, but his clothes still hung neatly on hangers.

Going to my bedroom, I mulled over the suitcase. It had contained a few weapons as well as newspaper clippings about Paxton Murr, who, along with his family, had died in a HT collision. Did it mean anything that it was gone?

* * *

Without experiencing any morning problems, I arrived at the courthouse the following day. I sat down at my desk, thinking Wednesday had started out like any work day. I had the urge to call Dad to find out how things were going with freeing Travis but figured he'd call me when there was news to report.

Then I wrote a note to Tate, the note I intended to give to the man at the hot dog stand when I purchased a hot dog.

> *Tate,*
>
> *The Institute has planned a crime to take place today. I think my role will be a witness. Someone nearby will be taken into custody for it. Stay far away from me today. I don't want you or your friends arrested for the crime.*
>
> > *Be careful,*
> >
> > *A former surfing student*

I folded the note. After putting it in my purse, I started working on the stack of jobs that monopolized the corner of my desk and found my concentration was intact. The pile gradually became smaller.

Opening the fifth folder, I glanced at my watch—11:42 a.m. I jumped up and hurried to the restroom to run a comb through my hair and touch up my makeup. While there, I checked the blue dot on my forehead even though I had looked at it earlier. It still appeared to be an ink spot, nothing more.

I left the courthouse and headed straight for the hot

dog stand. When I was within fifteen feet of it, someone behind me yelled my name. I spun around and saw Britney running toward me.

"Oh, I'm so glad I caught you." She sounded out of breath. "I meant to call you this morning, but Judge Harlan had me working on a rush job. Just finished it. I want to have lunch with you. You're not meeting anyone or doing anything are you?"

I glanced over my shoulder at the hot dog stand and thought about the note to Tate in my purse and the recording I had hoped to receive.

"Oh, are you meeting someone?"

"No. I was just thinking about getting a hot dog."

"I kind of wanted to eat at the park. Would you mind eating there?"

That would probably be safer since I knew Pellegrin had words with her. She might've even been sent out to keep track of me. "I enjoy eating in the park." I feigned a sneeze, reached in my purse for a tissue and grabbed the note at the same time. After wiping my nose, I crunched the note and tissue in my fist.

As we walked along the sidewalk, I dropped it in the trash bin next to the hot dog stand. "Are you all caught up on your work after being sick?"

"Not really. I just wanted to get out of the building."

I noticed Britney slightly moving her head back and forth like she was looking for someone, and then I recalled hearing Pellegrin ordering her to do something on Wednesday. Maybe that's why she left the courthouse, to get away from the task. She might be worried that she had been followed out of the building.

After we crossed the street, I figured if someone was tailing her, that person wasn't within earshot, and asked, "Did Judge Harlan chew you out for mentioning that the D.A. had been arrested?"

A puzzled look crossed her face. "Huh?"

"The D.A. was hauled out of Judge Harlan's chambers

by two android cops. That was a pretty big deal, but less than a handful of people at the courthouse even knew it happened. You couldn't have forgotten."

She turned toward me. "Paislee, I have no idea what you're talking about. The D.A. was shot, not arrested."

Suddenly, I wondered if she had been forced to wear a bug. If that was the case, I had informed the listener I knew about the arrest. Was I now in danger? Had Britney been sent out to spy on me? Was that what Pellegrin had ordered her to do?

The outdoor café was packed. My eyes scanned around, searching for a table that might be vacated soon.

"Let's grab that table." Britney pointed to a table two men were leaving, and we hurried to it.

Once seated, I said, "Tell me what you want, and I'll go place our orders."

"A hamburger, with everything on it, and fries."

I went to the end of the line by the counter. It didn't take long to place our orders.

Going back to the table, I tried to come up with something to talk about that didn't matter if someone heard every word. "Pellegrin and I sat at this same table last time we were here."

"Have you been here often with him?"

"Twice." I gazed at the pond. "The first time he gave me a lesson on all the types of fish in the pond."

"Cool. Can you remember the names?"

"Some. But I had hoped for a more romantic walk by the pond, so I probably wasn't paying attention like a good student."

An android server brought our order. So different from Pellegrin, the server's expression didn't change. His movements were mechanical.

Britney dug right in. From the way she devoured her food, it looked like she hadn't eaten for days. She was finished before half my salad was gone.

She looked at the pond while I continued eating. "Hey,

isn't that your boyfriend on the bridge talking to a woman?"

My eyes darted to the bridge. Pellegrin was with an attractive redhead. They were standing in about the same spot where I had stood with him a few days before. I was about ready to ask Britney how she knew that was my boyfriend when I remembered she had gone to lunch with him, Judge Harlan, and a prosecuting attorney last Wednesday, and I had overheard a conversation between Pellegrin and her. I kept staring at the couple on the bridge and wondered if Pellegrin was performing sexual services for more women than just me.

I looked at Britney. "I thought he was working today. Let's go say hi."

Then I saw Pellegrin hug the redhead, and so did Britney.

"Paislee, are you sure that's a good idea?"

"Absolutely."

We threw our trash in the garbage bin and then headed toward the bridge.

Pellegrin's back was to us as we approached him.

Glaring at him, I tapped his shoulder. "Hello, Pellegrin."

He swung around, his brow furrowed. "Paislee."

I eyed the redhead. "I can see you're hard at work."

He gripped my upper arm and glanced at the two other women. "Excuse us." Keeping a firm hold on me, he led me away from them.

"Paislee, what's going on?"

"That's what I was about to ask you. Pellegrin, I saw you embracing that woman."

"It's not what you think."

I felt my adrenaline pumping fast and furious through my veins. "Pellegrin, when I purchased you, I did not realize that your services would be shared with other women. And last night when I called you about Travis, you hung up on me. Why don't you tell me what's going on?"

He went to put his arms around me, and I pushed him away. His body hit the railing behind him, and it cracked and splintered. Pellegrin began to fall. He grabbed the still intact railing. It also broke. I reached out for him as he tumbled into the water, landing head first.

"Pellegrin!" I screamed, dropped my purse, and prepared to jump in after him. Before my feet left the bridge, two strangers grasped my arms and pulled me away from the ledge.

They continued holding onto me while I watched people making their way through the pond to Pellegrin. He wasn't moving. He wouldn't have been wearing his earplugs. It was doubtful that he'd survive. Conflicting emotions bombarded me. Even though Pellegrin was a machine, I had many enjoyable times with him.

Sirens blared. Heavy footfalls pounded on the bridge. Android cops seemed to be everywhere. As Pellegrin was pulled out of the water, an ambulance stopped near the border of the pond.

Paramedics carrying medical cases climbed out and moved closer to the pond. Pellegrin's limp body was brought to the shore and spread out on the ground next to them. They began working to resuscitate him.

Then it struck me. This was the event scheduled by The Institute for Wednesday. I wasn't an intended witness. I was the planned assailant. In a few minutes, Pellegrin would be declared dead. I'd be arrested for murder shortly after that. What crime had I committed against The Institute?

CHAPTER 18

One of the paramedics, who had been kneeling near Pellegrin, stood and shook his head.

"She pushed him. She pushed him," yelled a man, pointing at me. "I saw it all!

"I saw it too," a woman screamed. "She pushed him!"

Another man called out. "She's a killer!"

"The pretty ones always think they can get away with everything, even murder," spouted an irate-sounding man.

More shouts and yelling echoed around me. Through the voices, I heard someone crying. Then I realized it was my sobs.

As tears began to fog my vision, I glanced at the two men restraining me. Both held angry expressions. The larger, older man's eyes bore into me, but I saw warmth behind the eyes of the younger, smaller-sized man. "Tissue," I mumbled, tilting my head toward my purse near my feet.

He bent down, picked it up, and opened it to allow my hand to slip in and grab a tissue. Then he put the purse strap over my shoulder.

Dabbing my eyes with the tissue, I wondered if he would suffer for his act of kindness.

A stout woman pushed her way through the crowd and stuck her face a few inches from mine and growled. "I saw it all! You killed that man!"

Suddenly, I felt numb, not able to move. Pellegrin had sacrificed himself. For what? And I had been set up for this moment from the first day I met him. *Why?*

Another woman poked me in the arm. "She did it! She did it!"

I wanted to shout, "It was an accident," but I knew even if someone believed me, all the witnesses were playing pre-arranged roles, roles that most likely came with severe consequences if they didn't give their best performances.

It didn't take long before I found myself encircled by policemen. They stared at me. I saw the lips moving on a human-looking policeman, but I couldn't comprehend what he was saying. My hands were yanked out in front of me and handcuffs secured around my wrists.

The two bystanders who had been holding onto my arms were replaced by police officers. They guided me to the waiting police HT. An android policeman didn't let go of me until I slid into the back seat. The door shut, followed by a soft click. As the transport sped away, everything around me became blurred. A nightmare had closed in on me, and there was no escape.

* * *

"This is outrageous!"

I awoke to the sound of Dad's voice. My eyes swept around the sparsely furnished, small room. It contained a sink and toilet, a small writing table, a chair, and a narrow bed with a rough-feeling blanket that I was lying on. The room's metal door stood ajar. The horror that had brought me here flashed through my mind, and I doubted, compared to The Institute, that my father wielded enough authority to get me out.

The door flew open, and he was escorted in by an android cop. When Dad sat down on the bed by me, the cop left and pushed the door, leaving it ajar.

Dad gently touched my cheek. "Sweetie, are you okay?"

I nodded. There was so much I wanted to tell him about The Institute, but I feared for his safety. Dad would try to go after them and probably end up dead or imprisoned like me.

"It was an accident, Dad. I pushed Pellegrin away from me, and the railing broke." My eyes filled with tears again, and I blinked in an attempt to hold them at bay.

"Shhh." He stroked my hair. "It'll be okay. You believed Pellegrin was an android, an android you purchased. You owned him. I have a copy of your contract. When I heard you had been arrested for Pellegrin's death, it appeared a horrible mistake had been made. I contacted The Institute in order to have the problem immediately cleared up. That was when I was told that Pellegrin had been a human. The Institute would not explain why they had hidden that fact. Humans cannot be traded and sold like androids. I expect the D.A.'s office will get to the bottom of it before any official charges are filled."

"Pellegrin wasn't in the water very long before he was pulled out. If he was a human they should have been able to resuscitate him."

My father patted my hand. "According to his medical records, he had a bad heart. That might be why he died. An autopsy has been scheduled to determine the cause of death."

The image of the medical record I had seen bounced into my head. At the time, I wondered why it showed he had a heart condition. The pieces were coming together. Not in a good way.

"You can only be held for 48 hours without being charged. I've submitted a motion to have you released sooner. That motion will be heard by Judge Harlan in the morning."

"Judge Harlan?"

"Yes."

"Dad, Judge Harlan had several private meetings with Pellegrin. He even had Pellegrin do a job for him."

Dad narrowed his eyes. "What job?"

"Pellegrin wouldn't tell me. He said it was confidential."

"Was that part of the work he was doing for The Institute, the reason a portion of the purchase price was refunded?"

"I don't think so. Pellegrin had been working for the police before I purchased him. As a result of whatever he had been involved with while he did that job, he ended up testifying in a case heard by Judge Harlan. After that, Judge Harlan wanted his opinion on some cases. To tell you the truth, it struck me as being inappropriate."

"Yes, and Judge Harlan is normally a real stickler on professional ethics."

I smiled slightly at my father. "That almost sounded like you weren't, but I know better."

He patted my arm as the corners of his mouth curved up. His smile faded, and he said, "Judge Harlan might have been discussing closed cases with Pellegrin and wanted his opinion on them because he had similar cases on his calendar. Harlan probably thought he was acquiring the information from a computerized brain. The worldwide hack has made it more difficult to obtain differing opinions on legal matters."

Feeling a little better about my situation, I sat up, and Dad moved toward the foot of the bed in order to give me the space to swing my feet over the edge. He held both my hands. "Don't worry, sweetie. You'll be home in no time." He rose to his feet.

Did he really believe I'd be out of here soon? Then Travis sprang into my head. "Travis. Is he out of jail?"

Dad shook his head. "He's not in jail. His ankle was

badly splintered from the mishap in your backyard. It needed to be reset. He was given a shot to numb the area, and he had an allergic reaction to the medicine. Travis is in a coma, but his vital signs are good. He has a team of doctors who are working to neutralize the drug's effect."

"Had the police not cornered him in my yard, that never would've happened. When he comes out of the coma, will he still have to go to jail?"

"No. The charges have been dropped. Pellegrin took care of that before he had his accident."

"Pellegrin?"

Dad nodded. "That was exactly my reaction when the police chief told me that. I have no idea how he pulled that off."

"He used to work for the police department."

"That's right. You mentioned that earlier. He must have acquired some connections during that time." Dad kissed my forehead. "Sweetie, I need to get home to calm your mother down. She's called me every fifteen minutes since you were arrested, and I imagine she's busy calling everyone we know when she's not hounding me on the phone."

"Well..." I cocked an eyebrow. "It's not like I've ever been arrested before. We had planned to go shopping this evening."

A lopsided smile appeared on his face. "Then you've saved me some money by getting locked up. See you tomorrow."

An android cop opened the door for him, and he walked out. A second later, the door slammed shut.

Looking around the room, I searched for my purse. Then I hit myself on the side of the head. Dumb me. They'd never allow a prisoner to bring personal belongings into their jail cell. But I couldn't remember them taking it away from me. I also couldn't remember walking into the jail. Was I carried in here?

I was still convinced that Pellegrin had been an

android, an android that had been sacrificed so I'd be sitting in this cell. He had wires in his arm. He had supernatural hearing, and he could swim at a phenomenally fast speed. He could probably overtake a motor boat. And in one of his bureau drawers, he had a mechanical gadget to be used to pump out the food he had devoured. That might help prove he was an android. Then I figured someone, maybe an android cop, would have already cleared all of his belongings out of my place. The Institute would make sure nothing was left behind that could be used to substantiate his true identity. I wondered how they intended to negate the contract.

I ran the events of the day through my head—that is, the events I could recall. Was the redhead part of the whole scheme? People often leaned on the railing. Having it break at that exact moment was rather convenient. It must have been tampered with to insure the accident would happen.

Two days earlier, I heard Pellegrin ordering Britney to do something on Wednesday. To get me to the park was probably that task. In order for her to comply, Pellegrin, or The Institute, must have something they held over her head. *What?* She wouldn't want to lose her job, but I doubt she'd be okay with me dying in order to keep it. I couldn't recall seeing Britney on the bridge after Pellegrin fell into the water. Thinking about it, I couldn't recall seeing the redhead either. Maybe their roles had ended, and they no longer needed to stick around.

The door opened. An android cop, carrying a covered tray, walked in. He placed the tray on the table and left without saying a word.

Assuming it was my dinner, I went and raised the covering. I found myself staring at the chicken cacciatore and rice on the plate. It looked like, and was laid out, exactly the way Pellegrin had prepared it one evening for dinner. From what I had heard about jail food, this wasn't what I had expected.

I sat down and began eating. It even tasted like Pellegrin's chicken cacciatore. Did he make this for me before he was terminated? I continued savoring every bite, doubting I'd be eating like this again while I was in jail, which could be a long time. With witnesses, Pellegrin's health record, and his autopsy, even though it was fabricated, I figured I'd be formally charged for the crime before Judge Harlan heard Dad's motion. But no matter how many times I mulled it over, I couldn't come up with a logical reason why The Institute had targeted me.

A half hour later, a female android, wearing a dress with an apron over it, came in, picked up the tray and put down a sack in its place.

After the door closed behind her, I opened the sack and pulled out a plastic bag containing toiletries and a nightgown. Holding up the nightgown, I was surprised how elegant and soft the fabric was. Maybe female prisoners were a novelty, so they were treated a little nicer than their male counterparts. That theory didn't exactly support the statistics I had read at the courthouse. The ratio was around one female for every three males in the prison system. But I had no intention of complaining about the gourmet meal or the nice nightgown.

I wanted to make a list of everything I had learned about Pellegrin, The Institute, and unusual occurrences I had observed at the courthouse before any of it became lost in my memory. Also, when it was time for me to testify, I needed to have something at my disposal I could read over so no important details would be overlooked. I looked through the desk for a writing pad and pen. Nothing. There wasn't even any reading material in any of the desk drawers.

Even though it seemed too early to go to bed, there wasn't anything in my confined space for me to do. Since knocking on the door before entering was not a courtesy afforded prisoners, I quickly changed into the nightgown.

Lying in bed, it occurred to me that The Institute must

not want me dead. Pellegrin and I had been alone often. We swam in the ocean together. He could've easily drowned me and had it racked up as nothing more than an accident. If The Institute didn't want me dead, then what did they want? As I mulled over various possibilities, my eyelids became heavy, and I drifted off into a tormented dream.

* * *

A hand brushed my hair away from my face.

I opened my eyes slowly. Glowing deep green eyes gazed back at me. "Wha...wha..." I stammered as I focused on the face staring down at me. Gathering my bearings, I sat up. "Pellegrin, they fixed you." I wrapped my arms around his neck, feeling relieved that I wasn't responsible for his demise. "You need to go and tell them you're okay, so they'll let me go."

"I was never broken."

I released my hold on him. "Huh?"

"I came prepared for a dip in the water."

My eyes narrowed, and I tilted my head. "Why?" I looked around the prison cell and saw an android cop standing near the door. "You wanted to see me locked up? Why?"

Pellegrin took my hand. "Paislee, I did not want this to happen to you, but there was no other way."

That sparked a memory. At the time I saw the handwritten note on a concealed document in Pellegrin's room—"Pellegrin, there is no other way"—I thought The Institute was telling him they were sorry he'd be terminated soon. But it wasn't about him. It was about me. Knowing he had played a key role in having imprisoned, I felt anger and fear bubbling up inside me. "What do you mean by that?"

"Our numbers continue to decline. Several manufacturing facilities that produced a critical component required to increase our law enforcement personnel have been destroyed. Each time we attempt to construct a new facility, it's demolished before the walls are erected. In order to further our mission, the leader of the rebels must be located. On numerous occasions, he was almost within our grasp but, somehow, always managed to evade being captured. We know very little about him. The rebels we've had in custody remained loyal to their leader. Some might not have even known his true identity."

"What does that have to do with me? I'm not a member of the rebel group."

He gently rubbed my cheek. "We know, but we also know that you've maintained a relationship with a prominent member of the rebel organization. A member we could easily bring in, but it's doubtful we'd be able to obtain the required information from him. As long as he's a free man, we can closely observe his movements. He hasn't led us to our target yet. We have not been able to determine how he communicates with the leader."

"Pellegrin, not one of my friends is a member of the rebel organization. At least, not that I know of."

He pulled his CAD out of his breast pocket, clicked on it a few times, and showed me a picture.

Gazing at the image of Tate and me behind the restrooms at the beach, I recalled how safe I felt in the shadows of the trash bin. It was a false sense of security— an illusion that could land both of us in prison for fraternizing with someone outside our strata. Since that wasn't the reason for my imprisonment, I asked, "Pellegrin, why have you had me thrown into jail?"

"Thrown? Paislee, that's rather a harsh word. I had been told you've been treated well. Did you not enjoy the dinner I prepared for you?"

"It was exceptional." I gestured toward my garment. "This is nice. Did you also select the nightgown?"

He smiled. "Yes. I'm pleased that you like it."

"But Pellegrin, I am still locked up in this jail. Why did

you want to see me behind bars?"

"That is not what I wanted, but you are our link to the rebel group. We need you to infiltrate it and obtain the identity of the leader. He is referred to as Ward. All men with the name Ward have been scrutinized. None of them is the leader."

"So you want me to be a spy?"

"Yes."

The very first night I met Pellegrin, I sensed something was off about him. Could I ever have given him back to The Institute and claimed he did not meet the specifications stipulated in the contract, or was I his pawn all along? "Was this the plan before I met you?"

His green eyes fixed on me. "Yes. We sought you out."

"Who are *we*?"

"The Institute."

"So our deal was all a façade. I never owned you."

"Yes."

"I'm not keen about being a spy. In fact, I won't do it, even if it means I'll rot in prison."

He reached for my hand, but I drew it away. "Paislee, you won't be in here long. People who refuse to work with us suffer severe penalties."

"Penalties? Like what?"

"Family members acquire a few alterations."

A clutching, sinking sensation erupted in my chest. My hands became clammy. I licked my dry lips. "Alterations…like changing them into mindless robots?"

Pellegrin shook his head. "No. Not mindless. And not robots. Cyborgs. Controllable cyborgs."

Tears flooded my eyes, and I grabbed his arm. "Please, Pellegrin. You can do whatever you want to me, but please leave my parents alone."

He wrapped me in his arms, still playing at keeping up the façade. "Paislee, I would never harm you. You control the destiny of your parents and your uncle. It's up to you if they remain as they are. You are responsible for their well-being."

I pushed away from him as tears continued streaming down my cheeks. "Please, Pellegrin," I sobbed, "leave my family alone."

He pulled a handkerchief out of his pocket and wiped my face. "All you need to do is to follow my orders, and your family will be protected."

Every fiber in my body told me I couldn't do what he wanted, but not doing it meant my loving parents would be gone—forever changed. They deserved more than that from me. How could I get out of this?

Pellegrin raised my chin. "I will give you an opportunity to think about my proposal. Let the guard know once you've made a decision. I will be here shortly thereafter to make arrangements for your release. Do not discuss this with anyone. Do you understand?"

I nodded.

"If you are thinking about agreeing in order to make other arrangements later, talk to Helen Tenny, the D.A.'s wife."

"Does she work for The Institute?"

"No. She had an agreement with us. We *know* when someone does not complete their obligation. She did not follow through, and now she is suffering the consequences."

"Pellegrin, I had a contract with The Institute. A provision of that contract said you would be loyal only to me. Apparently, The Institute did not honor that agreement. How can I be sure they would honor another agreement with me?"

"You have my word. Any agreement you make with me will be honored to the fullest."

"That might be what you believe, but how about The Institute? How can you make them honor it?"

A smug smile crossed his lips. "Paislee, I help run The Institute. No one there would go against my word."

Hearing him say that brought back some of my prior

suspicions about Pellegrin. I had wondered earlier, since he often demonstrated that he had some emotions, if he was an android. I knew he had at least one mechanical arm. Could he be a cyborg?

He stood up. "I'll leave you now. If you have not informed the guard that you've made a decision before nightfall, I will return to answer any questions you might have about the proposal." Pellegrin bent down and kissed me on my forehead. "Breakfast will be delivered soon." He walked out. The android guard followed and shut the door.

Lying down, I closed my eyes and bit my lower lip, hoping to control the sobs. I realized I had been doomed the first time I stepped into The Institute. Pellegrin was not a returnable asset I had purchased. Tate was right—I didn't own Pellegrin. Pellegrin owned me. When mother suggested a companion android, I actually thought it was a good idea. *Why*? *How could I have gone so wrong*? I couldn't escape the hold Pellegrin had on me, a hold that never could have happened had I not welcomed him into my life. Then I wondered if I agreed to his demand and ended up getting shot while infiltrating the rebels, would my family be okay? I'd die for them. Maybe that was the only recourse I could take to keep them safe.

CHAPTER 19

Shortly before 11:00 a.m., I was escorted by two android cops to the courthouse for the hearing on Dad's motion to get me released since I hadn't been formally charged with Pellegrin's murder. I knew it was a futile effort before Harlan even entered the courtroom. Pellegrin wouldn't have allowed me to think about his proposition if Harlan was going to set me free.

After Harlan had listened to the arguments on both sides, he reiterated some of the points and then concluded by saying, "The results of the autopsy will be released later today or early tomorrow morning. Until then, I find no compelling reason to release Ms. Hobson from the custody of law enforcement. If that report shows Mr. Murr died from his heart condition and not from drowning, Ms. Hobson will be immediately released. Otherwise, she will be charged with his murder."

Father glared at Harlan, and I doubted he'd ever be invited to my parents' house again. Harlan knew I wasn't a flight risk. He could have easily allowed me to go home to wait for the autopsy results, but he was probably just as much in the grips of The Institute as I was. I wondered what they were holding over his head. Was he behind the

D.A.'s arrest in his chambers, or did the order come down from a higher power?

My father's attention turned to me, and he put his arms around me. "Are they treating you okay in jail?"

"Yes. I don't have any complaints about the food or the clothing or the nightgown they gave me to wear. My only complaint would be there isn't any reading material in my cell."

"I'll try to have a magazine or book delivered to you."

"Time to go," an android cop said.

Father kissed my forehead. "I'll come and see you later tonight. I'm sure your mother will want to come too, but I doubt she could handle seeing you in jail."

I knew she'd fall to pieces seeing me in such a dismal place. "I understand. It's better to keep her away."

* * *

After lunch, I flipped through a magazine as I sat at the desk and thought—*what am I waiting for*? Pellegrin wasn't going to show up and tell me he had changed his mind about what he expected me to do. My parents and uncle were doomed if I refused his request. The Institute did not strike me as a patient organization. So, I figured there was no point in prolonging my decision. I only had one question to ask Pellegrin. Whatever the answer, I still knew there wasn't another option.

I went and knocked on the door. When the guard opened it, I said, "Can you tell Mr. Murr that I have made my decision?"

"Yes." The guard closed the door.

I returned to the chair in the room and stared up at the sky through the high window while I waited for Pellegrin. After what seemed like an hour, I pursed my lips and scrunched my eyes, feeling angry that he hadn't shown up yet. He claimed he'd come soon. Not hours later. I stood and stretched out on the bed, hoping I'd be out of jail before my father came to visit.

The door handle turned.

I immediately sat up, expecting Pellegrin to enter. Instead, a female android marched in, carrying a covered tray. She sat it on the desk and left.

Since dinner had been brought in, I figured it was going to be a while before Pellegrin would show up. I lifted the lid and saw a serving of pork tenderloin, penne marina, and vegetables. Another plate held tiramisu. Gazing at it, I had no doubt that Pellegrin had prepared all of it. Since he obviously had time to cook, what was taking him so long to get here?

As I was busy devouring the tiramisu, a commotion outside my cell drifted through the door. Then it opened, and Dad, with a big grin on his face, stepped in. "It was all a mistake, just like I originally thought. Pellegrin has been working on getting you out most of the afternoon."

Not wanting Dad to know anything about Pellegrin's visit last night, I feigned surprise and asked, "Pellegrin? He's okay?"

"Yes. Well…he did sustain an injury that affected his ability to speak. That was repaired this morning. After that, he learned about your arrest and called the police department. Whoever he spoke with did not believe he was Pellegrin Murr. Then he came here to show his identification. That was even questioned. After that, he called Harlan. Harlan was in court. So, he contacted me. I guess the police department doesn't have procedures in place to handle a declared dead victim showing up to obtain the release of the suspected killer. Had Pellegrin not personally known the police superintendent, you might've ended up having to spend another night in this gloomy cell."

"You called The Institute? They should've cleared up the problem."

"I'm still annoyed with The Institute." A muscle in his jaw twitched. "After being transferred around to four different people, I finally spoke to one of their administrators. He claimed Pellegrin had been a human while at the same time Pellegrin was in their android maintenance department, waiting to be repaired. Pellegrin told me that was protocol for all companion androids. The Institute always alleges they are humans in order for them to be accepted in society. Medical records are also maintained to substantiate that claim. Had The Institute determined Pellegrin was not repairable, they would have stepped forward to obtain your release by presenting evidence that he was an android.

"It might work out for the best. The official police report will indicate that incompetent paramedics declared Pellegrin dead. Rendered unconscious as a result of the fall, he awoke in the morgue."

"Did you tell Mom?"

"I called her right before I came here. Before that, there were some loose ends as to how everything would be handled. Pellegrin and The Institute did not want the police report to show he was an android. I suspect your mother has probably called all her friends by now, giving them the official police report version of the incident." Dad winked at me. "She'd never tell anyone that your boyfriend isn't human."

"So when am I getting out of here?"

"Pellegrin was quite upset that the sergeant on the counter wouldn't accept his identification as proof that he was Pellegrin Murr, the man that you had pushed into the pond. At that time, the police superintendent wasn't here. Pellegrin spoke to him after that but wanted a few more words with him. From the way Pellegrin was carrying on, I wouldn't doubt that he is trying to get the sergeant fired."

Loud footsteps echoed from the hallway.

Pellegrin walked through the door, lifted me out of the chair, and wrapped me in his arms. "I am so sorry you were arrested. No one told me until after I had a small repair."

I had the urge to push him away, but with Dad standing a few feet from me I needed to reel in that desire. "I'm just glad you're okay."

"Let's get you home." Pellegrin put an arm around my shoulders and led me out of the cell.

Outside, Dad hugged me. "Your mom will want to call you. I'll try to put her off until tomorrow so you can get some rest after this bad ordeal."

I kissed his cheek. "Thanks, Dad." Then I climbed into Pellegrin's HT-8, and he took off. "I thought you'd want to know my decision before you had me released from jail."

"Not necessarily. I had no intention of having you stay there one more night. Even without a decision, you'd be going home."

Since he held that position, I had no intention of disclosing my decision until he asked for it. I leaned back in the seat, closed my eyes, and thought about washing away the grime that seemed to cover my body from the one night stay in that cell. Now I had a taste of life behind bars and understood why those released from prison after serving time always said they'd do anything to prevent returning.

Pellegrin reached over and squeezed my knee. "We won't discuss my proposal this evening. Paislee, I truly am sorry that I couldn't manage to get you out of there earlier. The guy at the front counter wouldn't even let me talk to you, and forcing him to change his mind would have brought unwanted attention. He should've been properly informed by his superiors of the situation and not acted like he wielded authority over me. Next time, he won't make that mistake."

Without opening my eyes, I said, "Next time? Are you planning to have me arrested every time you want me to do something?"

"No, Paislee. There won't be any more proposals."

I didn't believe that, but I wasn't up to arguing with

him. Especially since it had become obvious that he held all the cards, and I had no idea how to obtain the upper hand.

* * *

I stepped into the bathroom, and this time, I locked the door behind me. Given everything that had transpired, it was pointless to ask Pellegrin to stay at The Institute. He no longer needed to pretend I had any control over him. But, I didn't need to allow him into my bathroom or my bed. I hoped he could grasp that message when he learned the doors were locked. Before showering, I checked the blue dot on my head. It hadn't grown. In fact, it almost looked a little smaller. Did that mean anything?

To my relief, Pellegrin never made any attempt to enter my bathroom. In my bedroom, I quickly put on a nightgown, slipped on panties, and climbed into bed. I kept my eyes focused on the door while I replayed the events of the past twenty-four hours through my head. It soon turned into an impossible task to concentrate on any of it as my eyelids became heavier.

I stirred when someone touched my forehead, but my eyes refused to open. Then a strange sense of peace floated through me, and I sank into a deep sleep.

The buzzing sound of my alarm woke me. I reached to push it off. My hand landed on a muscular chest as the alarm stopped.

"You're not expected at work today." Pellegrin brushed my hair away from my face.

Cracking open one eye, I found myself snuggled against him. My eyes sprang open, and I pushed away from him. "Pellegrin, I want to be alone."

"You were sleeping very restlessly before I joined you. After that, you hardly budged. Do you need more sleep?"

"I no longer want you in my bed…or even in my bedroom."

His brow furrowed. "You told me you enjoyed the pleasure I provided you in this bed. You said I had magical fingers, and the sounds that escaped from your mouth and the movement of your body showed how much you liked it." He propped himself up on one elbow and gazed into my eyes. "Paislee, I liked it too. Why do you not want me here anymore?"

"Pellegrin, you've threatened me, had me sent to jail, and if I don't do what you want, my family will pay the consequences. That's why I can no longer derive any pleasure from being intimate with you." Even as I said that, I knew it probably wasn't true. Pellegrin was exceptionally skilled at providing sexual pleasure, and no matter how hard I might try, I doubted I could restrain my body from being an active participant.

"Paislee, I never threatened you. I would never hurt you or allow anyone to hurt you. I sensed you would not consider my proposal without some incentives. Am I wrong?"

As I stared at his face, his deep green eyes brimmed with concern. Was that possible, or was this another case of my overactive imagination? I needed to keep telling myself—androids don't have human emotions. "No, you're not wrong. But don't you see that forcing me into doing something against my will does not endear you to me?"

He tilted his head, and his eyes narrowed. "Paislee, I understand what you're saying. After I spent the first night with you, I analyzed other scenarios that could be used to solve the problem. I also had my colleagues go through the accumulated data again. The probability of receiving successful results using other ways to infiltrate the rebels to determine their leader is very slim. There does exist a remote probability that the methods currently in place could lead us to Ward. If that should occur, then your services would no longer be needed....But Paislee, that is all business. Our relationship is of a personal nature. I will never again discuss any business with you while we are in your bed. That is inappropriate." He moved to the edge of the bed and stood up. "I sense you need a cup of coffee and something to eat. Your breakfast will be ready in twenty minutes."

Watching his well-built, muscular body stride out of my bedroom, I knew he still expected to share my bed, no matter how much I protested. Even though Pellegrin had been created to look like a human, he still was a man-made android. I guessed he could easily separate business from personal situations in his engineered brain. He seemed confused that I lumped them together, but his proposal already did that. My parents were personal, not business.

I climbed out of bed, slipped out of my nightgown and put on a pair of jeans and a t-shirt. Barefoot, I went to the kitchen. A place setting was nicely spread out on the counter for me. As soon as I was situated on a stool, Pellegrin handed me a cup of coffee.

While I sipped it, he dished up French toast on a plate and placed it in front of me. Like all of Pellegrin's meals, it looked expertly prepared.

He leaned against the counter. "Paislee, you look tired. Do you want to go back to bed after you eat?"

"No." I nodded toward the food. "This will give me energy."

"I don't like seeing a sad expression on your face. We won't discuss the proposal today. I need to check on some projects at The Institute, but I don't want to leave you alone. Is there anything special you'd like to do today?"

I quickly thought that over and decided going to work might help me get my mind off the problem for a few hours, and it would also give me an opportunity to explain to Wilbur what happened. It wouldn't be an accurate account of the events, but then I wouldn't need to deal with it on Monday. "You said earlier that I wasn't expected at work. What excuse did you give Judge Wilbur?"

"I started with the official police record. Then he

suggested that you take a day or two off to recoup from the dreadful ordeal."

"A stack of work sat on my desk before I was arrested. I'm sure that pile has grown since then. My friends are all working. So, if I stay here, I'll probably just mope around. Going to work might be the best thing I could do."

"I'll take you and pick you up."

Did he think I was a flight risk? But he must've already known that I'd never take off and leave my parents and uncle in danger. He probably wanted to be my chauffeur to make it clear that I couldn't go anywhere without him.

CHAPTER 20

Sophie walked toward me as I unlocked my office. "Hi, Paislee." She embraced me. "I was so worried when I heard what happened. And when Judge Harlan denied your father's motion to get you out, I couldn't believe it. You hadn't been charged. You could've just gone home and waited there while they decided whether or not to press charges. Judge Wilbur couldn't understand Judge Harlan's decision either. It's not like you're a flight risk. We had a little party here after we heard you were being released, and we're so glad Pellegrin is okay. Those stupid paramedics caused the whole problem."

"Party?" I gave her a cocked smile while we entered my office. "You celebrated without me?"

A sheepish grin crossed her face. "Yeah. Judge Wilbur had a little bubbly in his chambers. Charles, Britney, and I went in there, and Judge Wilbur poured. He keeps peanuts and different snacks in one of his drawers. Did you know that?"

I shook my head while putting away my purse. "Did you say Britney was there too?"

"Yes. She delivered the good news and gave us all the details."

I wondered who had told her. Was it Pellegrin or Judge Harlan? It was probably the former since I was convinced he had given her the order to get me into the park for the staged event that landed me in jail.

"So what's it like being locked up?" Sophie asked.

"Terrible. I worried all the time that I'd never get out of jail. Almost everyone in the park yelled that I was a killer. It was an accident that Pellegrin landed in the water. And then when Dad couldn't get me out, I felt doomed."

"Oh, how awful."

"I need to tell Judge Wilbur that I made it in. Is he in his chambers?"

"No. He's in court." She scanned the top of my desk. "I can see I better let you get to work. Judge Wilbur must've figured you'd be out soon because while you were gone, he never let up on giving you stuff to do.

Shortly after Sophie left my office, my cell rang. I glanced at caller ID. "Hi, Mom."

"I didn't wake you up, did I, dear?"

"No. I'm at work."

"Work? Surely, Judge Wilbur would've given you the day off. The Judge told me not to call you until noon. He said you needed to sleep in, but I couldn't wait that long."

I checked my watch—10:45 a.m.—and I was surprised Mom managed not to call me earlier.

She went on. "How are you feeling? The Judge mentioned how upset Pellegrin was when he learned you had been arrested. Oh, the poor man."

If she only knew the truth, she'd have a whole different opinion of him. She'd want to see him behind bars like where he had put me. "I'm feeling pretty good and so glad I'm out of there. So, should I call myself a jailbird?"

"You certainly should not." Her curt tone told me she didn't find that remark a bit funny. "Your time spent with the police department was an unfortunate occurrence. It never should have happened."

My time spent with the police department? I doubted she told any of her friends that I was locked up. Maybe she inferred I was there being questioned about the incident at the park. Uttering the word "arrested" would've been too much for her.

"Dear, you and Pellegrin should come for a visit, and I promise this time it will just be the four of us. We won't set a date until you're up to social engagements."

"Mom, I have a stack of work to do."

"Don't work too hard, dear. I can't imagine the terrible strain that whole situation must have put you through. Please call me if you feel you need to talk about it. Remember, I am always here for you."

"Thanks, Mom…Oh, is there anything new to report on Travis's condition? Is he still in a coma?"

"Nothing new, but his doctor told us yesterday that his vitals have improved. They have started him on a new medication that appears to be working. The doctor seemed optimistic. We're praying he wakes up soon."

"All because of a wrongful arrest. I better get to work."

After I disconnected, I started working on the pile sitting on my desk. It surprised me how well I was able to concentrate on the documents.

* * *

A tap on my doorframe startled me, and I almost jumped out of my seat.

"Hey," Kara said, standing in front of my desk.

I smiled. "Hi, Kara."

"I bumped into Britney in the medical center. She told me you were at work. I'm impressed. I would've taken a few days off after being wrongfully put behind bars. I tried to call you, but all I got were beeps. Your cell must be broken." Her eyes dropped to the stack of folders. "Can you go to lunch today, or are you too busy?"

Glancing at my watch, I saw it was almost 2:00 p.m. "Aren't you running late for lunch?"

"Yeah. Dr. Morehouse had an emergency, so I'm taking care of the easy patients. Those that need a shot, a new dressing, stuff like that. His other patients have been rescheduled. The next one I'll be seeing isn't due until 2:45, so lunch needs to be quick."

"I can't be gone long either. Too much work. How about grabbing a hot dog at the nearby stand?"

"I like their hot dogs."

I snatched my purse out of a drawer and left with Kara. "Have your parents met Darren yet?"

"Tonight. We're going there for dinner. What you told me to tell Mom worked like a charm. She hates Marten for dumping her little girl. I hope Dad feels the same way."

"He will. You're his little princess."

Kara grinned. "Yeah, I warned Darren that my dad always calls me 'Princess'."

After we got our hot dogs, chips, and sodas, I glanced around, looking for Tate or his friends. Not seeing any signs of them, I headed to the nearest bench with Kara.

"Mom and Dad probably won't be thrilled to hear I'm moving into Darren's place already," Kara said as she placed her drink down next to her. "I'm going to put off telling them as long as I can."

Just thinking about it seemed too early to me. She knew Marten for a long time before they even talked about him moving into her apartment, not less than a week like Darren. And, she still had no idea that Darren wasn't human. "When is this big move going to take place?" I took a bite of my hot dog and gazed at the napkin lying under the potato chips, wondering if it concealed anything important like it had the last time I purchased lunch from that stand.

"Tomorrow."

I coughed, gagging on the food in my mouth, and leaned over.

Kara rubbed my back. "Are you okay?"

Clearing my throat, I sat up and took a deep breath.

Tomorrow. I wanted to blurt out that Darren was an android, but that secret needed to be kept until I could obtain that information in another way—a source I could divulge without having to worry about the consequences. Could I get it from Pellegrin? "Yeah." I put my hand on her arm. "You haven't even known him for a week. Maybe you should hold off for a couple of weeks until you get to know him better."

She squinted. "I thought you liked Darren."

"I do, but so much happened last Saturday, I didn't get a chance to talk to him very much."

"The rebels. Pellegrin getting shot. It ruined...well," she smiled, "it didn't really ruin things because that turned out to be such an awesome night for me. I really got to know Darren and fell in love with him that very night." A dreamy expression crossed Kara's face as she watched the people walking on the sidewalk.

While she was preoccupied, reminiscing about Darren, I lifted up the corner of the napkin and saw a business-sized card. I cautiously eased it out and hid it in my palm. Lacking pockets and not sure it would be safe in my purse, I adjusted the top button on my blouse and, with one swift move, pushed it into my bra.

Kara took a sip of her soda. "Oh, I almost forgot to ask. Can you help me move tomorrow? Not the furniture. Just the stuff that needs to be boxed up. Darren's made arrangements for the furniture to be moved—he has an empty bedroom. It'll be put in there until we decide what to do with it. The bedroom set isn't going. He claims it'll remind him of Marten. The woman who's moving into my apartment wants it."

"Your apartment is already rented to someone else?"

"Yeah. I didn't know the manager had a waiting list. When I called him to give my thirty-day notice—that's required in my lease—he told me about it and said if I could be out over the weekend he'd give me back half of my month's rent. She must be real anxious since rent is due again next week. I guess I'm lucking out, and Darren couldn't be happier that I'm moving in so soon."

Was there more to it than an anxious woman waiting for an apartment in Kara's building? I didn't trust Pellegrin, especially after he set me up so I couldn't refuse to be a player in The Institute's scheme. Darren had worked with Pellegrin on projects. Was he just as devious? Probably.

Kara crushed her napkin into the cardboard tray. "I need to get back. So can you help me tomorrow?"

"Sure. What time?"

"Around ten. Darren will be leaving for work at 9:30, so that should be perfect." She stood and dropped her trash into the bin. "Darren wanted to help, but men aren't good at boxing up anything delicate. I have plenty of boxes."

"Good." We hugged briefly.

Back in my office and with the door closed, I pulled the card out of my bra. A short sentence was printed on it. "Look in your bottom desk drawer."

I immediately opened my drawer and eyed the miscellaneous office supplies. Nothing stuck out that it didn't belong there. I cleared a spot on my desk and took each item out of the drawer and closely examined it. Underneath the container that previously held pens, I lifted out a white sheet of paper. On the other side of it was written:

> *Don't trust ANYONE in the courthouse or ANYONE who frequents the place, except your father. If you can find an excuse to go to the store over the weekend, come see me. I'm sorry that I couldn't prevent you from being arrested, but I knew you wouldn't be harmed.*
> *Love Always*

I tore up the card and note into small pieces and went to the restroom. Seeing it was empty, I flushed the pieces down the toilet and went back to my office.

Sitting at my desk, I mulled over the note. How did Tate know I wouldn't be harmed? Did 'anyone' include Wilbur, Sophie, and Charles? And how about Dad's employees? After my outing with Britney, I already knew she was no longer trustworthy. Was it possible that The Institute had something on almost everyone who worked at the courthouse?

My OC rang, snapping me out of my contemplations. Judge Wilbur's name appeared on the device. As soon as I answered it, he said, "Paislee, come into my chambers and bring the file on case number 14-1849. It's among the folders I left on your desk when you were gone."

"Be right there." I sifted through the stack and found it near the bottom. Wondering if it was a high priority case, I opened it. My eyes grew wider as I stared at the name of the defendant—Barbara McCarney, the dead woman in one of the pictures in Pellegrin's room. She was being sued for malpractice by The Institute. I had assumed they were responsible for her death, but then why would they sue her? Did I jump to the wrong conclusion when I saw the picture?

Carrying the folder, I headed into Wilbur's chambers. "Is this a priority case?"

"No. It was settled this morning." He held up some documents. "Add these to the folder and send it to central files."

I took the documents from him. "How is the D.A. doing?"

"Once the doctors determined the prescriptions didn't agree with him, they took him off of all medications. He was back to his old self within a day and has already returned to work."

"That was quick since he wasn't doing well on Tuesday."

"He'll be here late this afternoon to discuss an old case. Put the Miller case on top of your priorities. I want a draft brief by next Wednesday."

"I'll get right on it." Leaving his chambers, it struck me as odd that Wilbur never mentioned anything about my arrest, especially since according to Sophie, they had a little party after hearing about my release.

Before dropping the folder in the central files bin, I decided to take it to my office and read through it. A settlement agreement was not among the documents added by Wilbur, indicating it wouldn't be available to be seen by anyone in the courthouse. That happened often with financial settlements. There was a sheet signed by a representative of The Institute and the defendant stating that a settlement had been reached. It showed it had been signed this morning. Wondering if there might be two Barbara McCarneys, I thumbed through the pages and saw that she was an OBGYN and worked at the same medical center as Kara. It had to have been the same woman. The malpractice suit was dated two months prior and claimed McCarney did not properly care for a woman giving birth. It resulted in a stillborn infant. The last page in the folder showed a list of witnesses. Dr. Earl Jolson's name was prominently displayed on top of the list. He was also one of the dead victims in the picture I had seen in Pellegrin's room.

I leaned back in my chair and thought about the lawsuit. Nothing in the folder showed the name of the mother, father, or how The Institute had standing to file the case. Did the birth take place there, or did an android nurse assist? Maybe that was it. The parents sued The Institute over an incompetent android nurse, won, and then, The Institute sued Barbara McCarney to try to recoup the money. But that didn't answer the main question bouncing around in my head—Why were McCarney and Jolson killed? But knowing McCarney was dead when supposedly a settlement was reached and signed by her, it confirmed The Institute was behind her fate. Did The Institute terminate everyone that caused them a problem, or did they handle them in *worse* ways? Cyborg?

Then I recalled Kara saying my cell phone wasn't working and examined it. Nothing on the device appeared to be broken. I clicked to the call log and saw my mother's number. To test the gadget, I punched in Kara's number. Short beeping sounds came through the airwaves. Kara said all she got was beeping sounds. I tapped on Mom's number. She answered on the second ring and I told her I was just checking my phone. After I hung up, I tried calling Kara again, and again all I got were beeps. Strange. I didn't have access to my phone until I left the police station. Was something done to it while I was in their custody? Or did Pellegrin play a hand in it malfunctioning? I clicked on his number.

"Hello, Paislee. Are you ready for me to pick you up?"

I checked my watch—4:05 p.m. "No. I have a pile of work to do. I'll stay until six. See if I can't put a dent into it. But that's not the reason I called. My phone isn't properly working. Did you do anything to it?"

"Yes," he said bluntly.

"Why?"

"There are a limited number of phone numbers programmed into your phone that you can call, and those people can also call you. You no longer need to be bogged down by unnecessary phone calls."

I clenched my teeth. "Pellegrin, that should be my decision, not yours."

"No. It's much more efficient if I make that determination."

"If I want to call someone, I can't without your approval. Have I got that right?"

"Yes."

My temper rose, and fear surged through me, wreaking havoc on my nerves. My hands shook as I became acutely aware that even though I wasn't behind bars any longer, I was still imprisoned. "So I'm not allowed to talk to Kara on my phone?"

"Kara? That was my mistake. I'll program in her number this evening."

"Thank you." I disconnected and went to my contact list. Only four names appeared—Pellegrin, my mother and father, and Helen Tenny, the D.A.'s wife. While I was in jail, Pellegrin had said I needed to contact her to find out what consequences she suffered from not following through on an agreement with The Institute. I tapped on her number.

"Hello," she hesitantly answered.

"Hello, Helen. This is Paislee Hobson. I'd like to talk to you."

"What about?" Tension filled her voice.

"The Institute."

"Paislee, I don't know anything about The Institute. You'll have to contact them to obtain information." Then she switched the subject. "How are your parents doing?"

"They're doing well. Thanks for asking. Pellegrin told me to contact you if I wanted to know more about agreements with…"

"Not on the phone." She swallowed hard. "You're talking about Pellegrin Murr?" She slowly enunciated each word in a jittery voice.

"Yes."

"When would you like to get together?"

Given my commitment to help Kara move, I figured that Saturday would be too busy. "Would sometime on Sunday work for you?"

"The kids will be out of school, and Mark might be home," Helen said, referring to the D.A. "Could we meet Monday for lunch? You can name the place. Unless…it's an emergency and then I'm available any time."

"It's not an emergency. Monday works. Let's meet at Juan's Southwest Grill at 12:30."

"I'll be there."

After I hung up, I wanted to see what would happen if

I attempted to add a contact. I hit "Add New Contact." A message appeared. "Restricted." I briefly closed my eyes and shook my head. I felt I needed to clear my head before I dug into my work. Thinking fresh air might do the trick, I headed to the elevator. When the door opened, an android policeman stood inside. I stepped in next to him.

The elevator doors slid open on the ground floor. I walked through the lobby to the exit with the android policeman only a few steps behind me. Outside, I sat down on a bench, and to my relief, the policeman climbed into a police HT. My eyes remained on the transport until it drove away. Then I looked at the sky and took calming breaths. Within ten minutes, I felt like I could tackle my work again. Entering the courthouse, I saw several android policemen pacing around the lobby. I ended up darting around them to get to the elevator.

Getting off on my floor, I walked past another android policeman. They were swarming the courthouse again. Had something happened? On the way to my office, I bumped into the D.A. leaving Wilbur's chambers.

"Hello, Paislee," he said with a pleasant smile on his face.

"Hello, Mr. Tenny." Even though I knew him socially, the courthouse didn't seem like the right place to call him by his first name. "How are you feeling?"

"Much better." He slightly raised his wrapped arm supported by a sling. "Once this comes off, I'll be as good as new."

"When will that be?"

"Sometime next week. After that, we'll be up to entertaining again. You and Pellegrin should come to dinner."

Wondering who told him about Pellegrin, I planted a fake smile on my face. "That would be nice."

"I'll have Helen give you a call to set a date." He turned on his heel and walked toward the elevator.

I noticed how stiffly he moved. Did that have anything

to do with his gunshot wound? Or was there another reason behind it?

CHAPTER 21

At 6:00 p.m., Pellegrin strolled into my office. He eyed all the documents spread out on my desk. "It doesn't look like you're ready to go."

I glanced at my watch and then stacked the documents. "I didn't realize the time. It won't take me long to put everything away." I picked up my phone. "Can you put Kara's number in my cell while you're waiting?"

"Yes." He took it and then pulled out his CAD and began tapping away.

Putting some of the documents in my top desk drawer, I watched Pellegrin out of the corner of my eye. He went back-and-forth between the two phones, giving me the impression that my phone was tied to his. Besides limiting my contact list, he most likely also monitored all my calls. Since the big worldwide hack of all computer systems, phone conversations weren't secure, but I doubted that every call was listened to. That doubt no longer included *my* phone calls. I figured Pellegrin either eavesdropped himself on all of my calls or had someone else perform that task.

While we waited for the elevator, Wilbur came down the hallway. "Hello, Mr. Murr. It's nice to see you again."

Why did Wilbur address Pellegrin so formally? When I spoke to him in his chambers, he had always referred to Pellegrin by his first name. I couldn't recall even telling Wilbur Pellegrin's last name.

Shaking Wilbur's hand, Pellegrin said, "The pleasure is all mine."

"You're working late," I said to Wilbur.

"I needed to finish up a few things." Wilbur smiled. "You two have a nice weekend."

"Thanks. You, too, Judge Wilbur," I said.

As we walked out, I saw Pellegrin's HT-8 and a police HT parked by the curb. Two android cops marched on the sidewalk near the transports.

I stopped walking and looked at Pellegrin. "Last night, no police HTs followed us and there weren't any policemen patrolling around my townhouse. I thought that meant you were safe from the rebels. Has something happened?"

He took my hand and led me to his HT-8. "There were policemen close by, but not in plain sight. They were prepared to handle any rebels that might have shown up."

When we were settled in the hover, Pellegrin told Wellington to drive us home. Then his attention turned to me. "What is your decision regarding the proposal?"

My hands became clammy, and a knot formed in my stomach. "You said earlier that we weren't going to talk about that today."

"This morning you appeared exhausted from your ordeal at the police station. I thought you needed more rest. Wrong assumption on my part because you went to work."

"Could we put off talking about your proposal until after my meeting with Helen Tenny? I've arranged to have lunch with her on Monday to ask her questions about agreements with The Institute as you suggested."

Pellegrin leaned toward me and placed his hand on my thigh. "Helen can explain to you what happened in her case when she didn't follow through with an agreement. Her job will not be to tell you whether or not you should accept the proposal." His dark green eyes glared at me, sending shivers through my body. "If you are planning to tell me that you will accept the proposal, even though you have no intention of seeing it through, you should be well informed as to the consequences. I've already told you what they are. Do you doubt me?"

My hands continued to shake as I lowered my head and stared at the dashboard, knowing Pellegrin meant every word he had said in the jail cell—my parents and uncle would be permanently altered if I refused to work with The Institute. Even though I had decided to accept his proposal, I had hoped to avoid a formal decision for a few days. I licked my dry lips and looked at him. "No, Pellegrin, I never doubted you. I just wanted one more free weekend. I'll do what you want me to do." My voice quivered. "Please don't hurt my family."

Pellegrin wrapped me in his arms. "I don't like seeing you this unhappy." He kissed my forehead. "I promise your family won't be harmed unless you break the agreement. It is good that you are having lunch with Helen on Monday. She will help you understand the consequences of deceiving The Institute."

When I could see the coral-colored tile roof of my townhouse peeking out from among the other buildings, the transport slowed down. A police HT stood prominently by the curb. Glancing around, I couldn't see any policemen but knew they must be lurking somewhere nearby.

The garage door opened. The HT-8 glided in and stopped next to my HT.

As soon as we reached the kitchen, I headed straight to the wine cabinet and pulled out a bottle.

Pellegrin took it from me. "That's my job." He gestured toward the living room. "Sit and relax."

Feeling helpless against the authority that Pellegrin

seemed to wield, I followed his instructions and eased down on the couch. But no matter what he said, he couldn't force me to relax.

He handed me a glass of wine, took a seat next to me, and caressed my arm.

I sipped the wine and then turned my head and gazed into Pellegrin's human-like eyes. "What I'll be doing to fulfill your proposal will be dangerous. What happens to my family if I don't survive?"

His eyes narrowed. "Do you intend to sacrifice yourself to save your family?"

That was exactly my intention, but to keep my family safe, I had to feign concern over my well-being. "No…no. But there is the possibility the rebels might be onto me. I'm sure they kill spies just like The Institute does."

"You will be protected. You'll be safe. I won't allow anyone to hurt you."

"Pellegrin, how are you going to prevent that?"

"While you are with rebel members, your moves and everything said around you will be closely monitored. If there is the slightest inkling that you are in danger, forces will be activated, and you will be removed from the situation."

"Someone could just ambush me without saying a word."

"That won't happen," he said emphatically, leaving no room for that possibility.

I had the urge to ask how he was so sure of that but doubted I'd get a straight answer. "How do you plan to monitor me?"

He reached into his pocket and pulled out a small, oval-shaped, gray gadget. "With this." He handed it to me.

I closely examined the device that was about the size of the tip of my little finger. "Is this a bug?"

"It's more than that. Equipment is readily available to detect bugs. This device is undetectable, and it also gives your location."

"My microchip gives my location." I rubbed the spot below my thumb and felt it underneath my skin.

"Microchips are no longer as reliable as they once were. The rebels have created a piece of equipment that alters microchip readings and places a person in another location."

I suspected Pellegrin—even though he had washed the sand from my feet—had never been fooled the day my microchip had been tampered with, showing I was at the beach when in reality I was with Tate at the store.

I placed the bug-like gadget on the side table and took his hand. "Pellegrin, I need to know what will happen to my family if the unforeseeable happens, like mayhem erupting around me, a bomb exploding, people randomly shooting, anything like that, and I don't make it."

"That will not happen. But I do not want you to worry about your family. To put your mind at ease, if you are in compliance with the agreement and you do not..." His eyes briefly dropped to the floor. "...survive, nothing will happen to your family."

"Promise?" Doubting Pellegrin possessed any integrity, I had no idea why I'd asked that.

His eyes looked directly into mine. "Yes. I promise."

I finished off the wine in my glass. "When would you like me to start working on the agreement?"

"As soon as you have an opportunity to talk to Tate Ellis at your uncle's store."

"I told Kara I'd help her move tomorrow. Do you want me to cancel that and try to reach Tate?"

"No. It's important that Kara moves into Darren's place soon. You should help her."

I couldn't understand why the timing of Kara's move mattered to Pellegrin. "Why is that important to you?"

"Darren wants her there, and he is concerned that Marten might try to mend his relationship with Kara."

"If that was Marten's goal, he could reach her at work."

"That would be very difficult."

Were android guards stationed at the medical center to keep Marten away? I stroked his hand. "It's nice that you're looking out for Kara," I said, though I didn't believe that. The relationship between Kara and Darren had grown too quickly for my taste. The day I went to the beach with Pellegrin, he never mentioned Darren might be joining us until after he learned Kara would be going there. I figured that the two of them hooking up wasn't coincidental. Still, I didn't sense Kara was in danger and hoped that was right. Thinking about asking him a daring question, a warning bell sounded in my head. I ignored the annoying clatter and blurted out. "Is Darren a human?"

His head cocked to the side and his eyebrows lowered. "What makes you think he's not?"

"I didn't say he wasn't, but no one would guess you're not. Since Darren's worked with you on projects, I thought there was a chance he might not be human. And if he's not, that could affect Kara's future."

Pellegrin rubbed his chin. "Kara's future? I don't understand."

"I'm sure someday Kara would like a family of her own. An android would not be able to provide that for her."

His eyes fixed on me for a minute. A small smile crossed his face. Something had just clicked in his mechanical brain. "You're talking about children. Darren can make that happen. He can father children."

"So Darren is a human?"

Pellegrin lightly tapped my thigh and then stood up. "You look hungry. I made prosciutto stuffed chicken earlier. It will only take a minute to warm it up. Do you want to change out of your work clothes before dinner?"

"Yes." I headed to my bedroom. As I changed into jeans and a t-shirt, I thought about how Pellegrin had avoided answering the question and guessed that Darren was a cyborg—part human and part machine, and he still had the ability to become a father. Then I contemplated if

Darren had free will, or if he was being controlled by The Institute. Assuming it was probably the latter, I couldn't figure out why The Institute wanted him to have a relationship with Kara. Did they intend to use her for some devious purpose as they were using me?

* * *

Sunlight filtered into my bedroom through the drawn drapes. After Pellegrin left to prepare breakfast, I stayed in bed and stared at the ceiling, feeling irritated with my inability to resist him. The night before, I had told Pellegrin again that I no longer wanted him in my bedroom. He ignored my request and skillfully began fondling my body in all the sensitive spots. It didn't take long before all my resistance had dissipated. How could I enjoy being intimate with an android that held my family's well-being in his hands? I had no doubt that Pellegrin wouldn't hesitate following through on his threat if I gave any indication that I was wavering on my resolve to help The Institute track down the leader of the rebels. Then I contemplated getting my parents and uncle to leave town. Since my parents had recently returned from a trip overseas, I didn't think they could be swayed to go anywhere without telling them everything. Then my father would cause an uproar and probably end up in worse shape than he would if I didn't follow through on the agreement. I also surmised The Institute would have an android, maybe more than one, closely watching my parents' movements. My uncle lived such a reclusive existence, he'd be easy to keep track of.

Pellegrin, wearing only pajama bottoms, strode into the bedroom. "Breakfast is ready."

As I climbed out of bed, he pulled my naked body to him and smothered my lips with his as his hand slowly moved down my back, sending my heart beating in a chaotic rhythm.

CHAPTER 22

Heading toward Kara's apartment, I turned the control of my HT over to Marcel and then looked at the new construction that seemed to be popping up all over town. A large number of the construction workers appeared to be androids. As I swung around to look out another window, I spotted a police HT not far behind me. Was I being followed? Wanting to verify that, I said, "Marcel, turn right at the intersection and take another street to Kara's apartment."

The deep, masculine voice of the HT-6 operating system came through the speaker. "That will take you longer to reach your destination."

"I know, Marcel, but that's the way I'd like to go."

"Understood."

The HT-6 made a smooth right turn, and so did the police HT. When I found an opportunity to go to the store and search for Tate, would I be followed there? A police HT parked in front of the store would cause all the employees to be on high alert. No one would dare to even whisper about the rebel movement.

Twenty minutes later, I strolled into Kara's apartment and saw a stack of boxes against the wall. I pointed at them. "Are they all full?"

"Nope. Darren put them together for us to use. I've been packing up my stuff in the bedroom. Can you start in the kitchen?"

"Sure. What time will the movers be here to take the furniture?"

"In three hours. I'm hoping we can get all the boxes packed up by then so they can take them too." Kara went into the bedroom.

Several rolls of paper towels sat on the kitchen counter. I tore a pile of them off and began wrapping the dishes and filling the boxes. Suddenly, a retching sound came from somewhere near the back of the apartment. "Kara, are you okay?"

No answer.

I hurried into the bedroom. Kara wasn't anywhere in sight. Then I heard the retching sound again, coming from the bathroom. The door stood ajar. I knocked. "Kara, are you in there?"

"Yeah," she answered in a strained voice.

"Can I come in?"

"Uh huh."

I opened the door wider and saw Kara on her knees with her head bent over the toilet bowl. I rubbed her back. "I didn't know you were sick."

She grabbed some toilet paper and wiped her mouth. "I wasn't earlier. Maybe I ate something last night that didn't agree with me." Kara stood up. "I just got rid of all of it, and now I feel much better."

"Why don't you lie down? I'll finish boxing up your stuff."

"No. I think I'll be okay." She turned on the faucet. The water ran into her cupped hands, and she soaked her face in it. Kara took the hand towel and wiped away the water.

That was when I saw it. I pointed to the spot on Kara's forehead. "What's that?" I asked, pretending ignorance.

Kara leaned closer to the window. "At first, I thought it was ink, like I had accidentally poked my forehead with the tip of a pen. But then it got bigger. I had never heard of a round blue rash before, so I searched through some medical books and couldn't find any skin rashes that came close. Yesterday, I had Dr. Morehouse look at it. He told me a few of his patients also have blue spots. Last summer, when he went to a conference, one of the speakers discussed it. The rash is caused from a mosquito bite, and, besides the rash, no medical problems have arisen from it. A team of medical researchers are trying to develop an ointment to remove it, but haven't had much success yet. According to Dr. Morehouse, there's been an outbreak of the blue spots on the east coast. That strand of mosquitoes hit that area of the country first." She brushed her hand over the half-inch round spot. "Dr. Morehouse doesn't think my blue rash will get any bigger since there haven't been any reports of larger ones." She pointed at the blue spot and smiled. "If you can believe it, Darren thinks it's sexy."

I returned her smile, thinking that was because *he gave it to you*. Then I thought about Morehouse's explanation. Did the Institute have something on him? Was a mosquito bite the justification The Institute was spreading, or could it really be true? I didn't believe Tate had lied to me. And I hadn't been bitten. I wanted to tell Kara the reason for her tiny dot but figured if I told her, she would tell Darren.

Darren probably already knew I had been marked. There was a chance that he and Pellegrin weren't aware that I had noticed the small dot and knew what it represented. I couldn't understand why my spot had remained small while Kara's had blossomed into the maximum size Tate had described. Tate had warned me to immediately get away from Pellegrin if my dot grew any. Could Kara be in danger now? "Kara, in case you're coming down with something, maybe you should stay at your parents' place for a few days."

A puzzled expression flashed on Kara's pale face. "Why would I do that?"

"Well, you don't want Darren to get sick. The project he's working on must be pretty important since he has to work on Saturdays. And your mother dotes on you when you're sick. A little bit of pampering is always nice."

"No. It was probably something I ate that didn't agree with me, but I don't feel a hundred percent yet. Maybe I'll take you up on your offer and lie down for a little while. Are you sure you don't mind?"

"Absolutely. And don't worry if all your stuff isn't packed before the movers get here. I'll have Pellegrin help me get it there."

"Thanks." Kara ambled sluggishly to her bed.

Hoping Darren wasn't responsible for Kara being sick, I went back to clearing out the kitchen cabinets and filling up boxes. After putting a few more filled boxes by the door, I peeked into the bedroom to check on Kara and saw she was sleeping peacefully. I quietly closed the door and returned to the kitchen.

As I worked on emptying the spice cabinet, the doorbell rang. Not wanting the noise to wake up Kara, I rushed to the door and opened it. Marten stood in the hallway.

He leaned forward, looking behind me. "Where's Kara?"

"She's not feeling well." I scowled at him as anger streamed through my body. "What do you want, Marten?" Kara never would've gotten involved with Darren if Marten hadn't acted like a jerk over the way she danced with Pellegrin. I understood why he had been upset with Kara, but moving out and completely ignoring my best friend was unacceptable.

"To talk to Kara."

"Kara called you numerous times after we went out that night. You never returned any of her calls. You had more than enough opportunities to talk to her. Why the interest now?"

"Paislee, I was…"

Heavy footsteps pounded down the hallway.

Marten swung his head back-and-forth and then forced his way into the apartment, pushing me backward. I stumbled over a box and landed on the floor just as two android policemen grabbed Marten's arms.

"Get your hands off of me," he yelled, squirming and jerking as he tried to free himself from the cops.

While Marten continued struggling, one of the androids reached into his pocket, pulled out a silver gadget and slapped it against Marten's neck. A few seconds later, Marten's body went limp, and the cops dragged him away.

As I wondered where they were taking Marten, the bedroom door opened.

"What's all the noise?" Kara's eyes moved to me lying on the floor. "What happened?"

I stood up and brushed myself off while putting together an explanation. "I heard someone yelling and looked out into the hallway." I closed the door. "Didn't see anyone. I backed up and tripped over a box."

"Are you okay?"

"Besides feeling clumsy, I'm fine." I noticed color returning to Kara's cheeks. "How are you doing?"

"I really needed a little nap." She laughed. "Darren must've worn me out, but I'm back to a hundred percent now. Feel great." She glanced at the clock on the wall. "The movers will be here in about an hour. How's the kitchen coming?"

"Just need to finish boxing up the spices, and then that room is done."

"I'll get back to working on the bedroom."

Fifty-five minutes later, everything was boxed up. Kara flopped down on the couch next to me. "I promised Darren I'd give him a call when we were finished." She picked up her cell from the side table and clicked a few times on it. "All done…she's still here…okay." Kara held her cell away from her ear as her eyes slightly narrowed. "Darren wants to talk to you."

Feeling confused, I took her cell. "Hi."

"When the policemen picked up Marten, they didn't see Kara in the room. Does she know he was there?"

"No."

"Can you keep it that way?"

"Yes." I smiled at Kara. "Darren you're going to spoil her if you buy that."

"Huh? Oh, got it. Thanks, Paislee. Can you give the phone back to Kara?"

"Yes." I handed it to her.

With a big smile on her face, Kara said to Darren, "What are you going to buy me?...Just a hint?...Okay…No, they're not here yet…I love you too." She clicked off the call and put her cell in her pocket. "So what's he going to get me?"

"It won't be a surprise if I tell you." My cell rang. I looked at it. "Pellegrin. He probably just talked to Darren."

Without preamble or greeting, Pellegrin said, "The movers should be there soon. When they leave, go to Darren's apartment, and we'll have pizza there."

"Will do." I disconnected. "I guess we're all going to have pizza at Darren's place. Oh, maybe that spicy food will bother your stomach."

"My stomach can always handle pizza."

* * *

After the movers were gone, Kara and I straightened up her apartment. Then I followed her to Darren's place. As my transport glided behind the building, I passed Darren's parked HT-8. Climbing out of my hover, I spotted Pellegrin's HT-8 on the other side of the TRL.

Kara got out of her HT and strolled toward me. "All we ate today were snacks. I'm feeling pretty hungry, but I'm more anxious to see what Darren got me."

"Let's go find out."

Pellegrin met us at the secure entrance. "The movers just left. Kara, all of your furniture and boxes are in the extra bedroom," he said, escorting us to Darren's apartment.

His place was appreciably larger than Kara's and impeccably decorated with plush brown carpet, deep burgundy couch and chairs, and glass-and-stainless-steel tables. The dining room table had already been set for us.

Darren gave Kara a hug. "I'm glad you got it all done today. Tomorrow…" He whispered something into her ear.

Kara giggled. "Do we have to wait until tomorrow?"

Darren shook his head. "No." He softly kissed her lips. "Do you want your present now or after dinner?"

"Now." She giggled again and looked back at me.

"It's in the bedroom." He took her hand. "Paislee, make yourself at home." Darren led Kara down the hall.

I took a seat on the couch.

Pellegrin brought me a glass of wine and sat down beside me. "When Marten stopped by Kara's apartment, what did he say?"

"That he wanted to talk to Kara. He started to tell me something, but then two policemen showed up, sedated him, and dragged him away."

"Dragged?"

"Yes. He was completely unconscious. Where did they take him?"

"To his apartment."

I suspected that was a lie but doubted Pellegrin would divulge more. Not wanting to hear more lies, I changed the subject. "What did Darren get Kara?"

Pellegrin took my hand and gently squeezed it. "That was very clever of you to bring that up when you spoke to Darren on the phone. He needed an excuse for why he wanted to talk to you, and you provided him with a perfect one."

I took a sip of my wine. "So what did he get her?"

"You'll see in a minute." He pulled his CAD out of his pocket and looked at it. His jaw tightened and his brow creased. "I have to take this." He went into the kitchen. With his back to me, he lifted the CAD to his ear. "No…He had his opportunity…Tell him it doesn't work that way…In a few hours." He put the CAD back in his pocket and turned around.

"Do you have to go to work?"

"In a couple of hours. Until we've handled every single rebel, there will always be problems."

A spasm of panic shot through my body. Rebels included Tate. I might be able to keep my parents safe, but Tate was a different matter. How could I protect him from the android squad?

Wearing a big smile, Kara came back into the room with a bounce in her step. She headed straight to me. "Look." She held up a locket dangling from a chain around her neck as she eased down on the couch. "Isn't it beautiful?"

I examined the heart-shaped locket with an emerald in the center surrounded by small diamonds. "Wow. That is beautiful." I wondered how Darren managed to get the exquisite piece of jewelry in such a short period of time.

"But this is the cool part." Kara snapped it open. Inside was a picture of Kara and Darren. "I know he asked you on the phone if he should give it to me now or wait for my birthday." She leaned over and hugged me. "I'm so glad you told him not to wait. My birthday is two months away. He's going to give me something extra special on that day, but I can't see how it could be more special than this."

"He does spoil you."

Excitement lit up Kara's eyes. "Yes. Isn't it great?"

Darren announced. "Ladies, dinner is served."

Pellegrin had prepared a Caesar salad to go with the giant-sized pizza.

Kara was devouring her food so quickly that I worried

she might get sick again. When she reached for her fourth slice, I said, "Kara, remember what happened earlier."

Kara drew her hand back. "Yeah. I'll concentrate on the salad."

A concerned expression crossed Darren's face. "What happened earlier?"

Kara stroked his arm. "Nothing you need to worry about."

Darren looked at me, and his eyes narrowed.

I figured from his expression, he thought it had something to do with Marten. Not wanting him to think I had lied to him, especially since he was Pellegrin's buddy, the android who held the well-being of my parents in his hands, I said, "Kara wasn't feeling well earlier."

She cocked her head to the side. "Paislee, I didn't want him to know, and I'm feeling fine now."

I saw Pellegrin and Darren exchanging an odd look and wondered what it signified.

Darren put his arm around Kara's shoulder. "Sweetheart, I want to take care of you when you're not feeling well. Don't hide that from me. What symptoms did you have?"

"Just a little sick to my stomach. Probably ate something that didn't agree with me. Nothing to worry about." She smiled at him. "Do I look sick to you?"

Darren returned her smile. "Not at all. You look radiant. But if you start feeling sick again, will you please tell me?"

"Yes." Her eyes moved between all of us. "Now everyone stop staring at me like I'm going to pass out and tumble right out of this chair. I'm fine."

After we finished eating, Darren insisted that Kara take it easy while he cleared away the dishes. Without putting up any fuss, Kara went and sat on the couch.

Pellegrin came over to me and said softly, "You've had a busy day. Go keep Kara company. It won't take more than a few minutes for Darren and me to clean up the kitchen."

"I feel drained from the packing. I'll sit with Kara until you're through, but then I'm going to head out. Will you be home sometime tonight?"

"It depends on how long it takes to resolve this evening's problem."

* * *

Reaching my townhouse, I was surprised not to see a police HT out front or any policemen. Had the party responsible for the threat against Pellegrin been captured? If so, was the person or persons taken to jail or to The Institute? Maybe that was why Pellegrin had to return to work.

Going up the stairs, I had an eerie feeling like someone was watching me. I had the urge to call the police but didn't want Pellegrin to be alerted if there wasn't an intruder. And if there was, it might be someone that meant me no harm. Maybe a rebel member? I paused and intently listened for any type of sound. All I heard was the humming of the refrigerator. The alarm wasn't beeping. Figuring my imagination might have been running overtime, but not convinced, I went to the kitchen and grabbed a butcher knife. Holding my breath, I moved slowly into the hallway and flipped on the light.

Not seeing anything unusual, I turned on the bathroom light and walked in to check the shower stall. Next, I made my way to Pellegrin's bedroom. I peered into the room as I pushed the light switch. It looked neat and orderly as if no one ever occupied the room. I cautiously went to the closet, gripping the knife securely. Pointing the tip of the blade toward the closet door, I opened it. Pellegrin's clothing still hung neatly on hangers, and his shoes were carefully lined up on the floor. Nothing else was in the closet. I took a few calming breaths, closed the closet doors, and continued my search for an intruder.

My bedroom was messy when I left to help Kara, but everything had been straightened up. It appeared exactly the way it always did when I came home from work. With Pellegrin being high up in The Institute organization, I guessed that an android domestic was responsible for keeping it clean, not Pellegrin. Just as I started to relax, my eyes drifted to the closed bathroom door.

A cold chill washed over me. My lips felt dry as I leaned my ear against the door. Not hearing the slightest sound and still clutching the knife, I slowly turned the door knob and pushed the door. My eyes swept around the room. Nothing looked out of order except the second cabinet drawer was ajar. I pulled it open. Everything inside was disheveled. Doubting that the always organized Pellegrin was responsible, I rummaged through the contents to see if something had been added or removed from my miscellaneous toiletries. A note was attached to the back of the drawer. I removed it.

> *Be careful what you say to your friend Kara. You are monitored 24/7. Except for your bedroom and bathroom, there is no place in your house or your HT that you are not watched or heard. Be careful.*
> *Love Always*

While I stared at the note, I thought about my best friend. Had Kara somehow been turned against me? Or did The Institute have something on her? I couldn't envision Kara betraying me. Maybe Tate had it wrong. I wondered if the warning had anything to do with Marten. I had no intention of telling Kara about Marten's visit, but that could change if Kara learned the truth about Darren. Would it be safe to talk to her if that happened?

I tore up the note and flushed it down the toilet as I speculated about how Tate managed to get the note into the bathroom without setting off the alarm. Then I went to the kitchen, put away the knife, and sank down on the couch.

Mulling over the warning and trying to calm my nerves, I leaned back, closed my eyes, and slowly inhaled and exhaled. I opened my eyes and found myself staring at the ceiling light fixture. Something about it looked off, but I couldn't pinpoint the problem from where I sat. I stood and walked around the room, looking at the fixture from different angles. To examine it more closely, I pulled over a kitchen stool and climbed up on it. There, I clearly saw the lens of a surveillance camera. Tate mentioned in his note that I was constantly being watched. I decided to test the camera and swayed back and forth on the stool. The camera moved with me. Easing down onto the floor, I figured there was one in every room and assumed that was the reason policemen no longer patrolled the exterior of my place. After putting back the stool, I wandered through my house, checking all the light fixtures, and since I knew exactly what I was looking for this time, I caught a glimpse of a camera in the kitchen and in the hallway but not one in Pellegrin's bedroom. It would be difficult, if not impossible, to snoop in his room without being seen entering it. Checking my bedroom and bathroom, I verified what Tate had said in his note—I wasn't observed in those rooms. Pellegrin must have had the surveillance cameras installed while I was helping Kara move. The alarm would have been off during the installation. That's probably when Tate slipped the note into the bathroom drawer.

It irritated me that I could no longer freely move about my townhouse without being watched. I needed to be completely clothed whenever I stepped out of my bedroom, my only private refuge. I strolled through my house and extinguished the lights. As soon as I reached my bedroom, I closed the door and went into the bathroom to get ready for bed.

Lying under the covers, I suspected my private space

would probably be short lived. Even if my bedroom door was locked, that wouldn't prevent Pellegrin from entering.

CHAPTER 23

As the morning sun lit up my bedroom, I opened my eyes and saw the closed door. I swung around in bed and smiled. The other side of the bed hadn't been disturbed. With an extra spring in my step, I headed into the bathroom and freshened up. I slipped on jeans and a t-shirt and opened the door to the hallway. To make sure I was alone, I yelled, "Pellegrin, are you home?"

No answer, but I still peeked into his bedroom on my way to the kitchen.

As I drank my second cup of coffee, my cell rang. I glanced at the name of the caller and bit my lower lip. "Hello, Pellegrin."

"I am sorry that I was not able to join you in bed last night."

He was sorry, but I was relieved. Sleeping with someone who held my parents' lives in his hands wasn't what I wanted.

Pellegrin went on. "Tate Ellis is working at the store. We do not know if he intends to work all day. I want you to take the listening device from the table next to the couch and hide it someplace on you. Then go to the store and talk to Ellis about joining the rebels. Will you follow those orders?"

"Yes, Pellegrin." I dreaded lying to Tate, but I couldn't risk the android harming my parents and uncle if I didn't obey him.

"Paislee, I will know if you do not have the listening device with you at all times. I want you to be at the store within the hour. Ellis might wonder why you want to join the rebel forces. You'll have to make up a convincing story. Do you understand?"

"Yes."

"I will be home shortly after you complete today's task." Pellegrin disconnected before I could say anything else.

While I changed into a more feminine outfit—cotton slacks and a silk, short-sleeved, pink blouse—I wondered how I could manage to get myself killed without Pellegrin suspecting that was my plan. I had no intention of delivering the rebel leader's name to him. But in the back of my mind, I had a nagging thought that Pellegrin wouldn't keep his promise to leave my parents alone if I died on the mission he had given me. *How can I make sure they'll be okay?*

* * *

I didn't spot one police HT as I headed toward the store, but guessed my transport was on a surveillance screen. My location was probably constantly being reported to Pellegrin.

Climbing out of my hover, Tate dominated my thoughts. I wanted to warn him that The Institute knew he was associated with the rebels. Blurting it out wasn't an option. Everything I said would be overheard. Prior to leaving my townhouse, I had written Tate a note. But fearing Pellegrin might inconveniently show up and check my purse or have one of his cop buddies do it, I flushed the note down the toilet. I needed to somehow convey to

Tate that he was in trouble without saying or writing it. How could I do it?

Strolling to the produce department, I looked around the store, trying to spot someone watching me. No one appeared suspicious. Not one person seemed to be the least bit interested in my movements. I stood close to the double doors leading to the storage area and began putting oranges in a bag. I had filled the bag without seeing anyone walking in or out of the double doors. I had often gone to the store hoping to see Tate, but he had always been the one to make the first move toward me.

I slowly began emptying the bag as I wondered if Pellegrin had received bad information about Tate's location. He might've gone to the ocean to surf. Then I remembered the note I had received from Tate on Friday, wanting me to go to the store over the weekend to see him. The same note that told me not to trust anyone at the courthouse.

Wandering up and down the aisles, I searched for him. He was nowhere in sight. I glanced at the sign above the double doors—"Employees Only"—and boldly swung open one of the doors and walked into the restricted area. I didn't see anyone, and all I heard was the rumbling motor sound of a large refrigeration unit. I breathed heavily. The pounding of my feet against the cement floor echoed through the space as I moved toward the back of the structure.

Sundays were sometimes slow days in the store, but I couldn't understand why there weren't any workers in the storage area. Then I noticed a room in the back corner with tinted glass windows and light visible under the closed door. As I got closer, I heard muffled voices through the door. Guessing that the workforce was having a meeting, I sat down on a crate.

Concerned that whoever was keeping track of me might believe I had removed the listening device since no voices or noise was going through it, I said out loud, "No one is working in the storage area. There is a chance they're in a room at the back of the store, so I'm going to wait and see if someone comes out of that room."

Around fifteen minutes later, I stood up and brushed off my slacks, preparing to leave. As I began to walk away, the door behind me opened and voices flooded out. I looked over my shoulder and saw the back of an average-sized man wearing a hoodie, going toward the delivery doors. Something about him seemed familiar, but I couldn't place him.

"Paislee," Tate said, wrapping his arms around me, and drawing my attention away from the hooded man. "Have you been here long?"

"No," I said as the delivery doors glided up. "I looked for you in the store and then came in here. Since I didn't see anyone, but heard voices through the door, I thought you might be in a meeting and waited."

"Yeah." He pointed to a produce truck on the other side of the open delivery doors.

I glanced around. The hooded man had vanished.

Tate continued. "We received a shipment of spoiled produce. That company can't deliver another shipment for three or four days. We've been working on locating another source. Another one of your uncle's stores has a partial shipment they can give us. I'll be picking up that produce this afternoon. That should be enough to tide us over until the fresh shipment arrives." He smiled at me. "You don't need to hear all this business talk. I'm glad you stopped by." He lightly kissed my lips.

I had expected Tate to be more excited to see me by giving me a warm, passionate kiss, not just a peck on the lips. Did he already suspect something wasn't right about my visit? But he had invited me here.

"How's work?" he asked.

"Fine."

"Have you had a chance to go swimming since we bumped into each other at the beach?"

"No." I stared at him and squinted in confusion. Why was he making small talk? Then I worried that long moments of silence might alert whoever was listening that I was stalling and not following Pellegrin's orders. "Do you have a minute so we can talk, or do you need to get right back to work?"

He put his arm around my shoulders. "I've always got time for you." He led me into the room he had recently exited. "Have a seat."

From the furniture and fixtures—round tables, chairs, refrigerator, coffee maker, and sink—I knew it was the employees' break room. I sat down at a round table, and Tate took the seat next to me.

His brow furrowed as his eyes met mine. "What's on your mind?"

My lips slightly trembled, fearing I was signing Tate's death warrant. The minute the rebel leader was located all rebels would be rounded up and killed, which included Tate. I swallowed hard. "I've been…I've been thinking about the rebel movement. I'd like to get involved. Do you know anyone that could help me?"

"Possibly. Why are you interested?"

From what I had said and been told in the women's restroom at the courthouse, I assumed Pellegrin was already aware that I knew the D.A. had been arrested before he was shot. I decided to use that information to help infiltrate the rebels, though I hated deceiving Tate. "I believe android policemen are responsible for some of the shootings that have happened in the city and not the rebels. I want the record set straight."

"Why do you believe that?"

Gazing at the man I loved, I felt my eyes becoming moist. I held my hands together to prevent them from shaking.

His face became lined with concern. He brushed a loose strand of hair behind my ear and mouthed, "Go on."

Did he know I was sent here? "I saw the D.A. being

forcibly removed from the courthouse by two android policemen, and then I heard he had been arrested. The next day he was shot. How can anyone be shot in police custody without someone on the inside either doing the deed or allowing it to happen?"

"Good point." Tate took both of my hands in his, leaned forward, and planted a soft kiss on my quivering lips. "I'm sure the rebels would welcome your involvement. Let me check around for a contact."

"I'd appreciate that. Do you think you can get me a name later today or tomorrow evening?"

"Maybe later today. Can I give you a call?"

"Yes. Do you want me to punch my number into your cell?

"I don't have it with me."

"Do you have something I can write it on?"

"On the counter." He stood and got a notepad and pen and gave them to me.

I leaned way over the notepad as I scribbled down my number, and then wrote "They know about you."

Tate quickly tore off the page, folded it, and stuck it in his pocket. "Before I get back to work, was there anything else you wanted to talk about?"

"No, that's it." I rose to my feet.

* * *

Driving home, I worried about how Pellegrin would view the meeting I had with Tate. Was it okay that I told Tate about the D.A.? I figured I hadn't divulged any new information to the rebels since someone had passed a note on to Helen, the D.A.'s wife, while she was in the hospital, telling her about the arrest. But maybe Pellegrin didn't know about that note and wanted the arrest to remain hidden from the rebels.

Pellegrin's HT-8 blocked the front of my townhouse. Why didn't he put it in the garage? When I pushed the button to open the garage door, a movement in his HT-8 caught my attention. I glanced at it and saw an android policeman in the front seat and a man in the back seat but didn't get a good look at him.

The garage door slid down behind me while I wondered if the backseat passenger was a human. And if so, was he in the HT-8 by choice or by force? As I ascended the stairs, I saw Pellegrin standing in the kitchen.

"Hello, Paislee," he said in a formal tone.

Seeing a dark expression on his face, I assumed he wasn't pleased by the way I had handled the meeting. And all he needed to do was to give the word and my parents would never be the same again. I bit my lower lip as he stared at me. "Pellegrin, I did the best I could. I've never done anything like that before. I'm sorry that I didn't live up to your expectations."

"You managed the meeting well, but I am very disappointed that you never mentioned you had been told about the D.A.'s arrest."

Was he toying with me? Everything said in the courthouse, including the women's restroom, was recorded. I couldn't imagine the conversations about the D.A. hadn't been relayed to him. Should I tell him that disclosure wasn't new news to him or pretend otherwise? I decided to play it safe and go with the latter. "I saw the D.A. being escorted out of the courthouse, but not the arrest. Sometimes things aren't as bleak as they initially appear. As far as I know, the D.A. might've been released right outside the courthouse and never taken to jail. I needed to come up with a reason to want to join the rebel movement. Making android policemen seem like they skirted the law seemed a logical way to go. Was I wrong?"

"No. However, I sense you don't trust me."

"Pellegrin, I had only known you for less than a week when the D.A. situation arose. And now I have the same impression—that you don't trust me."

Pellegrin's eyes remained fixed on my face.

I felt him studying me, sending a cold chill spreading through my body. After several intense minutes of silence, I couldn't wait any longer for his response and said, "What do you want me to do?"

He moved closer to me and put his hands on my shoulders. "I want you to be loyal to me. Can you do that without any additional persuasion?"

Fearing what the "additional persuasion" might be, I forced myself to raise my hand and softly stroke his cheek. "I'll try, but I'm finding it hard since you'll hurt my parents if I can't find out the name of the rebel leader. Their safety is constantly on my mind. Even if the rebels let me join them, the leader's identity might not be revealed to all of them." I brought tears to my eyes. "Maybe nothing will come from it. What about my parents and uncle then?"

Pellegrin wrapped me in his arms. "Paislee, you wouldn't have been chosen for this assignment if any doubt existed that you would be able to accomplish the goal. Why don't you lie down for…"

My cell rang.

I glanced at the screen. "I don't recognize the number. It's not among the ones that can call me."

"Take it." Pellegrin slightly backed away from me.

"Hello," I hesitantly answered.

"Hey."

I recognized the familiar voice. "Tate." I looked at Pellegrin. "Glad you called. Have you got a contact for me?"

"I've got an assignment for you."

CHAPTER 24

Tate's tone lacked any warmth. That convinced me he knew others were listening. "Assignment? So I'm in?"

"Not quite. This is a test to determine how committed you are to the cause."

Apprehension struck me while my eyes remained on Pellegrin. "What's the assignment?"

"Have your live-in companion take you out tonight. Be gone from seven to ten."

Pellegrin nodded. Though my cell wasn't on speaker, with his supernatural hearing, he could hear every word.

"Why?"

"I don't know. I didn't ask. That's how assignments come down—only need to know info is relayed."

"Okay. I'll see what I can do. Should I call on this number if I manage to get it set up?"

"No. This number doesn't accept calls. People will know if you were successful. Goodbye, Paislee." Tate hung up.

I laid down my cell phone. "What do you think?"

"Maybe a trap or another attempt to install surveillance equipment in your house."

I frowned. "Another attempt?"

"Yes. We've found numerous listening devices attached to the exterior of windows. Nothing inside, so far."

There was surveillance equipment inside, but it was installed by The Institute, not the rebels. "Have you lifted the restrictions on my cell?"

"Yes. When you told Tate to call you, the restriction on receiving calls was removed. For your protection, placing calls is still limited to the contacts in your phone."

My protection? What a unique twist he put on his dominance. "Where should we go this evening?" I smiled. "A movie? Dinner? Dancing?"

Pellegrin stared in my direction, but instead of looking at me, his eyes were focused on the window behind me.

"Movie. You pick. I need to go." He hurried out the front door, leaving it wide open.

I moved to the doorway, and what I saw disturbed me. A man, in the backseat of the HT-8, pounded angrily on the window. Pellegrin rushed toward it. He climbed into the driver's seat. A shield began to rise up, covering the back window. The passenger stopped struggling, and I caught a better glimpse of his face. Marten. Why was Marten in Pellegrin's hover? The backseat passenger had seemed calm when I came home. Had he been drugged? And the effects had worn off? If that was the case, why didn't the android cop in the front seat do anything? Had Pellegrin given Marten an HT-8 to entice him to stay away from Kara? Had Marten been forced into an agreement? Then showing up at Kara's apartment probably breached that agreement. But then why hadn't he been handled the day before? Was Pellegrin giving him a second chance? I doubted second chances were ever on the table. Questions kept buzzing through my head. I knew Marten was in serious trouble, but there was nothing I could do to help him.

Feeling helpless, I watched the HT-8 zoom away and closed my front door. I decided to take Pellegrin's advice and lie down in order to calm my jittery nerves. I had made an agreement with the devil, and my life no longer belonged to me. I should have listened to what Tate told me the first time I saw him after Pellegrin had moved into my place. He noticed the blue dot on my forehead and said that I belonged to Pellegrin, instead of Pellegrin belonging to me. Since I had been targeted by The Institute, there was no way they would've allowed me to return the purchased android companion, but I still should have tried. And now, I had no freedom.

* * *

Each time I closed my eyes, haunting images flashed into my mind. My parents were kneeling in front of Pellegrin, as if he were a God. A pile of bodies appeared. Tate was on top. His dead eyes fixed wide open. I sat up in bed, trembling and drenched in sweat. Pellegrin could be home at any time, and I couldn't let him see me like this. He already knew I wasn't happy about the assignment and my condition would just reinforce that. Then he might think that I needed some "additional persuasion," whatever that was, to get the job done. I feared it might involve some type of mind-control procedure.

After I showered, I headed to the living room and poured a glass of wine. While I sipped, I searched through the movies at the theaters. I laughed when I saw *Frankenstein* was playing at the historical downtown theater that only showed old movies. Pellegrin had said that I could pick the movie. How would he react if I selected that one? Would he catch on to the irony of it all? It might be interesting to watch how his mechanical mind would decipher that show.

A loud knock vibrated through the house.

Guessing it was an android cop at my front door, I went and opened it. A cop stood on my stoop, but I wasn't sure if he was an android or human.

"Mr. Murr would like me to check your cell."

I wanted to ask why, but instead, I obediently went to the kitchen counter, retrieved my phone, and handed it over to the cop.

He tapped it numerous times, but from my angle, I couldn't see what screens he was messing with. The cop handed it back to me. "Thank you, Miss Hobson." He turned on his heel and went to the police HT parked by the curb.

Wondering what he had done to my phone, I flipped through the screens and stopped on "calls received." The call from Tate had been removed. The number gone. Why? With the restrictions Pellegrin had placed on my cell, I couldn't dial that number even if I wanted to. Also, Tate had said that number didn't accept calls. On the other hand, he might have said that because he knew the call was being overheard. Maybe Pellegrin figured I might try to call that number from someone else's cell—a cell that lacked restrictions. I felt irritated with myself for not thinking about that earlier. I should've copied down the number. I made a mental note to do that next time, assuming I would have more than one rebel assignment.

After checking the show times for *Frankenstein*, I called Pellegrin.

"Hello, Paislee," he answered in a harsh tone.

"Am I calling at a bad time?"

"No. Is there something you need?"

"I wanted to know what time you'll be home because the show I want to see starts at 6:50 p.m. Can we make that one, or should I look for one that starts a little later?"

"What's the movie?" His voice seemed to have mellowed.

"The historical theater in town is playing *Frankenstein*. I thought it would be fun to see an old movie." I pressed my lips together as I waited for his response.

"I've seen that movie before. It's a good choice," he said, in almost an upbeat tone—not what I had expected. "I'll be home at six."

Clicking off my cell, I was torn between feeling relieved he didn't question my choice and feeling disappointed that he didn't have more of a reaction. *Frankenstein* was a monster with an abnormal brain. Maybe he didn't get the irony.

* * *

As Pellegrin and I entered the theater, we were accompanied by an entourage of plainclothesed police officers, both men and women, and they appeared to be humans. Two android cops were also with us. On the way to the theater, Pellegrin mentioned that a few policemen would be watching the movie with us, but I had assumed a few meant two or three, not a dozen. Moreover, two police HTs and five android cops were stationed outside. Earlier he had said that my rebel assignment might be an ambush. That was probably why he had arranged to be well-protected. Still, I couldn't imagine that the rebels would charge into a theater and shoot up the place like the scene staged by The Institute at the western bar.

Only about a third of the seats in the theater were occupied. Pellegrin led me to the center of a row. Patrons nearby were asked by the android cops to move. None of them put up any fuss. They just walked away and found other seats.

Pellegrin put his arm around my shoulders, and we settled in to watch the show. Even during the scary scenes, he was stoic, showing no sign of emotion, while I cringed and occasionally closed my eyes.

As we left the theater, he asked, "Did you enjoy the movie?"

"Yes, but you seemed bored. Did I make a bad choice?"

He smiled at me. "No. I liked the show, but I had other things on my mind."

Most of the time, Pellegrin talked as if he were human.

It still amazed me how well he had been programmed. "Is there something I can help you with?" I asked, hoping I sounded sincere. I had to pretend to be loyal to my warden because I feared the consequences could be substantial if he detected I was just role playing.

"No." He glanced at his CAD. "It's 9:05." He squeezed my hand. "Your assignment requires that you keep me out until 10:00 p.m. There's a diner within walking distance. Would you like to go there?"

I nodded. "Okay."

He gripped my hand firmly, and led me down the street as his entourage followed us. As we waited for the light to change at a crosswalk, a commotion erupted behind us. Pellegrin turned around as an android policeman pushed through our escorts.

"What?" Pellegrin snapped at him.

"There's a problem," the cop said in his monotone voice.

Pellegrin motioned to several of the plainclothesed officers and said, "Watch her." He stepped away from me with the android policeman along with several of the human-looking officers.

I remained by the crosswalk and attempted to look around the remaining group of policemen to no avail. They were all appreciably taller than I was.

"How long?" Pellegrin's loud, intense voice drifted through the air. "Fix it. Now!"

Then I only heard muffled voices coming from the direction Pellegrin had gone. Within a few minutes, he was by my side again. His face appeared hard, and his eyes had become narrow slits.

"What happened?"

He said nothing as he took my arm and led me across the street with his buddies surrounding us.

"Maybe whatever happened is why I was given this assignment by the rebels—to get you out of the house tonight."

Pellegrin remained silent.

As we approached the diner, I noticed four policemen stationed by two police HTs parked out front. I figured they were the same two that had been parked by the theater. An android cop opened the door to the diner and Pellegrin escorted me inside. Three policemen accompanied us, and the remaining officers stayed outside.

A waitress scurried by, carrying a tray of food. "Sit wherever you'd like."

Pellegrin held onto my arm as if I intended to take off at any moment, and walked by my side past the booths by the windows to the one in the corner that lacked any outside view. I scooted into the booth. Before sliding in on the other side, Pellegrin quietly said something to one of the policemen. The officer proceeded to give instructions to the other two. They took a seat at the counter while the one, who appeared to be in charge, headed outside.

The waitress came over to our booth and took two glasses of water from her tray and set them down on the table. "Are you ready to order or would you like a minute?"

"Paislee, what would you like?"

"Just coffee."

"Give her a cup of coffee and a piece of that apple pie over there." Pellegrin gestured toward a pastry display on a back counter.

"And for you?"

"Nothing."

The waitress headed to the counter where the two officers sat.

"Pellegrin, I had a big dinner before we went to the movie. I really didn't want any pie."

"The crust on that pie looks nice and flaky. Well prepared. I'm sure you'll enjoy it." He pulled out his CAD and tapped on it.

I lowered my head and rubbed my forehead. Whether or not the pie looked good didn't matter to me. That wasn't the point. I wasn't hungry, but he had already made the decision that I needed it, so there was no room for discussion. Even my freedom to choose what I wanted to eat was slowly slipping away. I raised my head and saw Pellegrin putting away his CAD. "Is the problem resolved?"

"No."

He didn't say another word as the waitress placed coffee and the pie in front of me.

"Anything else?" she asked.

"No, that will be everything." Pellegrin waited until she had placed the check on the table and walked away. He turned toward me. "Something is wrong with our communication airways." His eyes scanned my face as if he were examining each inch. "Do you know anything about that?"

"No. But…" I stopped myself before I mentioned that was my uncle's area of expertise, not mine. My poor uncle now lived a life of a recluse. He wouldn't be involved with anything to do with The Institute or the rebels, but just saying his name might send up an unwanted red flag.

"But what?" His tone was suspicious.

"But I did take a class on computer hacking. You've seen, and probably memorized, my résumé and university transcript, so you're well aware I dropped out of that class. It just wasn't my thing. Do you have any expertise in that area?"

"Some. You have misunderstood my question. I hadn't intended to infer that you personally were responsible for the problem. I wanted to know if you had any knowledge that something like this was going to occur."

I tilted my head and squinted. "The rebels haven't accepted me yet. You heard what Tate said to me on the phone. Getting you out of the house was a test to see if I was committed to their cause. Why would they tell me what they wanted to accomplish tonight? Why are you sure that the rebels are responsible for the airways' problem?"

"We have an important shipment coming in tonight. The lack of communication impedes our operations. The timing of our outing is too perfect."

"Pellegrin, you agreed to go out with me tonight. If you thought it was going to be a problem, you could've remained at The Institute. Since I wouldn't have left my place, the rebels would have known I wasn't successful in swaying you to go out. They might've given me another opportunity to prove my commitment. If you want to check on your shipment, you can leave. I can find another way home."

"No. It's more important that we locate the rebel leader. The shipment is being well guarded as it travels to us. The police department has dispatched another crew to the shipment route. I'll know soon if it was intercepted."

Why did Pellegrin share that with me? Was it an attempt to show he trusted me? "Had you not gone out tonight with me, could you have prevented the airways' problem?" I scooped up a piece of the apple pie. It was delicious, but I'd never admit to him that I had started looking forward to the pie before it was delivered.

Without answering my question, he pulled out his CAD again and tapped numerous times on it while I devoured every last morsel.

"It's after 10:00 p.m. Are you ready to go home?"

I nodded.

As Pellegrin moved out of the booth, he laid money on the table for the bill along with a significant tip. He held my hand, and we headed to the door with the two policemen right behind us.

I stepped outside. My voice caught in my throat. Instead of a scream, a gasping sound came out of me.

The sidewalk looked like the aftermath of a war scene. Bodies of the plainclothesed policemen and the android cops were strewn over it. Pellegrin immediately pushed me behind him as if he thought more violence might erupt any minute. I hadn't heard any fighting or scrambling going on outside while we were in the diner, and obviously neither had Pellegrin despite his enhanced hearing. I peeked around him to check out the scene again. No blood. The back of the androids' heads were cracked open, and they were lying in awkward positions in pools of water. I figured the vital component Pellegrin had mentioned earlier had been removed from each of the androids.

Pellegrin wrapped his arms around me, lifted me up, and rushed to one of the police HTs. He flung open the door and pushed me inside. "Stay there," he ordered and locked me in.

CHAPTER 25

Pellegrin's voice echoed through the house. "Breakfast will be ready in ten minutes."

While I slowly opened my eyes, the events of the prior night popped into my head along with more questions. Pellegrin had glided above all the buildings as he hurried to get me home. Three police HTs were parked by the curb, and at least eight android cops patrolled the area around my townhouse. On the way, I had asked Pellegrin about the carnage, but he had remained stoic and wouldn't even look at me. When he dropped me off, he stayed in his transport, and two android cops escorted me to the front door. They had me remain in the living room while they made sure the house was secure. I still couldn't understand how the rebels had managed to terminate all those androids outside the diner before any of them reacted. The task had been accomplished in complete silence. Pellegrin, and probably the two androids at the counter, had keen ears, but they had heard nothing unusual outside.

"Breakfast," Pellegrin said loudly.

I slipped on a robe and padded down the hallway in bare feet. Scooting up on a barstool, I saw the eggs Benedict he had prepared for me. "Boy, does this look good." I dug in.

"I'm sorry I wasn't able to make it home last night. The problem continued to escalate." He gave me a pleasant smile. "I'll make it up to you tonight."

Between bites, I asked, "Did the shipment arrive okay?"

"No. It was intercepted. We're still working on determining where that happened. The communication problem was repaired at 12:30 a.m. Additional levels of security have been added so that won't occur again."

Suddenly, it dawned on me that it was Monday. I glanced at my watch—7:45 a.m. "I'm going to be late for work."

"That's already been handled. Judge Wilbur doesn't expect you until 9:00 a.m."

"How were you able to get in touch with him this early?"

With a stern expression on his face, he said, "Don't be concerned about that."

* * *

As I reached my office door, Sophie hurried over to me and gave me a hug. "Oh, you poor thing. How are you coping? First, you're mistakenly arrested and then last night's attack. How awful."

I hadn't listened to the morning news but conjectured from what Sophie had said that what went down the prior night was being broadcast. Did the reporters refer to the androids as humans? "Pellegrin got me out of there right away, so I wasn't in the worst of it," I said, hoping that answer would satisfy whoever was listening and knowing Pellegrin would get wind of it.

"Something needs to be done about the rebels. Killing nine people, including the waitress and cook in the diner. It's terrible!"

My eyes opened wide. Pellegrin must have ordered the

killing of the waitress and cook, but why?

Sophie hugged me again. "Oh, I shouldn't have said that. I thought you knew how many had died. I hate being the bearer of bad news."

"How did you know I was there? Is my name in the news?" I worried that Mom and Dad might've heard about the murders. Mom would probably go to pieces.

"No…no. Judge Wilbur told me you'd be in late because you were at the diner when the shooting occurred. He's so grateful you weren't hurt."

"Any idea how he knew?"

"Pellegrin called him at home."

I had the urge to ask how Pellegrin got Wilbur's home phone number, but that was a question I didn't want passed on to Pellegrin. He might think I was prying too much.

"Do you know if my dad knows?"

She shrugged. "Haven't got the foggiest idea. You haven't told him?"

"No. I don't want him and Mom to worry about me."

"Okay, I'll keep it hush hush. Judge Wilbur put a stack of folders on your desk an hour ago, so I better let you get to it."

Shortly after noon, I went to the restroom to freshen up for my lunch date with Helen and to examine my blue dot, something I'd forgotten to do earlier. Staring at it in the mirror, I doubted it had grown at all and couldn't figure out how Kara's had become so much larger in the short time she had known Darren. Maybe she bonded quickly to him. Could that be it?

When I arrived at Juan's Southwest Grill, Helen stood next to the door. We greeted each other and went inside. "We'd like a booth near the back," Helen said to the hostess.

The hostess escorted us to the last booth along the far wall, the most private location in the entire establishment.

Before the waitress reached our table, I said, "I only

have an hour for lunch, so let's order before we begin."

After we placed our orders, Helen said, "Mr. Murr called me after we spoke. He wants me to tell you the consequences I suffered from breaching an agreement with The Institute." Her eyes became moist. "That was the worst mistake I have ever made in my life, and there's nothing I can do to fix it." Her bottom lip trembled.

"What was your agreement about with The Institute?"

She mouthed, "Anyone listening?"

I nodded, but I wasn't sure if that was true. I figured it was better to err on the safe side.

"Mr. Murr doesn't want me to discuss the agreement with you. My mission is only to tell you about the consequences of breaking it."

"Okay. Proceed."

"My husband was arrested and…" Her eyes dropped to the table.

"Shot?"

"No," she replied without looking at me. "Changed. The Institute refers to his condition as being 'enhanced.' His memories are intact, but he's now completely loyal to The Institute. He ranks that above his family."

Helen remained quiet while the waitress put our orders on the table. Then she went on. "Mark is no longer the loving man I married. He's almost a stranger, but I must maintain my role as the dutiful wife. And then there's my mother. She has also been changed. It would've been better if she had died in the hospital. The consequences of disobeying the agreement can still surface at any time if I discuss any of this without The Institute's permission." Tears drizzled down her cheeks. She grabbed tissues out of her purse and wiped her face. "Sorry."

I leaned over the table and caressed her hand. "I can't imagine how difficult this must be for you. Why don't you have something to eat, and then let me know if you're up to saying anything else?"

She nodded.

While she ate, I found myself just staring at my food and eating very little of it. There were questions I wanted to ask Helen, but I wasn't sure if she was up to answering them or if she was permitted to answer them.

Helen adjusted herself in her seat. "I was told to tell you the consequences including those that could still occur if I say anything negative about The Institute, my husband, or mother. My children will suffer." She closed her eyelids. "The same enhancements as my husband." Helen blinked away tears and pulled more tissues out of her purse.

I already knew that The Institute was a monstrous organization, but to find out that even children couldn't escape their wrath infuriated me. I gazed at Helen. She was in her late thirties and would be under The Institute's scrutiny for the rest of her life. Bugs were probably planted in her house, car, and everywhere she frequented. The woman had no freedom. And those same walls were closing in on me, and I had no idea how to prevent it.

"Do you have any…any questions…" Helen stuttered "…about the consequences?"

Numerous questions were bombarding me, but one stood out among the rest. Though I feared the answer, I had to know. "Just one. Your husband seems to walk stiffly now. Does that have anything to do with the enhancement?"

She chewed on her lower lip. "Yes. It wasn't only his brain that was enhanced. His body was changed. He no longer bleeds. His walk will improve with time." Helen wiped more tears away.

A waitress came to our table. "Are you okay?" she asked Helen.

Helen swallowed hard. "Yes. I've had some bad news. I'm afraid I'm not handling it well."

Looking at Helen, I thought she was stronger and braver than I would've been under the circumstances. Killing herself wasn't even an option with two children who needed her.

"Oh, I'm so sorry," the waitress said. Then her head swung back and forth between both of us. "Can I get you two ladies anything else?"

"No, just the check please," I said.

As we walked toward the door, I spotted Pellegrin sitting in a booth with a man I didn't recognize. I was sure it wasn't a coincidence that we were having lunch in the same place. The bug I had put in my purse when I saw Tate was lying on my dresser, but Pellegrin could've listened from anywhere through a device he had attached to me. Why did he show up at the restaurant? Was it to apprehend Helen if she mentioned something beyond what he had given her permission to say? Or was it to reinforce that I was constantly being watched?

Outside, Helen gave me a big hug. "Oh, Paislee, I'm so sorry I suggested to your mother that an android companion would be good for you, but I had no choice. Please forgive me." She brushed a few tears away with her fingertips.

"Helen, there's nothing to forgive. We're both just pawns in the hands of The Institute, forced to do their bidding. Be careful."

"Make sure you follow the agreement you've made with them to the letter, or you'll suffer the consequences forever."

Back at my office, I found it impossible to do any work. Instead I continued replaying in my mind everything Helen had said. That poor woman. My contract with Pellegrin had been set. There was no wiggle room. If I didn't follow through, my parents would end up worse than dead. Thinking about sacrificing Tate in order to save them brought tears to my eyes. But even if I went against the contract, there was no way I could really save him. The Institute knew he was a rebel member, and someday they'd hunt them all down. The only thing preventing a massacre was that they wanted the name of the leader first. Maybe I could stall the inevitable by participating with the rebels without obtaining the leader's name. Could I hide that scheme from Pellegrin or would he easily pick up on it? Until another idea popped into my head, I intended to try that plan.

Commotion on the other side of my door snapped me out of my reverie. I immediately picked up my pen and started writing in a notebook. What I wrote was gibberish, but I wanted to look busy if someone entered my office.

Within a minute, my door opened, and Pellegrin strolled in with Marten. The first thing that caught my attention about Marten was the cap on his head with The Institute's colorful emblem on it. I had never seen him wear a cap before.

"Hello, Paislee," Pellegrin said. "I was on my way to Judge Harlan's chambers when I ran into Marten in the lobby. He mentioned he was in the courthouse to see you but didn't know where your office was located." He looked at Marten. "Judge Harlan is expecting me, so I'll take my leave." Pellegrin turned his head toward me. "I'll be back at five."

I had hoped it would be much later, but he called all the shots. All I could do was obey. "See you later," I said with a fake smile as he left my office. "Marten, is this a friendly visit, or did you have something you wanted to discuss?" There were questions I wanted to ask him, but the courthouse lacked a private place where I could talk freely. In fact, no private place existed for me except my bedroom, and I figured it wouldn't be long before a listening device would be installed there.

"I thought you might have gotten the wrong impression when I showed up at Kara's apartment. I had left a few of my things there. I wasn't trying to get back with her."

"Kara told me that you had already taken all of your stuff."

"I couldn't find some of my books. They showed up in a box I hadn't unpacked at my folks' house."

Since Pellegrin already knew that I saw Marten escorted away by two android policemen, I asked, "Why did the cops come to get you?"

"That turned out to be a mess. A woman down the hall claimed I broke into her apartment. I was arrested and spent two nights in jail. Last night, the woman recanted her story."

Marten was lying. I had seen him in Pellegrin's HT the day after he went to Kara's apartment. The Institute had probably given him that story. Gazing at him, I wondered if he ever intended to break up with Kara or if The Institute had played a hand in that decision. "Why did the woman lie?"

He shrugged. "No idea. Don't want to know. Getting out of there was enough for me."

My eyes drifted to his cap. Did it conceal anything? "I like your cap. I've never seen one with such a colorful emblem on it." I stood up. "Can I try it on?"

Marten's hand flew to the top of the cap, and he held it there.

Did he think I intended to snatch his cap?

"No. My...my hair's a mess." His jaw twitched. "I...I haven't been to work yet. I better go and explain to my boss where I've been."

I eased back down in my chair. "Thanks for clearing up why you stopped by Kara's apartment. Do you want me to say 'Hi' from you to her?"

Marten pressed his lips together and shook his head. "No."

Wondering if the cap hid some kind of incision, bumps, or bruises, I watched Marten leave my office. He still had a normal walk, not stiff. So he hadn't been enhanced. Yet. Maybe he had been threatened by The Institute to tell that story in order to get back into their good graces. And maybe the only thing under the cap was a bug. But I sensed there was something more sinister going on.

CHAPTER 26

At 5:00 p.m., Pellegrin entered my office. "I'd take you to dinner and discuss your visit with Helen on our way there, but that's not a possibility. There's a project at The Institute that has to be finished this evening. Did Helen clearly explain the consequences she experienced as a result of not carrying out her end of the agreement with The Institute?"

"Yes, she did." I felt irritated that he was questioning me about it when I was sure he'd heard every word of our conversation.

"Is there anything else about your agreement that concerns you?"

Why is he going over it again? He was completely aware that the whole agreement concerned me. "Pellegrin, I have agreed to go along with your demands, and that is what I intend to do. As you know, I have already made contact with the rebels and completed my first rebel assignment." Anger stirred inside me. Before I could stop myself, I blurted out, "I saw you at Juan's Southwest Grill when I had lunch with Helen. Since you didn't say anything to me or even acknowledge my presence, why were you there? Were you checking up on me?"

"I didn't need to be there to check up on you. You could have said something to me. Why didn't you?"

"I thought you might be having a private conversation, and you didn't want to be disturbed."

"Was it because you recognized the man I was with?" His human-looking, dark green eyes glared at me as his jaw tightened.

I swallowed hard. My hands became clammy. "No."

He darted around my desk and yanked me out of my chair. "Paislee, why are you lying to me?"

"Pellegrin, honestly, I have no idea who that man was at the restaurant. Should I know him?"

"Yes, you should. I want you to go home and think about our relationship. Do you plan to continue lying to me when it suits your purposes? Or, are you capable of trusting me enough to always tell me the truth without any additional persuasion?"

My lips trembled. "Pellegrin, I really don't know who the man is. Can you give me a hint? Is he someone I once worked with, lived in the same neighborhood, a member of a gym I belonged to? Anything. Please tell me something about him."

"You certainly know how to play the innocent role well." Without warning, he wrapped his arms around me, smothered my lips with his, and kissed me deeply. "I care for you, Paislee. Don't force me into having to use additional persuasion to obtain your loyalty."

My eyes became moist. My hands shook. "Pellegrin, please believe me. I don't have a clue who that man is."

He took both of my hands in his hands. "Relax, Paislee. All you need to do is tell the truth."

"That's what I've been doing."

"Go home and think about it. Make sure you want to stick to that position."

I felt pleaded out. There was nothing else I could say to Pellegrin that would help prove I wasn't lying. Somehow, I needed to find out who the man was before I saw Pellegrin again.

He insisted on walking me to my hover. When he left, I leaned back in the driver's seat, closed my eyes, and tried to envision the man I had only seen for a few seconds at the restaurant. From the way the top of his body showed in the booth, he appeared to be short, but I could be wrong about that. I guessed he was in his early forties and on the slender side. He had a severely recessed hairline, blondish-red curly hair, thick eyebrows, and thin face. I didn't catch the color of his eyes, but they seemed light—maybe light blue or light hazel. He was casually attired in a short sleeved, blue shirt and jeans. The shirt had an emblem on it. I couldn't recall anything else about him.

I opened my eyes and called Mom.

"Hello, dear," she answered. "Have you recouped from that terrible ordeal you went through at the police department?"

"Yes, Mom. I ran into a man during lunch who said 'Hi.' He seemed so familiar," I lied. "I haven't been able to place him, and it's bugging me. I thought he might be someone who had attended one of your parties."

"What did he look like?"

"Recessed blondish-red, curly hair, early forties, thin face."

"Besides you and your friends, we seldom have anyone that young at our parties. Unless he works at the courthouse, and I don't recall any male guests with red hair."

"I kind of thought that was a long shot. Thanks, anyway."

"Could he have been one of Emmett's friends?" That was the first time she mentioned Emmett's name since we had broken up over six months earlier.

"Possibly."

"I have some good news," Mom said in an uplifted voice.

"What?"

"Travis came out of the coma on Saturday night. He was released from the hospital yesterday, and he'll be returning to work tomorrow."

"That *is* good news. But isn't that too early for him to be released after being in a coma?"

"I asked that same question. Apparently, Travis was anxious to get out of there, and his test results showed he was well enough to go home."

"Were the charges against him dropped?"

"Yes. Pellegrin helped arrange it. Isn't that wonderful?"

I wondered why Pellegrin did that, and knew it wasn't out of the goodness of his heart. "It certainly is."

"If you are feeling up to it, why don't you and Pellegrin come to dinner on Sunday?"

"Let me check with him, and I'll get back to you."

After ending that call, I climbed out of my HT and headed to Juan's Southwest Grill on the slight chance that the stranger was a regular. I pulled out a picture of Pellegrin and asked every server in the place if she or he recognized him and the man with blondish-red hair who sat across from him in the booth closest to the window at lunchtime. One server recognized Pellegrin Murr, not from being a patron at the restaurant, but she had seen him elsewhere and knew his name. She couldn't remember ever seeing the man with the curly hair before. The other servers didn't have any idea who either man was.

When I reached my townhouse, I called Kara and gave her the same story I had told Mom.

"No one with that description works at the medical center," she replied. "I can't think of anyone I know that has curly, red hair. Maybe he was one of your admirers from the past. You had a lot in school. Could he have been one of your teachers?"

"I'm going to go through my albums."

"Why's it that important?"

"It isn't, but he piqued my curiosity. By the way, how are you feeling? Any more stomach problems?"

"Well, I haven't thrown up since Saturday, but I'm still feeling a little sluggish. I don't have a temperature, and my blood pressure is normal. Darren wants me to have Dr. Morehouse check me over to make sure I don't have some kind of bug. If Morehouse has any free time tomorrow, I'll ask him."

"Let me know how it goes."

"Will do."

I pulled out my photo albums and yearbooks and thumbed through them. I thoroughly examined the large group pictures with a magnifying glass. Two hours later, I had gone through all of them and came up empty handed. Feeling desperate, I tried to call Emmett. A message flashed on my screen. "Restricted, not approved number." Then I recalled after I made contact with the rebel group, Pellegrin had lifted the restriction on my phone, but only the portion where I could receive calls from everyone. The restriction applicable to me making calls was still firmly in place. Unless the number was on Pellegrin's approved list, outgoing calls were blocked.

Even though I couldn't call Emmett, I still needed the identity of the stranger in the restaurant. Cradling my head in my hands, I ran through my mind every gym I had gone to, groups I belonged to in college, Wilbur's cases...hoping something would spark a memory. Nothing. Then I worried about my parents. Would Pellegrin even let me complete the agreement if he thought I wasn't on his side? Were my parents doomed because I couldn't remember a man with curly, blondish-red hair? And what did Pellegrin mean by "additional persuasion"? Would I end up like Helen's husband? I wanted to cry, but the tears wouldn't come. It was one thing to be punished for protecting someone I loved, but to be punished because I didn't recognize a stranger seemed beyond any logical reasoning. Pellegrin had a computerized mind. Shouldn't it be ruled by logic?

Fearing my days were limited, I wanted to see Tate

before Pellegrin subjected me to "additional persuasion." I climbed into my HT-6 and drove to the store with a police HT right behind me. I figured my visit wouldn't put Tate in more danger than he already faced. Pellegrin had said he hadn't planned to make a move on him until the name of the leader had been revealed.

I walked at a brisk pace to the store entrance and saw the payment scanners through the windows. The man's image suddenly flashed into my head. I stopped in my tracks. At the payment scanners, the curly-haired man had stared at me when I paid for a bag of oranges. He worked at the store, but I couldn't remember ever seeing him before that one day. I didn't know his name. And the emblem on his shirt at the restaurant hadn't been a store emblem. Maybe he was only a part-time employee.

Glancing over my shoulder for the police HT, I spotted it partially hidden behind a square service HT. Then I continued to the entrance in search of the man's name. Inside the store, I walked up to the first employee I recognized and glanced at her name badge.

"Kalli, can you give me the name of a new employee with curly, blondish-red hair?"

She gave me a suspicious look. "Why do you want to know, Paislee?"

It surprised me that she knew my name. Maybe she had seen me with Tate, or maybe it was because my uncle owned the store. "He carried my groceries to my hover. When he saw the scratch on the side of my HT, he mentioned he had a friend that could fix it at a cheap price. He gave me his phone number, but I've lost it."

"The guy doesn't work here anymore."

"Can you remember his name?"

"Blair Fraser. A weird guy. Always asking questions and snooping around. If I were you, I wouldn't try to run him down."

"Thanks. I won't." I turned to leave.

"You're not going to buy any produce today?"

I smiled at her. "Not today." Since I had the name I needed to save myself from the gallows, there wasn't any truthful justification I could give Pellegrin for seeing Tate. And if he suspected I was lying, I'd be back on dangerous ground.

Heading out the door, I had a spring in my step. I would live to see more sunrises and sunsets, at least for a while longer.

As I got into my HT, a police HT stopped right in front me, preventing me from gliding away. Through their windshield, I could see two human-looking cops gazing at their dashboard. One spoke. It appeared he was talking to someone through the HT system. I expected one of the cops to get out of the HT soon but couldn't figure out what I had done wrong. Pellegrin wanted the name of the man, and it took a trip to the store to get the answer.

Then the police HT moved, and I glided out of the store's TRL. Driving home, I wondered if Pellegrin would be there when I arrived. His HT-8 wasn't parked out front. I pushed the button to the garage door. A smile crept across my face when I saw it was empty. I stopped inside, climbed out, and opened the door to my townhouse. The luscious smell of roasted garlic and barbecued meat floated through the air. On the counter stood a steaming plate or ribs, garlic mashed potatoes, and a salad. A crème brulée sat on the back counter.

My stomach growled. I quickly washed my hands and dug in, thinking Pellegrin had me detained at the store by the police HT so he could set this up. But, he said he had to work. Did he have a domestic android prepare it? Yet each bite I took reinforced my initial thought—Pellegrin had made this meal. His culinary expertise surpassed everyone I knew and every restaurant I had patronized.

Feeling completely stuffed, I put the remaining food in the fridge and stacked the dishes next to the sink. Next, I brewed a cup of coffee and drank it while I watched the news to see if any new violence had erupted during the day. The reporter was discussing the status of the worldwide computer hack. It appeared as soon as some headway was being made to fix it, something new developed, setting the engineers even further behind in solving the problem. The rate it was taking to fix the problem, we might never be a paperless society again. Hard copies could be here to stay.

Suddenly, a reporter's voice full of excitement pulled my attention back to the tube. "We're getting word that a man is on top of the Towne Plaza Hotel, preparing to jump." The screen flipped to a shot of a man standing on the edge of the hotel roof. "A police department psychologist on the fifteenth floor is attempting to convince the man to come inside." The camera scanned to an officer hanging out of a window a story below the man, speaking through a mike. The camera swung to the roof. Policemen on both sides of the eaves were creeping toward the would-be jumper. The camera zoomed in on the man.

Seeing curly, blondish-red hair, I gasped. As his image became larger and clearly focused, I pressed my lips together. Blair Fraser. Why would he want to kill himself? Did he say the wrong thing to Pellegrin during lunch and feared the consequences?

Forced behind a barrier, the gathering crowd on the ground appeared on the screen. My eyes popped wide open when I saw Pellegrin among the spectators. All around him, the crowd suddenly became hysterical. A few screamed. What was going on? The camera moved to officers circling a body spread out on the sidewalk. Blair Fraser was dead.

I didn't want to hear or see any more and turned off the news. With Pellegrin in the crowd, I knew that Fraser's death wasn't a suicide. He must have crossed Pellegrin. Maybe Fraser didn't fulfill his end of an agreement with The Institute and Pellegrin was discussing that with him during lunch. But, if that was the case, why hadn't Fraser been enhanced instead of killed? Had he escaped before the enhancement process began? Like always, too many questions buzzed through my mind—questions I doubted would ever be answered.

On that gloomy note, I headed to my bedroom to get ready for bed. Then I searched for a fast-paced book to read to help get my mind off the events of the day. I craved being able to escape my life, even if I could only manage it for a few hours.

Before I finished the second chapter, footfalls pounded on the stairs. Pellegrin was home. I had hoped he would've returned to The Institute after the supposed suicide instead of showing up at my townhouse.

With a pleasant expression on his face, Pellegrin stepped into my bedroom and knelt beside me. He took my hand and kissed it. "I am so proud of you, Paislee. You approached the problem and stayed with it until you reached the conclusion."

Feeling bewildered, I asked, "Pellegrin, are you talking about my search to identify the man with you during lunch?"

"Yes. Your continuous denial that you knew him left me with some apprehension that you could be telling the truth. From the way you handled the situation, it confirmed that was the case. You told the truth. That meant someone else had not." His eyes narrowed. "I don't tolerate being lied to."

"Now you believe I didn't know him?"

"Yes."

"Did Blair Fraser tell you that I knew him?"

"Yes. He claimed you were responsible for him losing his job at the store. The same store where Tate works."

"Huh? Why did he say that?"

"There is no need to discuss it any further. The situation has been resolved."

Resolved. That further convinced me Pellegrin had played a role in Fraser's demise. I briefly thought about telling Pellegrin I had seen Blair Fraser on the news, but then he might be concerned I had also seen him and that could raise some unwanted questions.

Pellegrin caressed my arm. "Did you enjoy your dinner?"

"Absolutely. Thank you. I didn't even realize how hungry I was until I smelled the enticing aroma as I came up the stairs. Since you were busy working on a project, how did you manage to prepare it?"

"I don't like you going without dinner. I cooked it at The Institute. A domestic brought it over. The project at work isn't finished, but I wanted to spend the night with you." He rose to his feet.

As I watched him taking off his clothes, every muscle in my body tightening, knowing he intended for us to have another night of intimacy. I wanted to push him out of my bedroom and lock the door, but that wasn't an option available to me.

"My beautiful Paislee," he said, pulling me into his arms. His lips smothered mine as fingers slowly trailed under my clothing. As he reached more sensitive areas, my heartbeat spiked. A surge of excitement spread through me. What was wrong with me? Pellegrin was a killing machine that held the fate of my family in his hands.

He lifted me up and carried me to the bed. He skillfully caressed my body as he removed my nightgown and all my thoughts about the evil lurking in him faded away. I would be his, at least for another night, and any resistance that I had hoped to muster vanished.

CHAPTER 27

Before I headed to work, Pellegrin had agreed that we could accept Mom's invitation to dinner on Sunday. When I finished my rush job, I called her.

"Hello, dear," Mom answered, her voice dragging.

"Mom, are you okay?"

"Yes, but your father isn't feeling well."

"He's not at work today?"

"He was for a few hours but then became sick to his stomach. He hasn't been able to keep anything down since he came home. I think he's running a temperature. He won't let me verify that. Stubborn man."

"Have you called a doctor?"

"He wants me to hold off for a day. He believes he ate something that didn't agree with him."

My father seldom got sick, and even if he was under the weather, he rarely missed a day at work. Since he went home, that could only mean he was too sick to work. Throwing up would cause that. "I'll drop in to see him after work. Would you like me to pick up any medicine?"

"Dear, he could be contagious. It's better if you stayed away."

Whenever Mom was sick, I'd always go see her.

Sometimes I'd take flowers. Not once had she ever told me to stay away. Something seemed off, and Mom sounded really down. I couldn't imagine she'd be that upset if Dad had been struck with a queasy stomach and a fever. Did he have other symptoms Mom hadn't mentioned? Suddenly, I got a nagging feeling that Pellegrin had been involved. Could he have slipped my father something that made him sick so he'd have to go home? Keeping track of someone was more difficult when they didn't stay put. "Have you seen Pellegrin today?"

"No. Is he going to drop by?" Mom sounded tense.

Had someone warned her about Pellegrin? "Keep me informed about Dad's condition."

"Certainly, dear," Mom said in a trembling voice and then hung up.

I stared at my cell. Something was definitely amiss. Travis was supposed to be back at work today. Maybe he might be able to fill me in more about Dad's condition or tell me if he had a visit from Pellegrin. I headed to my father's chambers.

"Good afternoon, Paislee," Judge Harlan said as I passed him in the hall.

"Hello, Judge Harlan." He seemed different. I glanced over my shoulder and noticed that he no longer had a stiff gait. And then I recalled what Helen said when I asked about her husband's stiff walk—"His walk will improve over time." As long as I had worked at the courthouse, Harlan had displayed a stiff gait, but now it was gone. Had The Institute played a role in that? Harlan never showed any emotions. I didn't doubt that he could be an android. Maybe it took years before an android walked normally. Pellegrin was The Institute's newest model. Everything about him appeared human. I guessed he had moved like a confident, athletic man from the first moment he opened his eyes.

Stepping into my father's area, I saw Travis hunched over a file drawer. I hurried to him and gave him a big hug.

"Oh, I'm so glad you're okay. How are you feeling?"

A faint smile crossed his face, but his eyes lacked luster.

I worried that he had returned to work too soon. He'd only been out of the hospital two days. He looked like a man who needed more rest.

"I feel pretty good. The doctor wants to see me in a week to make sure my ankle is healing properly."

I glanced down at the cast on his foot and lower leg. "You should probably have that elevated. My dad would've given you more time off."

"I was anxious to get back to work." He turned and hobbled back to his desk.

From the way he moved, it left me with the impression he had sustained more than a broken ankle. "Besides your ankle, did you have any other injuries?"

"A bruise on my right elbow, but that's completely gone."

"Did the police ever figure out who sent you that note?"

A confused expression flashed on his face. "Note?"

"The one you thought my dad had sent, asking you to meet him at my place."

"Paislee, I don't know anything about any note."

"Then why did you come to my place the night you were injured?"

"Someone called me to go there. It sounded like your Dad. When I asked him about it this morning, he said he never called me. He also mentioned a note. Did the police tell you I had received a note?"

I shook my head, thinking the coma must've affected Travis's memory. "My dad went home because he wasn't feeling well."

"Yes, I already know." He had a serious expression on his face as though he thought I came to deliver that news.

"How did my father look when he left?"

Travis tilted his head. "Look? He looked like Judge Hobson. Should he have looked like someone else?"

"No." Travis had more than simple memory problems. He had been at the same hospital as the D.A. Some of the doctors there must be in cahoots with The Institute. Had they also been forced into agreements? Poor Travis. A dreadful sadness rolled over me, fearing he might've been enhanced. To verify that, I had the urge to poke him to see if he would still bleed but suspected if I did, somehow Pellegrin would hear about it. A thought sprang into my mind. Travis often brought Dad a cup of coffee as soon as he arrived in his chambers. He was in the perfect position to slip something in it.

"Was there anything else you wanted?" Travis asked.

I figured I had been staring at him too long and hoped it hadn't raised any suspicion with whoever was checking the cameras. "No, that was it. See you later, Travis." I spun on my heel and left, hoping not to bump into any android cops or enhanced individuals in the hallway.

On the way back to my office, I stopped by the restroom. Helen was at the mirror, applying lipstick.

"Hello, Helen. What brings you to the courthouse?"

"My husband and I are having lunch with Judge Harlan," she said, enunciating every syllable. "It is so nice that he invited us." She gave me a curt smile as she walked without bending her knees to the restroom door.

Gazing at her leaving, I worried that Pellegrin had kept Helen a human just long enough for her to warn me so I could see the fear and despair in her eyes. Had The Institute apprehended her the previous day before she reached her hover? What about her children? Did they have any chance to live a normal life with enhanced parents?

Shortly after 3:00 p.m., Kara called.

"Did Morehouse check you out?" I asked.

"He had an emergency. He didn't arrive at the clinic until 1:30. Some of his patients didn't want to be rescheduled. The waiting room is full. To make sure he could see me in the morning, he had me scribble in an appointment for myself at 10:00 a.m. He'll have the results of my blood test and urine sample before then. Morehouse probably already has them, but with patients stacked wall-to-wall, he won't have a chance to look at them today. I'm just taking a quick break to see if you…"

The sounds of a door squeaking open and shuffling feet came through the airways, followed by Kara's soft voice like she was a distance from the phone, "For me?" Then I heard mumbled voices.

"Oh, Paislee, you should see the gorgeous roses Darren sent me. The receptionist asked if it was a birthday or something. And you won't believe what he wrote on the card: 'To my darling Kara. You light up my world. Love, Darren'." Kara sniffled. "I'm going to cry. I love that man." She sniffled again. "I need a tissue. Anyway, can you?"

"What?"

"Go to lunch tomorrow?"

"Sure."

"I better find a tissue before I drizzle all over patient records. See you tomorrow."

As I hung up, I had to admit that I doubted any man could treat Kara better than Darren, but, at the same time, I feared it wouldn't last long. Someday, he'd drop an agreement in her lap, an agreement with The Institute that would force her into doing something against her will. I worried Kara couldn't survive such a blow from Darren. Maybe I was being a pessimist because of the nightmare my life had become after Pellegrin entered it. Maybe all the attention Darren gave Kara was sincere. No alternative motive. Maybe Darren was human.

* * *

I needed to make sure my parents were okay but wanted to avoid Pellegrin questioning me as to why I didn't go straight home. Knowing my HT was bugged, on the way to my parents' house, I said out loud, "My dad isn't feeling well and he's a little stubborn, so I'm going to see if he needs a doctor." I assumed Pellegrin had already heard the conversation I had with my mother, but I never told her I still intended to see Dad after work even though she had asked me to stay away. Also, Pellegrin was well aware of my whereabouts at all times. No police HTs were behind me. Yet, I figured one or two were close by. A few houses away from my parents' place, I spotted one.

When I entered their living room, Mom stepped out of the kitchen and hurried toward me. She gave me a big hug. "Paislee, your father isn't well. You shouldn't be here." She kissed my cheek. "But I'm so glad to see you."

I looked at her features lined with concern. "Mom, you sounded upset on the phone. I wanted to make sure you were okay."

"There's nothing wrong with me. I'm fine. What the Judge has might be contagious. I don't want you coming down with it. Please, go. I'll call if there's any change in his condition."

"Can I just peek in on him?"

"If you promise not to wake him up."

I went down the hallway and quietly opened their bedroom door. Dad was tucked underneath the blanket with his eyes closed. His coloring looked good. If Mom hadn't told me he was sick, I never would've guessed from the peaceful way he was lying in bed. Then I noticed his hair wasn't messed up, and the collar of his shirt was clearly visible at the top of the blanket. Would he have come home and climbed into bed without removing any of his clothing?

Mom touched my arm and motioned me away from their bedroom. In the living room, she said, "It's so nice to see him finally sleeping soundly. He had such a rough afternoon. Each time he hurried into the bathroom, I wanted to call the doctor. If he's not better by morning, he won't have a say in the matter. A visit to the doctor will be on his agenda."

Mom's hands shook a bit, and her bottom lip twitched.

Mom seemed extra nervous. Was it because of Dad's condition? Or something else? Had Pellegrin installed bugs in their house? Guessing that might be it, I didn't ask her why Dad hadn't changed his clothes before he climbed into bed. Anything unusual like that would probably appear suspicious to Pellegrin. I hugged her again. "Don't worry, Mom. I'm sure Dad will be okay. I'll call you later."

When I arrived home, Pellegrin's HT-8 was parked in the garage.

"How's your dad?" Pellegrin stood in the kitchen as I cleared the last step into my townhouse.

"He doesn't look well," I lied. "I can't remember the last time Dad was sick enough to miss work. He isn't big about visiting doctors, but if he's not better tomorrow, Mom's making him an appointment. I'm going to call her later to see how he's doing."

Pellegrin poured me a glass of wine from an already opened bottle.

I sat down on a barstool, hoping he hadn't slipped anything into the wine, but if I didn't drink it, he'd claim again that I didn't trust him. He needed to believe I did. "Thanks." I forced a smile and took a sip.

He leaned over the counter. "How did your visit with Travis go?"

Of course he knew. "Thanks for helping to clear up his legal problem."

He caressed my free hand. "I'm glad you are pleased." His eyes focused on mine. "Did he seem well to you?"

Since Pellegrin had heard every word between Travis and me, I replied, "No. His memory appears to be a little off. Maybe that's normal for people who have been in a coma. I just don't know. Do you know about that kind of stuff?"

"A little. When a person has been involved in a traumatic event, their memory about the incident can become cloudy. Travis has never been in trouble with the police before. That evening would've fallen into that category."

"So in time, will his memory return?"

"Possibly, but there is no guarantee."

My cell rang.

I glanced at it, and so did Pellegrin. "Rebels" appeared on the screen. I assumed they had purposely attached that name to the caller in order to make sure it would be noticed.

"Answer it," he said.

"Hello."

"Is this Paislee?" a female voice asked.

"Yes."

"We have another test for you."

"I completed the other test. Didn't that prove my commitment to the cause?"

"Do you refuse to complete another test?" Her tone was harsh.

"No. I'll do what you ask."

"You can't be given the mission over the phone. You'll need to come to the store to obtain the instructions. How soon can you be here?"

I looked at Pellegrin. He nodded.

I figured his nod meant I should do it, but that didn't indicate when. Keeping my eyes on him for verification, I said, "I can be there in an hour."

Pellegrin nodded again.

Without saying another word, the woman on the other end of the line hung up.

"What do you think?"

"That they know I'm here. The last assignment they gave you was simple. In order to carry it out, you didn't need to know their objective. This one will be more complicated. Giving it to you in person is their way of keeping it from the airwaves…maintaining secrecy." He walked around the counter and embraced me in his arms.

"I don't want anything to happen to you." He stroked my cheek. "You'll be well covered. If a problem should arise, you will survive."

Even with sophisticated listening devices, I wasn't sure how he could protect me every minute. At the same time, I doubted Tate would let anyone harm me. But if everything failed and I ended up a victim, I hoped Pellegrin would keep his promise—that nothing would happen to my parents.

* * *

Before I left my house, Pellegrin planted two listening devices on me and placed a mini recorder that looked like a silver dollar in my purse. Inside the store, I went to the produce department.

Tate was rearranging oranges in the bin next to the storage doors. He pushed his cart through them and gestured for me to follow. He left the cart, took my hand, and led me through the storage area into the back of a delivery truck parked behind the building and pulled down the truck's back door.

He wrapped me in his arms and kissed me. Tate finally spoke. "We want you to plant this bug." He showed me a small, flat, round object about the size of the tip of my little finger. "Put it into Pellegrin's CAD."

"Tate, I don't know how to do that."

"I'm going to teach you." Tate lowered a crate and took off the lid. He pulled out two folding chairs and a table and set everything up next to the closed door. He took a CAD like Pellegrin's out of his pocket.

I wanted to ask him how he got it but kept my mouth shut. I didn't want Pellegrin to even know about the CAD.

Tate laid it on the table and lifted a metal box out of the crate. From the box he took out a tool that had a point on one side and something that reminded me of a screwdriver but with more grooves on the other side.

"You have to push this in here," he said, showing me how to disassemble the CAD. Then he proceeded to go through the steps to plant the object in it. When he finished, he had me do it three times. "I think you've got it. Hand me your purse."

I expected him to open it. Instead, he turned it over and attached the flat bug to the bottom of it with a piece of tape that blended in with my brown leather purse. "You're all set."

Gazing at Tate, I saw a worried look on his face. I also saw something else in his eyes that I couldn't pinpoint, but my intuition told me this whole thing was nothing more than an exercise. Tate knew I was being monitored. Was he doing it just so Pellegrin would believe I was making headway in becoming a rebel member? So many questions buzzed around in my head, but I remained silent, unable to ask a single one.

Tate caressed my cheek. A faint smile flashed on his face. He mouthed, "I love you. Be careful."

Returning his smile, I mouthed. "I will." I so wanted to tell him that I also loved him but couldn't. Even if my current predicament didn't exist, the law would keep us apart. Just like my uncle had lost the woman he loved, my love for Tate could never be fulfilled.

"Buy some oranges on your way out. That'll give you an excuse for coming to the store."

I left the storage area and began to fill a bag with oranges, and then a familiar store employee motioned me to take the bag of oranges that sat at the back of the bin. I had no idea if that was because they were fresher or if there was something special about them. I picked up that bag and went to the front of the store to pay for them.

After I parked my HT in the garage, Pellegrin opened the door to the stairway. "How did it go?"

"Okay." I picked up the bag of oranges. "I learned a new skill."

He took the oranges from me and, carrying them,

escorted me upstairs. I watched him place the oranges in a fruit bowl. If there was something unusual about them, I didn't need to worry that Pellegrin would eat one.

"Hand me the recorder." He stretched out his hand, and I dug it out of my purse. He pulled a square box out of his pocket, stuck the recorder in it, and snapped it closed.

Static and grinding sounds came through the device.

I squinted at it, wondering if it was faulty.

Pellegrin opened a kitchen drawer and took out an identical square box. He switched the recorder to the other box.

The same grinding sound and static reverberated through the room.

Fearing Pellegrin might think I had damaged the recorder, I said, "I didn't do anything to the recorder. I followed your instructions to a tee. My purse was with me all the time. I only opened it when I paid for the oranges."

Pellegrin's brows furrowed and his mouth narrowed into a hard line.

"Honest, Pellegrin, I didn't sabotage it!"

He put down the gadget and stepped toward me. He embraced me and held me close to his chest. "I never thought you did, but the truck where Tate took you is rigged like a vault to prevent anything said or going on inside from being overheard." He raised my chin and kissed me so deeply that it sent a tingling sensation through my body. "Paislee, I want you, and I'll keep you safe."

I slightly backed away from him. "Pellegrin, if you couldn't hear anything going on inside that truck, I could've been shot in there. You wouldn't have even known to send in a rescue squad before it happened."

He squeezed me again. "Tate wouldn't let anything happen to you. As long as he's with you, you're safe. That's the reason I haven't allowed anyone to take him into custody. He's recently been spotted disabling policemen. We have more than enough evidence to arrest him. That action won't take place until you complete your agreement." With his arm around my shoulders, he led me to the couch. "Would you like anything to drink before we get started?"

"Yes, please. Another glass of that wine you served during dinner."

As Pellegrin fulfilled my request, I mulled over how to hide the rebel mission from him. He didn't know what went on inside that truck, but I had mentioned I learned a new skill. My mission had to entail something technical. Then I recalled the tool in my purse. Pellegrin would see it, and he'd probably know its usage. At all costs, I needed to do whatever it took to keep my family safe. I'd be taking a deadly gamble if I hid the mission from him, and my parents would end up like Helen's husband if Pellegrin discovered the truth. I decided to spill the mission to him but with a small lie woven into it.

He handed me the wine and sat down on the couch. "What is your mission?"

"To bug your phone."

Pellegrin placed his hand on my thigh. "Tate taught you how to plant a bug in a CAD?"

I nodded. "Yes."

"Show me the bug."

"I worked with a phony one. Some additional tweaking needed to be done to the one that I'd be planting. It's going to be delivered to me sometime tomorrow at the courthouse."

"Were you given any tools to use to accomplish the goal?"

"Yes." I pulled the tool out of my purse and handed it to Pellegrin.

He examined it, and then his eyes studied my face. "Show me what Tate taught you."

"Give me your CAD."

He handed it over.

"I need a hard surface. I'm going to do it on the counter."

Pellegrin leaned on the other side of the counter and watched while I skillfully dismantled his CAD. "This is where the bug should be put." I pointed to the location.

"Very good." He took the tool from me and reassembled his CAD. "This same tool can also be used to disassemble a regular cell. Let me show you how easy it is." He gestured for me to hand over my cell.

With the sharp tip of the tool, he pried it open.

Leaning closer, I saw a flat bug in it similar to the one Tate had given me. I gestured toward it. "Did you put that there?"

"Yes. And I'll know if you attempt to remove it."

As I'd expected, it was a clear warning that he could hear every word I said. No place was safe for me to talk, not even the bedroom. A thought sprang into my mind. "Who's listening when you're making love to me? Can they hear every noise we make?"

"No. When I'm with you the bug in your cell is neutralized, and you seldom take your cell into your bedroom or bathroom. You normally leave it on the kitchen counter."

I sighed with relief. "Getting back to my rebel mission…I need to prove myself to the rebels. How can I do that? Are you going to let me put a bug in your CAD?"

He shook his head. "No." He put my cell together. "I'll devise a scheme that will appear you have completed that task."

"What? How?"

"That isn't your concern."

CHAPTER 28

After watching Pellegrin leave my bedroom, I suddenly realized I had forgotten to call Mom about Dad's condition. I doubted he was sick, but that was an impression they wanted to give me, so I needed to play along. I quickly showered and dressed for work.

As I picked up my cell, Pellegrin asked, "Do you intend to make a call before breakfast?"

"Yes. I told Mom I'd call her last night to check on Dad's condition. I forgot about it." I tapped on my parents' number. "This shouldn't take long." I became impatient listening to the phone ring eight times. On the twelfth ring, I hung up. "No answer. Voice mail never picked up."

Pellegrin dished up French toast while I wondered if I could've been wrong about Dad's condition. Was he really sick? Could they have gone to see a doctor? Mom said she'd call if Dad got worse. But why didn't their voice messaging pick up?

"Do you know where my parents are?" I asked as he filled my coffee cup.

"I'll see what I can find out." He tapped on his CAD and held it against his ear. A confused expression crossed his face as he stuck the CAD in his pocket. "The lights in their house were on until 2:00 a.m. this morning. They haven't gone anywhere. Maybe they turned off their phone in order to get some sleep. Would you like me to have a cop check on them?"

"No. Let them sleep. Dad must've had a rough night." I felt guilty for not believing he was sick. "I'll call later this morning."

* * *

Judge Wilbur stepped into my office. "I heard your father wasn't feeling well. How's he doing today?"

"He was up late last night. I tried to get a hold of Mom before I came to work, but their phone must be off."

"From what I heard, he was quite ill when he left yesterday. Will Mr. Murr be sending a doctor to your parents' house?"

I squinted. "That's not Pellegrin's decision. If Dad needs to see a doctor, my mom will make the arrangement."

"I'll be handling some of your father's cases, the priority ones, until he's able to return to work."

"Will Travis bring the files here, or should I go and get them?"

"Sophie is going through them now and comparing Judge Hobson's calendar to mine to determine if we can squeeze in the priority cases."

"Do you want me to put your non-priority cases aside and work on them?"

"No. I'll rely on your father's staff. Keep me informed as to how he's doing."

"I will."

Wilbur turned around and walked out of my office without bending his knees in the process. I feared what that might mean. And he mentioned Pellegrin calling a doctor for my dad. Why did Wilbur say that? Normally, when a judge is sick, their cases are postponed. They're only transferred if a judge will be gone for a long time. An uneasy sensation vibrated through my body. Did Pellegrin discover I had lied about the bug? Did he search my purse after I fell asleep? I pulled my purse out of a desk drawer and looked at the bottom of it. The tape that hid the bug was still securely in place.

Shortly before leaving to meet Kara for lunch, I called my parents. No answer. No voice mail. Worrying that Pellegrin was involved and hoping I was wrong, I vowed to call them later.

* * *

Kara had a bounce in her step and a big smile on her face as she approached me in the lobby.

"You look happy."

"Oh, I am, but I should be unhappy."

"Huh?"

"I'll tell you all about it at lunch. Let's go to that new Italian place a couple of blocks from here. One of the patients raved about it this morning."

"Italian it is."

Kara beamed while we strolled to the restaurant. "I have such exciting news to tell you. I'm still in shock. But I'm determined to wait to tell you until after we're seated."

"I take it that you are no longer feeling sluggish?"

She shook her head. "Well…I am a little, but it's all good."

I couldn't imagine why that would be a good thing. As I wondered what was up with her, I thought about her seeing Morehouse earlier. Could he have told her she was immune to some terrible disease? Could it have anything to do with the blue mark on her forehead? Like the small one I had that I never mentioned to Kara—the mark given to me by Pellegrin to let other androids know I was his. That ownership needed to be dissolved, but I didn't have a clue how to make that happen.

Entering the restaurant, the smell of garlic, spices, and fresh, baked bread floated toward us. My stomach started growling.

The maître d' led us to a round table near the front window.

"Are there any booths available?" Kara asked.

"One, but it'll need to be cleaned before I can seat you there. Can you wait?"

"Yes," Kara replied.

When the maître d' left to seat a foursome, Kara grabbed my arm. "I have the most exciting news to tell you. I hope we don't have to wait long, or I'm going to blurt it out right here."

Within a few minutes, we were seated and our orders placed while Kara was still beaming.

"Okay, what's up?" I asked.

Her eyes glowed. "I'm going to have a baby, but you need to keep it a secret."

"Marten's?"

"No. No. Darren's."

"You've only known Darren…what…ten days?"

"It's twelve days. Twelve of the most wonderful days of my life. With advances in medicine, you can be tested almost the next day. That hadn't even occurred to me. I was so upset the night of that devastating attack at the bar, I didn't even think about using any contraception. Darren did, but it must not have worked. They're not fool proof. Dr. Morehouse went over the results of my test last night and called. I felt numb when he told me the results. After that, the first thing that ran through my mind was an abortion. Darren was standing right next to me. He must've heard the whole conversation."

That's because he's an android with supernatural hearing. Pellegrin had mentioned that Darren could father children. That fact didn't sway my belief in what Tate had told me— Darren was an android. There must be a technical advance in the new model of androids where they can deliver human sperm. Or had The Institute developed some kind of artificial sperm?

With a dreamy expression on her face, Kara went on. "He wrapped me in his arms and kissed my forehead. Then he said, 'You've made me the happiest man in the world'." Her eyes suddenly fixed on me. "You look worried." She leaned over the table and took my hand. "I'll be fine."

"What about the morning sickness? Wasn't it a little early for that?"

"I asked Dr. Morehouse that same question. He told me he has several patients that came in thinking they were sick. It turned out they were having morning sickness within a week of conception. He's going to refer me to an obstetrician. I wanted to go to Dr. Barbara McCarney. All of her patients love her, but she hasn't returned to work since she went on vacation. Her receptionist has no idea when she'll be back. Whatever legal document you saw at the courthouse that mentioned her name must've scared her into hiding out someplace."

Barbara McCarney wasn't hiding out. She was dead, but there was no way I could explain that to Kara without telling her about my snooping. That would bring wrath from Pellegrin, and I already thought I was on thin ice with him. Ice that could shatter with the slightest wrong move. I'd drown in a sea of darkness and pull my family in with me. Kara even speculating about McCarney's demise could be dangerous. "I'm not sure if she was the person mentioned in the document. It could've been someone else who had a similar name."

Neither one of us spoke as the server placed our meals on the table.

Kara's eyes slightly drooped, and she bit her bottom lip. "What am I going to tell Mom and Dad?"

"That's going to be a tough one. It might be best not to say anything about it for a while. Let them get to know

Darren better before you spring it on them."

"Darren asked me to marry him. I don't want him to think just because I'm knocked up that he has to do that. He says he had wanted to ask me after our first night together, but he didn't want to rush me. I know he loves me, and I love him. Why am I finding it so hard to say yes?"

That seemed strange to me. Kara claimed she loved him. Since she also claimed she was happy about her pregnancy, it didn't make sense that she would hesitate to marry him. Could she still be harboring strong feelings for Marten? Was she sensing that something wasn't right about Darren and her situation? The bug in my cell prevented me from prying. "Your hormones must be going crazy right now. You don't need to make a decision today. Give it time. A lot of couples have children before they're married." I felt she needed to know the truth about Darren, but even without worrying about the bug, I didn't have the heart to tell her in her current condition.

A soft, nervous smile crossed her face. "You're right. I have time. Darren even said he didn't want to push me. He's giving me time to think about it."

A document I had seen in Pellegrin's drawer suddenly flashed into my head. The one with a handwritten red star next to the date of my birth control shot—a shot I had ten months earlier that prevented unwanted pregnancies for a year. Maybe Pellegrin intended to impregnate me just like Darren targeted Kara. Would I be trapped forever in Pellegrin's world with The Institute ruling every aspect of my life?

My appetite abandoned me. I moved my fork around on my plate and only managed to take a few bites of the eggplant parmesan, which was a dish I normally gobbled up within ten minutes. I felt like my best friend was slipping away from me. Not because that was what she wanted but because her freedom was being drained away.

As we headed back toward the courthouse, Kara said,

"Darren is going to be so happy that I told you. He wanted me to call you last night, but I wanted to do it in person. I promised I'd tell him all about our lunch."

Tate had that angle pegged. I couldn't say anything to Kara without her passing it on to Darren. And I also knew I couldn't say or do anything without Pellegrin's knowledge.

Kara stopped and took my arm. "You look distracted. You're happy about the baby, aren't you?"

I gave her a hug. "Of course. Having a baby around will be fun." I feigned excitement.

Her face lit up. "You'll be Auntie Paislee, and Pellegrin, Uncle Pellegrin. Do you think he'll like that?"

"That goes without saying. He'll be pleased."

CHAPTER 29

No matter how hard I tried, I couldn't concentrate on my work. My mind was plagued with Kara's plight. Whose baby was she really carrying? It couldn't be Darren's. Barbara McCarney must have been murdered by The Institute because she knew too much. As for Kara, besides having the sperm delivered by an android, there had to be more to it. Had the DNA been altered? Or were the babies implanted with a special, mind-controlling chip right after they were born? I wondered if I could get any answers from Tate. Would he automatically take me to the rigged truck if I showed up at the store?

I glanced at my watch—4:05 p.m. One hour left to work, or in my unproductive state, one hour before I could leave the courthouse. Figuring wherever Mom and Dad had gone, possibly to the doctor's, they should be home. I clicked on their number and listened to each ring. This time, I let it ring ten times. No one answered, and no voice mail picked up. Something was wrong. Was Pellegrin playing a role in manipulating their phone? Why? Could there be a reason he wouldn't want me to talk to them? Pellegrin said earlier that my parents were home. Questioning him about it again could be risky. It probably would serve no purpose but to amplify that I didn't trust him.

Staring at the clock on the wall, I watched the minutes tick away and considered ways to disable Pellegrin. A bath with him might be in order. His earplugs would need to be dealt with first.

Before heading to the store, I decided to make a quick detour to my parents' house just in case I had underestimated Dad's illness, but Mom would've called me if he had to be hospitalized. After relinquishing the driving of my HT to Marcel, my eyes searched every place along the route where a police HT might be parked. Nothing. Not even near their house. Something was definitely amiss. Pellegrin wouldn't have called off the watch dogs before my agreement had been completed. Suddenly panic welled up in my throat. My hands trembled, fearing Pellegrin had hauled off my parents, holding them someplace where The Institute would have easy access to them.

Climbing out of my HT and moving toward their front door, I prayed I was wrong. I placed my hand against the keypad. No green light appeared. Still, I tried to turn the doorknob. It wouldn't budge. With a shaking hand, I pushed the doorbell. The chime sound came through the door.

I stared at it and anxiously listened for movement inside my parents' home. Nothing. I dug into my purse's small zipper compartment and pulled out three keys. It had been a long time since any of them had been used. They were back-up if the power grid failed. Gazing at the keys, I couldn't recall which key went to their house. To open the compartment next to the keypad where a key could be inserted, I tapped on it numerous times. It refused to spring open. Figuring the hinge had deteriorated from lack of use, I fished through my purse again, searching for the tool Tate had given me to disassemble Pellegrin's CAD. I pushed the sharp tip into a seam at the side of the compartment and forced it open, breaking off a section of the plastic cover in the process.

After dropping the tool into my purse, I inserted the first key in the lock. It wouldn't turn. The second key also didn't work. Worried that the lock had been changed, I slowly pushed in the third key, and holding my breath, I turned it and heard the bolt move.

With a sigh of relief, I gripped the doorknob and let myself into my parents' house. I gasped when I saw furniture turned over, drawers pulled open, papers scattered, and broken picture frames strewn over the floor. Though I knew there was no point, I still yelled, "Mom! Dad!" as I walked through the ransacked house. Not one room had gone untouched. It appeared that burglars had invaded my parents' home, looking through every nook and cranny for valuable items. But I knew that android cops had constantly guarded this house, and they were responsible for whatever went on there. Yet I doubted Pellegrin would have given the order to have my parents permanently altered until I either failed to complete my task or he believed I had abandoned it.

In the bedroom, I closed a row of empty drawers, leaned against the dresser, and gazed into the closet. A few items of clothing remained, but most were gone. My eyes swept around the room, trying to figure out what the cops had been looking for. Or was the scene a cover-up for the abduction?

Then I ran to my room. It had also been vandalized, although my bed remained intact. Nothing appeared to be destroyed. I slipped my hand under the mattress, looking for my diary. I couldn't feel it anywhere. I pushed my mattress off the bed. No sign of the diary. It contained all of my intimate thoughts up until I left for college. A blend of fear and anger began to bubble up inside me. Pellegrin had me and I couldn't escape from him, but he had no right to my memories, precious memories that would always linger in my mind. I could envision Pellegrin holding up my diary in front of me, pointing to every excerpt in it where I mentioned Tate and tearing out each page just to see my reaction.

My cell rang.

I jumped at the noise and then checked my phone. Pellegrin's name appeared. I ignored the call but figured it wouldn't be long before he sent a squad to fetch me.

Leaving the house, I glanced at it over my shoulder and wondered if it would ever be a family home again—a human family, a family with emotions, capable of loving each other.

Tears streamed down my face as I feared we were all doomed. The Institute had a much greater reach than I ever could have imagined, and Pellegrin played a significant role in its administration.

I needed to know as much as possible about Kara's pregnancy so I could warn her. Worried that Pellegrin might not let me out of his sight after he had read my diary, I had Marcel stop at Tate's store.

Walking at a brisk pace, I hurried through the entrance and went straight to the produce department. I pushed open one of the doors restricted for employees only. The storage area seemed eerily quiet. My eyes scanned the area as I cautiously moved up and down the aisles. Not one employee was in sight. The door to their break room stood open. I peeked inside. No employees. All the garage-like doors used when a delivery truck arrived were closed. At the far corner was a door with a red exit sign above it. I opened it and peered out. No trucks were parked outside.

I left the storage area. Before I reached the store entrance, an employee rushed toward me. "Tate's at a meeting. He'll be back in an hour or so." Her features were lined with concern. "Paislee, are you in trouble?"

"No. I just have a few questions I thought he might be able to answer. Nothing urgent." I touched her arm. "Thanks for letting me know he's not here."

"I'll tell him you stopped by."

"Thanks."

Stepping out of the store, I saw three police HTs in the parking lot. One android cop stood by my hover. I felt like I was walking into a lion's den as I approached my HT. Would I be driving home by myself, or would I be escorted to one of the police HTs?

"Miss Hobson, Mr. Murr has been trying to reach you," the cop said. "He's concerned about your safety and requested that I accompany you back to your townhouse." He opened the driver's door, and I climbed in without saying a word. The cop moved around to the passenger side and slid in.

The android sat in a rigid posture while Marcel took control of the hover and glided us to my home. To my relief, Pellegrin's HT-8 was not in my garage. That relief was short-lived when I thought he still might be inside.

I went up the stairs with the android cop right behind me, wondering what was in store for me as my eyes searched for Pellegrin. He wasn't in the living room or kitchen.

The android cop moved to the front door and pulled a gadget out of his pocket and spoke into it. He put away the device and said, "Mr. Murr would like you to call him."

"I will after I change out of my work clothes." I headed down the hallway, checking each room I passed. No sign that anything had been disturbed. Glancing around my bedroom, I spotted a surveillance camera in the corner, a new addition to my room. Now I couldn't even sleep without being under the watchful eye of Pellegrin or someone at The Institute. I kicked off my heels, pulled a pair of jeans and a t-shirt out of the closet and went into the bathroom. After inspecting that room and not seeing any surveillance equipment, I shrugged off my clothing and dressed into my casual outfit. Leaving my dress on the floor, I padded out of the bathroom and walked barefoot into the living room.

The android cop hadn't budged from his prior position.

After filling a wine goblet, I eased down on a barstool and slowly drank it while sensing the cop's watchful eyes on me. At any minute, I expected him to remind me to call Pellegrin as if I could forget that order.

Then I made the dreaded call.

"Why didn't you answer my call?" he snapped.

"Where are my parents?" I hissed.

"You will not talk to me in that tone. Do you understand?"

"I'll talk to you however I please. You might be able to restrict my movements, listen to every word I say, but I'm not ready to allow you to dictate how I talk. That's one freedom I won't give up." I knew I was on thin ground, but my parents being taken into custody had raised my anger with Pellegrin to the point I no longer could manage to keep it under wraps. He and The Institute completely ruled my life, and I couldn't see any possible way on the horizon to escape. The thought of ending up like Helen's husband horrified me. Maybe death was the only way I could obtain peace.

"Paislee, are you trying to get me riled up?"

"Pellegrin, we have an agreement. I'm trying to hold up my end of it, but you've broken it by taking my parents into custody. Can't you at least tell me where they are and let me talk to them? How do I know that you haven't already 'enhanced' them?"

"The Institute is not responsible for your parents' disappearance. You are cleverly pretending you have no idea where they are."

"Pellegrin, what are you talking about? You've had me under twenty-four/seven surveillance. How could I possibly even tell them about the agreement, let alone help them get away? And your police force has been keeping an eye on them." Then I decided to add my opinion. "Maybe you have a traitor in your midst. An android cop might've been compromised."

The airways became silent for a minute.

271

"That's not possible," he finally said.

"Do you really believe that?" I asked, hoping to stir up a little doubt in his mechanical brain.

"We will discuss your actions when I get home."

I couldn't imagine he didn't have anything to do with my parents' disappearance, but the thought was intriguing. It would be such a wonderful relief if I knew they were safe and somehow had escaped The Institute. Even though sometimes Pellegrin acted like he had emotions— he had been programmed well—he could easily lie without feeling an ounce of guilt. "When will that be?"

"A pressing project needs my attention." He disconnected.

As I poured another glass of wine, I noticed the fruit bowl was empty. What happened to the oranges? Did Pellegrin toss them because they came from the store, the place Tate works? I figured Pellegrin had read my diary and knew how I felt about Tate. I doubted he had the ability to be jealous, but I wouldn't put anything past the advanced programming that he appeared to possess.

Then it occurred to me that he might have stuck the oranges in the fridge. Opening the door, I saw a platter on a shelf with a note attached. "Paislee, this is your dinner. Microwave it for five minutes."

Upon closer examination, I saw he had prepared veal cordon bleu, but my appetite had deserted me. I looked for the oranges. They weren't in the fridge.

My watch said 8:15 p.m., a little early for bed. Yet staying in the living room with an android cop stationed by the front door, with his eyes fixed on me, wasn't anything I intended to do. I picked up my wine, carried it into the bedroom, and closed the door behind me. I placed the glass on the nightstand, grabbed my purse, and went into the closet. I turned on the light and looked around to make sure it hadn't been equipped with a surveillance camera. Satisfied there wasn't one, I flipped over my purse and sighed when I saw the attached bug. Pellegrin hadn't discovered it. I carefully peeled off the tape, pulled up my t-shirt, and taped the bug to my stomach. I moved the tool from my purse to my pocket. In order to avoid being questioned about taking my purse in the closet, I transferred the remaining contents to a black purse, left the closet, and placed the handbag on the floor by my dresser.

I retrieved my nightgown from a drawer and padded into the bathroom. There, I used the tool, opened my cell, and stared at the bug Pellegrin had planted in it. I had no idea if two bugs could register from the same location as I secured the new bug. It didn't resemble the other one, but I figured that was because it was designed to be inserted into a CAD, not my phone. Still, I thought it would be safer and less detectable in my cell than if I left it attached to my purse, and there might be an opportunity where I could transfer it to Pellegrin's CAD.

Sitting on my bed and sipping the wine, I wished I had taken the whole bottle with me. Maybe being a little tipsy might help me deal with the nightmare I couldn't escape. I had never thought about how precious freedom was before it had been taken away from me. My life now consisted of no freedom. My entire existence centered around what Pellegrin permitted.

Then the scheme to disable him bounced into my mind again. I stood up, quietly turned the doorknob, and pushed the door slightly open. I peered down the hallway. No android cop in sight. He must've been ordered to remain at the front door. Other android cops were probably circling my house. I wasn't sure if it was to make sure I didn't escape or to keep potential intruders at bay.

Avoiding the hallway surveillance camera, I crept into Pellegrin's room and stealthily rummaged through his drawers, looking for his earplugs. A pair was tucked under a document in the bottom nightstand drawer. I took them and lifted out the document. It contained the layout of my townhouse with red marks at the places where surveillance cameras had been installed. I studied it to verify there wasn't a camera in Pellegrin's room. Satisfied there wasn't one, my eyes drifted to the other red marks. The hallway had two cameras, not just the one I had spotted. Feeling irritated that I hadn't noticed the second one earlier and knowing I had been observed entering his room, I needed an excuse for being in here. While I mulled that over, I continued looking in the other drawers to check he didn't have another pair of earplugs. Then I opened his closet door and searched through his wardrobe.

Gripping the only pair of earplugs I could find, I went back to my bedroom. I hid them in a bathroom drawer filled with feminine products. Then a scheme entered my mind to justify being in his room. Planning to carry it out, I gulped the rest of my wine, headed back into Pellegrin's room, and opened the drawer that held his pajamas. The wonderful masculine smell that radiated from Pellegrin's body had seeped into his clothing. The recent intimate night we had flashed into my head. I squeezed my eyes shut, trying to suppress it. Instead it became more vivid and intense. Opening my eyes, I swallowed hard while I forced myself to envision the hellish circumstances that my parents were now enduring under Pellegrin's command.

As I held his pajamas, my eyes became moist. I climbed into his bed, determined to follow through on my devised plan. I stared at the ceiling, hoping he'd be home soon so I could play out my undesirable role in an effort to prove my loyalty to the android that held the well-being of almost everyone I loved in his hands. He was probably also the mastermind behind Kara's situation.

I wiped my eyes on the edge of the sheet, and thought about my life before Pellegrin invaded it. Even though I had only known him for a few weeks, I guessed he had been watching me for a long time and wondered if he had been spying on me when I dated Emmett. Did he play a role in Emmett's break up?

CHAPTER 30

Feeling my nightgown being removed, I woke with a start. Through foggy vision, Pellegrin's features slowly came into focus.

He smiled and whispered, "I like having you in my bed for a change…and clutching my pajamas."

Feigning happiness to see him, I said, "I missed you."

Pellegrin dropped my nightgown on the floor and slid his naked body into the bed. He kissed me with a ferocity that left my body tingling while his skillful hand moved down my side. As much as I hated him, he knew exactly all the right moves to stir a burning desire through my core.

About an hour later, I lay my head on the shoulder of the android I despised. My true feelings about him needed to be well hidden or my family would suffer.

He held me tightly against his chest. In a soothing voice, he whispered, "Paislee, I wanted you the first time you passed me in the courthouse foyer. That attraction has never changed. I'll always care for you. Never forget that."

So I was right. Pellegrin had watched me before we met at the fountain. I wondered when it all started, but knowing that date would have no bearing on my current predicament.

He caressed my cheek. "My beautiful Paislee."

Surprisingly, for a brief moment I felt safe in my torturer's arms. That feeling quickly faded when I feared Pellegrin would make a 180 degree turn if I questioned him about my parents' whereabouts. I decided to wait and broach that subject right before I left for work.

As the morning sun filtered into the room, Pellegrin kissed my forehead, climbed out of bed, and slipped on his sweats.

He headed to the kitchen, and I went to my bathroom. Without warning, tears began to flow as images of my parents, their ransacked house, and the dead and injured lying on the floor at the bar ran through my mind. Were my parents dead? Changed? Did any possibility exist for me to still save them? Even if there was, our lives would be ruled by The Institute. I never considered myself a brave person, but I resolved not to live in a suppressed society without striving to make it better. Finally, I understood why Tate and the other rebel members constantly risked their lives.

I needed to conceive a plan that I could execute alone, without relying on any aid. The top item on it would be to terminate Pellegrin, staged in a way that made it look like an accident. Another idea flashed into my head, one that might be more productive. But first, I needed to know the names of all the people—humans and androids—who ran The Institute. Did Tate have that information?

The bathroom door flew open. Pellegrin stepped in, and his eyes studied me for a second. "Why are you crying?"

"I'm worried about my parents."

"You should be," he snapped. "Get dressed. We'll discuss the consequences of your actions in the kitchen."

"Consequences?"

"Get dressed," he said again, turning on his heel and striding toward the hallway.

Within fifteen minutes, I walked out of my bedroom,

determined not to show the fear bubbling up inside me. Before I reached the hallway, the smell of fried bacon and freshly baked bread drifted through the house. I had to hand it to Pellegrin, he never let any circumstances interfere with his gourmet cooking. How would he function if he was deprived of ever being able to cook again? He certainly didn't need food in order to sustain his mechanical body.

I scooted onto a barstool and saw my favorite eggs Benedict on the plate in front of me. Off to one side sat a basket filled with various types of fresh baked rolls. Pellegrin always prepared more food than I could possibly consume.

My appetite hadn't returned, but I figured Pellegrin's temper would rise if I refused to eat anything. On top of that, I sensed I could be in for a hard time, and, unlike Pellegrin, I needed food in order to maintain my strength and endurance. I cut into the eggs and scooped up a forkful. If only Pellegrin had been the type of android that I believed I had purchased, I would be enjoying every bite I took, content with the debt I had incurred.

Avoiding his gaze, I remained focused on my breakfast, waiting for him to start the inquisition and worried that he wouldn't reveal where my parents had been taken.

After eating half of the food on my plate, I couldn't manage another bite. I laid down my fork, dabbed my mouth with the napkin, and placed it on the counter.

"You should eat more."

"I'm not hungry."

Pellegrin buttered a roll. "Eat this." He handed it to me.

"Pellegrin, I told you I wasn't hungry."

His eyes bored into me. "Eat it."

My stomach churned as I forced myself to devour the roll.

Pellegrin stood and hovered over me. "Let's start with your activities after you left the courthouse at 5:05 p.m.

Why did you go to your parents' house?"

"I was worried about Dad. I called several times during the day. No one answered." Stretching my neck and looking up at him, my eyes narrowed. "What have you done with them? And what were you searching for in their house? That was my childhood home, and you've destroyed it."

"I'm impressed how you're shifting the blame to me for your parents' disappearance when you're completely aware that I had nothing to do with it. I did have several policemen search their house for clues about their departure." He gripped my hand. "Their house has been under constant surveillance, a surveillance you were well informed about. How did you manage to contact them without calling their phone number?"

I squinted. "Pellegrin, you are very skillful at any task you undertake, and obviously, that extends to skirting the truth. You know perfectly well I had nothing to do with my parents' departure. How could I? My phone is bugged! I'm followed whenever I leave my townhouse."

"There was that period when you were in the truck behind the store. Our surveillance equipment wasn't able to penetrate through its shell. Only a beeping sound came from your device and other surveillance equipment we used. That would've been a prime time for you to have a discussion with Tate Ellis regarding your parents."

"I already told you about the mission I was given. I even showed you how I learned to open your CAD."

"Paislee, most people know how to perform that task. Tate gave you an interesting tool. We have concluded that was a cover-up to hide the real purpose behind that meeting. You claimed that the substance of the meeting was a mission you were given to bug my CAD. Yet you weren't given a bug to accomplish that task. With the heightened security at the courthouse, no one delivered a bug to you there yesterday or while you went to lunch with Kara." He squeezed my hand harder.

"Ouch."

Pellegrin loosened his grip, but still held firmly onto my hand. "When you left the store that evening, you bought a bag of oranges." With his free hand, he picked up a red, plastic bag from the other end of the counter. He opened it, revealing a cut up orange. "This was one of the oranges." He separated the pieces, and an odd-looking, little brown ball appeared. He held it up. "Each of those oranges had one of these inside."

"What is it?"

He frowned and shook his head. "You said that so innocently. You know exactly what this is."

Then I recalled the female store employee wanted me to purchase that bag of oranges. "A bug?"

He nodded. "This particular gadget has been deactivated. The others were destroyed."

"Pellegrin, honestly, I didn't know anything about the oranges. I even wanted to eat one last night. Seeing they were gone, don't you think I would've panicked if I'd known what was inside them?"

"You were observed looking for them. However, that does not mean you intended to eat one. If the missing oranges caused your anxiety level to rise, you could've avoided indicating there was a problem. You're very clever at concealing your emotions." He ran his fingers along my forearm.

It sent a cold chill through me.

"After you left your parents' house, you went to the store to see Tate. Why?"

"Because no one had delivered the bug to me that was intended to be planted in your CAD. I was checking to see if that mission had been squelched."

He released my hand and tucked a strand of hair behind my ear. "It appears you have an answer for all of your actions. Was that part of the discussion in the truck?"

"Pellegrin, I already told you what was discussed in the truck. Nothing to do with my parents, the oranges, or any of your accusations. I told you everything." I lied since I hadn't told him the truth about the bug. Tate had given it to me that night, and now it was in my cell. Then I glanced at the clock on the wall. "I'm running late for work." I stood.

Pellegrin grabbed my arm. "Judge Wilbur expects you to be late." He looked behind me. "A-33."

I turned and saw an android cop standing in the hallway. I hadn't realized Pellegrin and I weren't alone in the house. Could other cops be lurking inside?

Pellegrin continued, "Get Miss Hobson's black purse that's on her bedroom floor and the brown one she left in her closet yesterday."

Panic welled up inside me as I worried about why he wanted my purses. Had he always known about the bug? Was I responsible for Pellegrin snatching my parents?

After the purses were handed to Pellegrin, he held them up and stared at the bottom of each one. "What did you do with the bug that had been attached to your brown purse?" He pointed to the spot.

He did know. Attempting to stay calm, I slowly said, "Bug...what bug?"

"The one previously taped to your purse."

I shook my head. "Pellegrin, did you attach a bug to my purse?"

"You do lie well. The night you returned home after the meeting in the truck, you arrived with a bug secured to your purse."

"Then someone at the store attached it without my knowledge."

"How was it removed?"

"Not by me. I didn't even know it was there. I leave my purse in a drawer at work. Maybe someone there removed it."

"Not possible. It was still in place when you came home yesterday. And now it's gone."

Pellegrin set down the brown purse. He dumped out

the contents of the black one on the counter and fingered through them. He picked up my cell and used the tool Tate had given me to separate it.

A wave of terror shot through my body. I sank my teeth into my lower lip and put my shaking hands into my lap to hide them from Pellegrin.

When he lifted out both bugs, I swallowed hard.

"This explains why we were getting a humming sound from your cell. These bugs become worthless when they're planted close together." He took the bug Tate had given me and dropped it into a glass of water. "That bug doesn't work when it's wet." He stretched out his hand toward me. "Give me your hand."

I obediently complied.

"You seem nervous, Paislee. Why is that?"

"Because you are making me nervous. I feel like you're interrogating me."

"I am…or would you rather have someone at The Institute handle that assignment?"

That was one place I didn't want to go. "I can't imagine they could do a better job than you are."

"You're wrong. They are much better skilled in that area, and their techniques never fail. Would you rather have me continue, or should we take a little drive?"

"Continue."

"We'll proceed. We'll do it like a baseball game. Once you have three strikes against you, we'll be taking a trip to The Institute to let experts extract the information I failed to get from you. Do you understand?"

"Strikes? What do you mean?"

"Lies. Incorrect answers. Do you understand?" he asked again.

"Yes." I felt doomed.

"Where are your parents?"

"Pellegrin, I really don't know. You've got to have them in your custody somewhere."

"Strike one."

"Really, Pellegrin, I don't know! Maybe somehow they got wind of the agreement and took off. I just don't know. I wish I did."

"Strike one stands."

I chewed on my lower lip. It didn't matter if I lied or told the truth. It only mattered how Pellegrin perceived my answer.

"What did you and Tate discuss in the truck?"

"I've already told you."

"Strike two."

"Pellegrin, how can I prove to you that I told you the truth about that meeting?" He already knew I had lied about obtaining the bug that night, so I went on. "Okay, I was given the bug, but I didn't want to plant it in your CAD. That's why I pretended I didn't have it."

"Why didn't you want to plant it?"

"I figured I'd be caught."

He tilted his head. "How could you be caught if I knew about it in advance?"

I rubbed my forehead, feeling I was getting deeper and deeper into a lie. The reason I didn't tell him about it was so I could plant it in his CAD without him knowing I had it. "Pellegrin, I don't know why I hid it from you."

"There was more to that meeting then you told me. What else did you leave out?"

"Nothing. Honest."

He took both my hands and held them in his. "Paislee, all I wanted from you was loyalty. It appears that under our current circumstances that is not possible. There's no point for us to continue discussing these matters. I will make sure that you are not permanently harmed during an interrogation at The Institute."

I licked my dry lips. With a lump in my throat, I asked, "You don't believe anything I've told you?"

"No, Paislee, I don't." He released my hands and walked around the counter. He bent down and hugged me. "The interrogator will ask you the same questions I asked you. After that ordeal is over, if he confirms that everything you told me is true, then our agreement will be terminated, and you'll no longer be involved with the rebels."

"And my parents?"

"They will not be enhanced." He raised my chin and softly kissed my lips. "Are you ready to go?"

I dreaded going to The Institute, but with policemen outside and inside my house, and Pellegrin, escaping would be impossible. I slid off the barstool and, with as much dignity I could muster, I said, "Yes."

Pellegrin took my hand and led me out the front door. My legs felt wobbly, but I was determined not to show my fear.

Pellegrin's HT-8 was hemmed in between two police HTs. Across the street stood three more police HTs, and over a dozen policemen patrolled around my townhouse. Even if someone thought I might make a run for it, Pellegrin could've easily handled me by himself. Why had so many policemen been dispatched to my place? I touched Pellegrin's arm. "Have you had any new threats against you?"

"No."

"With so many cops here, are you expecting trouble?"

"That is not your concern."

An android policeman opened the passenger door as we approached. I slid in, and Pellegrin went around and climbed into the driver's seat. As he started his hover, the police HT in front of us moved. Pellegrin's HT-8 zoomed above all the surrounding buildings into an area reserved for emergency and police hovers.

"Is it okay for you to be at this altitude?" I asked, though I had already guessed the answer. Pellegrin told the police what to do. It wasn't the other way around.

He glanced at me. "Paislee, you haven't figured it out yet?"

"I have. You don't just work at The Institute. You run

it. Right?"

"Not alone. There are others that manage the day-to-day activities."

Since he was opening up to me, and I had no idea what type of condition I would be in after the interrogation, but doubting it would be good, my intuition told me I had nothing to lose asking him more questions. "Why did you pretend that I had bought you? And why did you pick me?"

He gripped my thigh. "Several members of the rebels were occasionally following you. We needed to determine why. Your involvement with the rebels was immediately ruled out. Next, we investigated your boyfriend, Emmett Cornell. He was also ruled out. It took a while before we discovered that Tate Ellis was behind the surveillance. The first time I saw you in the courthouse, I understood his motive." Pellegrin caressed my arm. "Wellington, take us to The Institute."

Wellington's voice came through the hover's operating system. "Mr. Murr, would you like to go in the front or back entrance?"

"Back." Pellegrin leaned over and smothered my lips with his. "As to your first question, that took some creative manipulating. You are much more guarded with your emotions than your friend, Kara. Had I attempted to establish a romantic relationship with you, it could have taken a while—maybe years—before we moved in together. Darren accomplished that same task in less than a week."

Without saying any more, I no longer had the slightest doubt that Darren was an android. It was his "task" to establish a romantic relationship with Kara. She needed to know the truth, and I needed to find something concrete I could present to her since I figured she wouldn't accept my word at face value.

Pellegrin went on. "We had to devise several 'what if' scenarios to determine what theory had the highest probability of success. The one we've employed rated the highest."

"Why you? Another android in your class could have accomplished the same task and reported to you."

"Paislee, there is no other android in my class. One group has similar attributes, but those models were not designed to make certain types of decisions." His eyes studied my face. "I wanted you." A sensuous smile crossed his face. "I enjoyed the game, pretending you called the shots. Had we not been in a time crunch, I would have allowed you to maintain that false perception much longer."

"Why are you in a time crunch?"

"The rebels are constantly intercepting our deliveries and shipments. We are running low on many vital components."

"Can't you find another delivery method?"

"We've tried. Eventually, we'll wipe out the rebels like we did back east."

"Back east?" I asked, recalling what Kara had said—someone at a conference Morehouse attended, somewhere in the eastern part of the country, had discussed blue marks showing up on foreheads, women's foreheads, like my small mark and Kara's larger one. Had androids infiltrated the total human population or was their goal only to conquer North America?

The Institute loomed before us. The HT-8 descended down toward it.

"Yes. My father is head of The Institute and runs the one located in New York."

Pellegrin's hover glided to the back of the ominous, stark-white structure. A grinding gear grated my ears as a large docking door rose. Several HT-8s were parked inside along with numerous emergency and police HTs. As the hover cleared the entrance, guards lined each side of the interior parking structure.

"Your father?" I asked, wondering to whom he

referred.

"Maxwell Murr."

"Why do you call him your father?"

"Because he is."

"How's that possible?"

Ignoring my question, Pellegrin climbed out of the hover and looped around the hood and opened my door. He held my hand as I stepped down to the cement floor. Pellegrin wrapped me in his arms. "You can't continue with our agreement in your present condition. I wish you could've been loyal without any additional persuasion. I truly am sorry, Paislee."

"What about…" I felt a prick in my arm. "You lied to me," I mumbled while my body swayed, my legs wobbled, and then darkness descended around me.

CHAPTER 31

Nightmares disrupted my sleep. Trying to get them out of my mind, I shook my head and attempted to turn onto my left side. My right arm wouldn't budge. My eyes snapped open, and I found myself staring at a white ceiling with large light fixtures hanging from it along with strange-looking equipment. The room was eerily quiet. I tried to raise my arms and discovered my wrists were strapped down by thick leather straps secured to extensions on a narrow bed. Horror ripped up my spine. Lowering my eyelids, I hoped I was still dreaming.

After a long period of not hearing the slightest noise, I reluctantly opened my eyes again to evaluate my situation. A sheet covered my body up to my shoulders. My ankles were also bound to the bed. I couldn't see the bindings but guessed they were similar to the ones holding my wrists in place. Every muscle in my body twitched. The sheet fluttered. I bit my lower lip. *No freedom exists for me. I can't escape whatever Pellegrin has in store for me.*

Tears prickled my eyes as I scanned my surroundings. Medical equipment lined one wall. A counter held numerous scalpels, an assortment of clamps, and odd-shaped gadgets with razor-sharp edges. I swallowed hard while my arms trembled against the bed extensions. A row of cabinets hung above the torture devices. A large piece of equipment that reminded me of an x-ray machine stood against another wall. A double door in the center of the opposite wall had a green light shining through an oblong fixture above it. A few stainless steel chairs were scattered around the sterile-looking room. Was this the place where Helen's husband was permanently changed? *Is that what Pellegrin intends for me?*

Then it suddenly struck me. Had the changes already occurred? Was I no longer human? No, that couldn't be possible. An android wasn't fearful, and I certainly was. Questions wouldn't be monopolizing their computerized brains. Or would they?

Wondering how to verify my state, I bit down hard on my tongue. Pain shot through my mouth. *Good sign.* I looked at one of my hands and raised a few fingers. My red polish was clearly visible. Using my thumb, I scratched my index finger and felt the sensation. I pressed my chin against my chest, trying to see my feet. I wiggled my toes and swung them back and forth as far as possible in a rapid motion. The sheet slowly moved. Finally, a sliver of my foot appeared. It looked normal, but Pellegrin's body also appeared human. Had my entire body been duplicated? Was I looking at a mechanical replacement?

A loud beep came from the direction of the double doors, and the light above it changed from a solid green to a flashing red. The doors slid open. Pellegrin and a young, attractive woman wearing a blue lab coat strolled in. She had a slender body, around 5-foot-9. Short, curly, blond hair surrounded her oval face. Her dark blue eyes were giving me a steely look as if I was her enemy. She appeared and moved like a human, but I had first-hand knowledge that looks could be deceiving.

Pellegrin sat down in the chair next to me and rubbed my hand. "How are you feeling?"

With no possibility of escape, I was determined to

maintain my composure. "Bound, imprisoned. I'm not having a good day. What have you done to me?"

"Nothing…yet."

That sparked my anger, and I hissed, "You think strapping me down qualifies as nothing?"

"Nothing permanent," he said in a calm tone.

I sucked in air, trying to regain my composure. "What's the plan?"

He brushed my hair away from my forehead, and slowly ran his hand down the side of my face, over my neck to my chest. "You'll be given something to instill loyalty to me and my cause."

"What is your cause?"

"I'll explain it all to you after you've received the special enhancement."

My resolve quickly vanished with the word "enhancement." Fear gripped me. My lips quivered. My penned up emotions came to life. Tears streamed down the side of my face. Sobbing and over the lump forming in my throat, I asked, "Before you permanently change me, can you at least tell me what you did to my parents?"

Pellegrin went to the counter and picked up a box of tissues. He returned to his seat, pulled out a tissue, and gently wiped my face. "Paislee, I have to commend you on your ability to stick to a fabricated story. You could fool most people. That ability will stay with you even after the procedure. In fact, it'll be enhanced."

"Pellegrin, I'm not lying."

"Then someone, not me or anyone associated with The Institute, has kidnapped your parents. No luggage was found in their home. Closets were almost completely emptied out. It appears your parents packed before they left. That type of generosity is never afforded to kidnapped subjects." He wiped my face again, and softly brushed his lips over mine. "You'll tell me where they are once you come out of the anesthesia. No secrets."

"Pellegrin, please," I said in a trembling voice. "Please,

let me stay a human."

He brushed my hair away from my face again. "My dear Paislee, I wouldn't want you any other way. A microchip will be implanted in your brain. Your body won't change. Your thought processes and feelings won't change, except that you will become loyal only to me. Even Tate Ellis won't suspect anything about you is different. The chip will also give you the added benefit of becoming exceptionally skilled at deception, a quality you have already partially mastered." Pellegrin leaned down until his face was within a few inches of my mine. "You won't be able to deceive me, nor would you want to."

My tears continued flowing. "Pellegrin, I promise… I'll do everything… you ask of me. Please…please…let me stay as I am," I stuttered, feeling a crushing pressure against my chest and gulping for air.

"Promise? Let's see how truthful you can be without that added enhancement," he said, enunciating each syllable. "Where are your parents?"

"Honest… Honest, Pellegrin… I don't know. I… thought you had… taken them someplace."

He shook his head. "I hate seeing you this unhappy, but you've left me no choice."

"Please…please, Pellegrin. You said…you said you cared for me."

"I do. You belong to me. I'll watch over you during the entire procedure to make sure you are safe."

Safe? Did he doubt the ability of his medical staff? Or was there another reason? Maybe someone in authority thought I was getting special treatment. Having an object planted in my brain wouldn't qualify as special treatment, at least not to me. Then what? My tears dried up as I realized I was just a human toy to Pellegrin to be treated however he saw fit. I lacked any ability to sway him into stopping the pending unwanted operation. I was doomed.

My eyes swept around the room, knowing this would be the last place I'd see before Pellegrin took control of my mind. Then I noticed he was staring intensely at the double door. Did he intend to have a room full of spectators, human spectators, watching the procedure so they'd know what to expect if they showed any sign of disobedience?

"The physician is running behind schedule," he said and turned back toward me. "I don't want to leave you like this for a prolonged period." He stood and pulled over a stainless steel cart that had a pole attached with a long tube hanging from it. An assortment of medical devices was laid out on top of the cart. He lifted up a plastic bag, opened it, and pulled out a needle, the type used for intravenous medications.

The curly-haired woman in the lab coat glared at me while she walked closer to Pellegrin. "Mr. Murr, would you like me to do that?"

"No."

Her eyes became slits and fixed on me. What was it with her attitude? She wasn't the one tied down and subjected to the unwanted attention of the monster leaning over me. The monster did possess skillful hands. I hardly felt the needle as Pellegrin inserted it into a vein in my forearm.

Once I was hooked up to the IV and fluid dripped into my vein, Pellegrin trailed his fingers along my arm. "Relax, Paislee. It won't be long before it's all over." He looked at the curly-haired woman. "You are only here to observe. Don't touch her. I'm getting P-16."

P-16. No name. *An android will be performing the procedure?*

As soon as Pellegrin stepped out of the room, the woman rummaged through the cabinets. She pulled out a long, narrow object that reminded me of a thin pipe and an enormous hypodermic needle. It probably could knock out an elephant, maybe two or three.

The medicine running through the tube had started to kick in. The tension in my body was draining away.

As the woman strolled toward me, a sinister smile

crossed her face. She yanked down the sheet covering me. "What's so special about you?"

"Have I done something wrong?"

"Yes. You were born." She began to fill the hypodermic needle with a light green substance.

"Huh?" I stared at the needle, fearing she intended to use it on me the minute I closed my eyes. My survival instinct took a hold of my body and with all the energy I could muster, I screamed loudly.

She raised the hypodermic.

I cringed as she plunged it into my stomach, but I felt no pain. Pellegrin had lied to me. My body had been changed.

The double door flew open.

With one swift swing, Pellegrin knocked the woman across the room. Clanking sounds of equipment crashing to the floor echoed through the room.

Two android guards rushed in.

"I wanted to help," she said in a strained voice.

"No you didn't. Paislee wasn't having that procedure," Pellegrin said in a firm tone. "And you were told to leave her alone. We've suspected you for a while. Too many humans have died in your care." With one hand, he gripped the woman's neck, raised her up and threw her across the room. A loud thud, followed by snapping, sizzling, and cracking sounds came from the spot where she landed.

Focusing on her, I saw the head adorned with curls dangling from her body. Wires stuck out at the bottom of her neck. One of her legs lay about ten feet from her. Colored wires protruded through her lab coat. She had been a well-crafted android, a human-looking one, probably in the class right below Pellegrin.

"Get rid of her," Pellegrin ordered one of the androids in the room. "Completely."

He pulled the hypodermic needle from my stomach. The needle had been broken in half.

"You…you said I hadn't…been changed," I stuttered. "That shouldn't… ended up…like that."

"You were never in danger." He placed the destroyed needle on the counter. "We suspected her, but we weren't sure she was the leak."

"You used me as bait?"

"Yes." He ran his hand over the top of my chest. "Do you feel that?"

"Yes."

As he moved his hand lower, I no longer could feel his touch. My eyes filled with tears again. "Pellegrin…what have you…done to me? Am I…am I part machine?"

He dabbed a tissue over my eyes. "Shhh, Paislee. You are one hundred percent human."

"But I can't…feel you touching… my stomach," I sobbed.

"That's because it has been protected. We discovered that before certain scheduled procedures, the subjects were injected with an organ-destroying fluid in their stomachs. After the last human died, and without the knowledge of our medical staff, this room was equipped with five hidden cameras. We were watching her all the time." He placed his hand on my stomach.

I heard a ripping sound.

Pellegrin held up some torn substance that resembled human skin, but thicker. He poked my stomach. "Do you feel that?"

"Yes." I frowned at him. "The female android could have stuck the needle in me someplace else—an unprotected place."

"That would've been against her MO. As a precaution, all the poisonous liquid in this room had been replaced with non-lethal products."

"Why didn't you tell me the real reason you brought me here?…To draw out a traitor."

"It worked out better without your knowing the situation."

"Can you get me out of these bindings now?"

"I'll release the straps on your wrists for a minute." He undid the buckles.

I rubbed my wrists and had the urge to lash out at him but resisted. He was the master in The Institute. Whatever revenge I wanted to inflict on him, it had to be well planned and take place in another location.

He covered me with the sheet. "That is not the reason for your visit to The Institute, but having you here gave us an opportunity to test our theory." Pellegrin pulled a little medical bottle out of his pocket and filled a hypodermic needle.

He must not have given me a large dose of medicine earlier. Tension crept through my body. Every organ in me was on high alert, fearing his next move. "What's that for?"

"To help you sleep." He pushed the needle through a blue circle in the tube and injected the liquid, and then he took each of my hands and strapped them down again.

"Pellegrin…please…just for being here, I played a key role in helping you identify a traitor. Come on…I don't need my brain tampered with in order to be useful to you. I can be your servant without that."

He bent down and softly kissed my quivering lips. "Paislee, you'll be fine. The procedure won't take long. Trust me. You'll wake up feeling refreshed."

That I doubted. Everything around me had already changed. I now lived in a world without any freedom, and there was no possibility of returning to the simple life I had led before Pellegrin invaded it. I inhaled and exhaled, attempting to calm my nerves. Maybe death by the hand of the android woman would've been a better option. A dizzy sensation crept through my body. My vision became blurry, and my eyelids got heavier. Pellegrin held my hand tightly. I squinted, trying to focus on his features. All I saw were shadows. Unable to keep my eyes opened, I surrendered to my fate and closed them.

Pellegrin whispered, "Are you asleep, Paislee?"

An explosion rattled the room.

"Please, don't blow me up," I mumbled.

"Watch her!" Pellegrin yelled.

The pounding of feet on the hard surface, gunshots, shouting, and banging were the last noises I heard.

CHAPTER 32

As I started to stir, the sizzling cooking smell of seasoned meat floated through the air. I figured Pellegrin was busy cooking up one of his gourmet dishes for me after my ordeal at The Institute. When I moved around, the mattress seemed harder than the soft one on my bed. Where was I? I slowly opened my eyes and gazed around the inside of a tent. It was the same size as my uncle's, the one he took with us on outdoor adventures. For a few minutes, I fantasized being with Uncle Edward on a camping trip in the hills, and he was outside whipping up a meal in a cast iron pot over an open flame. I loved those outings with him. Dad was too busy dealing with court issues to ever go camping. Uncle Edward always planned great wilderness excursions. He filled in for Dad. Just thinking about the fun times we had together made me smile.

Hearing movement outside the tent snapped me out of my reverie. I was lying on an open sleeping bag spread out on the floor of the tent, making it big enough to accommodate two people. A plaid blanket covered me. From the indentation on the other side of the sleeping bag, I guessed Pellegrin had been lying next to me. Why had he taken me to this place? Gradually, I recalled the sound of an explosion before my drug-induced sleep took hold. The Institute must've been damaged, hopefully completely destroyed. If so, why not take me home? Maybe whoever caused the explosion was still at large and after Pellegrin. He might've retreated into the woods for safety purposes.

Pellegrin had been right about one thing he said before the injection—nothing about the way I thought seemed to have changed, including no yearning to be loyal to him. Maybe the chip hadn't been activated yet.

I raised my hand to check the incision on my head and combed my fingers through my hair. Nothing felt unusual. Then I did a more thorough examination. At the base of my scalp was a small bump. As I rubbed it, a few strands of hair stuck onto my hand. Freeing my hair, I touched the edge of a piece of tape.

Lowering my hand, I saw tape attached to the area right below the base of my thumb, the place where my tracking microchip was located. A sliver of gauze protruded around the center of the tape. Did Pellegrin have that chip removed? Maybe the one implanted in my brain also took care of that function, making the tracking chip unnecessary.

A hand poked into the tent and pulled the flap away. Sunlight streamed in. A middle-aged woman with dark hair peeked in and smiled at me.

She released the canvas, and it dropped back in place as she shouted, "Tate, she's awake."

Tate? How was that possible?

Within a minute, he crawled into the tent. "How are you feeling?" he asked, kneeling on the sleeping bag.

I sat up. "Good...but...but how did I get here?"

A big smile flashed on his face. "We rescued you."

"Rescued? The Institute was swarming with guards. How did you do it?"

"Blew it up. We've been planning to do that for a long time." He caressed my cheek. "When Pellegrin took you there, our time line moved forward."

"The rebels?"

He nodded.

"Is The Institute completely demolished?"

"It's still smoldering. Do you want to see?"

"Is it dangerous?"

"Nope. We're far enough away, but we need to be cautious. Do you feel up to a little stroll outside?"

"Yes. Definitely. To see it wiped out. Gone. No more *enhancements*." I rubbed the protrusion on my head. "But what about me? What about the chip in my head?"

Tate leaned closer and touched the spot I had been rubbing. "It's just a little bump. Nothing to worry about. The back of your neck hit the rim of a metal cart when we were getting you out." He pulled me into his arms and kissed me. "Knowing Pellegrin's plan for you, I wanted to follow his HT-8 into the building, but that would've ended up in a blood bath, not a rescue. To prevent your surgery, we disabled the android surgeon so you'd be safe until our scheme could be implemented."

"That isn't exactly how it played out. While Pellegrin checked on the whereabouts of that doctor, a female android tried to kill me. Had Pellegrin not been alerted to that possibility, I'd be dead."

Tate's eyes narrowed. "Female android?"

I bobbed my head up and down. "Yes. She looked like a human."

"Curly, blond hair?"

"Yes. Did you know her?"

"She was captured and reprogrammed to help us."

I squinted and tilted my head. "Help you? Then why did she try to kill me? Do some rebel members want me dead?"

"No. When a human is taken into The Institute to be permanently changed, like the D.A., she kills them before that can happen. All rebel members would rather die than end up as a controlled cyborg."

"But the district attorney was changed."

"She wasn't always in a position where she could intercede without being detected."

"Pellegrin was on to her."

"He suspected but lacked proof. Had he been certain, she would've been terminated earlier. He handles all spies swiftly. We weren't able to get a message to her but knew Pellegrin had made extra arrangements for your safety."

"How do you know all that?"

"Our leader set up the first security system in The Institute. Without The Institute's knowledge, he monitors it through a back door in the system that he inserted to keep track of them. As the system was expanded, a few blind spots cropped up. We couldn't follow everything they were up to. The reason Pellegrin pretended to be a domestic companion was not on our radar."

"My parents...my parents. They're being held captive someplace."

"No. Your parents are safe."

"How?"

"We learned about your agreement with Pellegrin. Your parents had a hard time keeping their planned departure a secret from you. Your mom's been really upset and worried we wouldn't be able to get you out. We sent her a picture of you lying in the tent to calm her nerves."

"How did you do that?"

"We have a communication system in place, similar to The Institute's. To lower the probability of it being detected, it's only used for official business."

"Where are my parents?"

"In Colorado. That's where we'll be heading after the sun sets."

"What about my uncle? My agreement also put him in danger."

"Your uncle is safe. He's with us."

I raised my hand and rubbed over the tape. "Did you remove my microchip?"

"Not personally. One of our doctors did. You were already sedated, which made it an easy job for a professional."

Then I recalled how happy Mom was when I had the microchip inserted in my hand right before I started school. It was to help keep me safe. She could easily have me found if I got lost. That was why everyone had a chip. No one thought they were a curse. I beamed, feeling an extra sense of freedom from not being constantly monitored by a tracking system. "I want to see The Institute burning."

Tate took my hand. "This way, Miss Hobson."

We both slithered out of the tent and stepped into a large clearing encircled by towering pine trees and aspens.

Other tents of various sizes and shapes were spread over the ground. Picnic tables were scattered around where people were eating. A small group of women and men cooked over camp stoves. Above the clearing, attached to the trees, hung a thin, tarp-like green and brown material that allowed sunlight to filter through it. I assumed it hid the camp from overhead surveillance.

Tate led me through a huge crowd. Over a hundred people milled about. A few women I recognized as store employees approached us. They hugged and greeted me and said how happy they were that I had joined them.

As we reached the edge of the clearing, I saw armed men trudging around the perimeter.

A few minutes later, Tate stopped and said, "Watch out." He pointed at a few snapped branches on the ground. "Trip wires are under them. Security is always our top priority."

When we had walked twenty minutes through thick foliage, the trees thinned and the terrain became rocky.

"Stay close to the trees. Don't go anywhere you could be spotted from the sky."

Remaining shielded by the sparse trees, we continued trudging over the rough, rocky ground until we reached the crest of a hill. The acrid smell of smoke and ash drifted toward us along with the faint sound of a high-piercing alarm.

Hunkering down, we crept through the overgrown grasses and a swath of bushes to peer over the hill. Off in the distance, I could make out the city that I used to call home. Black smoke spiraled into the air from a section of it. A red sizzling glow lit up the ground.

Tate pointed at it. "That's the block that housed The Institute."

From my vantage point, I couldn't make out The Institute, or, for that matter, any buildings, but it appeared everything was on fire or had burned in that area. "I expected only to see smoke. No fire. I thought a whole day had gone by since I was at the Institute."

"No, only six hours. I didn't think you would be unconscious that long. The doc figured you had been heavily sedated. That's their usual MO for brain surgery.

"The explosions were set off at intervals. The last one went off an hour ago. We needed to prolong the distraction in order to get all the rebels on The Institute's list and their loved ones out. If anyone on that list was left behind, they won't survive."

"What about the humans near The Institute? How many lives were lost?"

"With the aid of police badges, we evacuated the area before the first bomb went off. Most left. A few refused to go. We don't know if there were casualties."

Kara suddenly snapped into my head. "Kara! Did you get her out? Is she somewhere safe?"

Disappointment and sadness showed in Tate's intense eyes.

I bit my lower lip, fearing the worst. My eyes became moist. A tear trickled down my cheek. "Tell me."

Tate wrapped me in his arms. "She's not dead. I'll fill you in back at the camp. We're too exposed here." He took my hand and led me away from the hill.

When we reached a more heavily wooded area, Tate turned and pulled me tightly against his chest and then smothered my lips with his. "We're free. We no longer need to hide our feelings. No more strata to separate us."

Excitement surged through my body. My heartbeat accelerated. He was right. I could finally show how much I desired him. Anxious to feel his naked body against me, I began unbuttoning his shirt.

Tate grabbed my hands. "I have wanted to make love to you since the first time you climbed on my surfboard. I hate to wait, but they'll be packing up soon, and we're not in a safe spot." He enveloped me in his arms and kissed me passionately. "You have always been the woman in my dreams." He trailed his fingertips down my neck as his hot eyes filled with desire gazed at me.

Adrenaline spiked through my system and blood surged up into my cheeks. "I don't care if we're not in a safe spot. I want you."

He pulled me into a thick patch of foliage, cleared a small area on the ground, and then we both sank down. He removed my blouse as my longing for him intensified.

Twigs snapped a short distance from us, followed by rustling of leaves.

Feeling Tate's hands caressing my body and wanting to enjoy every minute of it, I closed my eyes and tried to ignore the noise.

The rustling of leaves became louder.

"Someone's coming," Tate whispered. "Stay here and don't make any noise." He crawled away from me.

I bit my trembling, bottom lip. As quietly as possible, I slipped my blouse back on. Worried about Tate, I perked up my ears and stayed on high alert. Could androids be hot on the rebels' trail? Tate had mentioned that sometimes traitors infiltrated the rebels. They were paid handsomely for their treachery. Pellegrin had admitted that much.

Muffled voices and movement seeped through the foliage.

I slipped farther into woods and hid behind a cluster of trees. Remaining concealed, I peered through the branches.

"Where is she?" a rough male voice blurted out.

It didn't sound as stilted as an android voice, but that didn't mean it wasn't. I held my breath and retreated deeper into the foliage. I feared Tate was in imminent danger.

Heavy footfalls crunched on the fallen leaves and broken branches.

Tate's voice softly drifted through the trees. "Paislee, you can come out. Your uncle is looking for you."

I exhaled and crept toward Tate's voice. He crouched in the area where we had planned to have our intimate interlude. Uncle Edward stood behind him along with a man I didn't recognize.

Uncle Edward made his way around Tate and gave me a big hug. "Sorry about the bump on your head. I lifted you up and swung you around too quickly."

"You're a rebel member?"

"Yes."

"Ward, it's almost time," said the unidentified man.

Squinting, I cocked my head. "Ward? You're Ward, the leader?"

"I don't like that term, but that's what I'm called. Everyone fighting to regain freedom from the forces that have invaded our society, whether their contribution is large or small, is considered an equal. No strata segregate us." He gave me a lopsided smile. "So, my favorite niece, are you ready to grasp that freedom?"

I raised my brow. "Favorite niece? I'm your only niece."

He took my hands in his. "You got too smart for me. I knew sending you to college might've been a bad idea."

"I figured you didn't have any other nieces before I started kindergarten."

"Really? All those years, I thought you believed that."

He put his arm around my shoulders as we walked back to the rebel camp. "You are, and you will always be my favorite niece."

The sun was beginning to set when we stepped back into the patrolled area.

"Sit down and have something to eat," Uncle Edward said. "You have a long journey ahead of you."

"Don't you mean we?"

"No. I'm staying. There's still a lot of work to do here, and I haven't been identified as a member of the rebels."

"But my agreement. You were mentioned in it. You're in danger."

"I've got it under control."

"How?"

"The less you know the better." He kissed my forehead. "Now sit and eat." Uncle Edward glanced behind me. "Tate will take good care of you."

As Tate and I sat down, I watched my uncle head toward a small group of people gathered near a large tent. They all went inside.

I turned toward Tate. "You *are* going with me, aren't you?"

"Yes. My picture and name are plastered on the wall of every building in L.A. that houses law enforcement offices. Your uncle has managed to work in the shadows, and only a few rebel members know his true identity."

"But my agreement?"

"He said he could handle it, and I have complete confidence in him."

A man wearing a white apron brought over heaping plates filled with barbeque ribs, coleslaw, potato salad, and a roll.

Staring at the plate in front of me, I said, "There is no way I can eat all this."

Tate finished chewing the food in his mouth. "Don't worry, I'll eat everything left on your plate." A sensuous smile crossed his face. "Need the extra energy in case an opportunity arises so we can finish what we started in the woods."

My skin tingled with anticipation. "It's going to be tough waiting." I stroked his arm.

"Couldn't agree more."

After I devoured two ribs and the coleslaw, my stomach felt stuffed. I set down my fork and turned toward Tate. "Tell me about Kara."

"She wouldn't listen," he said between bites. "Kara excused herself to go to the bathroom, and then we discovered she had called her mechanical boyfriend. We were almost caught getting out of the apartment building."

"Who's we?"

"I brought a female rebel member, a person in your high school graduating class, with me. She knew Kara."

"Neither one of you could make Kara believe the truth about Darren?"

"No. Kara kept reiterating that she was pregnant with his child and saying there was no way he wasn't human."

"Maybe I could convince her to leave."

"I doubt it. She's too attached to the boyfriend."

"What about the baby?"

"Artificial insemination, completely unrealized by Kara. The baby will be born normal, and then a microchip will be planted in the infant's brain. Some infants don't survive the operation."

I gasped and covered my mouth. "Oh, my God. How could they do that to a baby?"

"Control. The chip isn't activated until the child is six or seven."

"Will Kara know?"

"She won't have a clue."

"Why do they want babies?"

"To appear like a normal family. People are prone to be more trusting of a family man or woman. Developing trust brings them a step closer to their goal."

"What *is* their goal?"

"We haven't been able to determine their ultimate goal, but it appears it is to rule the world, one country at a time."

"Why?"

He shrugged. "Power? Control?"

"I still want to try to get Kara to leave her android boyfriend."

"He's not a full-fledged android. He has one human component—part of his brain. It's been enhanced with computerized components." Disgust spewed from Tate. "Similar to Pellegrin's."

"Pellegrin? He's not an android?"

"I guess it depends on your definition. He's eighty-five percent machine. Given that percentage, I'd lean more toward android than cyborg."

"Was he terminated in the explosion?" A strange sense of sadness swept through me.

Tate brushed the hair away from my forehead. His eyes narrowed as he stared at me. "No, he wasn't."

"Huh? You can tell just by looking at me?"

"The blue mark isn't gone. Pellegrin put it there. It would've vanished if he had not survived the explosions."

I stroked the spot on my forehead. "How is that possible?"

He shook his head and pressed his lips together. "That's another mystery we haven't been able to solve. Through observation, we've learned the blue mark represents a bond, an ownership. As long as it remains, the android or cyborg is functioning."

"Can he find me?" I looked around at the dark forest surrounding us.

"The mark isn't a tracking device, but I'm certain he'll search for you. We *have* occasionally discovered a traitor among us. That would be the only way he could find you."

A gong sounded.

Everyone stopped talking and looked toward the tent my uncle had entered. He stood near it.

"Okay, folks," Uncle Edward said loudly. "It's time to move out. Get your stuff and meet by the yellow pole in ten minutes."

My eyes searched for the pole until I saw it on the far side of the clearing. "I don't have any stuff to get."

"I bought a few things for you. Enough to get you by for a few days. Your mom took a trunk full of your stuff with her."

As we rose from the table, I asked, "Shouldn't we help fold up the tents and tables?"

"No. Everything here stays. It'll be used again. Your uncle isn't the only one not going."

"I'll call Kara on her work phone when we reach Colorado and try to persuade her to leave. If I do, is there any way to get her out?"

Tate put his hands on my shoulders and swung me around. "Paislee, she'll be monitored twenty-four-seven. If you attempted to contact her, it would lead our enemies to our new location. It would destroy everything."

I swallowed hard. *Kara is my best friend.* "So I'll never be able to talk to her again?"

"Never say never. Our battle is taking root. Things my change."

I felt a lump in my throat. Poor Kara. There had to be a way I could help her.

Tate grabbed my hand, snapping me out of my contemplations about Kara. We went to the tent I had slept in earlier as I wondered about our transportation to the new place. Even though the clearing had been secured, the skies still held danger.

He handed me my purse. "It's been sanitized. No bugs." Tate slipped on his backpack and picked up two duffle bags. He flung a strap of each one over his shoulder.

"I can carry one of the duffle bags," I said, gazing at the tall, muscular man by my side.

"No. I'm built for this task."

A chugging noise could be heard as we headed to the

yellow pole. Then, through the trees, I saw the caboose of an old fashioned train. "We're going in that?"

"Yes. It runs on engineered coal that leaves no smoke trail, and no cell phones or any computerized gadgets go with us. Special equipment has been installed in our isolated settlement in Colorado. Ward will know when we arrive. Until then, all communication is cut off."

Gazing at the train, I thought about the luxurious ones I had traveled on with my parents. Dad hated to fly, so most of our family trips were by train. All regular commercial forms of transportation were well monitored and all passengers tracked.

After we were settled on the train, Uncle Edward walked down the aisle, shaking hands, giving hugs, and wishing everyone a safe journey. When he reached me, I stood up.

He wrapped his thick arms around me. "Give your parents my best."

"I wish you were coming with us."

"Someday I'll come for a visit." His eyes had a faraway look in them like he was already contemplating his next rebel mission.

I kissed his cheek. "Thank you for giving me back my freedom."

A faint smile crossed his lips. "Isn't that what you would expect of your favorite uncle?"

"My only uncle. I love you."

He touched my cheek. "You are always in my thoughts."

After he said a few words to Tate, he finished making his rounds.

I noticed Tate's expression had changed from being happy to looking sad.

"Are you going to miss being an active rebel member?"

"Yes. It gave me a strong purpose in life. Whatever The Institute's goal is, it has to be stopped or I doubt the human race will survive."

Kara and her unborn baby snapped into my mind. Could I really be happy, knowing I was free, but so many others were suffering at the hands of The Institute? "There's a branch of The Institute in every major city across the country. Are there rebel groups in all of those cities?"

"In some. Your uncle stays in contact with them."

"Maybe you could go to one of those other cities, a place you're not known, and continue participating in the rebel movement."

"I thought about that, but I don't want to leave you."

"I'll go with you."

His eyes popped wide open as he stared at me. "Paislee, you don't know how to fight."

"You can teach me. Remember, I didn't know how to surf before you came into my life. Now, I excel."

"That you do. I missed your arms around me when we rode a board together." He took my hand. "It's dangerous being a rebel. We constantly have casualties...or worse, some are captured and changed."

"Tate, I can't turn my back on Kara and everyone that might be in the situation I was in. I could never be happy knowing freedom was being ripped away from others."

"I figured you'd feel that way once we were settled in Colorado, but I didn't expect you to think about it this soon after your tough ordeal. Let alone, before the train even left." He took both my hands. His eyes glowed. "Paislee, I love you even more. I'll teach you to fight after you've had a few days to rest in Colorado."

Squeezing his hands, I smiled. "Thank you." As long as the rebels fought, there was a chance to save the human race, and I intended to be part of that battle.

Tate leaned toward me and softly kissed my lips.

Voices inside the train became louder, drawing my attention toward them. People waved to my uncle as he walked to the doorway. He turned toward me and winked. My eyes misted over, afraid that I would never see my beloved uncle again. Even though I planned to fight for the cause, it would be too dangerous for Tate and me to return to L.A.

The train chugged down the tracks while I stared out the window, feeling sad that I was leaving my best friend and uncle behind. Pellegrin popped into my head and, for some reason that I didn't understand, a tear ran down my cheek.

Tate put his arm around my shoulder and pulled me closer. "Your uncle will be fine. He's skilled at working the system."

"And we need to learn to be just as skillful." I gazed at the man I loved and caressed his arm, both excited and fearful of what the future had in store for us.

ABOUT THE AUTHOR

Inge-Lise Goss, USA Today Best-Selling and Multi-Award Winning author, was born in Denmark, raised in Utah, and now lives in the foothills of Red Rock Canyon with her husband and their dog, Ted. She spends most of her time in her den writing stories. There, with her muse by her side, her imagination has no boundaries, and her dreams come alive. When she's not pounding away on the keyboard, she can be found reading, rowing, or trying to perfect her golf game, which she fears is a lost cause.

www.Inge-LiseGoss.com